ST. LEON
A TALE OF THE SIXTEENTH CENTURY

BY
WILLIAM GODWIN

He put his hand to the wound; the Animal stirred not.

ADVERTISEMENT.

The Publishers of the Collection of "Standard Novels" are extremely desirous that I should furnish them with a few lines, by way of introduction to the appearance of St. Leon in its present form. I am however at a loss how to oblige them. In the original Preface I frankly stated the sources upon which I had drawn for the idea and conduct of the work. I have therefore no remarks to offer, but these which follow:—

In 1794 I produced the novel of Caleb Williams. I believed myself fortunate in the selection I had made of the ground-plot of that work. An atrocious crime committed by a man previously of the most exemplary habits, the annoyance he suffers from the immeasurable and ever-wakeful curiosity of a raw youth who is placed about his person, the state of doubt in which the reader might for a time be as to the truth of the charges, and the consequences growing out of these causes, seemed to me to afford scope for a narrative of no common interest. I was not disappointed. Caleb Williams was honoured with the public favour.

The consequence was that I was solicited to try my hand again in a work of fiction. I hesitated long. I despaired of finding again a topic so rich of interest and passion. In those days it was deemed a most daring thought to attempt to write a novel, with the hope that it might hereafter rank among the classics of a language. The most successful English writer in that province of literature had scarcely gone beyond three. It had not then been conceived that the same author might produce twenty or thirty, at the rate of two or three per annum, and might still at least retain his hold upon the partiality of his contemporaries. To Sir Walter Scott we are indebted for this discovery.

At length, after having passed some years in a state of diffidence and irresolution, I ventured on the task. It struck me that if I could "mix human feelings and passions with incredible situations," I might thus attain a sort of novelty that would conciliate the patience, at least, even of some of the severest judges. To this way of thinking St. Leon was indebted for a "local habitation, and a name."

One of my most valued friends Mr. Northcote has often told me, that the public may sometimes be interested in the perusal of a book, but that they never give themselves any trouble about the author. He therefore kindly advised me on no occasion to say any thing in print about myself. The present race of readers seem scarcely disposed to verify this maxim. They are understood to be desirous to learn something of the peculiarities, the "life, character, and behaviour," of an author, before they consign him to the gulph of oblivion, and are willing to learn from his own testimony what train of thoughts induced him to adopt the particular subject and plan of the work, upon the perusal of which they are engaged.

June, 1831.

PREFACE.

The following passage from a work, said to be written by the late Dr. John Campbel, and entitled Hermippus Redivivus, suggested the first hint of the present performance:—

"There happened in the year 1687, an odd accident at Venice, that made a very great stir then, and which I think deserves to be rescued from oblivion. The great freedom and ease with which all persons, who make a good appearance, live in that city, is known sufficiently to all who are acquainted with it; such will not therefore be surprised, that a stranger, who went by the name of signor Gualdi, and who made a considerable figure there, was admitted into the best company, though nobody knew who or what he was. He remained at Venice for some months; and three things were remarked in his conduct. The first was, that he had a small collection of fine pictures, which he readily showed to any body that desired it; the next, that he was perfectly versed in all arts and sciences, and spoke on every subject with such readiness and sagacity, as astonished all who heard him; and it was, in the third place, observed, that he never wrote or received any letter, never desired any credit, or made use of bills of exchange, but paid for every thing in ready money and lived decently, though not in splendour.

"This gentleman met one day at the coffee-house with a Venetian nobleman, who was an extraordinary good judge of pictures: he had heard of signor Gualdi's collection, and in a very polite manner desired to see them, to which the other very readily consented. After the Venetian had viewed signor Gualdi's collection, and expressed his satisfaction, by telling him that he had never seen a finer, considering the number of pieces of which it consisted; he cast his eye by chance over the chamber-door, where hung a picture of this stranger. The Venetian looked upon it, and then upon him. 'This picture was drawn for you, sir,' says he to signor Gualdi, to which the other made no answer, but by a low bow. 'You look,' continued the Venetian, 'like a man of fifty, and yet I know this picture to be of the hand of Titian, who has been dead one hundred and thirty years, how is this possible?'—'It is not easy,' said signor Gualdi, gravely, 'to know all things that are possible; but there is certainly no crime in my being like a picture drawn by Titian.' The Venetian easily perceived, by his manner of speaking, that he had given the stranger offence, and therefore took his leave.

"He could not forbear speaking of this in the evening to some of his friends, who resolved to satisfy themselves by looking upon the picture the next day. In order to have an opportunity of doing so, they went to the coffee-house about the time that signor Gualdi was wont to come thither; and not meeting with him, one of them, who had often conversed with him, went to his lodgings to enquire after him, where he heard, that he had set out an hour before for Vienna. This affair made a great noise, and found a place in all the newspapers of that time.

It is well known that the philosopher's stone, the art of transmuting metals into gold, and the elixir vitæ, which was to restore youth, and make him that possessed it immortal; formed a principal object of the studies of the curious for centuries. Many stories, beside this of signor Gualdi, have been told, of persons who were supposed to be in possession of those wonderful secrets, in search of which hundreds of unfortunate adventurers wasted their fortunes and their lives.

It has been said of Shakespear, that he

Exhausted worlds, and then imagined new:
but the burthen sustained by Shakespear was too heavy for the shoulders of any other individual. I leave the first part of the task above mentioned to be divided among those celebrated novelists, living and dead, who have attempted to delineate the scenes of real life. In this little work I have endeavoured to gain footing in one neglected track of the latter province. The hearts and the curiosity of readers have been assailed in so many ways, that we, writers who bring up the rear of our illustrious predecessors, must be contented to arrive at novelty in whatever mode we are able. The foundation of the following tale is such as, it is not to be supposed, ever existed. But, if I have mixed human feelings and passions with incredible situations, and thus rendered them impressive and interesting, I shall entertain some hope to be pardoned the boldness and irregularity of my design.

Some readers of my graver productions will perhaps, in perusing these little volumes, accuse me of inconsistency; the affections and charities of private life being every where in this publication a topic of the warmest eulogium, while in the Enquiry concerning Political Justice they seemed to be treated with no great degree of indulgence and favour. In answer to this objection, all I think it necessary to say on the present occasion is, that, for more than four years, I have been anxious for opportunity and leisure to modify some of the earlier chapters of that work in conformity to the sentiments inculcated in this. Not that I see cause to make any change respecting the principle of justice, or any thing else fundamental to the system there delivered; but that I apprehend domestic and private affections inseparable from the nature of man, and from what may be styled the culture of the heart, and am fully persuaded that they are not incompatible with a profound and active sense of justice in the mind of him that cherishes them. True wisdom will recommend to us individual attachments; for with them our minds are more thoroughly maintained in activity and life than they can be under the privation of them; and it is better that man should be a living being, than a stock or a stone. True virtue will sanction this recommendation; since it is the object of virtue to produce happiness, and since the man who lives in the midst of domestic relations will have many opportunities of conferring pleasure, minute in the detail, yet not trivial in the amount, without interfering with the purposes of general benevolence. Nay, by kindling his sensibility, and harmonising his soul, they may be expected, if he is endowed with a liberal and manly spirit, to render him more prompt in the service of strangers and the public.

Nov. 26, 1799.

TRAVELS OF ST. LEON.

CHAPTER I.

There is nothing that human imagination can figure brilliant and enviable, that human genius and skill do not aspire to realize. In the early ages of antiquity, one of the favourite topics of speculation was a perfect system of civil policy; and no sooner had Plato delineated his imaginary republic, than he sought for a spot of earth upon which to execute his plan. In my own times, and for upwards of a century before them, the subject which has chiefly occupied men of intrepid and persevering study, has been the great secret of nature, the opus magnum, in its two grand and inseparable branches, the art of multiplying gold, and of defying the inroads of infirmity and death.

It is notorious that uncommon talents and unparalleled industry have been engaged in this mighty task. It has, I know, been disputed by the audacious adversaries of all sober and reasonable evidence, whether these talents and industry have in any case attained the object they sought. It is not to my purpose to ascertain the number of those whose victory over the powers and inertness of matter has been complete. It is enough that I am a living instance of the existence of such men. To these two secrets, if they are to be considered as two, I have been for years in the habit of resorting for my gratification. I have in my possession the choice of being as wealthy as I please, and the gift of immortal life. Every thing that I see almost, I can without difficulty make my own; for what palaces, pictures, parks or gardens, rarities of art or nature, have not a price at which their owner will consent to yield them? The luxuries of every quarter of the world are emptied at my feet. I can command, to an extent almost inconceivable, the passions of men. What heart can withstand the assault of princely magnificence? What man is inaccessible to a bribe? Add to these advantages, that I am invulnerable to disease. Every sun that rises, finds the circulations of my frame in the most perfect order. Decrepitude can never approach me. A thousand winters want the power to furrow my countenance with wrinkles, or turn my hairs to silver. Exhaustless wealth and eternal youth are the attributes by which I am distinguished from the rest of mankind.

I do not sit down now to write a treatise of natural philosophy. The condition by which I hold my privileges is, that they must never be imparted. I sit down purely to relate a few of those extraordinary events that have been produced, in the period of my life which is already elapsed, by the circumstances and the peculiarity to which I have just alluded.

It is so obvious, as to make it almost improper to specify it, that the pursuit in which so many of my contemporaries are engaged, and the end of which I have so singularly achieved, is in its appearance infinitely more grand and interesting than that which occupied the thoughts of Plato and the most eminent writers of antiquity. What is political liberty compared with unbounded riches and immortal vigour? The immediate application of political liberty is, to render a man's patrimony or the fruits of his industry completely his own, and to preserve them from the invasion of others. But the petty detail of preservation or gradual acquisition can never enter into competition with the great secret, which endows a man in a moment with every thing that the human heart can wish. Considered in this light, how mean and contemptible does the ambition of the boasted ancients appear, compared with ours? What adept or probationer of the present day would be content to resign the study of God and the profounder secrets of nature, and to bound his ardour to the investigation of his own miserable existence?

It may seem perhaps to many, that the history of a person possessed of advantages so unparalleled as mine, must be, like the history of paradise, or of the future happiness of the blessed, too calm and motionless, too much of one invariable texture and exempt from vicissitude, to excite the attention or interest the passions of the reader. If he will have patience, and apply to the perusal of my narrative, he will in no long time perceive how far his conjecture is founded in sagacity and reason.

Some persons may be curious to know what motives can have induced a man of such enormous wealth, and so every way qualified to revel in delights, to take the trouble of penning his memoirs. The immortality with which I am endowed seems to put out of the question the common motives that relate to posthumous fame.

The curiosity here mentioned, if it really exists, I cannot consent to gratify. I will anticipate nothing. In the progress of my story, my motive for recording it will probably become evident.

I am descended from one of the most ancient and honourable families of the kingdom of France. I was the only child of my father, who died while I was an infant. My mother was a woman of rather a masculine understanding, and full of the prejudices of nobility and magnificence. Her whole soul was in a manner concentrated in the ambition to render me the worthy successor of the counts de St. Leon, who had figured with distinguished reputation in the wars of the Holy Land. My father had died fighting gallantly in the plains of Italy under the standard of Louis the Twelfth; a prince whose name was never repeated to me unaccompanied with the praises due to his military prowess, and to the singular humanity of disposition by which he acquired the title of The father of his people. My mother's mind was inflamed with the greatness of my ancestors, and she indefatigably sought to kindle in my bosom a similar flame. It has been a long-established custom for the barons and feudal vassals of the kings of France to enter with great personal expense into the brilliant and dazzling expeditions of their sovereigns; and my father greatly impaired his fortune in preparations for that very campaign in which he terminated his life. My mother industriously applied herself to the restoration of my patrimony; and the long period of my minority afforded her scope for that purpose.

It was impossible for any boy to be treated with more kindness and considerate indulgence than I was during the period of my adolescence. My mother loved me to the very utmost limits perhaps of human affection. I was her darling and her pride, her waking study, and her nightly dream. Yet I was not pampered into corporeal imbecility, or suffered to rust in inactivity of mind. I was provided with the best masters. I was excited, and successfully excited, zealously to apply myself to the lessons they taught. I became intimately acquainted with the Italian writers of the twelfth and thirteenth centuries. I was initiated in the study of the classics, to the cultivation of which the revival of letters at this time gave particular ardour. I was instructed in the principles of the fine arts. There was no species of accomplishment at that time in vogue, that my mother was not anxious I should make my own. The only science I neglected was the very science which has since given rise to the most extraordinary events of my life. But the object to which my attention was principally called, was the pursuit of military exercises, and the cultivation of every thing that could add to the strength, agility, or grace of my body, and to the adventurousness and enterprise of my mind. My mother loved my honour and my fame more than she loved my person.

A circumstance that tended perhaps more than any other to fix the yet fluctuating character of my youthful mind, was my being present as a spectator at the celebrated meeting between Francis the First and Henry the Eighth, king of England, in a field between Ardres and Guines. My mother refused to accompany me, being already arrived at an age in which curiosity and the love of festive scenes are usually diminished, and the expenses incurred by all the nobility who attended upon this scene being incompatible with the economy to which she rigidly adhered. I was therefore placed under the protection of the Marquis de Villeroy, her brother, and, with two servants who attended me, formed a part of his suite.

I was at this time fifteen years of age. My contemplations had been familiar with ideas of magnificence and grandeur, but my life had been spent in the most sequestered retirement. This contrast had a particular effect upon my disposition; it irritated to a very high degree my passion for splendour and distinction; I lived in the fairy fields of visionary greatness, and was more than indifferent to the major part of the objects around me. I pined for every thing the reverse of my present condition; I cultivated the exercises in which I was engaged, only as they were calculated to prepare me for future achievements.

By the incident I have mentioned, I was transported at once from a scene of modest obscurity, to a scene of the most lavish splendour that the world perhaps ever contemplated. I never remembered to have seen even Paris itself. The prevailing taste of Europe has for some time led very much to costliness in dress. This taste, in its present profusion, I believe took its rise in the field of the Vale of Ardres. The two kings were both in the vigour of their youth, and were said to be the handsomest men of the age in which they lived. The beauty of Henry was sturdy and muscular; that of Francis more refined and elegant, without subtracting in any considerable degree from the firmness of his make. Henry was four years older than his brother monarch. The first of them might have been taken as a model to represent a youthful Hercules, and the last an Apollo.

The splendour of dress that was worn upon this occasion exceeds almost all credibility. Every person of distinction might be said in a manner to carry an estate upon his shoulders; nor was the variety of garments inferior to the richness. Wolsey, a man whose magnificence of disposition was only surpassed by the pride of his soul, was for the most part the director of the whole. He possessed the most absolute ascendancy over the mind of his master, at the same time that Francis artfully indulged his caprice, that he might claim from him in return a similar indulgence in weightier matters.

The pomp of processions, and the ceremony of opening this memorable festival, went first; a sort of solemn and half-moving pageant, which the eye took in at leisure, and took in till it was filled. This was succeeded by every thing that was rapid, animated, and interesting: masques and exhibitions of all kinds; and, which was still more to me, and which my soul devoured with indescribable ardour, joustings, tilts, and tournaments without end. The beauty of the armour, the caparisons of the steeds, the mettle of the animals themselves, and the ardour and grace of the combatants, surpassed every thing that my fancy had ever painted. These scenes were acted in the midst of a vast amphitheatre of spectators, where all that was noble and eminent of either country was assembled—the manliness of aspiring youth, and the boundless varieties of female attraction. All were in their gayest attire; every eye was lighted up with complacency and joy. If Heraclitus, or any other morose philosopher who has expatiated on the universal misery of mankind, had entered the field of Ardres, he must have retracted his assertions, or fled from the scene with confusion. The kings were placed at either end of the lists, surrounded with their courtiers. Every eye through this vast assembly was fixed upon the combatants; the body of every one present was inclined this way or that, in unconscious sympathy with the redoubted knights. From time to time, as the favourites of either party prevailed, the air was rent with shouts and acclamations.

What added to the fascination of all that I have yet mentioned, was that now, for the first time in an equal degree perhaps for centuries, the stiffness of unwieldy form was laid aside, and the heart of man expanded itself with generosity and confidence. It burst the fetters of ages; and, having burst them, it seemed to revel in its new-found liberty. It is well known that, after a few days of idle precaution and specious imprisonment on both sides, Francis one morning mounted his horse, and appeared, without guards or any previous notice, before the tent of Henry. The example was contagious, and from this time all ceremony was laid aside. The kings themselves entered personally into the combats of their subjects. It was a delightful and a ravishing spectacle, to witness the freedom of the old Roman manners, almost of the old Roman Saturnalia, polished and refined with all that was graceful and humane in the age of chivalry.

It may easily be imagined what an effect a scene like this was calculated to produce upon a youth of my age and my education. I recollected with anguish that the immaturity of my years precluded me from taking any active part in the spectacle. My appearance however was sufficiently advantageous. I was presented to Francis the First. He did me the honour to question me respecting my studies; and, finding in me some knowledge of those arts and that literature, of which he was himself so zealous a favourer, he expressed to my uncle a great satisfaction with my figure and acquisitions. I might from this time have been taken to court, and made one of the pages to this illustrious monarch. But the plan of my mother was different. She did not wish for the present that my eye should be satiated with public scenes, or that the public should grow too familiarly acquainted with my person. She rightly judged that my passion for the theatre of glory would grow more impetuous, by being withheld for some time from the gratifications for which it panted. She wished that I should present myself for the first time among the nobility of France an accomplished cavalier, and not suffer the disadvantage of having exposed in the eye of the world those false steps and frailties, from which the inexperience of youth is never entirely free. These motives being explained to the king, he was graciously pleased to sanction them with his approbation. I accordingly returned to finish the course of my education at my paternal château upon the banks of the Garonne.

The state of my mind during the three succeeding years amply justified the sagacity of my mother. I was more eager for improvement than I had ever yet been. I had before formed some conceptions of the career of honour from the books I had read, and from the conversation of this excellent matron. But my reveries were impotent and little, compared with what I had now seen. Like the author of our holy religion, I had spent my forty days without food in the wilderness, when suddenly my eyes were opened, and I was presented with all the kingdoms of the world, and all the glory of them. The fairy scene continued for a moment, and then vanished; leaving nothing behind it on all sides, but the same barrenness and gloom by which it had been preceded. I never shut my eyes without viewing in imagination the combats of knights and the train of ladies. I had been regarded with distinction by my sovereign; and Francis the First stood before my mind the abstract and model of perfection and greatness. I congratulated myself upon being born in an age and country so favourable to the acquisition of all that my soul desired.

I was already eighteen years of age, when I experienced the first misfortune that ever befel me. It was the death of my mother. She felt the approach of her dissolution several weeks before it arrived, and held repeated conversations with me, respecting the feelings I ought to entertain, and the conduct it would become me to pursue, when she should be no more.

"My son," said she, "your character, and the promise of your early years, have constituted my only consolation since the death of your excellent father. Our marriage was the result of a most sincere and exclusive attachment; and never did man more deserve to be loved than Reginald de St. Leon. When he died, the whole world would have been nothing to me but one vast blank, if he had not left behind him the representative of his person, and the heir to his virtues. While I was busied in your education, I seemed to be discharging the last duty to the memory of my husband. The occupation was sacred to the honour of the dead, even before it became so peculiarly pleasing to me upon its own account, as I afterwards found it. I hope I have in some measure discharged the task, in the manner in which my lord your father would have wished it to have been discharged, if he had lived. I am thankful to Heaven, that I have been spared so long for so dear and honourable a purpose.

"You must now, my son, stand by yourself, and be the arbitrator of your own actions. I could have wished that this necessity might have been a little further deferred; but I trust your education has not been of that sort which is calculated to render a young man helpless and contemptible. You have been taught to know your rank in society, and to respect yourself. You have been instructed in every thing that might most effectually forward you in the career of glory. There is not a young cavalier among all the nobility of

France more accomplished, or that promises to do greater honour to his name and his country. I shall not live to witness the performance of this promise, but the anticipation even now, pours a long stream of sunshine on my departing hour.

"Farewell, my son! You no longer stand in need of my maternal care. When I am gone, you will be compelled more vividly to feel that singleness and self-dependence which are the source of all virtue. Be careful of yourself. Be careful that your career may be both spotless and illustrious. Hold your life as a thing of no account, when it enters into competition with your fame. A true knight thinks no sacrifice and suffering hard, that honour demands. Be humane, gentle, generous, and intrepid. Be prompt to follow wherever your duty calls you. Remember your ancestors, knights of the Holy Cross. Remember your father. Follow your king, who is the mirror of valour: and be ever ready for the service of the distressed. May Providence be your guardian. May Heaven shower down a thousand blessings, upon your innocence, and the gallantry of your soul!"

The death of my mother was a severe blow to my heart. For some time all the visions of greatness and renown which had hitherto been my chosen delight appeared distasteful to me. I hung over her insensible corpse. When it had been committed to the earth, I repaired every day to the spot where it was deposited, at the hour of dusk, when all visible objects faded from the eye, when nature assumed her saddest tints, and the whole world seemed about to be wrapped in the darkness of the tomb. The dew of night drizzled unheeded on my head; and I did not turn again towards the turrets of the château, till the hour of midnight had already sounded through the stillness of the scene.

Time is the healer of almost every grief, particularly in the sprightly season of early youth. In no long period I changed the oppression of inactive sorrow, for the affectionate and pious recollection of my mother's last instructions. I had been too deeply imbued with sentiments of glory, for it to be possible, when the first excess of grief was over, that I should remain in indolence. The tender remembrance of my mother itself, in no long time, furnished a new stimulus to my ambition. I forgot the melancholy spectacle of the last struggles of her expiring life; I even became accustomed no longer to hear her voice, no longer to expect her presence, when I returned to the château from a short excursion. Her last advice was now all that survived of the author of my existence.

CHAPTER II.

I was in this state of mind, when early one morning in the beginning of summer, soon after I rose, I was startled by the sound of trumpets in the plain near the château. The bugle at the gate was presently sounded; the drawbridge was let down; and the Marquis de Villeroy entered the court-yard, accompanied by about thirty knights in complete armour. I saluted him with respect, and the tenderness excited by recent grief. He took me by the hand, after a short repast in the hall, and led me to my closet.

"My son," said he, "it is time to throw off the effeminacy of sorrow, and to prove yourself a true soldier of the standard of France."

"I trust, my lord," replied I, with modest earnestness, "that you well know, there is nothing after which my heart so ardently aspires. There is nothing that I know worth living for but honour. Show me the path that leads to it, or rather show me the occasion that affords scope for the love of honour to display itself, and you shall then see whether I am backward to embrace it. I have a passion pent up within me, that feeds upon my vitals: it disdains speech; it burns for something more unambiguous and substantial."

"It is well," rejoined my uncle. "I expected to find you thus. Your reply to my admonition is worthy of the blood of your ancestors, and of the maternal instructions of my sister. And, were you as dull as the very stones you tread on, what I have to tell you might even then rouse you into animation and ardour."

After this short preface my uncle proceeded to relate a tale, every word of which inflamed my spirits, and raised all my passions in arms. I had heard something imperfectly of the state of my country; but my mother carefully kept me in ignorance, that my ambition might not be excited too soon, and that, when excited, it might be with the fullest effect. While I impatiently longed for an occasion of glory, I was far from apprehending, what I now found to be true, that the occasion which at this period presented itself, was such, that all the licence of fiction could scarcely have improved it.

The Marquis de Villeroy described to me the league now subsisting against France. He revived in my memory, by terms of the most fervent loyalty, the accomplishments and talents of my royal master. He spoke with aversion of the phlegmatic and crafty disposition of his imperial rival; and, with the language of glowing indignation, inveighed against the fickleness of the capricious Henry. He described the train of disasters, which had at length induced the king to take the field in person. He contrasted, with great effect, the story of the gallant Chevalier Bayard, the knight without fear and without reproach, whose blood was still fresh in the plains of the Milanese, with that of the Constable of Bourbon, the stain of chivalry, whom inglorious resentment and ungoverned ambition had urged to join the enemies of his country, in neglect of his loyalty and his oath. He stimulated me by the example of the one, and the infamy of the other; and assured me that there never was an opportunity more favourable for acquiring immortal renown.

I wanted no prompter in a passion of this sort; and immediately set about collecting the whole force of my clients and retainers. I shook off the inglorious softness of my melancholy, and was all activity and animation. The lessons of my youth were now called into play. I judged it necessary to invite the assistance of some person of experience to assist me in marshalling my men; but I did much of what was to be done myself, and I did it well. It was my first employment in the morning: and the last that was witnessed by the setting sun. My excellent mother had left my revenues in the best order, and I spared no expense in the gratification of my favourite passion.

However eager I felt myself to take the field, the desire to appear in a manner worthy of a Count de St. Leon restrained me; and I did not join the royal army till the Imperialists, having broken up the siege of Marseilles, and retreated with precipitation into Italy, the king had already crossed the Alps, entered the Milanese, and gained uncontested possession of the capital.

From Milan Francis proceeded to Pavia. Glory was the idol of his heart; and he was the more powerfully excited to the attack of that place, because it was the strongest and best fortified post in the whole duchy. The more he displayed of military prowess, the more firmly he believed he should fix himself in his newly acquired dominions; the inhabitants would submit to him the more willingly, and the enemy be less encouraged to enter into a fresh contention for what he had acquired. Such at least were the motives that he assigned for his proceedings: in reality perhaps he was principally induced by the brilliancy which he conceived would attend on the undertaking.

It was a few weeks after the opening of the siege, that I presented myself to my royal master. He received me with those winning and impressive manners by which he was so eminently distinguished. He recollected immediately all that had passed at our interview in the Vale of Ardres, and warmly expressed the obligations which France had at various times owed to my ancestors. He spoke with earnest respect of the virtues and wisdom of my mother, and commended the resolution by which she had in former instances held me back from the public theatre. "Young gentleman," said the king, "I doubt not the gallantry of your spirit; I see the impatience of a martial temper written in your face: I expect you to act in a manner worthy of your illustrious race, and of the instructions of a woman who deserved to be herself a pattern to all the matrons of France. Fear not that I shall suffer your accomplishments to rust in obscurity. I shall employ you. I shall assign you the post of danger and of renown. Fill it nobly; and from that hour I shall rank you in the catalogue of my chosen friends."

The siege of Pavia proved indeed to be a transaction, in the course of which military honour might well be acquired. It was defended by a small, but veteran garrison, and by one of the ablest captains that Europe at that time possessed. He interrupted the approaches of the besiegers by frequent and furious sallies. In vain, by the aid of our excellent artillery, did we make wide and repeated breaches in the fortifications. No sooner did we attempt to enter by the passage we had opened, than we found ourselves encountered by a body composed of the choicest and bravest soldiers of the garrison. The governor of the city, who, though grey-headed and advanced in years, was profuse of every youthful exertion, was ordinarily at the head of this body. If we deferred our attack, or, not having succeeded in it, proposed to commence it anew with the dawn of the following day, we were sure to find a new wall sprung up in the room of the other, as if by enchantment. Frequently the governor anticipated the success of our batteries; and the old fortification was no sooner demolished, than we beheld, to our astonishment and mortification, a new wall, which his prudence and skill had erected at a small interval within the line of the former.

One of these attacks took place on the second day after my arrival at the camp of our sovereign. Every thing that I saw was new to me, and inflamed me with ardour. The noise of the cannon, which had preceded the attack, and which was now hushed; the inspiring sounds of martial music which succeeded that noise; the standards floating in the air; the firm and equal tread of the battalion that advanced; the armour of the knights; the rugged, resolute, and intrepid countenances of the infantry;—all swelled my soul with transport hitherto unexperienced. I had beheld the smoke of the artillery, in the midst of which every thing was lost and confounded; I had waited in awful suspense till the obscurity should be dissipated; I saw with pleasure and surprise the ruin of the wall, and the wideness of the breach. All that had been recorded of the military feats of Christian valour seemed then to stand crowded in my busy brain; the generosity, the condescension, the kindness, with which the king had addressed me the day before, urged me to treble exertion. I was in the foremost rank. We surmounted the ditch. We were resisted by a chosen body of Spaniards. The contention was obstinate; brave men, generous and enterprising spirits, fell on the one side and the other. I seized the cloth of a standard, as, in the playing of the wind, it was brought near to my hand. Between me and the Spaniard that held it there ensued an obstinate struggle. I watched my opportunity, and with my sword severed the flag from its staff. At this moment the trumpets of the king sounded a retreat. I had received two severe wounds, one in the shoulder and the other in the thigh, in the contest. I felt myself faint with the loss of blood. A French officer, of a rude appearance and gigantic stature, accosting me with the appellation of boy; commanded me to surrender the standard to him. I refused; and, to convince him I was in earnest, proceeded to wrap it round my body, and fastened it under my arm. Soon after I became insensible, and in this situation was accidentally found by my uncle and his companions, who immediately took me and my prize under their care. As soon as I was a little recovered of my wounds, the king seized an opportunity, after having bestowed loud commendations upon my gallantry, of conferring the honours of knighthood upon me in the face of the whole army.

While our tents were pitched under the walls of Pavia, I was continually extending the circle of my acquaintance among the young gentry of France, who, like myself, had attended their sovereign in this memorable expedition. I had some enemies, made such by the distinctions I obtained during the siege. But they were few; the greater part courted me the more, the more I showed myself worthy of their attachment. Envy is not a passion that finds easy root in a Frenchman's bosom. I was one of the youngest of those who attended on the siege; but my brothers in arms were generous rivals, who in the field obstinately strove with me for superior glory, but over the convivial board forgot their mutual competitions, and opened their hearts to benevolence and friendship. "Let us not," was a sentiment I heard often repeated, "forget the object that led us from our pleasant homes to pour from the heights of the Alps upon the fields of Italy. It is to humble the imperious Spaniard—to punish the disloyal Bourbon—to vindicate the honour of our beloved and illustrious monarch. Those walls cover the enemy; yonder mountains serve to hide them from our assault; let no Frenchman mistake him who marches under the same standard for an adversary."

The trenches had not been opened before Pavia till about the beginning of November. The winter overtook us, and the siege was yet in progress; with some apparent advantage indeed to our side of the question, but by no means promising an instant conclusion. The season set in with unusual severity; and both officer and soldier were glad, as much as possible, to fence out its rigour by the indulgences of the genial board. My finances, as I have said, were at the commencement of the expedition in excellent order: I had brought with me a considerable sum; and it was not spared upon the present occasion.

There were however other things to be attended to, beside the demands of conviviality. The king became impatient of the delays of the siege. The garrison and the inhabitants were reduced to great extremities; but the governor discovered no symptoms of a purpose to surrender. In the mean time intelligence was brought, that Bourbon was making the most extraordinary exertions in Germany, and promised to lead to the enemy a reinforcement of twelve thousand men from that country; while the imperial generals, by mortgaging their revenues, and pawning their jewels, and still more by their eloquence and influence with those under their command, were able to keep together the remains of a disheartened and defeated army in expectation of his arrival. There was some danger therefore, if the siege were not speedily terminated, that the king might ultimately be obliged to raise it with ignominy, or to fight the enemy under every disadvantage. Francis however was not to be deterred from his undertaking. He swore a solemn oath, that Pavia should be his, or he would perish in the attempt.

Thus circumstanced, he conceived a very extraordinary project. Pavia is defended on one side by the Tesino, the scene of the first of the four famous battles by which Hannibal signalised his invasion of Italy. The king believed that if this river could by the labour of his army be diverted from its course, the town must instantly fall into his hands. He was encouraged to the undertaking, by recollecting a stratagem of a similar nature by which Cyrus formerly made himself master of the city of Babylon. It was a thought highly flattering to the grandeur of his soul, to imagine that posterity would in this instance institute a parallel between him and Cyrus the Great.

The plan for diverting the course of the Tesino produced a new and extraordinary scene. It was, as may well be believed, a work of uncommon labour. A new channel was to be scooped out and deepened; and, while the stream was turned into this channel, piles were to be sunk, and an immense mound of earth created, as an effectual impediment to the waters resuming their former course. This was a heavy burthen to the soldier, in addition to the disadvantage of being encamped during the course of a winter remarkably severe for the climate in which we fought. By any other army the task would have been performed with cloudiness and discontent, if not complained of with repining and murmurs. But here the gaiety of the French character displayed itself. The nobility of France, who attended their sovereign in great numbers, accompanied the infantry in their labour. We laid aside the indulgence of the marquée, of tapestry and carpets; we threw off our upper garments; and each seized a spade, a barrow of earth, or a mattock. We put our hands to the engines, and refused no effort under pretence that it was sordid or severe. While the trees were leafless, and nature appeared bound up in frost, sweat ran down our faces and bedewed our limbs. The army were encouraged by our example. An employment which, under other circumstances, would have been regarded as rigid, was thus made a source of new hilarity and amusement. It was a memorable sight to behold the venerable and grey-headed leaders of the French army endeavouring to exert the strength and activity of their early years. To me, who had but lately arrived at the stature of manhood, and who was accustomed to all the exercises which give strength and vigour to the frame, this new employment was in no degree burdensome. I felt in it the satisfaction that a swift man experiences when he enters the lists of the race; I congratulated myself upon the nature of my education; if it be a sin to covet honour, that guilt was mine; and, so great was my appetite for it, that I was inexpressibly rejoiced to observe the various ways in which it might be gratified.

Strange as it may seem, this scene of a winter-camp, in the midst of blood and sweat, surrounded with dangers, and called on for unparalleled exertions, appears to me, through the vista of years that is now interposed between, to have been one of the happiest of my life. The gay labours and surprises of the day were succeeded by a convivial evening, in which we did not the less open our hearts, though frequently liable to be interrupted in our midnight revels by the inexhaustible activity and stratagems of the enemy. In this various and ever-shifting scene, I forgot the disasters that occurred, and the blood that flowed around me. All sense of a large and impartial morality was, for the time at least, deadened in my breast. I was ever upon the alert. The diversity of events neither suffered my spirits to flag, nor reflection to awake. It is only upon such occasions, or occasions like these, that a man is able fully to feel what life is, and to revel in its exuberance. Above all, I was delighted with the society and friendship of my brother-officers. They honoured me; they loved me. I seemed to feel what sympathy was; and to have conscious pleasure in making one in a race of beings like myself. Such were my sensations.

It must not, however, be imagined, that all about me felt in these respects as I did. I was deeply indebted in this particular to my youth and my fortune. The old endeavoured to brace themselves in vain; they sunk under the continual pressure. The poor soldier from the ranks laboured incessantly, and I laboured as much as he; but he had little opportunity to recruit his vigour and renovate his strength. There was yet another class of persons in the camp, whose gaiety was much less interrupted than mine. These were, the king, and the generals who commanded under him. They could not be entirely devoid of thought and consideration. They suffered much anxiety from the length of the siege; and felt that every period of delay increased the doubtfulness of the event.

Antonio de Leyva, governor of the city, necessarily felt himself alarmed at the extraordinary project in which we were engaged, and made every exertion to prevent it. One evening the king sent for me to his tent, and told me in confidence that the enemy intended that very night to make three several attacks upon our mound, one on each side of the stream, and one by means of boats in the centre. Two of these, he said, were merely intended as feints; the west bank of the Tesino was the point against which their principal exertions would be directed. On that side he was resolved to command in person; the boats with which he proposed to resist their flota he confided to one of the most famous and valuable officers of his army; the detachment on the east bank he purposed to intrust to my uncle and myself. He observed, that the detachment he could spare for that purpose, after having formed the other two bodies, and reserved a sufficient number for the defence of the camp and the works, would be small; and he warned me to the exertion of a particular vigilance. It would be doubly unfortunate, if a body, the attack upon which was to be merely a feigned one, should nevertheless be routed. "Go," added he, "fulfil my expectations; deport yourself answerably to the merit of your first achievement; and depend upon it that you will prove hereafter one of the most eminent supporters of the martial glory of France."

The Marquis de Villeroy divided our little force into two bodies: with the larger he lay in wait for the enemy near the scene of the expected attack: the smaller he confided to my direction, and placed so that we might be able to fall upon the rear of the garrison-troops as soon as they should be fully engaged with our comrades. In the situation assigned me I took advantage of the skirts of a wood, which enabled me to approach very near to the expected route of our assailants, without being perceived by them. The night was extremely dark, yet the vicinity of my position was such, that I could count the numbers of the adversary as they passed along before my hiding-place. I was alarmed to find that they amounted to at least the triple of what we had been taught to expect. They were no sooner past, than I despatched to the king a young knight, my particular friend, who happened to be with me, to urge the necessity of a reinforcement. At the same time I sent a messenger to my uncle, by a circuitous route, to inform him of what I had observed, and the step I had taken, and to entreat him to defer the attack as long as consistently with propriety it should be possible. The enemy, however, had no sooner arrived at the place of his destination, than the troops of the marquis, no longer capable of restraint, rushed to engage. The Spaniards were at first surprised, but a short time led them to suspect the weakness of their assailants; nor was the assistance I brought to my uncle sufficient to turn the fortune of the fight. We lost many of our men; the rest apparently gave ground; and it was a vain attempt, amidst the darkness of the night, to endeavour to restore order and rally them to the assault. We were already almost completely overpowered, when the succours we expected reached us. They were, however, unable to distinguish friend from enemy. A storm of mingled rain and snow had come on, which benumbed our limbs, drove fiercely in our faces, and rendered every object alike viewless. The carnage which in this situation took place was terrible. Our blows were struck at random. A Frenchman was not less dreadful than a Spaniard. When the battle ceased, scarcely one of the enemy was left alive; but we observed with astonishment and horror the number of the besiegers who had probably, in the midst of the confusion, been cut to pieces by their own countrymen.

I am now arrived at the period which put an end to the festivity and jocundness of the campaign. All after this was one continued series of disaster. About the close of January, our work, though not wholly interrupted, was considerably retarded by a succession of heavy rains. This was injurious to us in many ways; our project, which was executed in the midst of waters, rendered additional damp a matter of serious consideration. We were also seized with an apprehension of still greater magnitude, which was speedily realised. The snows being at length completely dissolved, and the quantity of water continually increasing, we perceived one afternoon strong symptoms that our mound, the principal subject of our labour and source of our hope, was giving way in various places. The next morning at daybreak, it rushed down every where at once with wonderful violence and noise. It is difficult to describe the sensation of anguish which was instantly and universally diffused. The labour of many weeks was overthrown in a moment. As we had proceeded in our work, we every day saw ourselves nearer the object to which we aspired. At this time our project was almost completed, and Pavia was in imagination already in our hands, to gain possession of which had cost us such unremitted exertions, the display of so much gallantry, and the loss of so many soldiers. We were confounded at the catastrophe we saw. We gazed at each other, each in want of encouragement, and every one unable to afford it.

Still, however, we were not destitute of advantages. The garrison began to be in want both of ammunition and provisions. They were in a general state of discontent, almost of mutiny, which scarcely all the address and authority of the governor were able to suppress. If the town continued longer unrelieved, it was sure to fall into our hands. But even this our last hope was considerably diminished by the intelligence we received the very day after the destruction of our mound, that the imperial army, after having received large reinforcements, was approaching in considerable force. The king had some time before, in the height of his confidence, and elation of his heart, sent off a detachment of six thousand men to invade the kingdom of Naples; for upon that, as well as the Milanese, he had inherited pretensions from his immediate predecessors.

But, though the enemy was superior in numbers, and a part perhaps of their forces better disciplined than ours, they laboured under several disadvantages to which we were not exposed. The Emperor, though his dominions were more extensive, did not derive from them a revenue equal to that of Francis. As he did not take the field in person, the war appeared to his subjects only a common war, proceeding upon the ordinary motives of war. But my countrymen were led by their sovereign, were fresh from the recent insolence of an invasion of their own territory, and fought at once for personal glory and their country's honour. The king, who commanded them, seemed expressly formed to obtain their attachment and affection. His nobles became enthusiastic by the example of his enthusiasm, and willingly disbursed their revenues to give prosperity and éclat to the campaign.

The first question that arose upon the approach of the enemy was, whether we should break up the siege, and attend in some strong post the slow, but sure, effect of their want of money, and the consequent dispersion of their troops, or wait their attack in our present posture. The former advice was safe; but to the gallant spirit of Francis it appeared ignominious. He was upon all occasions the partisan of rapid measures and decisive proceedings; and his temper, with the exception of a few wary and deliberate counsellors, accorded with that of our whole army. For some days we congratulated ourselves upon the wisdom of our choice; we presented to the enemy so formidable an appearance, that, notwithstanding the cogent motives he had to proceed, he hesitated long before he ventured to attack us. At length, however, the day came that was pregnant with so momentous expectation.

If through the whole limits of our camp there was not a man that did not feel himself roused upon this glorious occasion, to me it was especially interesting. The scene accorded with the whole purpose of my education, and novelty made it impressive. I lived only in the present moment. I had not a thought, a wish, a straggling imagination, that wandered beyond the circuit of the day. My soul was filled; at one minute wild with expectation, and at another awed into solemnity. There is something indescribably delicious in this concentration of the mind. It raises a man above himself; and makes him feel a certain nobleness and elevation of character, of the possession of which he was to that hour unconscious. Fear and pain were ideas that could find no harbour in my bosom: I regarded this as the most memorable of days, and myself as the most fortunate of mortals. Far indeed was I from anticipating the disgraceful event, in which this elation of heart speedily terminated.

The sun rose bright in a cloudless sky. The cold of the season was such, as only to give new lightness and elasticity to the muscles and animal spirits. I saw few of those objects of nature, which in this delightful climate gave so sacred a pleasure to the human soul. But in my present temper there was no object of sight so ravishing, as the firm and equal steps of the martial bands, the impatience of the war-horse, and the display of military standards; nor any music so enchanting, as the shrillness of the pipe, the clangor of the trumpet, the neighing of steeds, and the roaring of cannon. It is thus that man disguises to himself the real nature of his occupation; and clothes that which is of all things the most nefarious or most to be lamented, with the semblance of jubilee and festival.

The Imperialists were at first unable to withstand the efforts of French valour. They gave way on every side; we pursued our advantage with impetuosity. To the slaughter of whole ranks mowed down with tremendous celerity, to the agonies of the dying, I was blind; their groans had no effect on my organ, for my soul was occupied in another direction. My horse's heels spurned their mangled limbs, and were red with their blood. I fought not merely with valour, but with fury; I animated those around me by my example and my acclamations. It may seem contrary to delicacy to speak with this freedom of my own praises; but I am at my present writing totally changed and removed from what I was, and I write with the freedom of a general historian. It is this simplicity and ingenuousness that shall pervade the whole of my narrative.

The fortune of the day speedily changed. The cowardice and desertion of our Swiss allies gave the first signal of adversity. The gallant commander of the garrison of Pavia sallied out in the midst of the fight, and suddenly attacked us in the rear. A stratagem of the Imperial general effected the rout of our cavalry. The whole face of the field was utterly reversed.

It would be in vain for me to attempt to describe even the small part that I beheld of the calamity and slaughter of the French army. At this distance of time, the recollection of it opens afresh the almost obliterated wounds of my heart. I saw my friends cut down, and perish on every side. Those who, together with myself, had marched out in the morning, swelled with exultation and hope, now lay weltering in their blood. Their desires, their thoughts, their existence, were brought to a fatal termination. The common soldiers were hewed and cut to pieces by hundreds, without note and observation. Many of the first nobility of France, made desperate by the change of the battle, rushed into the thickest of the foe, and became so many voluntary sacrifices; choosing rather to perish, than to turn their backs with dishonour.

In the battle I had two horses killed under me. The first of them suffered a sort of gradual destruction. He had already received one wound in the nostrils, and another in the neck, when a third shot carried away two of his feet, and laid him prostrate on the earth. Bernardin, my faithful attendant, observed what was passing, and immediately brought me a fresh charger; but I had not long mounted him, when he received a wound which killed him on the spot. I was myself hurt in several places, and at length the stroke of a sabre brought me to the ground. Here I remained for a long time insensible. When I recovered, and looked around me, I found myself in entire solitude, and could at present perceive no trace either of the enemy or of my own people. Soon, however, I recollected what had passed, and was but too well assured of the defeat my countrymen had sustained. Weak and battered as I was, I attempted to retire to a place of greater security. I had scarcely changed my ground, before I saw a trooper of the enemy rushing towards me, with the intention to take away my life. Fortunately I observed a tree at hand, to the shelter of which I hastened; and, partly by moving the branches to and fro, and partly by shifting my position, I baffled my adversary, till he became weary of the attempt. A moment after, I saw one of my most intimate and familiar companions killed before my eyes. It was not long, however, before a party of fugitive French came up to the spot where I stood, and I, like the rest, was hurried from the field. My uncle perished in the battle.

It is wonderful how men can harden their hearts against such scenes as I then witnessed. It is wonderful how they can be brought to co-operate in such demoniac fury, and more than demoniac mischief, barbarity, and murder. But they are brought to it; and enter, not from a deplorable necessity, but as to a festival, in which each man is eager to occupy his place, and share the amusements. It seemed to me at that time, as it seems to me now, that it should be enough for a man to contemplate such a field as I saw at Pavia, to induce him to abjure the trade of violence for ever, and to commit his sword once more to the bowels of the earth, from which it was torn for so nefarious a purpose.

These sensations, though now finally established in my mind, were, at the time of which I am writing, but of fleeting duration. The force of education, and the first bent of my mind, were too strong. The horror which overwhelmed me in the first moments of this great national defeat subsided; and the military passion returned upon me in its original ardour. My convictions, and the moral integrity of my soul, were temporary; and I became myself a monument of that inconstancy and that wonder, to which I have just alluded.

Various circumstances, however, prevented this passion from its direct operation. The character of France was altered by the battle of Pavia, though mine remained the same. It was in the fullest degree decisive of the fortune of the war. Milan, and every other place in the duchy, opened their gates to the conqueror; and, in a fortnight, not a Frenchman was left in the fields of Italy. Of the whole army only a small body effected an orderly retreat, under the command of the Duke of Alençon. Many persons of the highest distinction perished in the battle: many were made prisoners by the enemy. France by this event found the list of her noblesse considerably reduced in numbers; add to which, those whose loss she sustained, were almost all of them taken from among the most distinguished and meritorious in the catalogue.

But what constituted the principal feature in this memorable event was, that the king himself was found in the number of the prisoners; nor was he released by his ungenerous competitor till after more than a twelvemonth's confinement. During this period Francis tasted of the dregs of adversity. Inclined in the first instance to judge of his rival by himself, he expected a liberal treatment. In this he was deeply disappointed. After a detention of many months in the Milanese, the scene of his former successes, he was transferred to Madrid. He was personally neglected by the emperor, while his disloyal subject was treated with singular distinction. The most rigorous terms were proposed to him. All this had the effect, in one instance, of sinking him into a disease of languor and dejection which he was not expected to survive; and, in another, of inducing him to execute an instrument by which he abdicated the crown, and declared his resolution of remaining a prisoner for life. His confinement was at length terminated by his solemnly engaging to compulsory articles, which he was determined to break as soon as he found himself at liberty; an alternative peculiarly grating to the liberality of his spirit. This reverse of fortune materially changed his character. The fine spirit of his ambition was from this time evaporated; and, while he still retained the indefeasible qualities of his soul, and was gallant, kind-hearted, and generous, he bartered, as far as was compatible with his disposition, the enterprising and audacious temper he had previously manifested, for the wary and phlegmatic system of his more fortunate competitor. His genius cowered before that of Charles; and the defeat of Pavia may, perhaps, be considered as having given a deadly wound to the reign of chivalry, and a secure foundation to that of craft, dissimulation, corruption, and commerce.

CHAPTER III.

The lists of military ambition then being closed, if not permanently, at least for a time, my mind took a new bias; and, without dismissing its most cherished and darling passion, pursued a path in the present emergency, to which the accidents of my youth had also guided me. If my mother had survived, she would probably either not have consented to my serving at the siege of Pavia, or at least would have recalled me to the obscurity of my paternal château as soon as the campaign was at an end. I had not fully completed the twentieth year of my age, at the period of the memorable battle in which my sovereign was made prisoner. I was left without adviser or guide; even the Marquis de Villeroy, my mother's brother, of whatever consequence his admonitions to me might have proved, was taken from me in this fatal engagement. The king himself, perhaps, had it not been for the dreadful calamities in which he was now involved, might have condescended to interest himself in some degree in my welfare. By the course of events, I was left, yet a minor, and with an ample revenue at my disposition, to be wholly guided by the suggestions of my own mind.

In the portion of his reign already elapsed, the splendid and interesting qualities of Francis had given a new spring to the sentiments of the nation. He was the most accomplished and amiable prince of the time in which he lived. There was but one of all the sovereigns of Christendom that could cope with him in power,—the Emperor Charles; and as Charles's peculiarities were of a sort that Frenchmen were accustomed to regard with aversion and contempt, so there had not been a doubt among my compatriots, of the side upon which the superiority would ultimately rest. By the events of the day of Pavia they were confounded and overwhelmed. They did not despair of their country; they soon felt, and felt to its utmost extent, the rank which France held among the European states. But the chain of their ideas was interrupted; they could not but be conscious that the fortune of the kingdom had received a grievous check. The illustrious career which they had in fancy already traversed, was postponed to a distant period.

The consequences which flow from a suppressed ambition may easily be imagined. The nobility of France exchanged the activity of the field for the indulgences of the table: that concentrated spirit which had sought to expand itself upon the widest stage, now found vent in the exhibition of individual expense: and, above all, the sordid and inglorious passion for gaming, a vice eminently characteristic of the age, now especially gained strength, and drew multitudes into its destructive vortex. It was, perhaps, impossible for a young man to have entered the theatre of the world under less favourable auspices.

In what I have already written, I felt myself prompted to enlarge with complacency upon the sentiments and scenes of my youth; and I have yielded to the suggestion. The same internal admonition makes me shrink from entering with minuteness into the detail of my ruin. I recollect my infatuation with abhorrence; I fly from the memory with sensations inexpressibly painful; I regard it as a cloud that overshadowed and blackened for ever the fair prospects of my earlier years.

I shall not enumerate all my youthful companions, or all my youthful follies. I committed a mistake obvious enough, at this immature period of my existence, when I mistook profusion and extravagance for splendour and dignity; and the prudent economy which my mother had practised, served, in the present instance, as the pander to my vices. The whole tendency of my education had been to inspire me with a proud and restless desire of distinction; and I was not content to play a second part in the career of my vices, as I should not have been content to play a second part in the genuine theatre of honour and fame. In all that was thoughtlessly spirited and gaily profligate, I led the way to my compeers, and was constantly held up by them as an example. By this conduct I incurred the censure of the rigorous and the old; but the voice of censure reached me much seldomer than that of adulation. My person and demeanour were the topics of general applause. I was tall and well-proportioned; my frame was slender and agile, but with an appearance of the fullest health; my countenance was open, commanding, and animated: my rank and situation in the world gave me confidence; the fire and impetuosity of my temper rendered my gestures easy, rapid, expressive, and graceful. The consequence of all this was, to confirm me in a plan of life which I early laid down to myself, and from which I never in any instance deviated. I put aside those rules, as splenetic and hypercritical, which confessors preach, and with which the preceptors of young men are accustomed to weary and alienate the minds of their pupils. The charge of being disorderly and unthinking I despised; that of imprudence, even when meant for blame, sounded in my ear like the voice of encomium. But, accustomed from education to sentiments of honour, and from habit to the language of eulogy, it is difficult for any man to be more firmly bent than I was to incur no breath of dishonour, or to draw the line more peremptorily between the follies of youth and the aberrations of a gross and unprincipled spirit.

It may be alleged, indeed, and with considerable justice, that the habit of gaming is an exception to this statement. It was with hesitation and reluctance that I entered into this habit. I saw it as it was, and as every ingenuous and undebauched mind must see it, base and sordid. The possession of some degree of wealth I regarded, indeed, as indispensable to a man who would fill a lofty and respectable character in the world; a character that, by uniting the advantages of exterior appearance with the actions of a hero, should extort the homage of his species. But, in the picture I drew of this man in my mind, I considered wealth as an accident, the attendant on his birth, to be dispensed with dignity, not to be adverted to with minuteness of attention. Deep play is certainly sufficiently inconsistent with this character. The direct purpose of the gamester is to transfer money from the pocket of his neighbour into his own. He rouses his sleepy and wearied attention by the most sordid of all motives. The fear of losing pierces his heart with anguish; and to gain—to obtain an advantage for himself which can scarcely exceed, and which seldom equals, the injury his competitor suffers,—is the circumstance which most transports his heart with delight. For this he watches; for this he calculates. An honourable gamester does not seize with premeditation the moment when his adversary is deprived, by wine or any other cause, of his usual self-possession. He does not seek with sober malice to play upon his passions. He does not enter with avidity into the contest with an unpractised but presuming rival: but he cannot avoid rejoicing, when he finds that accident has given him an unusual advantage. I have often thought that I could better understand how a man of honour could reconcile himself to the accursed and murderous trade of war, than to the system of the gaming table. In war, he fights with a stranger, a man with whom he has no habits of kindness, and who is fairly apprised that he comes against him with ruinous intent. But in play, he robs, perhaps, his brother, his friend, the partner of his bosom; or, in every event, a man seduced into the snare with all the arts of courtesy, and whom he smiles upon, even while he stabs.

I am talking here the mere reason and common sense of the question as it relates to mankind in general. But it is with other feelings that I reflect upon the concern I have myself individually in the subject. Years roll on in vain; ages themselves are useless here; looking forward, as I do, to an existence that shall endure till time shall be no more; no time can wipe away the remembrance of the bitter anguish that I have endured, the consequence of gaming. It is torture! It is madness! Poverty, I have drained thy cup to the dregs! I have seen my wife and my children looking to me in vain for bread! Which is the most intolerable distress?—that of the period, in which all the comforts of life gradually left me; in which I caught at every fragment of promise, and every fragment failed; in which I rose every morning to pamper myself with empty delusions; in which I ate the apples of purgatory, fair without, but within bitterness and ashes; in which I tossed, through endless, sightless nights, upon the couch of disappointment and despair?—or the period, when at length all my hopes were at an end; when I fled with horror to a foreign climate; when my family, that should have been my comfort, gave me my most poignant agony; when I looked upon them, naked, destitute, and exiles, with the tremendous thought, what and who it was that had caused their ruin? Adversity, without consolation,—adversity, when its sting is remorse, self-abhorrence and self-contempt,—hell has no misery by which it can be thrown into shade or exceeded!

Why do I dwell upon, or at least why do I anticipate, this detested circumstance of my story? Let me add one remark in this place, and pass on to the other particulars of this epoch of my prodigality. It is true, I must take this shameful appellation to myself—I was a gamester. But, in the beginning, I took no concern in that species of science which is often implied in the appellation. My games were games of hazard, not of skill. It appeared to my distempered apprehension to be only a mode in which for a man to display his fortitude and philosophy; I was flattered with the practice of gaming, because I saw in it, when gracefully pursued, the magnanimity of the stoic, combined with the manners of a man of the world; a magnanimity that no success is able to intoxicate, and no vicissitude to subvert. I committed my property to the hazard of the die; and I placed my ambition in laughing alike at the favours of fortune and her frowns. In the sequel, however, I found myself deceived. The fickle goddess sufficiently proved that she had the power of making me serious. But in her most tremendous reverses, I was never influenced to do any thing that the most scrupulous gamester regards as dishonourable. I say not this for the purpose of giving colour and speciousness to my tale. I say it, because I have laid it down to myself in this narrative as a sacred principle, to relate the simple, unaltered truth.

Another characteristic of the reign of Francis the First, is its gallantries. It is well known how much the king was himself occupied with attachments of this sort; his government was rather the government of women than of politicians; and the manners of the sovereign strongly tended to fix the habits of his subjects. A very young man rather takes the tone of his passions from those about him, than forms one that is properly his own; and this was my case in the present instance as well as in the preceding. Originally of an amorous constitution, I should perhaps have quieted the restlessness of my appetites without ostentation and éclat, had not the conduct of my youthful associates in general led me to regard gallantry as an accomplishment indispensably necessary in a young man of rank. It must be confessed, indeed, that this offence against the rigour of discipline has a thousand advantages over that of gaming. Few women of regular and reputable lives have that ease of manners, that flow of fancy, and that graceful intrepidity of thinking and expressing themselves, that is sometimes to be found among those who have discharged themselves from the tyranny of custom. There is something irresistibly captivating in that voluptuousness which, while it assumes a certain air of freedom, uniformly and with preference conforms itself to the dictates of unsophisticated delicacy. A judicious and limited voluptuousness is necessary to the cultivation of the mind, to the polishing of the manners, to the refining of sentiment and the developement of the understanding; and a woman deficient in this respect may be of use for the government of our families, but can neither add to the enjoyments, nor fix the partiality, of a man of animation and taste.

But whatever there may be in these considerations, certain it is that the conduct I pursued in matters of gallantry led me into great and serious expenses. The mistresses with whom I chanced to associate had neither the inexpressible captivation of madame de Chateaubriant, nor the aspiring and impressive manners of the duchess d'Etampes. They had, however, beauty and vivacity, frolic without rudeness, and softness without timidity. They had paid some regard to points of knowledge and taste, considering these as additional means for fixing the partiality of their paramours, and knowing that they had no security for the permanence of their prosperity but in the variety of their attractions. In their society I was led into new trains of reflection, a nicer consideration of human passion and the varieties of human character, and, above all, into a greater quickness and delicacy in matters of intellectual taste. My hours, for the most part, rolled swiftly and easily away, sometimes in the society of the young, the gay and the ambitious of my own sex, and sometimes in the softer and more delicious intercourse of the fair. I lived in the midst of all that Paris could at that time furnish of splendid and luxurious. This system of living was calculated to lull me in pleasing dreams, and to waste away existence in delirious softness. It sufficiently accorded with the sad period of our sovereign's captivity, when my young compatriots sought to drown the sense of public and patriotic considerations in copious draughts of pleasure; nor did the monarch's return immediately restore to France her former haughtiness and pride.

The course of sensuality in which I was now engaged, though it did not absolutely sink into grossness, may well be supposed to have trodden upon the very edge of licence. I and my companions were young; we were made fearless and presuming by fortune and by rank; we had laid aside those more rigorous restraints which render the soberer part of mankind plausible and decent, by making them timid and trite. I will not contaminate the minds of my innocent and inexperienced readers by entering into the detail of the follies in which I engaged.

One thing it is necessary to remark, as essential to the main thread of my story. My expenses of all kinds, during this period of self-desertion, drained my resources, but did not tarnish my good name. My excesses were regarded by some as ornamental and becoming, but by all were admitted as venial. The laurels I had won in the field of military honour were not obscured by my subsequent conduct. I was universally ranked among the most promising and honourable of the young noblemen of France. I had some rivals;

I did not pass through this turbulent and diversified scene without disputes; but no one cast a reflection upon my name, no one ventured to speak of me with superciliousness and opprobrium. Nor was my temper more injured than my reputation. From every dispute I extricated myself with grace and propriety; I studied the pleasure and ease of all with whom I associated; and no man enjoyed more extensively than I did the sweets of friendship, as far as the sweets of friendship can be extensively enjoyed.

CHAPTER IV.

I had been now two years in habits of life and a mode of expense extremely injurious to my patrimony, when a circumstance occurred, which promised completely to deliver me from the ruinous consequences of my own folly. This was no other than my encounter with that incomparable woman, who afterwards became the partner of my life, and the mother of my children. I cannot even now recollect her without tears: the sentiment which her very name excites in my mind is a mingled feeling, on the one hand, of the most exquisite and unspeakable delight, a feeling that elevates and expands and electrifies my throbbing heart; and, on the other, of the bitterest anguish and regret. I must develope the source of this feeling.

Marguerite Louise Isabeau de Damville was, at the period of our first meeting, in the nineteenth year of her age. Her complexion was of the most perfect transparency, her eyes black and sparkling, and her eyebrows dark and long. Such were the perfect smoothness and clearness of her skin, that at nineteen she appeared five years younger than she was, and she long retained this extreme juvenility of form. Her step was airy and light as that of a young fawn, yet at the same time firm, and indicative of strength of body and vigour of mind. Her voice, like the whole of her external appearance, was expressive of undesigning, I had almost said childish, simplicity. Yet, with all this playfulness of appearance, her understanding was bold and correct. Her mind was well furnished with every thing that could add to her accomplishments as a wife or a mother. Her indulgent parents had procured her every advantage of education, and circumstances had been uncommonly favourable to her improvement. She was encouraged and assisted in the art of drawing, for which she discovered a very early talent, by Leonardo da Vinci; and she formed her poetical taste from the conversation and instructions of Clement Marot. But, amidst the singular assemblage of her intellectual accomplishments, there was nothing by which she was so much distinguished, as the uncommon prudence of her judgments, and the unalterable amiableness of her manners. This was the woman destined to crown my happiness, and consummate my misery. If I had never known her, I should never have tasted true pleasure; if I had been guided by her counsels, I should not have drained to the very dregs the cup of anguish.

The house of her father, the Marquis de Damville, was the resort of all the most eminent wits and scholars of that period, particularly of Marot, Rabelais, Erasmus and Scaliger. This was my first inducement to frequent it. My education had inspired me with an inextinguishable love of literature; and the dissipation in which I was at this time involved could not entirely interrupt the propensity. The most thoughtless and extravagant period of my life had occasional intervals of study and reflection; and the gay, animated, and ingenious conversation of the men I have mentioned, had always peculiar charms for me.

I had continued for some time to visit at the Marquis's hotel, before I encountered the beautiful Marguerite. The first time I saw her, she made a deep impression upon me. The Marquis, who was one of the most benevolent and enlightened of mankind, had been led by my character and manners to conceive a warm friendship for me. He saw the ruin in which I was heedlessly involving myself, and believed that it was not yet too late to save me. As he thought that there was no method so likely to effect my reformation as the interposition of domestic affections, he was not unwilling to encourage the attachment I began to feel for his daughter. On my part I wanted but little encouragement. I no sooner observed her manners, and became acquainted with her merits, than my heart was unalterably fixed. I became as it were a new man. I was like one, who, after his eyes had grown imperceptibly dim till at length every object appeared indistinct and of a gloomy general hue, has his sight instantaneously restored, and beholds the fabric of the universe in its genuine clearness, brilliancy, and truth. I was astonished at my own folly, that I could so long have found gratification in pleasures mean and sensual. I was ashamed of my own degradation. I could not endure the comparison between the showy, unsubstantial attractions of the women I had hitherto frequented, and the charms of the adorable Marguerite. The purity of her mind seemed to give a celestial brilliancy and softness to the beauties of her person. The gross and brutal pursuits of the debauchee are often indeed described by the same epithets as the virtuous and refined passion with which I was now for the first time inspired; but experience convinced me that they differed in their most essential features.

The Marquis saw the state of my mind, and addressed me thus. "Count," said he, "I feel the most ardent friendship for you. I am inexpressibly concerned for your welfare. You will be convinced of this, when I have furnished you with a clue to my late conduct towards you. I regard you, if not as a ruined man, at least as a man in the high road to ruin. Your present habits are of the most dangerous sort; they appear to you perfectly conformable to principles of the strictest honour; nay, they come recommended to you by a certain éclat and dignity with which they seem to be surrounded. I could say to you, Recollect yourself. Be not misled by delusive appearances. Consider the present state of your fortune, and the state in which your mother left it. You cannot be ignorant how greatly it is impaired. How has this circumstance arisen? Have your revenues been expended in the service of your country? Have you purchased any thing by them that will confer on you lasting renown? Put together the sum of actions, which, piece by piece, you have been willing to regard as indifferent and innocent, if not as graceful and becoming. You cannot but be struck with their monstrous deformity. Is it possible that you can be ignorant of the nature of poverty? There is such a thing as honourable poverty. The poverty of Cincinnatus was honourable, who impoverished himself by paying the fine which was factiously imposed on his son, and then was contented to pass his time alternately between the highest situations and the most rigid simplicity. The poverty of a man of genius, such as Rabelais, if not honourable, is interesting, when we compare his merits and worth with that of many of those persons upon whom fortune has blindly lavished her favours. It is honourable, if he have declined the means of enriching himself by the sacrifice of his independence and his principles. But of all earthly things the most contemptible is the man who, having wasted his goods in riotous living, yet hungers after the luxuries that have proved his bane, and feasts himself upon the steam of dainties of which he has lost the substance. Poverty, always sufficiently disadvantageous in a degenerate age, where attention and courtship are doled forth with scales of gold, is tremendous to him. He is the scorn of all mankind. Wherever he is a guest, he is invited only to be trampled upon and insulted. He is capable of nothing, and is a burden to society and mankind. The helplessness of age advances upon him with stealing steps, and he is destined to gather all its miseries and none of its consolations.

"I might have talked to you thus, but I refused it. I apprehend something of the nature of advice. I know that it can seldom be attended with its genuine effect, and will never be received with deference and pleasure, where its motives are capable of misconstruction. If I had talked to you thus, I might have appeared to be indulging the tyranny of age; I might have seemed to assume an unbecoming air of superiority and command: it could not have been clear that I was honestly interested in that, about which I affected so much concern. I doubt not the ingenuousness of your nature. I doubt not that you would have been struck with the picture. But I must be permitted to doubt the adequate and lasting effect of my expostulation. I was not willing by my forwardness and loquacity to wear out one of the great springs of human improvement.

"I have determined on your reform. For that purpose I think it necessary to combine my remonstrances and advice, with a change of your habits and situation. You have tasted largely of what are commonly called the pleasures of life, but there are pleasures that you have not tasted. At this moment you anticipate them; and anticipate them with the ardour of a lover. But you know not yet all the gratifications that attend upon domestic affections.

"I am willing to bestow upon you my daughter. I consent to prove the purity of my advice, and the sincerity of my regard, by committing her happiness to the risk. She is a treasure, the equal of which perhaps the world does not hold. I speak not of her personal attractions. But in understanding, accomplishments, and virtue, I firmly believe no woman living can compare with her. In possessing her, you will be blessed beyond the lot of princes. But, at the same time that I shall thus put happiness within your grasp, remember that I commit to your disposal the happiness of Marguerite. You are a worthy and an honourable man; your talents and your virtues will constitute her felicity. Her portion will redeem the injury which your patrimony has suffered from your excesses, and you will have enough for yourselves, and for your mutual offspring. I cannot believe that, with such a deposit intrusted to you, you will consent to bring her to misery and ruin.

"I have one condition, however, to stipulate with you. I require of you, as the pledge of her happiness, that you break off your present modes of life; that you separate yourself from your connections, and retire into the country upon your paternal estate. You are yet too young to be in danger from that tyranny of custom, which often renders men more advanced in life incapable of relishing the simple and genuine pleasures. You will find contentment and joy in the society of my daughter, and in the bosom of your rising family. You will be happy in the circle of your own hearth, and have little to ask of the rest of mankind. If, in any ill-omened and inauspicious moment, the allurements of your present vices (forgive the plainness of my speech) should resume their power over you, I hope at least that I shall never live to see it; that I shall not be taught by bitter experience, that I have sacrificed to the disinterestedness of my friendship the happiness of my daughter and of my posterity!"

My heart weeps blood, while I record the admonitions of this noble and generous man. A nobler France did not contain through all her boundaries. Refined by literature, polished by the best society his age could afford, grown grey in the field of honour, and particularly distinguished by the personal attachment and confidence of his sovereign. What was all this advice to me? What return did I make to this unparalleled kindness and friendship? I ruined this admirable woman! I involved her in poverty and shame! With the most savage barbarity I prepared for her an immature grave! Can I forget this? Of what avail to me are immortal life and immortal youth? Oh, Marguerite, Marguerite! For ever thy image haunts me! For ever thy ghost upbraids me! How little have I proved myself worthy of such a partner! Rather what punishment, what plagues, what shame and detestation have I not deserved! Praised be Heaven, the last prayer of the Marquis of Damville at least was granted! He did not live to witness my relapse, my profligacy, and insanity.

I resume the thread of my story.—I listened to the address of the Marquis with reverence and admiration. I accepted his conditions with joy. I married his adorable daughter, and conducted her to my paternal estate in the Bourdelois. Now only it was that I tasted of perfect happiness. To judge from my own experience in this situation, I should say, that nature has atoned for all the disasters and miseries she so copiously and incessantly pours upon her sons, by this one gift, the transcendent enjoyment and nameless delights which, wherever the heart is pure and the soul is refined, wait on the attachment of two persons of opposite sexes. My beloved Marguerite guided and directed me, at the same time that she was ever studying my gratification. I instructed her by my experience, while she enlightened me by the rectitude and decision of her taste. Ours was a sober and dignified happiness, and its very sobriety served to give it additional voluptuousness. We had each our separate pursuits, whether for the cultivation of our minds, or the promotion of our mutual interests. Separation gave us respectability in each other's eyes, while it prepared us to enter with fresh ardour into society and conversation. In company with each other, hours passed over us, and appeared but minutes. It has been said to be a peculiar felicity for any one to be praised by a man who is himself eminently a subject of praise: how much happier to be prized and loved by a person worthy of love? A man may be prized and valued by his friend; but in how different a style of sentiment from the regard and attachment that may reign in the bosom of his mistress or his wife? Self-complacency and self-satisfaction may perhaps be numbered among the principal sources of contentment. It is necessary for him who would endure existence with patience, that he should conceive himself to be something,—that he should be persuaded he is not a cipher in the muster-roll of man. How bitter is the anguish we are sometimes doomed to sustain in this respect from the marks we receive of other men's indifference and contempt? To feel that we are loved by one whose love we have deserved, to be employed in the mutual interchange of the marks of this love, habitually to study the happiness of one by whom our happiness is studied in return, this is the most desirable, as it is the genuine and unadulterated condition of human nature. I must have some one to sympathise with; I cannot bear to be cut off from all relations: I desire to experience a confidence, a concord, an attachment, that cannot rise between common acquaintance. In every state we long for some fond bosom on which to rest our weary head; some speaking eye with which to exchange the glances of intelligence and affection. Then the soul warms and expands itself; then it shuns the observation of every other beholder; then it melts with feelings that are inexpressible, but that the heart understands without the aid of words; then the eyes swim with rapture; then the frame languishes with enjoyment; then the soul burns with fire; then the two persons thus blest are no longer two; distance vanishes, one thought animates, one mind informs them. Thus love acts; thus it is ripened to perfection; never does man feel himself so much alive, so truly etherial, as when, bursting the bonds of diffidence, uncertainty and reserve, he pours himself entire into the bosom of the woman he adores.

Marguerite de Damville was particularly distinguished from every other woman I ever knew by the justness of her taste and the vividness of her feelings. This circumstance was a fund of inexhaustible delight and improvement to me. We were both of us well acquainted with the most eminent poets and fine writers of modern times. But when we came to read them together, they presented themselves in a point of view in which they had never been seen by us before. It is, perhaps, more important that poetry, and every thing that excites the imagination or appeals to the heart, should be read in solitude, than in society. But the true way to understand our author in these cases, is to employ each of these modes in succession. The terrible, the majestic, the voluptuous and the melting, are all of them, in a considerable degree, affairs of sympathy; and we never judge of them so infallibly, or with so much satisfaction, as when, in the presence of each other, the emotion is kindled in either bosom at the same instant, the eye-beams, pregnant with sentiment and meaning, involuntarily meet and mingle; the voice of the reader becomes modulated by the ideas of his author, and that of the hearer, by an accidental interjection of momentary comment or applause, confesses its accord. It was in this manner that we read together the admirable sonnets of Petrarch, and passed in review the sublime effusions of Dante. The letters of Eloisa to Abelard afforded us singular delight. We searched into the effusions of the Troubadours, and, among all their absurdities and inequality, we found a wildness, a daring pouring forth of the soul, an unpruned richness of imagination, and, from time to time, a grandeur of conception and audacious eccentricity of thought, that filled us with unlooked for transport. At other times, when not regularly engaged in this species of reading, we would repeat passages to each other, communicate the discoveries of this sort that either had made in solitude, and point out unobserved beauties, that perhaps neither of us would have remarked, but for the suggestions of the other. It is impossible for two persons to be constituted so much alike, but that one of them should have a more genuine and instantaneous relish for one sort of excellence, and another for another. Thus we added to each other's stores, and acquired a largeness of conception and liberality of judgment that neither of us would have arrived at if separate. It is difficult to imagine how prolific this kind of amusement proved of true happiness. We were mutually delighted to remark the accord of our feelings, and still more so, as we perceived that accord to be hourly increasing, and what struck either as a blemish in the other, wearing out and disappearing. We were also led by the same means to advert to the powers of mind existing in each, the rectitude of judgment and delicacy of feeling. As our attachment hourly increased, we rejoiced in this reciprocation of benefits, while each gave or received something that added to value of mind and worth of character. Mutual esteem was incessantly kept alive, and mutual esteem is the only substantial basis of love. Each of us hourly blessed our common lot, while each believed it impracticable elsewhere to have found so much worth blended with so much sweetness.

But we did not confine ourselves to the library and fireside. We walked, we rode, we travelled together; we observed together the beauties of nature, and the system of the universe; we traversed many provinces of France, and some parts of Italy and Spain; we examined the characters of mankind, as they are modified by the varieties of natural descent, or the diversities of political government. In all this we found peculiar gratification. There is something in the scent and impression of a balmy atmosphere, in the lustre of sunshine, in the azure heaven and the purple clouds, in the opening of prospects on this side and on that, in the contemplation of verdure and fertility, and industry and simplicity and cheerfulness, in all their variations, in the very act and exercise of travelling, peculiarly congenial to the human frame. It expands the heart, it makes the spirit dance, and exquisitely disposes us for social enjoyment. The mind becomes more elevated and refined, it assumes a microscopical and unwonted sensibility; it feels things which, in ordinary moments, are unheeded and unknown; it enjoys things too evanescent for a name, and too minute to be arrested; it trembles with pleasure through every fibre and every articulation.

One thing is necessary to be mentioned in this place, though, while it adds to the fidelity of delineation, I am aware it breaks the tone of feeling, and the harmony of the picture. But it is not my intention in this history to pass myself for better than I am. I have laid down to myself the sacred maxim of absolute truth and impartiality. I must confess, therefore, with whatever anguish, my extreme inferiority to my incomparable partner. She had all the simplicity of genuine taste. The more she delivered herself up to nature, the greater was her content. All superfluous appendages and show appeared to her as so many obstacles to enjoyment. She derived her happiness from the tone of her own mind, and stood in no need of the gaping admiration and stupid wonder of others to make her feel herself happy. But I retained the original vice of my mind. The gestures of worship and the voice of applause were necessary to me. I did not suffice to myself. I was not satisfied with the tranquil and inglorious fruition of genuine pleasures, forgetting the vain and anxious tumult of the world, and forgotten by those who figured on its theatre. It may be, that Marguerite could, and ought, by insensible degrees, to have rooted out this disease of my mind. But I am concerned only with the statement of facts; and I know that no such thing was the effect of our intercourse.

This absurd passion did not, however, at this time, lead me to any fatal extremities. It contented itself with the frivolous gratification resulting from a certain portion of ostentation and expense. I maintained a considerable train of servants: my apartments were magnificent, and my furniture splendid. When we travelled, it was with an attendance little short of princely. Idiot that I was, to regard this as an addition to the genuine pleasures which I have above enumerated! When we were at home, every accidental guest was received and entertained with extraordinary pomp, a pomp not directed to add to his accommodation, but that was designed to leave him impressed with astonishment and admiration at the spirit of his host. Often, indeed, did I feel this ostentation an encumbrance: often did I languish for the ease and freedom which result from a mediocrity of circumstances. But this I called, doing honour to my ancestors and my country, and vindicating the consideration due to the house of St. Leon.

To quit this painful recollection.—A circumstance which tended at this time to fill the measure of my happiness, consisted in the dear pledges which Marguerite bore me of our mutual affection. It is impossible for him who has not experienced it, to conceive the accumulation which a genuine tenderness derives from this source. The difficulties are many that attend upon pregnancy; trifles are at that period sources of fatigue and injury; it is necessary that the person should be protected, and the mind tranquil. We love to watch over a delicate plant, that appears to call for all our anxiety and attention. There is in this case the sentiment, without the repulsive circumstances that attends upon our sympathy with a dangerous and alarming disease. Marguerite, by her sensibility and growing attachment, abundantly rewarded my cares. At length the critical period arrives, when an event so extraordinary occurs, as cannot fail to put the human frame in considerable jeopardy. Never shall I forget the interview between us immediately subsequent to her first parturition, the effusion of soul with which we met each other after all danger seemed to have subsided, the kindness which animated us, increased as it was by ideas of peril and suffering, the sacred sensation with which the mother presented her infant to her husband, or the complacency with which we read in each other's eyes a common sentiment of melting tenderness and inviolable attachment!

This, she seemed to say, is the joint result of our common affection. It partakes equally of both, and is the shrine in which our sympathies and our life have been poured together, never to be separated. Let other lovers testify their engagements by presents and tokens; we record and stamp our attachment in this precious creature, a creature of that species which is more admirable than any thing else the world has to boast, a creature susceptible of pleasure and pain, of affection and love, of sentiment and fancy, of wisdom and virtue. This creature will daily stand in need of an aid we shall delight to afford; will require our meditations and exertions to forward its improvement, and confirm its merits and its worth. We shall each blend our exertions, for that purpose, and our union, confirmed by this common object of our labour and affection, will every day become more sacred and indissoluble.—All this the present weakness of my beloved Marguerite would not allow her to say. But all this occurred to my reflections; and, when we had time tranquilly to compare our recollection of the event, it plainly appeared that in all this our hearts and conceptions had most truly sympathised.

The possessing a third object, a common centre of anxiety to both, is far from weakening the regard of such a couple for each other. It does not separate or divert them; it is a new link of connection. Each is attached to it the more for the sake of either; each regards it as a sort of branch or scion, representing the parent; each rejoices in its health, its good humour, its smiles, its increase in size, in strength, and in faculties, principally from the idea of the gratification they will communicate to the other. Were it not for this idea, were it possible the pleasure should not be mutual, the sentiment would be stripped of its principal elevation and refinement; it would be comparatively cold, selfish, solitary, and inane.

In the first ten years of our marriage my wife brought me five children, two sons and three daughters. The second son only died in his infancy. My predominant passion at this time was that of domestic pleasures and employments, and I devoted myself, jointly with the mother, to the cultivation of the minds of my children. They all in a considerable degree rewarded our care; they were all amiable. Taught by the example of their parents, they lived in uncommon harmony and affection. Charles, the eldest, was a lad of a bold and active disposition; but the sentiments of virtue and honour that were infused into him, both by Marguerite and myself, found a favourable reception, and promised to render those qualities, which, if left to themselves, might have been turbulent and dangerous, productive of the happiest consequences. Julia, his eldest sister, was uncommonly mild and affectionate, alive to the slightest variations of treatment, profoundly depressed by every mark of unkindness, but exquisitely sensible to demonstrations of sympathy and attachment. She appeared little formed to struggle with the difficulties of life and the frowns of the world; but, in periods of quietness and tranquillity nothing could exceed the sweetness of her character and the fascination of her manners. Her chief attachment was to her mother, though she was by no means capable of her mother's active beneficence and heroic fortitude. Louisa, the second daughter, resembled her mother in person, and promised to resemble her in character. Marguerite, the youngest, differed from the whole family, in the playfulness and frolic of her disposition. Her vivacity was inexhaustible, and was continually displaying itself in innocent tricks, and smart, unexpected sallies. Nothing could possibly be more ingenuous than this admirable infant; nothing more kind, considerate, and enthusiastic in her tenderness and grief, when an occasion occurred to call forth these sentiments. But the moment the sorrowful occasion was over, she would resume all her vivacity; and even sometimes, in the midst of her tears, some trait of her native humour would escape. I know not whether all the family were not more attached to the little Marguerite than to any other individual member, as she certainly oftenest contributed to their amusement and pleasure.—Such was the amiable circle, one and all of whom have been involved by me in the most tremendous ruin and disgrace.

CHAPTER V.

Charles was now nine years of age. His mother and myself had delighted ourselves with observing and forwarding the opening of his infant mind, and had hitherto been contented with the assistance of a neighbouring priest by way of preceptor. But, as he was our only son, we were desirous that he should obtain every advantage of education. We were neither of us illiterate; but, in the course of twenty-three years, which had elapsed since I was myself of Charles's age, the progress of literature and the literary passion in Europe had been astonishingly great, and I was anxious that he should realise in his own person every benefit which the fortunate and illustrious period of human affairs in which he began to exist seemed to hold out to him. Beside, there was an impetuosity and forwardness in his character, that seemed ill to brook the profound solitude and retirement in which his mother and I were contented to live. His case demanded companions of his own age, a little world of fellow-beings, with whom he might engage in their petty business and cares, with whose passions his own might jostle or might sympathise, who might kindle his emulation, and open to him the field of fraternal associations and amity.

There was, however, a considerable difficulty attendant on this question. The schools of real literature in France, where languages were properly taught, and science might be acquired, were at this time exceedingly few. The nearest university was that of Toulouse, at the distance of twenty-six leagues. This was, practically speaking, as far from us as Paris itself. Was then our darling child to be torn from his parents, from all he was accustomed to see, and all by whom he was loved, to be planted in the midst of strangers, to have his mind excited to observation, and the spirit of generous contention roused, at the risk of suppressing the tender affections of his soul, and the sentiments of duty, reliance, and love? There seemed, however, to be no alternative. It was necessary that a temporary separation should take place. Intellectual improvement was a point by all means to be pursued; and we must direct our efforts to keep alive along with it those winning qualities, and that softness of heart, which had hitherto rendered Charles so eminently our delight. Such were our fond speculations and projects for the future.

It was at length determined that I should proceed along with him to Paris. I could there observe upon the spot the state of the university, and the means of learning that existed in the metropolis; and could consult with some of those eminent luminaries with whom I had become acquainted at the house of the Marquis de Damville. Marguerite declined accompanying me upon this occasion. Her father was dead: she could not think of quitting her daughters for any considerable time; and our nuptial engagement of residing always in the country gave her a repugnance to the removing with her whole family to Paris. It was left probable that she might come to me when the business was settled, if at that time it was determined to leave her son at the capital; and that she might then reconduct me to the place, which had been the scene of all my happiness, but which I was destined never to revisit in peace.

Preliminaries being at length fully adjusted in the manner that appeared suitable to the importance of the occasion, I set off for the metropolis of my country, which I had seen only once, and that for a very short period, in the course of ten years. That visit had been produced by a very melancholy circumstance, the death of the Marquis de Damville. Marguerite and myself had then been summoned, and arrived at his hotel but a few days before he expired. Though extremely weakened by the mortal disease under which he laboured, he retained all the faculties of his mind, and conversed with us in the most affectionate and endearing terms. He congratulated us upon our mutual felicity; nor could the situation in which we found him, upon the brink of an everlasting oblivion of all earthly things, abate the sincerity and fervour of his delight. He thanked me for my carriage and conduct as a husband, which, he said, might with propriety be held up as a model to the human species. He applauded himself for that mingled discernment and determination, which, as he affirmed, had so opportunely secured my virtue and his daughter's happiness. He trusted that I was now sufficiently weaned from those habits which had formerly given him so much alarm. At the same time he conjured me, by every motive that an overflowing enthusiasm could suggest, to persist in my good resolutions, and never to change that residence, where I had found every degree of delight of which the human mind is in its present condition susceptible. "Do not," said he, "be drawn aside by ambition; do not be dazzled by the glitter of idle pomp and decoration; do not enter the remotest circle of the vortex of dissipation! Live in the midst of your family; cultivate domestic affection; be the solace and joy of your wife; watch for the present and future welfare of your children; and be assured that you will then be found no contemptible or unbeneficial member of the community at large!"

Such were the last advices of the Marquis de Damville. Excellent man! how ill were your lessons remembered! how ill your kindness remunerated! He died in the sixth year of our marriage. The serious impression which this event produced in my mind gave me small inclination to enter into any species of society, and disposed me to quit Paris as soon as every respect had been paid to the obsequies of the deceased.

Upon my arrival in the metropolis on the present occasion, I immediately sought to renew my acquaintance with those amiable and eminent persons, who had for the most part constituted the circle of the Marquis de Damville. They received me with that interest and attention that I have usually found attendant on a cultivated mind. The pleasure was considerable, that resulted from meeting them thus again, after ten years' cessation of intercourse. A few of them, indeed, were dead, and others dispersed by various accidents in different parts of France or of Europe. The greater part, however, I still found in that celebrated city, which might well be considered as the metropolis of the civilised world. The king had early been distinguished by his love of letters and the arts; and added years, while they abated in his mind the eagerness of ambition and glory, gave new strength to his more cultivated propensities. The liberality of his conduct, and the polished ease that characterised his manners, produced a general predilection in favour of the capital in which he resided.

I found all my former friends matured and improved by the silent influence of time. Their knowledge was increased; their views rendered wider; their conversation was more amusing and instructive, their manners more bland and unaffected. But, if their characters had experienced revolution, mine was more materially changed. I had before encountered them with all the heat and presumption of youth, with no views so much present to my mind as those of chivalry and a factitious honour, with no experience but that of a camp. I was impetuous, volatile, and dissipated. I had not rested long enough upon any one of the flowers of intellect to extract its honey; and my mind was kept in a state of preternatural agitation by the passions of a gamester. It was now become cool, moderate, and tranquil. The society of Marguerite had contributed much to the improvement of my character; I had lived in no idle and brutish solitude, but in the midst of contemplation and letters; and I had the passions of a husband and a father, in the extremest degree attached to his family. These passions will be found, perhaps, to be the true school of humanity: the man, whose situation continually exercises in him the softest and most amiable charities of our nature, will almost infallibly surpass his brethren in kindness to sympathise with, and promptness to relieve, the distresses of others.

Will it be accounted strange that, in Paris, surrounded by persons of various knowledge and liberal benevolence, I found myself under the influence of other feelings, than any I had lately experienced? I was like a man who had suffered long calamity in a famished vessel or a town besieged, and is immediately after introduced into the midst of luxury, to a table loaded with the most costly dainties. Every viand has to his apprehension an exquisite relish, and every wine a delicious flavour, that he never perceived in them before. Let no one infer that my love for Marguerite was diminished; it has already sufficiently appeared in the course of my narrative, that no happiness could be more consummate than mine was with this admirable woman. Had I been called upon to choose for the seat of my future life, between my paternal château in the Bordelois, with Marguerite to grace my abode, on the one hand; and all the gratifications that Paris could afford, on the other, I should not have hesitated even for an instant. But the mind of man is made capacious of various pleasures; and a person of sound and uncorrupted judgment will perhaps always enjoy with emotion the delights which for a long time before he had not encountered, however enviable his content may have been under their absence. I delighted to converse with the men of genius and refinement with whom Paris at this time abounded. It was a feast of soul of which I had rarely partaken in my rural retreat. I delighted to combine excellence with number, and, to a considerable degree at least, variety of intercourse with sentiments of regard and friendship. In these select societies I found no cold suppressions and reserve. Their members were brethren in disposition, similar in their pursuits, and congenial in their sentiments. When any one spoke, it was that the person to whom he addressed himself might apprehend what was passing in his thoughts. They participated with sincerity and a liberal mind in each other's feelings, whether of gay delight or melancholy disappointment.

Thus situated, I forgot for a time my engagements with Marguerite. The scenes of St. Leon, its fields, its walks, its woods and its streams, faded from my mind. I forgot the pleasure with which I had viewed my children sporting on the green, and the delicious, rural suppers which I had so often partaken with my wife beneath my vines and my fig-trees at the period of the setting sun. When I set out for Paris, these images had dwelt upon my mind, and saddened my fancy. At every stage I felt myself removed still further from the scene where my treasures and my affections were deposited. But, shortly after, new scenes and new employments engaged my thoughts. The pleasures which I sought but weakly at first, every time they were tasted increased my partiality for them. I seemed for a time to be under the influence of an oblivion of my former life. Thus circumstanced, the folly which had so deep a root in my character, took hold of me. I hired a magnificent hotel, and entertained at my own expense those persons in whose society I principally delighted. My circles became more numerous than those of the Marquis de Damville, and were conducted in a very different style of splendour and profusion. I corresponded with Marguerite; but I continually found some new pretext for lengthening my stay; and she on her part, though the kindest and most indulgent of women, became seriously alarmed and unhappy.

As my parties were more numerous than those of the Marquis de Damville had been, they were more mixed. Among others, I occasionally associated with some of those noblemen who had been the companions of my former dissipation and gaming. An obvious consequence resulted from this. Parties of play were occasionally proposed to me. I resisted—I yielded. My first compliances were timid, hesitating, and painful. I recollected the lessons and exhortations of my excellent father-in-law. At length, however, my alarms abated. I reproached myself with the want of an honourable confidence in my own firmness, and the cowardice of supposing that I was not to be trusted with the direction of my conduct.

One evening I ventured beyond the cautious limits I had at first prescribed myself, and won a considerable sum. This incident produced a strong impression upon me, and filled my mind with tumult and agitation. There was a secret that I had concealed almost from myself, but which now recurred to me with tenfold violence. I was living beyond the means I had to discharge my expenses. My propensity of this sort seemed to be fatal and irresistible. My marriage with Marguerite had occurred opportunely, to heal the breaches I had at that time made in my fortune, and to take from me the consciousness of embarrassments which I should otherwise have deeply felt. The death of the Marquis, however deplorable in other respects, happened at a period when the spirit of profusion and magnificence which characterised me had again involved my affairs in considerable difficulty. It might be supposed that these two cases of experience would have sufficed to extirpate my folly; but they had rather the contrary effect. In each of them the event was such as to prevent extravagance and thoughtlessness from producing their genuine results; and, of consequence, they appeared less criminal and mischievous in my eyes than otherwise they probably would have appeared. I rather increased than diminished my establishment upon the death of my father-in-law. I had no reasonable prospect of any property hereafter to descend to me, that should exonerate me from the consequences of further prodigality. But I did not advert to this. I saw myself surrounded by my children; they were the delight and solace of my life; and yet I was needless of their interests. Sometimes I resolved upon a more rigid economy: but economy is a principle that does not easily lay hold of any but a heart framed to receive it. It is a business of attentive and vigilant detail. It easily escapes the mind, amidst the impetuosity of the passions, the obstinacy of rooted propensities, and the seduction of long established habits. Marguerite, indeed, did not share with me in these follies; the simplicity and ingenuousness of her mind were such, that she would have been as happy in a cottage as a palace; but, though she did not partake my vices, an ill-judged forbearance and tenderness for my feelings did not permit her effectually to counteract them. This is, perhaps, the only defect of character I am able to impute to her.

After I had won the sum to which I have alluded, I retired to my hotel full of anxious thoughts. It produced upon me, in some degree, the same effect as ordinarily belongs to a great calamity. I lay all night sleepless and disturbed. Ruin and despair presented themselves to my mind in a thousand forms. Heedless prodigality and dilapidated revenues passed in review before me. I counted the years of my life. I had completed the thirty-second year of my age: this was scarcely half the probable duration of human existence. How was I to support the remaining period, a period little assorted to difficulties and expedients; and which, in the close of it, seems imperiously to call for every indulgence? Hitherto, an interval of four or five years had repeatedly sufficed to involve me in serious embarrassment. My children were growing up around me; my family was likely to become still larger; as my offspring increased in years, their demands upon my revenues would be more considerable. Were these demands to be slighted? Were my daughters, nay, was the heir of my rank and my name, to be committed to the compassion of the world, unprovided and forlorn? What a cheerless prospect! What a gloomy and disconsolate hue did these ideas spread upon that future, which the health of the human mind requires to have gilded with the beams of hope and expectation? I had already tried the expedient of economy; and I had uniformly found this inestimable and only sheet-anchor of prudence gliding from my deluded grasp. Could I promise myself better success in future? There seemed to be something in my habits, whether of inattention, ostentation, or inconsistency, that baffled the strongest motives by which parsimony and frugality can be enforced.

Why did these thoughts importunately recur to me in the present moment? They were the suggestions of a malignant genius,—thoughts, the destination of which was to lead me into a gulf of misery and guilt! While I was going on in a regular train of expense, while I was scooping the mine that was to swallow me and my hopes together, I had the art to keep these reflections at bay. Now that I had met with an unexpected piece of good fortune, they rushed upon me with irresistible violence. Unfortunate coincidence! Miserable,—rather let me say, guilty, abandoned miscreant!

As soon as I rose in the morning, I went to the closet where, the evening before, I had deposited my recent acquisitions. I spread out the gold before me. I gazed upon it with intentness. My eyes, a moment after, rolled in vacancy. I traversed the apartment with impatient steps. All the demon seemed to make his descent upon my soul. This was the first time that I had ever felt the struggle of conscious guilt and dishonour. I was far indeed from anticipating that species of guilt, and that species of ruin, which soon after overwhelmed me. My mind did not once recur to the possibility of any serious mischief. I dwelt only, as gamesters perhaps usually do, upon the alternative between acquisition and no acquisition. I did not take into the account the ungovernableness of my own passions. I assumed it as unquestionable, that I could stop when I pleased. The thoughts that tortured me were, in the first place, those of a sanguine and unexperienced adventurer in a lottery, whose mind rests not for a moment upon the sum he has risked, but who, having in fancy the principal prize already in his possession, and having distributed it to various objects and purposes, sometimes fearfully recurs to the possibility of his disappointment, and anticipates with terror what will be his situation, if deprived of this imaginary wealth. I had now, for the first time, opened my eyes to the real state of my affairs, and I clung with proportionable vehemence to this plank which was to bear me from the storm. In the second place, I felt, though darkly and unwillingly, the immorality of my conception. To game may, in some instances, not be in diametrical opposition to liberality of mind; but he who games for the express purpose of improving his circumstances must be an idiot, if he does not sometimes recollect that the money lost may be as serious a mischief to his neighbour, as the money gained can possibly be a benefit to himself. It is past a question, that he who thus turns his amusement into his business loses the dignity of a man of honour, and puts himself upon a level with the most avaricious and usurious merchant.

Though I was far from having digested a specific plan of enriching myself by these discreditable means, yet the very tumult of my thoughts operated strongly to lead me once more to the gaming-table. I was in no humour to busy myself with my own thoughts; the calmness of literary discussion, and the polished interchange of wit, which had lately so much delighted me, had now no attraction for my heart; the turbulence of a scene of high play alone had power to distract my attention from the storm within. I won a second time. I felt the rapidity and intenseness of my contemplations still further accelerated. I will not over again detail what they were. Suffice it to say, that my hopes became more ardent, my conception of the necessity of this resource more impressive, and my alarm lest this last expedient should fail me more tormenting.

The next time I lost half as much as the sum of my winnings. I then proceeded for several days in a nearly regular alternation of gain and loss. This, as soon as the fact unavoidably forced itself upon my mind, only served to render my thoughts more desperate. No, exclaimed I, it was not for this that I entered upon so tormenting a pursuit. It is not for this that I have deserted the learned societies which were lately my delight, and committed myself to a sea of disquiet and anxiety. I came not here, like a boy, for amusement; or, like one who has been bred in the lap of ignorance and wealth, to seek a relief from the burden of existence, and to find a stimulus to animate my torpid spirits. Am I then to be for ever baffled? Am I to cultivate a tract of land, which is to present me nothing in return but unvaried barenness? Am I continually to wind up my passions, and new-string my attention in vain? Am I a mere instrument to be played upon by endless hopes and fears and tormenting wishes? Am I to be the sport of events, the fool of promise, always agitated with near approaching good, yet always deluded?

This frame of mind led me on insensibly to the most extravagant adventures. It threw me in the first place into the hands of notorious gamblers. Men of real property shrunk from the stakes I proposed; as, though they were in some degree infected with the venom of gaming, their infection was not so deep as mine, nor with my desperation of thought. The players with whom I engaged were for the most part well known to every one but myself, not to be able to pay the sums they played for, if they lost; nay, this fact might be said in some sense to be known to me as well as the rest, though I obstinately steeled myself against the recollection of it. One evening I won of one of these persons a very large sum, for which I suffered him to play with me upon honour. The consequence was simple. The next morning he took his departure from Paris, and I heard of him no more.

Before this, however, the tide of success had set strongly against me. I had sustained some serious vicissitudes; and, while I was playing with the wretch I have just mentioned, my eagerness increased as my good luck began, and I flattered myself that I should now avenge myself of fortune for some of her late unkindnesses. My anguish—why should I call the thing by a disproportionate and trivial appellation?—my agony—was by so much the greater, when I found that this person, the very individual who had already stripped me of considerable sums, had disappeared, and left me without the smallest benefit from my imaginary winnings.

No man who has not felt, can possibly image to himself the tortures of a gamester, of a gamester like me, who played for the improvement of his fortune, who played with the recollection of a wife and children dearer to him than the blood that bubbled through the arteries of his heart, who might be said, like the savages of ancient Germany, to make these relations the stake for which he threw, who saw all my own happiness and all theirs through the long vista of life, depending on the turn of a card! Hell is but the chimera of priests, to bubble idiots and cowards. What have they invented, to come into competition with what I felt! Their alternate interchange of flames and ice is but a feeble image of the eternal varieties of hope and fear. All bodily racks and torments are nothing compared with certain states of the human mind. The gamester would be the most pitiable, if he were not the most despicable creature that exists. Arrange ten bits of painted paper in a certain order, and he is ready to go wild with the extravagance of his joy. He is only restrained by some remains of shame, from dancing about the room, and displaying the vileness of his spirit by every sort of freak and absurdity. At another time, when his hopes have been gradually worked up into a paroxysm, an unexpected turn arrives, and he is made the most miserable of men. Never shall I cease to recollect the sensation I have repeatedly felt, in the instantaneous sinking of the spirits, the conscious fire that spread over my visage, the anger in my eye, the burning dryness of my throat, the sentiment that in a moment was ready to overwhelm with curses the cards, the stake, my own existence, and all mankind. How every malignant and insufferable passion seemed to rush upon my soul! What nights of dreadful solitude and despair did I repeatedly pass during the progress of my ruin! It was the night of the soul! My mind was wrapped in a gloom that could not be pierced! My heart was oppressed with a weight that no power human or divine was equal to remove! My eyelids seemed to press downward with an invincible burden! My eyeballs were ready to start and crack their sockets! I lay motionless, the victim of ineffable horror! The whole endless night seemed to be filled with one vast, appalling, immovable idea! It was a stupor, more insupportable and tremendous than the utmost whirl of pain, or the fiercest agony of exquisite perception!

One day that my mind was in a state of excessive anguish and remorse (I had already contrived by this infernal means to dispossess myself of the half of my property), my son came unexpectedly into my chamber. For some time I had scarcely ever seen him: such is a gamester! All the night, while he slept, I was engaged in these haunts of demons. All the day, while he was awake, and studying with his masters, or amusing himself, I was in my bed-chamber, endeavouring to court a few broken hours of sleep. When, notwithstanding the opposition of our habits, I had the opportunity of seeing him, I rather shunned to use, than sought to embrace it. The sight of him had a savour of bitterness in it, that more than balanced all the solace of natural affection. It brought before me the image of his mother and his sisters; it presented to my soul a frightful tale of deserted duties; it was more galling and envenomed than the sting of scorpions.

Starting at the sound of the opening door, I called out abruptly, and with some harshness, "Who is there? What do you want?"

"It is I, sir," replied the boy; "it is Charles, come to pay his duty to you!"

"I do not want you now; you should not come, but when you know I am at leisure," answered I somewhat disturbed.

"Very well, sir; very well: I am going." As he spoke his voice seemed suffocated with tears. He was on the point of shutting the door, and leaving me to myself.

"Charles!" said I, not well knowing what it was I intended to do.

He returned.

"Come here, my dear boy!"

I took his hand, I drew him between my knees, I hid my face in his neck, I shook with the violence of my emotion.

"Go, go, boy: you perceive I cannot talk to you."

I pushed him gently from me.

"Papa!" cried he, "I do not like to leave you. I know I am but a boy, and can be but of little use to you. If mamma were with you, I would not be troublesome. I should cry when I saw you were grieved, but I would ask no questions, and would leave you, because you desired it. I hope you have not had any bad news?"

"No, my boy, no. Come to me to-morrow, and I will be at leisure, and will talk a great deal to you."

"Ah, papa, to-morrow! Every day that I did not see you, I thought it would be to-morrow! And there was one to-morrow, and another to-morrow, and so many, that it seemed as if you had forgotten to speak to me at all."

"Why, Charles, you do not doubt my word? I tell you that to-morrow you shall see me as long as you please."

"Well, well, I will wait! But do then let it be all day! I will not go to college, and it shall be a holiday. Papa, I do not like my lessons half so well as I did, since I have neither you nor mamma that I can tell what they are about."

"Good-bye, Charles! Be a good boy! remember to-morrow! Good-bye!"

"Papa! now I am sure you look a good deal better than you did at first. Let me tell you something about the lesson I read this morning. It was a story of Zaleucus the Locrian, who put out one of his own eyes, that he might preserve eye-sight to his son."

This artless story, thus innocently introduced, cut me to the soul. I started in my chair, and hid my face upon the table.

"Papa, what is the matter? Indeed you frighten me!"

"Zaleucus was a father! What then am I?"

"Yes, Zaleucus was very good indeed! But, do you know, his son was very naughty. It was his disobedience and wickedness that made him liable to such a punishment. I would not for the world be like Zaleucus's son. I hope, papa, you will never suffer from my wilfulness. You shall not, papa, indeed, indeed!"

I caught the boy in my arms. "No, you are very good! you are too good! I cannot bear it!"

"Well, papa, I wish I were able to show you that I love you as well as ever Zaleucus loved his son!"

I was melted with the ingenuousness of the boy's expression. I quitted him. I paced up and down the room. Suddenly, as if by paroxysm of insanity, I seized my child by the arm, I seated myself, I drew him towards me, I put my eye upon him.

"Boy, how dare you talk to me of Zaleucus? Do you mean to insinuate a reproach? Do I not discharge a father's duty? If I do not, know, urchin, I will not be insulted by my child!"

The boy was astonished. He burst into tears, and was silent.

I was moved by his evident distress. "No, child, you have no father. I am afraid you have not. You do not know my baseness. You do not know that I am the deadliest foe you have in the world."

"Dear papa, do not talk thus! Do not I know that you are the best of men? Do not I love you and mamma better than every body else put together?"

"Well, Charles," cried I, endeavouring to compose myself, "we will talk no more now. Did not I tell you, you should not come to me but when you knew it was a proper time? I hope you will never have reason to hate me."

"I never will hate you, papa, do to me what you will!"

He saw I wished to be alone, and left me.

CHAPTER VI.

In the evening of the same day, my beloved Marguerite arrived unexpectedly at Paris. In the beginning of our separation, I had been to the last degree punctual in my letters. I had no pleasure so great, as retiring to my closet, and pouring out my soul to the most adorable of women. By degrees I relaxed in punctuality. Ordinary occupations, however closely pursued, have a method in them, that easily combines with regularity in points of an incidental nature. But gaming, when pursued with avidity, subverts all order, and forces every avocation from the place assigned it. When my insane project of supplying the inadequateness of my fortune by this expedient began to produce an effect exactly opposite, I could not, but with the extremest difficulty, string my mind to write to the mistress of my soul. I endeavoured not to think, with distinctness and attention, of the persons whose happiness was most nearly involved with mine. I said to myself, Yet another venture must be tried; fortune shall change the animosity with which she has lately pursued me; I will repair the breaches that have been sustained; and I shall then return with tenfold avidity to subjects that at present I dare not fix my mind upon. My letters were accordingly short, unfrequent, and unsatisfactory; and those of Marguerite discovered increasing anguish, perturbation, and anxiety. What a change in the minds of both had the lapse of a few months produced! Not that my attachment had suffered the diminution of a single particle; but that attachment, which had lately been the source of our mutual felicity, was now fraught only with distress. My mind was filled with horrors; and Marguerite expected from me an encouragement and consolation in absence, which, alas, I had it not in my power to give!

I had now continued in Paris for a time vastly greater than I had originally proposed. After having remained more than ten days without receiving one word of intelligence, a letter of mine was delivered to Marguerite, more short, mysterious, and distressing to her feelings, than any that had preceded. The ten days' silence, from me who at first had never missed an opportunity of pouring out my soul to her, and contributing to her pleasure, was exquisitely painful. There is scarcely any thing that produces such a sickness of the heart as the repeated prorogation of hope. But, when the letter arrived that had been so anxiously looked for, when the hand-writing of the superscription was recognised, when the letter was treasured up for the impatiently desired moment of solitude, that the sacred emotions of the heart might suffer no interruption, and when it at last appeared so cold, so ominous, so withering to the buds of affection, the determination of Marguerite was speedily formed. The relations that bound us together were of too mighty a value to be dispensed or to be trifled with. She felt them as the very cords of existence. For ten years she had known no solace that was disconnected from my idea, no care but of our own happiness and that of our offspring. Benevolent she was almost beyond human example, and interested for the welfare of all she knew; but these were brief and mutable concerns; they were not incorporated with the stamina of her existence. I was the whole world to her; she had no idea of satisfaction without me. Her firmness had been sufficiently tried by the interposal of separation and absence. How was she to interpret the obscurity that had now arisen? Had I forgotten my family and my wife? Had I been corrupted and debauched by that Paris, the effects of which upon my character her father had so deeply apprehended? Had I, in contempt of every thing sacred, entered into some new attachment? Had the attractions of some new beauty in the metropolis made me indifferent to the virtue of my children, and the life of their mother? Perhaps the length of our attachment had infected me with satiety, and the inconstancy of my temper had been roused by the charms of novelty. Perhaps the certainty of her kindness and regard had no longer allurements for me; and I might be excited to the pursuit of another by the pleasures of hope combined with uncertainty, and of a coyness, that seemed to promise compliance hereafter, even while it pronounced a present denial. These were the images that haunted her mind; they engendered all the wildness, and all the torments, of a delirious paroxysm; she resolved that no time should be sacrificed to needless uncertainty, and that no effort of hers should be unexerted to prevent the mischief she feared.

It was evening when she arrived. I was upon the point of repairing to that scene of nightly resort, the source of all my guilt and all my miseries. I enquired of my son's valet where he was, and how he had been in the course of the day. He was gone to bed: he had appeared unusually sad, sometimes in tears; and, while he was undressing, had sighed deeply two or three times. While I was collecting this account in my own apartment, the gates of the hotel opened, and a number of horsemen entered the court-yard. I was somewhat surprised; because, though I was accustomed to see much company, few of my acquaintance visited me at so late an hour, except on the evenings appropriated to receive them. I crossed the saloon to enquire. One of the servants exclaimed, "It is Bernardin's voice: it must be my mistress that is come!"

Nothing could be further from my mind than the thought of her arrival. I flew through the passage; I was on the spot the moment that the servant prepared to conduct his mistress from the litter; I received Marguerite in my arms, and led her into the house. If I had expected her arrival, I should infallibly have met her at this moment with anxiety and confusion; I should have gone round the circle of my thoughts, and should not have had confidence to encounter the beam of her eye. But the event was so unexpected as to drive all other ideas from my mind; and, in consequence, I enjoyed several minutes,—ages, rather let me say,—of the sincerest transport. I kissed the mistress of my soul with ecstasy; I gazed upon her well known lineaments and features; I listened to the pleasing melody of her voice; I was intoxicated with delight. Upon occasions like this, it seems as if every former joy that had marked the various periods of intercourse distilled its very spirit and essence, to compose a draught, ten times more delicious and refined than had ever before been tasted. Our meeting was like awaking from the dead; it was the emancipation of the weary captive, who exchanges the dungeon's gloom for the lustre of the morning, and who feels a celestial exhilaration of heart, the very memory of which had been insensibly wearing away from his treacherous brain. All my senses partook of the rapture. Marguerite seemed to shed ambrosial odours round her; her touch was thrilling; her lips were nectar; her figure was that of a descended deity!

Her pleasure was not less than mine. It is indeed absurd, it may be termed profanation, to talk of solitary pleasure. No sensation ordinarily distinguished by that epithet can endure the test of a moment's inspection, when compared with a social enjoyment. It is then only that a man is truly pleased, when pulse replies to pulse, when the eyes discourse eloquently to each other, when in responsive tones and words the soul is communicated. Altogether, we are conscious of a sober, a chaste, and dignified intoxication, an elevation of spirit, that does not bereave the mind of itself, and that endures long enough for us to analyse and savour the causes of our joy.

For some time we rested on a sofa, each filled and occupied with the observation of the other. My eyes assured Marguerite of the constancy of my affection; my kisses were those of chaste, undivided, entire attachment.

Our words were insignificant and idle, the broken and incoherent phrases of a happiness that could not be silent. At length Marguerite exclaimed, "It is enough; my fears are vanished; I have no questions to ask, no doubts to remove. Yet why, my Reginald, did you suffer those doubts to gather, those fears to accumulate? Surely you knew the singleness of my affection! How many painful days and hours might you have saved me, almost by a word!"

"Forgive me, my love," replied I. "Waste not the golden hour of meeting in recrimination! Feeling, as your angelic goodness now makes me feel, I wonder at myself, that I could for one moment have consented to separation; that I could have thought any thing but this existence; or that, having experienced the joys that you have bestowed, I could lose all image of the past, and, dwelling in a desert, imagine it paradise!"

"Recrimination!" rejoined Marguerite. "No, my love; you make me too happy to leave room for any thing but gratitude and affection! Forgive me, Reginald, if I pretend that, in meeting you thus, I find myself your superior in happiness and love. You only awake from lethargy, forgetfulness of yourself and—of me; but I awake from anguish, a separation, that I desired not at first, and of which I hourly wished to see an end, from doubts that would intrude, and refused to be expelled, from the incessant contemplation and regret of a felicity, once possessed, but possessed no longer! Melancholy ideas, gloomy prognostics overspread my sleepless nights, and bedewed my pillow with tears! This it is, that, at last, has driven me from my family and daughters, resolved to obtain the certainty of despair, or the dispersion of my fears! Have I known all this, and think you that I do not enjoy with rapture this blissful moment?"

While we were thus conversing, Charles entered the room. He was not yet asleep when his mother arrived: he heard her voice; and hastened to put on his clothes, that he might rush into her arms. The pleasure Marguerite had conceived from our meeting, and the affectionate serenity that had taken possession of her soul, infused double ardour into the embraces she bestowed on her son. He gazed earnestly in her face; he kissed her with fervency; but was silent.

"Why, Charles!" said she, "what is the matter with you? Are not you glad to see me?"

"That I am, mamma! So glad, that I do not know what to do with myself! I was afraid I never should have been glad again!"

"Pooh, boy! what do you mean? You were not mother-sick, were you?"

"Yes, indeed, I was sick, sick at heart! Not that I am a coward! I think that I could have been satisfied to have been without either my father or you for a little while. But papa is so altered, you cannot think! He never smiles and looks happy; and, when I see him, instead of making me joyful, as it used to do, it makes me sad!"

"Dear Reginald!" replied the mother, looking at me, "is it possible that, while my heart was haunted with fear and suspicions, separation alone should have had such an effect on you?"

"I dare say it was that," interposed the boy. "I could not make papa smile, all I could do: but, now you are come, he will soon be well! How much he must love you, mamma!"

The artless prattle of my son struck anguish to my soul; and awakened a whole train of tormenting thoughts. Alas! thought I, can it indeed be love, that thus contrives against the peace of its object? Would to God, my child! that my thoughts were as simple and pure as thy innocent bosom!

"And yet," added the boy, as if recollecting himself, "if he could not see you, sure that was no reason for him to avoid me? He seemed as much afraid of me, as I have seen some of my play-fellows of a snake! Indeed, mamma, it was a sad thing that, when I wanted him to kiss me and press me to his bosom, he shrunk away from me! There now! it was just so, as he looks now, that papa used to frown upon me, I cannot tell how often! Now is not that ugly, mamma?"

I could no longer govern the tumult of my thoughts. "Peace, urchin!" cried I. "Why did you come to mar the transport of our meeting? Just now, Marguerite, I forgot myself, and was happy! Now all the villain rises in my soul!"

My wife was so astonished at the perturbation of my manner, and at the words I uttered, that she was scarcely able to articulate. "Reginald!" in broken accents she exclaimed—"my love!—my husband!"

"No matter," said I. "It shall yet be well! My heart assures me it shall!—Be not disturbed, my love! I will never cause you a moment's anguish! I would sooner die a thousand deaths!—Forget the odious thoughts that poor Charles has excited in me so unseasonably! They were mere idle words! Depend upon it they were!"

While I was speaking, Marguerite hid her face upon the sofa. I took her hand, and by my caresses endeavoured to soothe and compose her. At length, turning to me,— "Reginald!" said she, in a voice of anguish, "do you then endeavour to hide from me the real state of your thoughts? Was the joy that attended our meeting perishable and deceitful? After ten years of unbounded affection and confidence, am I denied to be the partner of your bosom?"

"No, Marguerite, no! this was but the thought of a moment! By to-morrow's dawn it shall have no existence in my bosom. Why should I torment you with what so soon shall have no existence to myself? Meanwhile, be assured, my love (instead of suffering diminution) is more full, more fervent and entire, than it ever was!"

At this instant my mind experienced an extraordinary impression. Instead of being weaned, by the presence of this admirable woman, from my passion for gaming, it became stronger than ever. If Charles had not entered at the critical moment he did, I should have remained with Marguerite, and, amidst the so long untasted solace of love, have, at least for this night, forgotten my cares. But that occurrence had overturned every thing, had uncovered the wounds of my bosom, and awakened conceptions that refused to be laid to sleep again. The arms of my wife, that were about to embrace me, suddenly became to me a nest of scorpions. I could as soon have rested and enjoyed myself upon the top of Vesuvius, when it flamed. New as I was to this species of anguish, tranquilly and full of virtuous contentment as I had hitherto passed the years of my married state, the pangs of a guilty conscience I was wholly unable to bear. I rose from my seat, and was upon the point of quitting the room.

Marguerite perceived by my manner that there was something extraordinary passing in my mind. "Where are you going, Reginald?" said she.

I answered with a slight nod. "Not far," I replied, attempting an air of apathy and unconcern.

She was not satisfied. "You are not going out?" she enquired.

I returned to where I had been sitting. "My love, I was going out at the moment of your arrival. It is necessary, I assure you. I hope I shall soon be back. I am sorry I am obliged to leave you. Compose yourself. You are in want of rest, and had better go to bed."

"Stop, Reginald! Afford me a minute's leisure before you depart! Leave us, Charles! Good night, my dear boy! Kiss me; remember that your mother is now in the same house with you; and sleep in peace."

The boy quitted the room.

"Reginald!" said the mother, "I have no wish to control your desires, or be a spy upon your actions; but your conduct seems so extraordinary in this instance, as to dispense me from the observation of common rules. I have always been a complying wife; I have never set myself in contradiction to your will; I appeal to yourself for the truth of this. I despise, however, those delicacies, an adherence to which would entail upon us the sacrifice of all that is most valuable in human life. Can I shut my ears upon the mysterious expressions which Charles's complaints have extorted from you? Can I be insensible to the extraordinary purpose you declare of leaving me, when I have yet been scarcely half an hour under the roof with you? Before Charles came in, you seem to have entertained no such design."

"My love," replied I, "how seriously you comment upon the most insignificant incident! Is it extraordinary that your unexpected arrival should at first have made me forget an engagement that I now recollect?"

"St. Leon," answered my wife, "before you indulge in surprise at my earnestness, recollect the circumstances that immediately preceded it. Through successive weeks I have waited for some satisfactory and agreeable intelligence from you. I had a right before this to have expected your return. Uncertainty and a thousand fearful apprehensions have at length driven me from my home, and brought me to Paris. I am come here for satisfaction to my doubts, and peace to my anxious heart. Wonder not, therefore, if you find something more earnest and determined in my proceedings now, than upon ordinary occasions. Give me, I conjure you, give me ease and relief, if you are able! If not, at least allow me this consolation, to know the worst!"

"Be pacified, Marguerite!" I rejoined. "I am grieved, Heaven knows how deeply grieved, to have occasioned you a moment's pain. But, since you lay so much stress upon this circumstance, depend upon it, I will postpone the business I was going about, and stay with you."

This concession, voluntary and sincere, produced an effect that I had not foreseen. Marguerite gazed for a moment in my face, and then threw herself upon my neck.

"Forgive me, my beloved husband!" she cried. "You indeed make me ashamed of myself. I feel myself inexcusable. I feel that I have been brooding over imaginary evils, and creating the misery that corroded my heart. How inexpressibly you rise my superior! But I will conquer my weakness. I insist upon your going to the engagement you have made, and will henceforth place the most entire confidence in your prudence and honour."

Every word of this speech was a dagger to my heart. What were my feelings, while this admirable woman was taking shame to herself for her suspicions, and pouring out her soul in commendation of my integrity! I looked inward, and found every thing there the reverse of her apprehension, a scene of desolation and remorse. I embraced her in silence. My heart panted upon her bosom, and seemed bursting with a secret that it was death to reveal. I ought, in return for her generosity, to have given up my feigned engagement, and devoted this night at least to console and pacify her. But I could not, and I dared not. The wound of my bosom was opened, and would not be closed. The more I loved her for her confidence, the less I could endure myself in her presence. To play the hypocrite for so many hours, to assume a face of tranquillity and joy while all within was tumult and horror, was a task too mighty for human powers to execute. I accepted of Marguerite's permission, and left her. Even in the short interval before I quitted the house, my carriage was near to betraying me. I could perceive her watchful of my countenance, as if again suspicious that some fatal secret lurked in my mind. She said nothing further upon the subject however, and I presently escaped the inquisition of her eye.

It is scarcely necessary to describe the state of my mind as I passed along the streets. It is sufficient to say that every thing I had felt before from the passion of gaming was trivial to the sensations that now occupied me. Now first it stood confessed before me, a demon that poisoned all my joys, that changed the transport of a meeting with the adored of my soul into anguish, that drove me forth from her yet untasted charms a solitary wanderer on the face of the earth. My busy soul drew forth at length the picture of what this encounter would have been, if it had been sanctified with the stamp of conscious innocence. At one moment I felt myself the most accursed of mankind; I believed that he who could find, as I did, barrenness and blasting in the choicest of Heaven's blessings, must be miserable beyond precedent or hope. Shortly after, however, I reviewed again the image of my poison, and found in it the promise of a cure. The more desperate my case appeared to me, with the greater insanity of expectation did I assure myself that this one night should retrieve all my misfortunes. In giving to it this destination indeed, I should afflict the gentle bosom of my wife but too probably with some hours of uneasiness. But the event would richly repay her for so transitory a suffering; I would then open my whole mind to her. I would practise no more reserves; I should no longer be driven to the refuge of a vile hypocrisy. I would bid farewell to the frowns and the caresses of fortune. I would require of her no further kindnesses. If I were incapable myself of a rigid economy, I would commit implicitly to Marguerite the disposal of my income, whom I knew to be every way qualified for the office. With these reflections I nerved my mind to the most decisive adventures.

Why should I enter into a long detail of the incidents of this crisis? Soon, though not immediately, I began to lose considerable sums. I brought with me in the first instance a penetrating eye, a collected mind, an intellect prepared for unintermitted exertion. Misfortune subverted all this. My eye grew wild, my soul tempestuous, my thoughts incoherent and distracted. I was incapable of any thing judicious; but I was determined to persevere. I played till morning, nor could the light of morning induce me to desist. The setting sun of that day beheld me a beggar!

There is a degree of misery, which, as it admits of no description, so does it leave no distinct traces in the memory. It seems as if the weakness of the human mind alike incapacitated it to support the delirium of joy, and the extremity of sorrow. Of what immediately succeeded the period to which I have conducted my narrative I have no recollection, but a horror beyond all names of horror, wild, inexplicable, unintelligible. Let no one, however, imagine, that the temporary desertion of the soul is any alleviation of its misery. The mind that sinks under its suffering does not by that conduct shake off its burden. Rather, ten thousand times rather, would I endure all the calamities that have ever yet received a name, the sensations and history of which are capable of being delineated, than sustain that which has no words by which to express itself, and the conception of which must be trusted solely to the faculties and sympathy of the reader. Where is the cold and inapprehensive spirit that talks of madness as a refuge from sorrow? Oh, dull and unconceiving beyond all belief! I cannot speak of every species of madness; but I also have been mad! This I know, that there is a vacancy of soul, where all appears buried in stupidity, and scarcely deserves the name of thought, that is more intolerable than the bitterest reflections. This I know, that there is an incoherence, in which the mind seems to wander without rudder and pilot, that laughs to scorn the superstitious fictions of designing priests. Oh, how many sleepless days and weeks did I endure! the thoughts frantic, the tongue raving! While we can still adhere, if I may so express myself, to the method of misery, there is a sort of nameless complacency that lurks under all that we can endure. We are still conscious that we are men; we wonder at and admire our powers of being miserable; but, when the masts and tackle of the intellectual vessel are all swept away, then is the true sadness. We have no consciousness to sustain us, no sentiment of dignity, no secret admiration of what we are, still clinging to our hearts.

All this I venture to affirm, with the full recollection of what I suffered, when restored to my senses, present to my mind.

When the account was closed, and the loss of my last stake had finished the scene, I rose, and, quitting the fatal spot where these transactions had passed, entered the street, with a heart oppressed, and a bursting head. My eyes glared, but I saw nothing, and could think of nothing. It was already nearly dark; and the day which had been tempestuous, was succeeded by a heavy and settled rain. I wandered for some time, not knowing whither I went. My pace, which had at first been slow, gradually increased, and I traversed the whole city with a hurried and impatient step. The streets which had contained few persons at first, gradually lost those few. I was almost alone. I saw occasionally ragged and houseless misery shrinking under the cover of a miserable shed; I saw the midnight robber, watching for his prey, and ready to start upon the unwary passenger. From me he fled; there was something in my air that impelled even desperate violation to shrink from the encounter. I continued this incessant, unmeaning exertion for hours. At length, by an accidental glance of the eye, I found myself at the gate of my own hotel. Heedless of what I did, I entered; and, as nature was now completely exhausted within me, sunk down in a sort of insensibility at the foot of the grand staircase.

This stupor, after a considerable interval, gradually subsided. I opened my eyes, and saw various figures flitting about me; but I seemed to myself equally incapable of collecting my thoughts, and of speech. My understanding indeed shortly became clearer, but an insuperable reluctance to voluntary exertion hung upon me. I explained myself only in monosyllables; a sort of instinctive terror of disclosing what had passed to the admirable woman I had sacrificed maintained in me this perpetual reserve. For several days together I sat from morning till night in one immovable posture, nor was any thing of force enough to awaken me to exertion.

CHAPTER VII.

It was not long before the unhappy partner of my fortunes was informed of what had passed. The wretches who had stripped me of my all soon made their appearance to claim what was no longer mine. What would have been their reception, if I had sufficiently possessed myself to parley with them on the subject, I am unable to determine. I could not have preserved the wreck of my property from their grasp, but at the expense of an indelible stain upon my honour; yet my desperation would probably have led me to a conduct equally extravagant and useless. In the condition in which I was, the whole direction of the business devolved upon Marguerite; and never did human creature demean herself with greater magnanimity and propriety. She saw at once that she could not resist their claims but at the expense of my reputation; for herself she valued not riches, and had no dread of poverty; and, thus circumstanced, she had the courage herself to bring to me the papers they offered, the object of which I scarcely understood, and to cause me to annex that signature which was to strip her and her children of all earthly fortune. Her purpose was, as soon as this business was over, to cause us to quit France, and retire into some scene of virtuous obscurity. But she would not leave behind her for the last descendants of the counts de St. Leon any avoidable disgrace. Her mode of reasoning upon the subject was extremely simple. Obscurity she regarded as no misfortune; and eminent situation, where it fairly presented itself, as a responsibility it would be base to shrink from: ignominy alone she considered as the proper theme of abhorrence. For the fickleness and inconstancy of fortune it is impossible to answer; by one of those reverses in which she appears to delight, she might yet restore us to the lustre of our former condition; but, if the name of St. Leon was henceforth to disappear from the annals of France, she was desirous at least, as far as depended on her, that it should expire, like the far famed bird of Arabia, in the midst of perfumes.

When the whole situation of Marguerite is taken into consideration, the reader, like myself, will stand astonished at the fortitude of her conduct. She had come to Paris, unable any longer to tranquillise the agitation of her mind, and exhausted with fears, suspicions, and alarms. When she arrived, she experienced indeed one delusive moment of transport and joy. But that was soon over. It was succeeded by reflections and conjectures respecting the mysteriousness of my behaviour; it was succeeded by my unexpected departure, and the hourly expectation of my return. After the lapse of a night and a day, I returned indeed, but in what a condition! Drenched with rain, trembling with inanition, speechless and alone. Scarcely had she received notice of my arrival, and come forward to meet me, than she saw me fall, motionless and insensible, at her feet. She watched my recovery, and hung with indescribable expectation over my couch. She was only called away by the wretches, who came to advance their accursed claims, and to visit her with the intelligence of our ruin, as with a thunderbolt. Already enfeebled and alarmed by all the preceding circumstances, they spoke with no consideration to her weakness, they stooped to no qualifications and palliatives, but disclosed the whole in the most abrupt and shocking manner. Any other woman would have sunk under this accumulation of ill. Marguerite only borrowed vigour from her situation, and rose in proportion to the pressure of the calamity. She took her resolution at once, and answered them in the most firm and decisive language.

The period of inactivity and stupor that at first seized me was succeeded by a period of frenzy. It was in this condition that Marguerite conducted me and my children to an obscure retreat in the canton of Soleure, in the republic of Switzerland. Cheapness was the first object; for the most miserable pittance was all she had saved from the wreck of our fortune. She had not chosen for beauty of situation, or magnificence of prospects. The shock her mind had sustained was not so great as to destroy her activity and fortitude, but it left her little leisure for the wantonness of studied indulgence. The scene was remote and somewhat sterile. She conceived that, when I recovered my senses, an event which she did not cease to promise herself, solitude would be most grateful, at least to the first stage of my returning reason.

Hither then it was that she led me, our son, and three daughters. Immediately upon our arrival she purchased a small and obscure, but neat, cottage, and attired herself and her children in habits similar to those of the neighbouring peasants. My paternal estates, as well as those which had fallen to me by marriage, had all been swallowed up in the gulf, which my accursed conduct had prepared. Marguerite made a general sale of our moveables, our ornaments, and even our clothes. A few books, guided by the attachment to literature which had always attended me, were all that she saved from the wreck. A considerable part of the sum thus produced was appropriated by my creditors. Marguerite had the prudence and skill to satisfy them all, and was contented to retain that only which remained when their demands were discharged. This was the last dictate of her pride and the high-born integrity of her nature, at the time that she thus departed a voluntary exile from her native country. Two servants accompanied us in our flight, whose attachment was so great, that even if their attendance had not been necessary, it would have been found somewhat difficult to shake them off. Marguerite, however, was governed by the strictest principles of economy; and, whatever the struggle might have been with the importunity of humble affection in dismissing these last remains of our profuse and luxurious household, she would have thought herself obliged to proceed even to this extreme, if judicious parsimony had demanded it from her. But it did not. Our youngest daughter was at this time only twelve months old, and it would have been scarcely possible for the mother, however resolute in her exertions, to have discharged the cares due to such a family, at a time when the father of it was suffering under so heavy an affliction. One female servant she retained to assist her in these offices. She could not dispense herself from a very assiduous attention to me. She could never otherwise have been satisfied, that every thing was done that ought to be done, that every tenderness was exercised that might be demanded by my humiliating situation, or that sufficient sagacity and skill were employed in watching and encouraging the gleams of returning reason. The violence of my paroxysms, however, was frequently such as to render a manual force greater than hers necessary to prevent me from effecting some desperate mischief. Bernardin, a trusty servant, nearly of my own age, and who had attended upon my person almost from infancy, was retained by Marguerite for this purpose. I was greatly indebted for the recovery which speedily followed to the affectionate anxiety and enlightened care of this incomparable woman. It is inconceivable to those who have never been led to a practical examination of the subject, how much may be effected in this respect by an attachment ever on the watch, and an understanding judicious to combine, where hired attendance would sleep, and the coarseness of a blunt insensibility would irritate, nay, perhaps, mortally injure.

It is scarcely possible to imagine a wife more interesting and admirable than Marguerite appeared upon the present occasion. Fallen from the highest rank to the lowest poverty, she did not allow herself a mean and pitiful regret. No reverse could be more complete and abrupt, but she did not sink under it. She proved, in the most convincing manner, that her elevation was not the offspring of wealth or rank, but was properly her own. She gave a grace, even a lustre, to poverty, which it can only receive from the emanations of a cultivated mind. Her children were reconciled and encouraged by her example, and soon forgot those indulgences which had not yet had time to emasculate their spirits. The deplorable situation to which the father of the family was reduced was far from inducing her to cease from her efforts in the bitterness of despair. She determined for the present to be both a father and a mother to her children. She looked forward with confidence to my speedy recovery. Though I was the author of her calamities, she did not permit this consideration to subtract from the purity of her affection, or the tenderness of her anxiety. She resolved that no word or look of hers should ever reproach me with my misconduct. She had been accustomed to desire rank, and affluence, and indulgence for her children; that her son might run the career of glory which his forefathers ran, and that her daughters might unite their fates with what was most illustrious and honourable in their native country. But, if she were disappointed in this, she determined, as far as it should be in her power, to give them virtue and cheerfulness and content, a mind that should find resources within itself, and call forth regard and esteem from the rest of mankind.

My recovery was fitful and precarious, sometimes appearing to be rapidly on the advance, and at others to threaten a total relapse. Among the expedients that Marguerite employed to re-excite the slumbering spark of reason was that of paternal affection. Ever on the watch for a favourable opportunity, she sometimes brought to me her own little namesake, who, though only twelve months old, did not fail to discover unequivocal marks of that playfulness and gaiety which made so considerable a part of her constitutional character. Her innocent smiles, her frolic and careless laughter, produced a responsive vibration that reached to my inmost heart. They were, not unfrequently, powerful enough to check the career of my fury, or to raise me from the lowest pitch of despondence. Julia wept for me, and Louisa endeavoured to copy the offices of kindness she was accustomed to see her mother perform: Charles, who conceived more fully than the rest the nature of my indisposition, was upon all occasions solicitous to be admitted into my presence, and attended me for the most part with speechless anxiety, while his watchful, glistening eye uttered volumes, without the assistance of words. His mother at length yielded to his importunity, and he became established the regular assistant of Bernardin in the care of my person. The restlessness and impetuosity he had hitherto manifested seemed upon this occasion entirely to subside: hour after hour he willingly continued shut up in my chamber, eager for every opportunity of usefulness, and gratified with that complaisance with which the human mind never fails to be impressed, when it regards its actions as beneficent, or approves its temper as compassionate.

The restoration of my health was greatly retarded by the melancholy impressions which necessarily offered themselves to my mind when recollection resumed her seat. It was fortunate for me that this sort of retrospection appears not to be the first thing that occurs after a paroxysm of insanity. When the tide of incoherent ideas subsides, the soul is left in a state of exhaustion; and seems, by a sort of instinct, to shun the influx of tumultuous emotions, and to dwell upon such feelings as are mild, tranquil, and restorative. Once, however, when I was nearly recovered, the thought of what I had been, and the recollection of what I was, violently suggesting themselves to my mind, brought on a relapse, attended with more alarming and discouraging symptoms than my original alienation. At that moment Marguerite was, for the first time, irresistibly struck with the conception that mine was an incurable lunacy; and, as she afterwards assured me, at no period down to that instant had she felt herself so truly inconsolable. But even a sentiment of the last despair was incapable of superseding the active beneficence of Marguerite. Her assiduities, so far as related to this fatal calamity, were at length crowned with success. Her gloomy prognostics were not realised, and the distemper of my understanding quitted me for ever.

Wretched, however, as I have already remarked, beyond all common notions of wretchedness, were my thoughts, when my soul returned to its proper bias, and I fully surveyed the nature of my present situation. Marguerite, who, by her sagacity and patience, had recovered me from a state of the most dreadful disease, now exerted herself to effect the more arduous task of reconciling me to myself. She assured me that she forgave me from her inmost heart; nay, that she was thankful to Providence, which, in the midst of what the world calls great calamities, had preserved to her what she most valued, my affection, entire. She contrasted what had been the subject of her apprehensions before she came to Paris, with what had proved to be the state of the case afterwards. She averred, that the worst that had happened was trivial and tolerable, compared with the image that her fears had delineated. She had feared to find my heart alienated from her, and herself a widowed mother to orphan children. She dreaded lest I should have proved myself worthless in her eyes, lest I should have been found to have committed to oblivion the most sacred of all duties; and, for the gratification of a low and contemptible caprice, to have sacrificed all pretensions to honour and character. For that, indeed, her heart would have bled; against that, all the pride she derived from her ancestry and my own would have revolted; that would have produced a revulsion of her frame, snapping the chain of all her habits, and putting a violent close upon all the sentiments she had most fondly nourished. She dreaded, indeed, that she should not have survived it. But the mistake I had committed was of a very different nature. I had neither forgotten that I was a husband nor a father; I had only made an injudicious and unfortunate choice of the way of discharging what was due to these characters. What had passed was incapable of impeaching either the constancy of my affections or the integrity of my principles. She forgave me, and it was incumbent upon me to forgive myself.

She assured me that poverty, in her apprehension, was a very slight evil; and she appealed to my own understanding for the soundness of her judgment. She bid me look round upon the peasantry of the neighbourhood, upon a footing with whom we were now placed, and ask my own heart whether they were not happy. One disadvantage, indeed, they were subjected to,—the absence of cultivation and learning. She could never bring herself to believe that ignorance was a benefit; she saw the contrary of this practically illustrated in her own case, in mine, and in that of all the persons to whom, through life, she had been most ardently attached. She wished her children to attain intellectual refinement, possess fully the attributes of a rational nature, and to be as far removed as possible from the condition of stocks and stones, by accumulating a magazine of thoughts, and by a rich and cultivated sensibility. But the want of fortune did not in our case, as in the case of so many others, shut them out from this advantage: it was in our own power to bestow it upon them.

It was the part of a reasonable man, she told me, not to waste his strength in useless regrets for what was past, and had already eluded his grasp; but to advert to the blessings he had still in possession. If we did this in our present situation, we should find every reason for contentment and joy. Our pleasure in each other, and the constancy of our attachment, was unassailed and unimpaired. Where were there two married persons, she would venture to ask, who had more reason to applaud their connection, or to whom their connection was pregnant with so various gratifications? From ourselves we had only to turn our thoughts to our children; and we were surely as singularly fortunate in this respect as in each other. Charles, who had always been the subject of our pride, had lately exhibited such an example of patient sympathy and filial affection, as perhaps had never been equalled in a child so young. The sensibility of Julia, the understanding of Louisa, and the vivacity of Marguerite, were all of them so many growing sources of inexhaustible delight. Our children were intelligent, affectionate, and virtuous. Thus circumstanced, she entreated me not to indulge that jaundice of the imagination, which should create to itself a sentiment of melancholy and discontent in the midst of this terrestrial paradise.

Most virtuous of women, now perhaps the purest and the brightest among the saints in heaven! why was I deaf to the soundness of your exhortations, and the generosity of your sentiments? Deaf, indeed, I was! A prey to the deepest dejection, they appeared to me the offspring of misapprehension and paradox! Supposing, in the mean time, that they were reasonable and just in the mouth of her who uttered them, I felt them as totally foreign to my own situation. The language, as they were, of innocence; it was not wonderful that to an innocent heart they spoke tranquillity and peace. Marguerite looked round upon the present rusticity and plainness of our condition, and every thing that she saw talked to her of her merit and her worth. If we were reduced, she was in no way accountable for that reduction; it had been the test of her magnanimity, her patience, and the immutableness of her virtue. She smiled at the assaults of adversity, and felt a merit in her smiles. How different was my situation! Every thing that I saw reminded me of my guilt, and upbraided me with crimes that it was hell to recollect. My own garb, and that of my wife and children, the desertion in which we lived, the simple benches, the unhewn rafters, the naked walls, all told me what it was I had done, and were so many echoes to my conscience, repeating, without intermission and without end, its heart-breaking reproaches. Sleep was almost a stranger to me; these incessant monitors confounded my senses in a degree scarcely short of madness itself. It is the property of vice to convert every thing that should be consolation into an additional source of anguish. The beauty, the capacity, and the virtue of my children, the affection with which they regarded me, the patience and attentiveness and forbearance of their excellent mother, were all so many aggravations of the mischief I had perpetrated. I could almost have wished to have been the object of their taunts and execration. I could have wished to have been disengaged from the dearest charities of our nature, and to have borne the weight of my crimes alone. It would have been a relief to me if my children had been covered with the most loathsome diseases, deformed and monstrous. It would have been a relief to me, if they had been abortive in understanding, and odious in propensities, if their hearts had teemed with every vice, and every day had marked them the predestined victims of infamy. The guilt of having stripped them of every external advantage would then have sat light upon me. But thus to have ruined the most lovely family perhaps that existed on the face of the earth, the most exemplary of women, and children in whom I distinctly marked the bud of every excellence and every virtue, was a conduct that I could never forgive even to myself. Oh, Damville, Damville! best of men! truest of friends! why didst thou put thy trust in such a wretch as I am! Hadst thou no presentiment of the fatal consequences? Wert thou empowered to commit thy only child and all her possible offspring to so dreadful a risk? Indeed, it was not well done! It was meant in kindness; but it was the cruellest mischief that could have been inflicted on me. I was not a creature qualified for such dear and tender connections. I was destined by nature to wander a solitary outcast on the face of the earth. For that only, that fearful misery, was I fitted. Why, misguided, misjudging man! didst thou not leave me to my fate? Even that would have been less dreadful than what I have experienced!—Wretch that I am! Why do I reproach my best benefactor? No, let me turn the whole current of my invective upon myself! Damville was actuated by the noblest and most generous sentiment that ever entered the human mind. What a return then have I made, and to what a benefit!

All the previous habits of my mind had taught me to feel my present circumstances with the utmost acuteness. Marguerite, the generous Marguerite, stood, with a soul almost indifferent, between the opposite ideas of riches and poverty. Not so her husband. I had been formed, by every accident of my life, to the love of splendour. High heroic feats, and not the tranquillity of rural retirement, or the pursuits of a character professedly literary, had been the food of my imagination, ever since the faculty of imagination was unfolded in my mind. The field of the cloth of gold, the siege and the battle of Pavia, were for ever present to my recollection. Francis the First, Bayard, and Bourbon, eternally formed the subject of my visions and reveries. These propensities had indeed degenerated into an infantine taste for magnificence and expense; but the roots did not embrace their soil the less forcibly, because the branches were pressed down and diverted from their genuine perpendicular. That from a lord, descended from some of the most illustrious houses in France, and myself amply imbued with the high and disdainful spirit incident to my rank, I should become a peasant, was itself a sufficient degradation. But I call the heavens to witness that I could have endured this with patience, if I had endured it alone. I should have regarded it as the just retribution of my follies, and submitted with the most exemplary resignation. But I could not, with an equal mind, behold my wife and children involved in my punishment. I turned my eyes upon the partner of my life, and recalled with genuine anguish the magnificence to which she was accustomed, and the hopes to which she was born. I looked upon my children, the fruit of my loins, and once the pride of my heart, and recollected that they were paupers, rustics, exiles. I could foresee no return to rank, but for them and their posterity an interminable succession of obscurity and meanness. A real parent can support the calamity of personal degradation, but he cannot bear to witness and anticipate this corruption of his blood. At some times I honoured Marguerite for her equanimity. At others I almost despised her for this integrity of her virtues. I accused her in my heart of being destitute of the spark of true nobility. Her patience I considered as little less than meanness and vulgarity of spirit. It would have become her better, I thought, like me, to have cursed her fate, and the author of that fate; like me, to have spurned indignant at the slavery to which we were condemned; to have refused to be pacified; and to have wasted the last dregs of existence in impatience and regret. I could act that which had involved us in this dire reverse; but I could not encounter the consequences of my act.

The state of my mind was in the utmost degree dejected and forlorn. I carried an arrow in my heart, which the kindness of my wife and children proved inadequate to extract, and the ranklings of which time itself had not the power to assuage. The wound was not mortal; but, like the wound of Philoctetes, poisoned with the blood of the Lernean hydra, I dragged it about with me from year to year, and it rendered my existence a galling burden hardly to be supported. A great portion of my time was passed in a deep and mournful silence, which all the soothings that were addressed to me could not prevail on me to break. Not that in this silence there was the least particle of ill humour or sullenness. It was a mild and passive situation of the mind; affectionate, as far as it was any thing, to the persons around me; but it was a species of disability; my soul had not force enough to give motion to the organs of speech, or scarcely to raise a finger. My eye only, and that only for a moment at a time, pleaded for forbearance and pardon. I seemed like a man in that species of distemper, in which the patient suffers a wasting of the bones, and at length presents to us the shadow, without the powers, of a human body.

This was at some times my condition. But my stupor would at others suddenly subside. Mechanically, and in a moment, as it were, I shook off my supineness, and sought the mountains. The wildness of an untamed and savage scene best accorded with the temper of my mind. I sprung from cliff to cliff among the points of the rock. I rushed down precipices that to my sobered sense appeared in a manner perpendicular, and only preserved my life, with a sort of inborn and unelective care, by catching at the roots and shrubs which occasionally broke the steepness of the descent. I hung over the tops of rocks still more fearful in their declivities, and courted the giddiness and whirl of spirit which such spectacles are accustomed to produce. I could not resolve to die: death had too many charms to suit the self-condemnation that pursued me. I found a horrible satisfaction in determining to live, and to avenge upon myself the guilt I had incurred. I was far from imagining that the evils I had yet suffered were a mere sport and ostentation of misery, compared with those that were in reserve for me.

The state of mind I am here describing was not madness, nor such as could be mistaken for madness. I never forgot myself, and what I was. I was never in that delirium of thought, in which the patient is restless and active without knowing what it is that he does, and from which, when roused, he suddenly starts, shakes off the dream that engaged him, and stands astonished at himself. Mine was a rage, guided and methodised by the discipline of despair. I burst into no fits of raving; I attempted no injury to any one. Marguerite therefore could not reconcile herself to the placing me under any restraint. I frequently returned home, with my clothes smeared with the soil, and torn by the briars. But my family soon became accustomed to my returning in personal safety; and therefore, whatever was the uneasiness my wife felt from my excursions, she preferred the enduring it, to the idea of imposing on me any species of violence.

The state of my family presented a singular contrast with that of its head. Marguerite was certainly not insensible to the opposition between her former and her present mode of life; but she submitted to the change with such an unaffected cheerfulness and composure, as might have extorted admiration from malignity itself. She would perhaps have dismissed from her thoughts all retrospect to our former grandeur, had not the dejection and despair that seemed to have taken possession of my mind forcibly and continually recalled it to her memory. For my sufferings I am well assured she felt the truest sympathy; but there was one consideration attending them that imperiously compelled her to task her fortitude. They deprived me of the ability of in any degree providing for and superintending my family; it became therefore incumbent upon her to exert herself for the welfare of all. Had we never fallen under this astonishing reverse, I might have spent my whole life in daily intercourse with this admirable woman, without becoming acquainted with half the treasures of her mind. She was my steward; and from the result of her own reflections made the most judicious disposition of my property. She was my physician; not by administering medicines to my body, but by carefully studying and exerting herself to remove the distemper of mind. Unfortunately no distempers are so obstinate as mental ones; yet, had my distemper had any lighter source than an upbraiding conscience, I am persuaded the wisdom of Marguerite would have banished it. She was the instructor of my children; her daughters felt no want of a governess; and I am even ready to doubt whether the lessons of his mother did not amply supply to Charles his loss of an education in the university of Paris. The love of order, the activity, the industry, the cheerfulness of, let me say, this illustrious matron, became contagious to all the inhabitants of my roof. Once and again have I stolen a glance at them, or viewed them from a distance busied, sometimes gravely, sometimes gaily, in the plain, and have whispered to my bursting heart, "How miserable am I! how happy they! So insurmountable is the barrier that divides innocence from guilt. They may breathe the same air; they may dwell under the same roof; they may be of one family and one blood; they may associate with each other every day and every hour; but they can never assimilate, never have any genuine contact. Is there a happier family than mine in all the valley of this far-famed republic? Is there a family more virtuous, or more cultivated with all the refinements that conduce to the true dignity of man? I, I only am its burden and its stain! The pleasure with which I am surrounded on every side finds a repellent quality in my heart that will not suffer its approach. To whatever is connected with me I communicate misfortune. Whenever I make my appearance, those countenances that at all other times spoke contentment and hilarity fall into sadness. Like a pestilential wind, I appear to breathe blast to the fruits of nature, and sickliness to its aspect."

Marguerite expostulated with me in the most soothing manner upon the obstinacy of my malady. "My Reginald! my love!" said she, "cease to be unhappy, or to reproach yourself! You were rash in the experiment you made upon the resources of your family. But have you done us mischief, or have you conferred a benefit? I more than half incline to the latter opinion. Let us at length dismiss artificial tastes, and idle and visionary pursuits, that do not flow in a direct line from any of the genuine principles of our nature! Here we are surrounded with sources of happiness. Here we may live in true patriarchal simplicity. What is chivalry, what are military prowess and glory? Believe me, they are the passions of a mind depraved, that with ambitious refinement seeks to be wise beyond the dictates of sentiment or reason! There is no happiness so solid, or so perfect, as that which disdains these refinements. You, like me, are fond of the luxuriant and romantic scenes of nature. Here we are placed in the midst of them. How idle it would be, to wish to change our arbours, our verdant lanes and thickets, for vaulted roofs, and gloomy halls, and massy plate! Alas, Reginald! it is, I fear, too true, that the splendour in which we lately lived has its basis in oppression; and that the superfluities of the rich are a boon extorted from the hunger and misery of the poor! Here we see a peasantry more peaceful and less oppressed than perhaps any other tract of the earth can exhibit. They are erect and independent, at once friendly and fearless. Is not this a refreshing spectacle? I now begin practically to perceive that the cultivators of the fields and the vineyards are my brethren and my sisters; and my heart bounds with joy, as I feel my relations to society multiply. How cumbrous is magnificence! The moderate man is the only free. He who reduces all beneath him to a state of servitude becomes himself the slave of his establishment, and of all his domestics. To diminish the cases in which the assistance of others is felt absolutely necessary is the only genuine road to independence. We can now move wherever we please without waiting the leisure of others. Our simple repasts require no tedious preparation, and do not imprison us in saloons and eating rooms. Yet we partake of them with a more genuine appetite, and rise from them more truly refreshed, than from the most sumptuous feast. I prepare for my meal by industry and exercise; and when it is over, amuse myself with my children in the fields and the shade.—Though I love the sight of the peasants, I would not be a peasant. I would have a larger stock of ideas, and a wider field of activity. I love the sight of peasants only for their accessories, or by comparison. They are comparatively more secure than any other large masses of men, and the scenes in the midst of which they are placed are delightful to sense. But I would not sacrifice in prone oblivion the best characteristics of my nature. I put in my claim for refinements and luxuries; but they are the refinements and purifying of intellect, and the luxuries of uncostly, simple taste. I would incite the whole world, if I knew how to do it, to put in a similar claim. I would improve my mind; I would enlarge my understanding; I would contribute to the instruction of all connected with me, and to the mass of human knowledge. The pleasures I would pursue and disseminate, though not dependent on a large property, are such as could not be understood by the rustic and the savage.—Our son, bred in these fields, indeed, will probably never become a preux chevalier, or figure in the roll of military heroes; but he may become something happier and better. He may improve his mind, and cultivate his taste. He may be the counsellor and protector of his sisters. He may be the ornament of the district in which he resides. He may institute in his adoptive country new defences for liberty, new systems of public benefit, and new improvements of life. There is no character more admirable than the patriot-yeoman, who unites with the utmost simplicity of garb and manners an understanding fraught with information and sentiment and a heart burning with the love of mankind. Such were Fabricius and Regulus among the ancients, and such was Tell, the founder of the Helvetic liberty. For my part, I am inclined to be thankful, that this unexpected reverse in our circumstances has made me acquainted with new pleasures, and opened to my mind an invaluable lesson. If you could but be prevailed on to enter into our pleasures, to dismiss idle reproaches and pernicious propensities, our happiness would then be complete."

The expostulations of Marguerite often excited my attention, often my respect, and sometimes produced a sort of imperfect conviction. But the conviction was transient, and the feelings I have already described as properly my own returned, when the fresh and vivid impression of what I had heard was gone. It was in vain that I heard the praises of simplicity and innocence. I was well pleased to see those who were nearest to me not affecting contentment, but really contented with these things. But I could not be contented for them. The lessons of my education had left too deep an impression. I could myself have surrendered my claim to admiration and homage, as a penance for my misdeeds; but I could not figure to myself a genuine satisfaction unaccompanied by these accessories: and this satisfaction I obstinately and impatiently coveted for those I loved.

CHAPTER VIII.

While I murmured in bitterness of soul at the lowness to which my family was reduced, a still heavier calamity impended, as if in vengeance against the fantastic refinements of distress over which I brooded.

I was wandering, as I had often done, with a gloomy and rebellious spirit, among the rocks, a few miles distant from the place of our habitation. It was the middle of summer. The weather had been remarkably fine; but I disdained to allow the gratifications which arise from a pure atmosphere and a serene sky to find entrance in my soul. My excursions had for some days been incessant; and the sun, which matured the corn and blackened the grapes around, had imbrowned my visage, and boiled in my blood. I drank in fierceness and desperation from the fervour of his beams. One night, as in sullen mood I watched his setting from a point of the rock, I perceived the clearness of the day subsiding in a threatening evening. The clouds gathered in the west; and, as night approached, were overspread with a deep dye of the fiercest crimson. The wind rose; and, during the hours of darkness, its roarings were hollow and tempestuous.

In the morning the clouds were hurried rapidly along, and the air was changed from a long series of sultriness to a nipping cold. This change of the atmosphere I disregarded, and pursued my rambles. A little before noon, however, the air suddenly grew so dark, as to produce a sensation perfectly tremendous. I felt as if the darkest night had never exceeded it. The impetuous motion to which I had been impelled, partly by the fever in my blood, and partly by the turbulence of the season, was suspended. Mechanically I looked round me for shelter. But I could ill distinguish the objects that were near me, when a flash of lightning, blue and sulphureous, came directly in my face, with a brightness that threatened to extinguish the organ of vision. The thunder that followed was of a length and loudness to admit of no comparison from any object with which I am acquainted. The bursts were so frequent as almost to confound themselves with each other. At present I thought only of myself; and the recent habits of my mind were not calculated to make me peculiarly accessible to fear. I stood awe-struck; but rather with the awe that inheres to a cultivated imagination, than that which consists in apprehension. I seemed ready to mount amidst the clouds, and penetrate the veil with which nature conceals her operations. I would have plunged into the recesses in which the storm was engendered, and bared my bosom to the streaming fire. Meanwhile my thoughts were solemnised and fixed by observing the diversified dance of the lightnings upon the points of the rocks, contrasting as they did in the strongest manner with the darkness in which the rest of the scene was enveloped. This added contention of the elements did not, however, suspend the raging of the wind. Presently a storm of mingled hail and rain poured from the clouds, and was driven with inconceivable impetuosity. The hailstones were of so astonishing a magnitude, that, before I was aware, I was beaten by them to the ground. Not daring to attempt to rise again, I simply endeavoured to place myself in such a manner as might best protect me from their violence. I therefore remained prostrate, listening to the force with which they struck upon the earth, and feeling the rebound of their blows from different parts of my body.

In about twenty minutes the shower abated, and in half an hour was entirely over. When I began to move, I was surprised at the sensation of soreness which I felt in every part of me. I raised myself upon my elbow, and saw the hailstones, in some places lying in heaps like hillocks of ice, while in others they had ploughed up the surface, and buried themselves in the earth. As I looked further, I perceived immense trees torn from their roots, and thrown to a great distance upon the declivity. To the noise that they made in their descent, which must have been astonishingly great, I had been at the time insensible. Such were the marks which the tempest had left upon the mountains. In the plain it was still worse. I could perceive the soil for long spaces together converted into a morass, the standing corn beaten down and buried in the mud, the vines torn into a thousand pieces, the fruit trees demolished, and even in some places the animals themselves, lambs, sheep, and cows, strewing the fields with their mangled carcasses. The whole hopes of the year over which my eyes had glanced a few minutes before, for it was near the period of harvest, were converted into the most barren and dreary scene that any quarter of the globe ever witnessed. I was mounted upon a considerable eminence, and had an extensive prospect of this horrible devastation.

As I stood gazing in mute astonishment, suddenly a fear came over me that struck dampness to my very heart. What was the situation of my own family and their little remaining property, amidst this dreadful ruin? I was in a position where, though I nearly faced our habitation, a point of the rock intercepted it from my sight. The obstacle was but a small one, yet it would require a considerable circuit to overcome. I flew along the path with a speed that scarcely permitted me to breathe. When I had passed the upper rock, the whole extensive scene opened upon me in an instant. What were my sensations, when I perceived that the devastation had been even more complete here than on the side where I first viewed it! My own cottage in particular, which that very morning had contained, and I hoped continued to contain, all that was most dear to my heart, seemed to stand an entire solitude in the midst of an immense swamp.

Marguerite, whose idea, upon our retreat into Switzerland, had been that of conforming without reserve to the new situation that was allotted us, had immediately expended the whole of what remained from the shipwreck of our fortune, in the purchase of the cottage in which we dwelt, and a small portion of land around it, sufficient with economy for the support of our family. Under her direction the hills had been covered with vines, and the fields with corn. She had purchased cows to furnish us with milk, and sheep with their fleeces, and had formed her establishment upon the model of the Swiss peasantry in our neighbourhood. Reverting to the simplicity of nature, appeared to her like building upon an immovable basis, which the clash of nations could not destroy, and which was too humble to fear the treachery of courts, or the caprice of artificial refinement.

It was all swept away in a moment. Our little property looked as if it had been particularly a mark for the vengeance of Heaven, and was more utterly destroyed than any of the surrounding scenes. There was not a tree left standing; there was not a hedge or a limit that remained within or around it; chaos had here resumed his empire, and avenged himself of the extraordinary order and beauty it had lately displayed.

I was not overwhelmed with this astonishing spectacle. At that moment nature found her way to my heart, and made a man of me. I made light of these petty accessories of our existence; and the thought of my wife and my children, simply as they were in themselves, filled every avenue of my heart. For them, and them alone, I was interested: it was a question for their lives. To conceive what they might personally have sustained was a horror that seemed to freeze up all the arteries of my heart. I descended from the mountain. It was with the greatest difficulty, and not without many circuitous deviations, that I proceeded; so much was the surface changed, and so deep and miry the swamps. My terror increased, as I passed near to the carcasses of the animals who had fallen victims to this convulsion of the elements. I observed, with inconceivable alarm, that the dead or wounded bodies of some human beings were intermingled with the brute destruction. I stayed not to enquire whether they were yet in a state to require assistance; the idea that had taken possession of me left no room for the sentiment of general humanity.

A little further on I distinctly remarked the body of a woman at some distance from any habitation, who appeared to be dead, destroyed by the storm. Near her lay a female infant, apparently about six years of age. My attention was involuntarily arrested; I thought of Louisa, that sweet and amiable child, so like her admirable mother. The figure was hers; the colour of the robe corresponded to that in which I last saw her. The child was lying on her face. With all the impatient emotions of a father, I stooped down. I turned over the body, that I might identify my child. It was still warm; life had scarcely deserted it. I gazed upon the visage; it was distorted with the agonies of death: but enough to convince me still remained discernible; it was not Louisa!

I can scarcely recollect a period through all the strange vicissitudes of my existence to be compared with this. If I had not felt what I then felt, I could never have conceived it. Human nature is so constituted, that the highest degree of anguish, an anguish in which the heart stretches itself to take in the mightiness of its woe, can be felt but for a few instants. When the calamity we feared is already arrived, or when the expectation of it is so certain as to shut out hope, there seems to be a principle within us by which we look with misanthropic composure on the state to which we are reduced, and the heart sullenly contracts and accommodates itself to what it most abhorred. Our hopes wither; and our pride, our self-complacence, all that taught us to rejoice in existence, wither along with them. But, when hope yet struggles with despair, or when the calamity abruptly announces itself, then is the true contention, the tempest and uproar of the soul too vast to be endured.

This sentiment of ineffable wretchedness I experienced, when I stooped down over the body of the imaginary Louisa, and when I hastened to obtain the certainty which was of all things most terrible to me. The termination of such a moment of horror is scarcely less memorable than its intrinsic greatness. In an instant the soul recovers its balance, and the thought is as if it has never been. I clapped my hands in an ecstasy at once of joy and astonishment, so sure did I seem to have made myself of my misfortune; I quitted the body with an unburdened heart; I flew towards my home, that I might ascertain whether I was prematurely speaking comfort to my spirit.

At length I reached it. I saw the happy group assembled at the door. Marguerite had entertained the same terrors for me, with which I had myself so lately been impressed. We flew into each other's arms. She hid her face in my neck, and sobbed audibly. I embraced each of the children in turn, but Louisa with the most heartfelt delight. "Are you safe, papa?"—"Are you safe, my child?" were echoed on every side. A spectator, unacquainted with what was passing in our hearts, would certainly have stood astonished to see the transport with which we exulted, surrounded as we were with desolation and ruin.

After an interval, however, we opened our eyes, and began to ruminate upon the new condition in which we were placed. Marguerite and myself watched each other's countenances with anxiety, to discover what were likely to be the feelings of either in this terrible crisis. "Be of good heart, my love," said Marguerite; "do not suffer the accident which has happened entirely to overcome you." There was a mixed compassion, tenderness, and anxiety in the tone of voice with which she uttered these words, that was inexpressibly delightful.

"No, Marguerite," replied I, with enthusiastic impetuosity, "I am not cast down; I never shall be cast down again. Ruin is nothing to me, so long as I am surrounded with you and our dear children. I have for some time been a fool. In the midst of every real blessing, I have fashioned for myself imaginary evils. But my eyes are now opened. How easily is the human mind induced to forget those benefits with which we are constantly surrounded, and our possession of which we regard as secure! The feelings of this morning have awakened me. I am now cured of my folly. I have learned to value my domestic blessings as I ought. Having preserved them, I esteem myself to have lost nothing. What are gold and jewels and precious utensils? Mere dross and dirt. The human face and the human heart, reciprocations of kindness and love, and all the nameless sympathies of our nature,—these are the only objects worth being attached to. What are rank and station?—the homage of the multitude and the applause of fools. Let me judge for myself! The value of a man is in his intrinsic qualities; in that of which power cannot strip him, and which adverse fortune cannot take away. That for which he is indebted to circumstances, is mere trapping and tinsel. I should love these precious and ingenuous creatures before me better, though in rags, than the children of kings in all the pomp of ornament. I am proud to be their father. Whatever may be my personal faults, the world is my debtor for having been the occasion of their existence. But they are endeared to me by a better principle than pride. I love them for their qualities. He that loves, and is loved by, a race of pure and virtuous creatures, and that lives continually in the midst of them, is an idiot, if he does not think himself happy. Surrounded as I am now surrounded, I feel as irremovable as the pillars of creation. Nothing that does not strike at their existence can affect me with terror."

Marguerite viewed me with surprise and joy. "Now indeed," said she, "you are the man I took you for, and the man I shall henceforth be prouder than ever to call my husband. The sorrow in which you lately indulged was a luxury; and we must have done with luxuries. You will be our protector and our support."

Thus saying, she took me by the hand, and motioned me to view with her the devastation that had been committed. There was one path I had discovered, in which we might proceed some way with tolerable ease. The scene was terrible. We were indeed beggars. A whole province had been destroyed: all the corn and the fruits of the earth; most of the trees; in many places cattle; in some places men. Persons who had been rich in the morning saw all the produce of their fields annihilated, and were unable even to guess by what process fertility was to be re-established. The comparatively wealthy scarcely knew how they were to obtain immediate subsistence; the humbler class, who always live by the expedients of the day, saw nothing before them but the prospect of perishing with hunger. We witnessed, in one or two instances, the anguish of their despair.

Our prospect was scarcely in any respect better than theirs; yet we felt differently. We were more impressed with the joy of our personal escape. As my error respecting the value of externals had been uncommonly great, the sudden revolution of opinion I experienced was equally memorable. The survey, indeed, that we took of the general distress somewhat saddened our hearts; but the sadness it gave was that of sobriety, not of dejection.

It was incumbent upon us to make a strict examination into the amount of our property, and our immediate resources; and in this office I united myself with Marguerite, not only with a degree of cheerfulness and application, the perfect contrast of my whole conduct ever since our arrival in Switzerland, but which greatly exceeded any thing I had ever before exhibited in a business of this nature. We found that, though all our hopes of a harvest were annihilated, yet we were not destitute of the instant means of subsistence. The resources we possessed, whether in money or provisions, that were our dependence till the period when the new produce should supply their place, were uninjured. Our implements of husbandry remained as before. The land was not impoverished, but had rather derived additional fertility from the effects of the storm. What we had lost was chiefly the produce of our capital for one year, together with a part of that capital itself in the live stock that had been destroyed. This was a loss which a certain degree of care and scope in our external circumstances might easily have enabled us to supply. But the principle of supply was denied us. It was with considerable difficulty that all the economy of Marguerite had enabled her to support our family establishment, while every thing of this kind had gone on prosperously. Such a shock as the present we were totally disqualified to surmount. It compelled us to a complete revolution of our affairs.

Many indeed of our neighbours had scarcely any greater advantage in their private affairs than ourselves. But they possessed one superiority that proved of the greatest importance in this conjuncture; they were natives of the state in which they resided. In the cantons of Switzerland, the destruction of the fruits of the earth, occasioned by inclement seasons and tempests, is by no means unfrequent; and it is therefore customary, in plentiful years, to lay up corn in public magazines, that the people may not perish in periods of scarcity. These magazines are placed under the inspection and disposal of the magistracy; and the inhabitants looked to them with confidence for the supply of their need. No storm, however, had occurred in the memory of man so terrible and ruinous as the present; and it became evident that the magazines would prove a resource too feeble for the extent of the emergency.

The storm had spread itself over a space of many leagues in circumference, not only in the canton of Soleure, but in the neighbouring cantons, particularly that of Berne. The sufferers, in our own canton only, amounted to scarcely less than ten thousand. While the women and children, for the most part, remained at home, the houses having in general suffered little other damage than the destruction of their windows, the fathers of families repaired to the seat of government to put in their claims for national relief; and these alone formed an immense troop, that threatened little less than to besiege the public magazines and the magistrates. An accurate investigation was entered into of the losses of each, it being the purpose of government, as far as its power extended, not only to supply the people with the means of immediate subsistence, but also, by disbursements from the public treasury, to recruit the stock of cattle, and to assist every one to return, with revived hopes and expectation, to the sphere of his industry. The purpose was no doubt benevolent; but, in the mean time, the unhappy victims found in uncertainty and expectation a real and corroding anguish.

I advanced my claim with the rest, but met with a peremptory refusal. The harsh and rigorous answer I received was, that they had not enough for their own people, and could spare nothing to strangers. Upon this occasion I was compelled to feel what it was to be an alien, and how different the condition in which I was now placed from that I had filled in my native country. There I had lived in the midst of a people, to whom the veneration of my ancestry and name seemed a part of their nature. They had witnessed for several years the respectable manner in which I lived; the virtues of Marguerite were familiar to them; and they took an interest in every thing that concerned us, a sentiment that confessed us at once for kindred and patrons. It was the turn of mind only which is generated by rank, that had compelled us to quit their vicinity; we might have continued in it, if not in affluence, at least enjoying the gratifications that arise from general affection and respect. But here we were beheld with an eye of jealousy and distaste. We had no prejudice of birth and habit in our favour; indeed, in the reverse of fortune which had brought us hither, Marguerite had been less desirous of obtruding, than of withdrawing from the public eye, the circumstance of our rank. We were too recent inmates to have secured, by any thing of a personal nature, an advantageous opinion among our neighbours. They saw only a miserable and distracted father of a family, and a mother who, in spite of the simplicity she cultivated, sufficiently evinced that she had been accustomed to a more elevated situation. The prepossessions of mankind are clearly unfavourable to a new-comer, an emigrant who has quitted his former connections and the scenes of his youth. They are unavoidably impelled to believe, that his taking up his abode in another country must be owing to a weak and discreditable caprice, if it be not owing to something still more disadvantageous to his character.

The calamity therefore which we had suffered in common with most of the inhabitants of the province, finally reduced us to the necessity of a second emigration. The jealousy with which we were regarded, daily became more visible and threatening. Though, in consequence of the distribution made by order of the state, the price of commodities was not so much increased as might have been expected, we were considered as interlopers upon the portion of the natives; the sellers could with difficulty be persuaded to accommodate us, and the bystanders treated us with murmurs and reviling. While we were deliberating what course to pursue in this emergency, certain officers of government one morning entered our habitation, producing an order of the senate for our immediate removal out of the territory. It is of the essence of coercive regulations, to expel, to imprison, and turn out of prison, the individuals it is thought proper to control, without any care as to the mischiefs they may suffer, and whether they perish under or survive the evil inflicted on them. We were accordingly allowed only from six in the morning till noon, to prepare for our departure. Our guards indeed offered to permit me to remain three days to wind up my affairs, upon condition that my wife and children were instantly removed into another country, as a sort of hostages for my own departure. This indulgence however would have been useless. In the present state of the country no purchaser could be found for the little estate I possessed; and if there could, it must doubtless have been disposed of to great disadvantage at such an emergency. I know not how we should have extricated ourselves out of these difficulties, if a member of the senate, who, being one of my nearest neighbours, had been struck with admiration of the virtues of Marguerite, and with compassion for my family, had not paid me a visit shortly after the arrival of the officers, and generously offered to take upon himself the care of my property, and to advance me what money might be necessary for my emigration. This offer, which at any other time might have been regarded as purely a matter of course, under the present circumstances, when capital was so necessary for the revival of agriculture in the desolated country, implied a liberal and disinterested spirit. I accepted the kindness of my neighbour in both its parts, but for the reimbursement of his loan referred him to the French minister to the United Cantons, who, under all the circumstances of the case, and taking my estate as security for the money advanced, I thought it reasonable to believe would attend to my application.

CHAPTER IX.

My affairs being thus far adjusted, I took leave of my late habitation, and set off with my wife and children the same afternoon. In the evening we arrived at Basle, where we were permitted to remain that night; and the next morning were conducted in form out at the north gate of the city, where our attendants quitted us, with a fresh prohibition under the severest penalties, if we were found within the ensuing twelve months in any of the territories of the Helvetic republic.

Marguerite and myself had already formed our plan. We began with dismissing both our servants. An attendant was no longer necessary to me, nor a nurse for the infant. The suggestion of this measure originated in myself. My temper at this time, as I have already said, underwent a striking change. I was resolved to be happy; I was resolved to be active. It was hard to part with persons so long familiar to us, and who appeared rather in the character of humble friends than domestics; but an imperious necessity demanded it. "Let us," said I to Marguerite, "increase and secure our happiness by diminishing our wants. I will be your husbandman and your labourer; you may depend upon my perseverance. My education has fitted me to endure hardship and fatigue, though the hardships then thought of were of a different nature. You have ever delighted in active usefulness; and will not, I know, repine at this accumulation of employment. Let us accommodate ourselves to our circumstances. Our children, I perceive, are fated to be peasants, and will therefore be eminently benefited by the example of patience and independence we shall set before them."

The next object of our plan related to the choice of our future place of residence. This originated with Marguerite. She had heard much of the beauty and richness of the country bordering on the lake of Constance, and she thought that, while we denied ourselves expensive pleasures, or rather while they were placed out of our reach, there would be a propriety in our procuring for ourselves a stock of those pleasures which would cost us nothing. This was a refinement beyond me, and serves to evince the superiority which Marguerite's virtue and force of mind still retained over mine. The virtue I had so recently adopted was a strenuous effort. I rather resolved to be happy, than could strictly be said to be happy. I loved my children indeed with an unfeigned affection. It was with sincerity that I professed to prefer them to all earthly possessions. But vanity and ostentation were habits wrought into my soul, and might be said to form part of its essence. I could not, but by the force of constant recollection, keep them out of my wishes and hopes for the future. I could not, like Marguerite, suffer my thoughts, as it were, to riot and wanton in the pleasures of poverty. I could only reconcile myself to my fate by a sort of gloomy firmness. The tranquillity I seemed to have attained, was an unnatural state of my soul, to which it was necessary that I should resolutely hold myself down, and from which my thoughts appeared ever upon the alert to escape. Bitter experience had at length taught me a hard lesson; and that lesson I was determined to practise, whatever pangs my resignation might cost me.

We proceeded without hesitation in the direction we had resolved to pursue. Our whole journey exceeded the space of forty leagues in extent, and the expense necessarily attendant upon it (our family, even after its reduction, consisting of no less than six persons), drained our purse of a great part of the money which had been supplied to us by the benevolent senator. But he had agreed to undertake the disposing of the property we were obliged to leave behind us, and in the mean time, if any considerable interval occurred before that was accomplished, to furnish us with the sums that should be necessary for our subsistence. We placed the utmost reliance upon his fidelity, and dismissed from our minds all anxiety respecting the interval which our banishment had interposed between us and the resources necessary for our future settlement.

Upon our arrival at Constance, we found a letter from our friend; and though he transmitted to us no fresh supply, the complexion of his communication was upon the whole so encouraging, as to determine us, with no other delay than that of four days' rest from our journey, to pass to the other side of the lake, and explore for ourselves a situation suitable to our design. The western bank of the lake, with the exception only of the city of Constance, was part of the pays conquis of the United Cantons; the eastern bank was a territory dependent on the government of that city. It was in this territory that we purposed fixing our residence; and we trusted, that our affairs would shortly be put in a train to enable us to take possession of the spot we should select.

Thus driven once more into flight by the pressure of misfortune, and compelled to exchange for a land unknown the scenes which familiarity might have endeared, or tender recollections have made interesting, we did not sink under the weight of our adversity. This removal was not like our last. Switzerland was to none of us endeared like the vales of St. Leon. I was not now goaded and tormented by conscious guilt in the degree I had then been; Marguerite was not afflicted by the spectacle of my misery. Our present change, though it might be denominated a fall, was light in comparison with the former. The composure I had gained was new to me, and had to my own mind all the gloss of novelty. To my companions it proved contagious; they were astonished at my serenity, and drew from it an unwonted lightness of heart.

Thus circumstanced, our tour had its charms for us all; and there are few passages of my life that I have felt more agreeably. The lake itself is uncommonly beautiful, and its environs are fertile and interesting. It is surrounded with an abundance of towns, villages, country seats, and monasteries, sufficient to adorn and diversify the view, but not to exclude the sweetness of a rural scenery, or the grand features of nature. We coasted a considerable part of the lake, that we might judge in some degree, previously to our landing, which part of the shore promised best to yield us the object we sought. The autumn was now commencing; the air was liquid and sweet; the foliage was rich and varied; and the vine-covered hills exhibited a warmth and luxuriance of colouring, that no other object of nature or art is able to cope with. Surrounded with these objects, I sat in my boat in the midst of my children; and, as I was but just awakened to an observation of their worth and my own happiness, I viewed them with a transport that would be ill illustrated by being compared with the transport of a miser over his new-recovered treasure from the bowels of the deep.

O poverty! exclaimed I, with elevated and unconquerable emotion, if these are the delights that attend thee, willingly will I resign the pomp of palaces and the splendour of rank to whoever shall deem them worth his acceptance! Henceforth I desire only to dedicate myself to the simplicity of nature and the genuine sentiments of the heart. I will enjoy the beauty of scenes cultivated by other hands than mine, or that are spread out before me by the Author of the universe. I will sit in the midst of my children, and revel in the luxury of domestic affections; pleasures these, that may be incumbered, but cannot be heightened, by all that wealth has in its power to bestow! Wealth serves no other purpose than to deprave the soul, and adulterate the fountains of genuine delight.

Such was the spirit of exultation with which my mind was at this time filled. I am sensible that it was only calculated to be transitory. I might learn to be contented; I was not formed to be satisfied in obscurity and a low estate.

Thus happy, and thus amused, we spent two days in coasting the lake, landing frequently for the purposes either of variety or enquiry, and regularly passing the night on shore. On the evening of the second day we were struck with the neat appearance and pleasing situation of a cottage, which we discovered in our rambles, about a mile and a half from the lake. We found that it was to be sold, and it seemed precisely to correspond with the wishes we had formed. It was at a considerable distance from any populous neighbourhood, the nearest town being that of Merspurg, the usual residence of the bishops of Constance, which was distant from this spot not less than three leagues.

The cottage was situated in a valley; the hills being for the most part crowned with rich and verdant foliage, their sides covered with vineyards and corn, and a clear transparent rivulet murmuring along from east to west. In the distance a few similar cottages discovered themselves, and in front there was an opening between the hills, just wide enough to show us a few sails as they floated along the now even surface of the lake.

We approached the cottage, and found in it only one person, an interesting girl of nineteen, who had resided there from her birth, and had been employed for the last four years in attendance upon the closing scene of her mother. Her mother had been dead only a few weeks, and she was upon the point of removing, as she told us, to the house of a brother, the best creature in the world, who was already married, and had a family of children. While we were talking with her, we perceived a fine boy of about eleven years of age skipping along the meadow. He proved to be her nephew, and hastened to say that his father and Mr. Henry were just behind, and would be with her in a few minutes. We waited their arrival; and it was easy to see that Mr. Henry was by no means an indifferent object in the eyes of the beautiful orphan: she had probably conditioned that he should permit her to remain single as long as she could be of any use to her mother. The lovers were well satisfied that the girl's brother should be taken aside, that I might talk over with him the affair of the cottage. We made a tour of the fields that were part of the property of the deceased, and the terms of our intended purchase were easily adjusted.

Though we had now accomplished the immediate purpose of our expedition, yet, as we had found unusual exhilaration and sweetness in the objects it presented to us, we came to a resolution of continuing it still further, and completing the circuit of the lake. We were aware that it would be vain as yet to expect to receive the money requisite for completing our purchase; and as no pleasure, merely in the way of relaxation, could be more delightful than that we were now enjoying, so was it impossible that we could fill up our time in a more frugal manner than in this little voyage. Our gratification was not less, but more perfect, because it consisted of simple, inartificial, unbought amusements. The scenes around us were refreshing and invigorating; they were calculated, temporarily at least, to inspire gaiety and youth into decrepitude itself. Amidst these scenes we forgot our sorrows; they were a kind of stream, in which weariness and dejection plunged their limbs, and came forth untired and alert. They awakened in the mind all its most pleasing associations. Having already, as we believed, chosen the place of our future residence, we busied ourselves in imagining all the accompaniments that would grow out of it. We determined that poverty with health would not fail to be attended with its portion of pleasures. The scenes of nature were all our own; nor could wealth give them a more perfect, or a firmer, appropriation. The affections and charities of habitude and consanguinity we trusted we should feel uninterrupted; unincumbered with the ceremonies and trappings of life, and in that rural plainness which is their genial soil.

After a leisurely and delightful voyage of six days, we returned to Constance. We expected to have found on our return some further intelligence from the beneficent senator, but in this we were disappointed. The imagination however easily suggested to us a variety of circumstances that might have delayed the business he had undertaken; and it was no forced inference to suppose that he deferred writing, because he had nothing important to communicate. At first therefore we suffered little uneasiness from the delay; but as time proceeded, and the silence of our protector continued, the affair began to assume a more serious aspect. The little stock we had brought with us in our exile was in a rapid progress of decay. We had managed it with frugality; though not at first with that anxious solicitude, the necessity of which we now began to apprehend. We had procured for ourselves two small and inconvenient apartments in an obscure alley of the city of Constance. We were in the act of meditating what steps it would be necessary to take in this unfortunate emergency, when intelligence was brought us of the sudden decease of the person upon whose kindness and exertions we depended.

He was succeeded in his estate by his nephew, a man of whom we had heard something during our residence in the neighbourhood, and whose habits we understood to be diametrically the reverse of his predecessor's. In short, he had been represented to us as illiberal, morose, selfish, and litigious; a man who, having suffered in one part of his life the hardships of poverty, scrupled no means, honourable or otherwise, of removing it to the greatest practicable distance. He had already reaped the succession some weeks, when we heard of the event that put him in possession of it; and the letters which I had more than once addressed to our protector had probably fallen into his hands. These circumstances afforded no favourable augury of the treatment we might expect from him. The first thing which seemed proper was to write to him, which I accordingly did. I acquainted him with the nature of the transaction between myself and his uncle, and signified how necessary it was that we should come to a conclusion as speedily as possible. I represented to him pathetically the condition to which I was born, and the opulence in which I had passed many years of my life, together with the contrast afforded by the present reduced and urgent circumstances of my family. I entreated him to exert his generosity and justice in behalf of an unfortunate exile, whom untoward events had deprived of the power of doing justice to himself.

To this letter I received no answer. Uncertain as to the cause of my correspondent's silence, or even whether my letter had been received, I wrote again. My heart was wrung with this new adversity. I was forbidden, under pain of perpetual imprisonment, to return to the territories of the republic, and I had no friend to solicit in my behalf. In Constance I was utterly a stranger. In Switzerland, my unfortunate habits of life, the depression and solitude in which I had been merged, deprived me of the opportunity of forming connections. The deceased was the only person who had been disposed to interfere for me. It was too probable that the silence of his successor was an indication of the hostility of his views. I saw nothing before me but the prospect of my family perishing with want, deprived of their last resource, exiles and pennyless. Thus destitute and forlorn, what could we do? to what plan could we have recourse? We had not so much as the means of providing ourselves with the implements of the humblest labour. If we had, could I, under my circumstances, resolve upon this? Could I give up the last slender pittance of my children while there was a chance of recovering it; and, by surrendering them to the slavery of perpetual labour, devote them to the lowest degree of ignorance and degradation? No; I still clung to this final hope, and was resolved to undertake any thing, however desperate, rather than part with it. Such were my feelings; and, in the new letter which I now despatched, I poured out all the anguish of my soul.

A reply to this letter was at length vouchsafed. The heir of my protector informed me, that he knew nothing of the business to which I alluded; that he had come into possession of the lands I described, together with the other property of his late uncle, and regarded himself as holding them by the same tenure; that he found in the accounts of the estate a sum of money advanced to me, which he might with the strictest justice regard as a debt, and pursue me for it accordingly. He should be liberal enough however so far to give credit to my story, and to consider the sum in question as advanced upon a pledge of land: in that case, I might regard myself as sufficiently fortunate in having obtained even that amount at a time when, but for the humanity or weakness of his uncle, my estate would not have sold for a farthing. Meanwhile, the forbearance which he proffered would, he observed, depend upon my conduct, and be retracted if I afforded him cause for resentment. He added, that he despised my menaces and commands, and that, if I took a single step against him, I should find it terminate in my utter ruin.

Nothing could be more profligate than the style of his letter. But its impotence was equal to its wickedness. It was absurd to threaten to inflict ruin on a man whom ruin had already overtaken. Before the letter arrived, I had disbursed the whole sum I brought with me from Switzerland. This entire annihilation of my resources seemed to steal on me unperceived. Finding that all reply to my importunity was either refused, or deferred to an uncertain period, I would willingly at all risks have sought the villain who thus obdurately devoted me and my family to destruction, and have endeavoured to obtain justice in person. But it was now too late. Before I felt the case thus desperate, my finances were so far reduced as to make it impracticable for me to leave my wife and children enough to support them in my absence, even if I had determined myself to set out upon this perilous expedition pennyless. I resolved that, if we did perish, we would perish together.

Penury was now advancing upon us with such rapid strides, that the lowest and most scanty resources no longer admitted of neglect. Had a case thus desperate been encountered with timely attention, it is not improbable that some of the various talents I had acquired in the course of my education would have furnished me with a means of subsistence not altogether plebeian or incompetent. But, with the uncertainty of my situation, and totally unaccustomed as I was to regard my person or mind as a machine fitted for productive labour, I had not looked to this question, till the urgency of the case deprived me of every advantage I might otherwise have seized. I was glad therefore to have recourse to menial occupation, and sought employment under the gardener of the episcopal palace, for whose service I was sufficiently qualified by my ten years' retreat in the Bordelois. That I might better adapt myself to the painful necessity of my situation, I previously exchanged some of my own clothes for garments more suitable to the business I now solicited. It was not till I had arrived within a very few days to the end of my resources; that even this expedient, by a sort of accident, recurred to my mind. Marguerite, though fully aware of the urgency of the case, had, as she afterwards told me, imposed on herself a compulsory silence, fearing for the inflamed and irritated frame of my mind, and aware that the course of events would ultimately lead me to a point with which she dreaded to intermeddle. This was for her a trying moment; my lately recovered insanity obliging her to contemplate in silence our growing distress, and to wait the attack of hunger and want that threatened to destroy us, with an apparent tranquillity and cheerfulness.

For me, so entire a revolution had taken place in my sentiments, that I spurned with contempt, so far as related to myself, that pride of rank and romantic gallantry of honour, which had formerly been my idols. I submitted with a sort of gloomy contentment to the situation upon which my destiny drove me. I regarded it as the natural result of my former misconduct; and derived a sentiment of ease and relief from thus expiating, as it were, with the sweat of my brow, the temptations to which I had yielded. Had I been myself only reduced thus low, or had the produce of my labour been sufficient to purchase competence for my wife and the means of instruction for my family, I can safely affirm that I should have found no consequence so direct from my own degradation as the means of silencing the reproaches of conscience and reconciling me to myself. But when I returned in the evening with the earnings of my day's labour, and found it incompetent to the procuring for those who depended on me the simplest means of subsistence, then indeed my sensations were different. My heart died within me. I did not return after the fatigues of the day, which, to me who had not been accustomed to unremitted labour, and who now began to feel that I was not so young as I had been at the siege of Pavia, were extremely trying,—I did not return, I say, to a night of repose. I became a very woman when I looked forward, and endeavoured to picture to myself the future situation of my family. I watered my pillow with my tears. Often, when I imagined that my whole family were asleep, I gave vent to my perturbated and distracted mind in groans: Marguerite would sometimes overhear me; and with the gentlest suggestions of her admirable mind would endeavour to soothe my thoughts to peace. For the present, as I have said, my earnings were incompetent, and we found it necessary to supply the deficiency by the sale of the few garments, not in immediate use, that we still possessed. What then would be the case when these were gone, and when, in addition to this, it would be necessary to purchase not only food to eat, and a roof to shelter, but also clothes to cover us?

CHAPTER X.

These deficiencies I anxiously anticipated; but there was another evil, upon which I had not calculated, that was still nearer and more overwhelming. The mode of life in which I was now engaged, so different from any thing to which I had been accustomed, excessive fatigue, together with the occasional heat of the weather, the uneasiness of my mind, and the sleeplessness of my nights, all combined to throw me into a fever, which, though it did not last long, had raged so furiously during the period of its continuance, as to leave me in a state of the most complete debility. While the disorder was upon me, I was sensible of my danger; and, as the brilliant and consolatory prospects of life seemed for ever closed upon me, I at first regarded my approaching dissolution with complacency, and longed to be released from a series of woes, in which I had been originally involved by my own folly. This frame of mind however was of no great duration; the more nearly I contemplated the idea of separation from those I loved, the smaller was my resignation. I was unwilling to quit those dear objects by which I still held to this mortal scene; I shrunk with aversion from that barrier which separates us from all that is new, mysterious, and strange. Another train of ideas succeeded this, and I began to despise myself for my impatience and cowardice. It was by my vices that my family was involved in a long train of misfortunes; could I shrink from partaking what I had not feared to create? The greater were the adversities for which they were reserved, the more ought I to desire to suffer with them. I had already committed the evil; in what remained, it was reasonable to suppose I should prove their benefactor and not their foe. It was incumbent on me to soothe and to animate them, to enrich their minds with cheerfulness and courage, and to set before them an example of philosophy and patience. By my faculties of industry I was their principal hope; and, whatever we might suffer combined, it was probable their sufferings would be infinitely greater, if deprived of my assistance. These reflections gave me energy; and it seemed as if the resolute predilection I had conceived for life contributed much to my recovery.

One thing which strongly confirmed the change my mind underwent in this respect, was a conversation that I overheard at a time when I was supposed to be completely in a state of insensibility, but when, though I was too much reduced to give almost any tokens of life, my faculties of hearing and understanding what passed around me were entire. Charles came up to my bedside, laid his hand upon mine as if to feel the state of the skin, and, with a handkerchief that was near, wiped away the moisture that bedewed my face. He had been fitted for many nurse-like offices by the unwearied attention he had exerted towards me in the paroxysm of my insanity. Having finished his task, he withdrew from the bed, and burst into tears. His mother came up to him, drew him to the furthest part of the room, and in a low voice began the conversation.

"Do, my dear boy, go down stairs, and get yourself something to eat. You see, your papa is quiet now."

"I am afraid that will not last long; and then he will be so restless, and toss about so, it is dreadful to see him."

"I will watch, Charles, and let you know."

"Indeed, mamma, I cannot eat now. I will by and by."

"You must try to eat, Charles, or else you will make yourself quite ill. If you were ill too, it would be more than I could support."

"I will not be ill, mamma. I assure you I will not. But, besides that I have no stomach, I cannot bear to eat when there is hardly enough for my sisters."

"Eat, boy. Do not trouble yourself about that. We shall get more when that is gone. God is good, and will take care of us."

"I know that God is good; but for all that, one must not expect to have every thing one wishes. Though God is good, there are dreadful misfortunes in the world, and I suppose we shall have our share of them."

"Come, Charles, though you are but a boy, you are the best boy in the world. You are now almost my only comfort; but you will not be able to comfort me if you do not take care of yourself."

"Dear mamma!—Do you know, mamma, I heard that naughty man below stairs count up last night how much rent you owed him for, and swear you should not stay any longer if you did not pay him. If I were a little bigger, I would talk to him so that he should not dare to insult us in our distress. But, not being big enough, I opened the door, and went into the room, and begged him for God's sake not to add to your distress. And, though he is so ugly, I took hold of his hand, and kissed it. But it felt like iron, which put me in mind of his iron heart, and I cried ready to burst with mortification. He did not say hardly a word."

"He must be paid, Charles: he shall be paid."

"Do you know, mamma, as soon as I left him I went to the bishop's gardens, and spoke to the gardener? I asked him, if he had heard that my papa was ill, and he said he had. He said, too, he was very sorry, and wanted to know what hand we made of it for want of the wages. I told him, we were sadly off, and the man of the house had just been affronting me about his rent. But, said I, cannot you give me something to do, to weed or to rake? I can dig a little too, and scatter seed. He asked, if I knew weeds from flowers. Oh, that I do! said I. Well then, said he, there is not much you can do; but you are a good boy, and I will put you on the bishop's list. But now, mamma, I have not the heart to work, till I see whether papa will get well again."

While poor Charles told his artless tale, Marguerite wept over him, and kissed him again and again. She called him the best child in the world, and said that, if I were but so fortunate as to recover, with such a husband and such a son, she should yet be the happiest of women.

"Oh, my poor father!" exclaimed Charles. "Ever since the great hail-storm, I have every hour loved him better than before. I thought that was impossible, but he is so gentle, so kind, so good-humoured, and so patient! I loved him when he was harsh, and when he was out of his mind; but nothing so well then as I have done since. People that are kind and smile always do one good; but nobody's smiles are like my father's. It makes me cry with joy sometimes, when I do but think of them. Pray, papa," added he, coming up to the bedside, and whispering, yet with a hurried and passionate accent, "get well! Do but get well, and we will be so happy! Never was there a family so happy or so loving as we will be!"

While he spoke thus, I endeavoured to put out my hand, but I could not; I endeavoured to smile, but I was unable: my heart was in a feeble, yet soothing, tranquillity. The accents of love I had heard, dwelt upon my memory. They had talked of distress, but the sentiment of love was uppermost in my recollection. I was too weak of frame to suffer intellectual distress; no accents but those which carried balm to my spirit, seemed capable of resting upon my ear. From this hour I regularly grew better, and, as I recovered, seemed to feel more and more vividly how enviable it was to be the head of a loving and harmonious family.

My recovery however was exceedingly slow, and it was several weeks before I had so far recruited my strength as to be capable of my ordinary occupations. In the mean time the pecuniary difficulties to which we were exposed hourly increased, and the cheerful but insignificant labours of Charles could contribute little to the support of a family. The melancholy nature of our situation might perhaps have been expected to prevent the restoration of my health. At first however it had not that effect. The debilitated state of my animal functions led me, by a sort of irresistible instinct, to reject ideas and reflections which I should then have been unable to endure. I saw the anxiety and affection of my family, and I was comforted. I saw the smiles of Marguerite, and I seemed insensible to the languor, the saddened cheerfulness, they expressed. I did not perceive that, while I was provided with every thing necessary in my condition, my family were in want of the very bread that should sustain existence.

My health in the mean time improved, and my perceptions became proportionably clearer. Symptoms of desolation and famine, though as much as possible covered from my sight, obtruded themselves, and were remarked. One day in particular I observed various tokens of this nature in silence, and with that sort of bewildered understanding which at once labours for comprehension and resists belief. The day closed; and what I had perceived pressed upon my mind, and excluded sleep. Now for the first time I exerted myself to recollect in a methodical way the state of my affairs; for the severity of my illness had at length succeeded to banish from me all ideas and feelings but what related to the sensations it produced, and to the objects around me; and it was not without effort that I could once more fully call to mind the scenes in which I had been engaged. The truth then by regular degrees rose completely to view; and I began to be astonished, that my poor wife and children had been able in any manner to get through the horrible evils to which they must have been exposed. This thought I revolved in my mind for near two hours; and the longer I dwelt upon it, the more perturbed and restless I grew. At length it became impossible for me to hold my contemplations pent up in my own bosom. I turned to Marguerite, and asked her, whether she were asleep.

She answered in the negative: she had been remarking my restlessness, and tenderly enquired respecting its cause.

"How long," said I, "is it since I was taken with the fever?"

"A month to-morrow," replied she. "It was of the most malignant and distressing kind while it lasted, and I did not expect you to live. But it has left you a fortnight; and I hope, Reginald, you find yourself getting strong again."

"And so we are here in Constance, and we have left Switzerland———?"

"Three months, my love!"

"I remember very well the letter we received from monsieur Grimseld; has any further intelligence reached us from that quarter?"

"None."

"None! No supply of any kind has reached you?"

"My dear Reginald, talk of something else! You will soon, I hope, be well: our children are all alive; and the calamity, that has not succeeded to separate us, or to diminish our circle of love even by a single member, we will learn to bear. Let us fix our attention on the better prospects that open before us!"

"Stay, Marguerite! I have other questions to ask. Before you require me to bear the calamities that have overtaken us, let me understand what these calamities are. While we waited for intelligence from Switzerland, we expended the whole sum that we brought with us, and I was obliged to hire myself to the episcopal gardener for bread; was it not so?"

"Indeed, Reginald, you are to blame! Pray question me no further!"

"This was our condition some time ago; and now, for a month past, I have been incapable of labour. Marguerite, what have you done?"

"Indeed, my love, I have been too anxious for you, to think much of any thing else. We had still some things, you know, that we could contrive to do without; and those I have sold. Charles too, our excellent-hearted son, has lately hired himself to the gardener, and has every night brought us home a little, though it was but little."

"Dear boy! What children, what a wife, have I brought to destruction! Our rent too, surely you have not been able to pay that?"

"Not entirely. In part I have been obliged to pay it."

"Ah! I well remember how flinty-hearted a wretch has got the power over us in that respect!"

"He has not turned us out of doors. He threatened hard several times. At last I saw it was necessary to make an effort, and the day before yesterday I paid him half his demand. If I could have avoided that, we might have had a supply of food a little longer. I intreated earnestly for a little further indulgence, but it was in vain. It went against the pride and independence of my soul to sue to this man; but it was for you and for my children!"

"Remorseless wretch! Then every petty resource we had is gone?"

"Indeed I do not know that we have any thing more to sell. I searched narrowly yesterday; but I will examine again to-day. The poor children must have something to support them, and their fare has of late been dreadfully scanty."

"Their fare! What have they eaten?"

"Bread; nothing else for the last fortnight!"

"And yourself?"

"Oh, Reginald! it was necessary, you know, that I should keep myself alive. But, I assure you, I have robbed them as little as I could."

"Horror, horror! Marguerite, what is it you dream of? I see my wife and children dying of hunger, and you talk to me of hope and of prospects! Why has this detail of miseries been concealed from me? Why have I been suffered, with accursed and unnatural appetite, to feed on the vitals of all I love?"

"Reginald! even selfishness itself would have taught us that! It is to your recovery that we look for our future support!"

"Mock me not, I adjure you, with senseless words! You talk idly of the future, while the tremendous present bars all prospect to that future. We are perishing by inches. We have no provision for the coming day! No, no; something desperate, something yet unthought of, must be attempted! I will not sit inactive, and see my offspring around me die in succession. No, by Heaven! Though I am starving like Ugolino, I am not, like Ugolino, shut up in a dungeon! The world is open; its scenes are wide; the resources it offers are, to the bold and despairing, innumerable! I am a father, and will show myself worthy of the name!"

"Reginald! torture me not by language like this! Think what it is to be indeed a father, and make yourself that! Be careful of yourself; complete your recovery,—and leave the rest to me! I have conducted it thus far, nor am I yet without hope. Eight days ago I applied to the secretary of the palace, representing your case as a retainer of the bishop, disabled by sickness, and with a family unprovided for. Till yesterday I got no answer to my memorial; and then he informed me, that you had been so short a time in employ, that nothing could be done for you. But to-day I will throw myself at the feet of the bishop himself, who arrived last night only from the other side of the lake."

Every word that Marguerite uttered went to my heart. It was not long before the dawn of the day, and the truths I had heard were further confirmed to me by the organ of sight. The sentiments of this night produced a total revolution in me, and I was no longer the feeble convalescent that the setting sun of the preceding day had left me. The film was removed from my eyes, and I surveyed not the objects around me with a glassy eye and unapprehensive observation. All the powers I possessed were alert and in motion. To my suspicious and hurried gaze the apartment appeared stripped of its moveables, and left naked, a mansion in which for despair to take up his abode. My children approached me; I seemed to read the wan and emaciated traces of death in their countenances. This perhaps was in some degree the painting of my too conscious thoughts. But there needed no exaggeration to awaken torture in my bosom, when, thus stimulated, I observed for the first time the dreadful change that had taken place in Marguerite. Her colour was gone; her cheeks were sunk; her eye had the quickness and discomposure expressive of debility. I took hold of her hand, and found it cold, emaciated, and white. I pressed it to my lips with agony; a tear unbidden fell from my eye, and rested upon it. Having finished my examination, I took my hat, and was hastening to escape into the street. Marguerite noted my motions, and anxiously interposed to prevent my design. She laid her hand on my arm gently, yet in a manner full of irresistible expostulation.

"Where would you go? What have you purposed? Do not,—Oh, do not, destroy a family, to whom your life, your sobriety, and prudence, are indispensable!"

I took her hand within both mine. "Compose yourself, my love! I have been your enemy too much already, to be capable now, so much as in thought, of adding to my guilt! I need an interval for musing and determination. I will return in a very short time, and you shall be the confidant of my thoughts!"

With wild and impatient spirit I repassed in idea the whole history of my life. But principally I dwelt in recollection upon the marquis de Damville, that generous friend, that munificent benefactor, whose confidence I had so ill repaid. "Damville!" exclaimed I, "you trusted to me your daughter, the dearest thing you knew on earth; you believed that the wretch did not live who could be unjust to so rich a pledge. Look down, look down, O best of men! from the heaven to which your virtues have raised you, and see of how much baseness man—yes, the man you disdained not to call your friend—is capable! But, no! a sight like this might well convert the heaven you dwell in to hell! You trusted her to me; I have robbed her! You enriched her mind with the noblest endowments; I have buried them in the mire of the vilest condition! All her generous, her unwearied exertions are fruitless; by my evil genius they are blasted! I have made her a mother, only that she might behold her children perishing with hunger! They stretch out their hands to me for the smallest portion of that inheritance, which I have squandered in more than demoniac vice! This, this is the fruit of my misdeeds! I am now draining the last dregs of that mischief, of which I have so wickedly, so basely, been the author!"

As I returned I met Marguerite, who was come from her attempt upon the bishop. He had received her paper, and delivered it to his secretary, that very secretary who had already disappointed all her expectations from that quarter. She had attempted to speak, to adjure the bishop, whatever he did, not to deliver her over to a man by whom her hopes had been so cruelly frustrated; but the tumult of the scene drowned her voice, and the hurry and confusion overpowered her efforts. They, however, drew such a degree of attention on her, that, in the dissentions which religious broils at that time spread in Constance, she was suspected of pressing thus earnestly towards the person of the bishop with no good design, and in fine was rudely thrust out of the palace. She had not recovered from the agitation into which she had been thrown, when I met her. I eagerly enquired into the cause of her apparent distress; but she shook her head mournfully, and was silent. I easily understood where she had been, and the failure of her experiment.

"All then," said I, "is at an end. Now, Marguerite, you must give up your experiments, and leave to me the cure of evils of which I only am the author. I will return this instant to the garden of the palace, and resume the situation I formerly occupied."

"For God's sake, Reginald, what is it you mean? You have just acquired strength to seek the benefit of air. The least exertion fatigues you. At this moment, the little walk you have taken has covered you with perspiration. You could not dig or stoop for a quarter of an hour without being utterly exhausted."

"Marguerite, I will not sit down tamely, and see my family expire. In many cases it is reasonable to bid a valetudinarian take care of himself. But our situation is beyond that. I must do something. Extraordinary circumstances often bring along with them extraordinary strength. No man knows, till the experiment, what he is capable of effecting. I feel at this moment no debility; and I doubt not that the despair of my mind will give redoubled energy to my efforts."

While I spoke thus, I was conscious that I had little more than the strength of a new-born child. But I could not endure at such a time to remain in inactivity. I felt as much ashamed of the debilitated state in which my fever had left me, as I could have done of the most inglorious effeminacy and cowardice of soul. I determined to relieve my family, or perish in the attempt. If all my efforts were vain, I could not better finish my career, than exhausted, sinking, expiring under a last exertion, to discharge the duties of my station.

We returned into the house. Marguerite took from a closet the last remnant of provisions we had, the purchase of poor Charles's labour of the preceding day. There was a general contest who should escape from receiving any part in the distribution. Charles had withdrawn himself, and was not to be found. Julia endeavoured to abscond, but was stopped by Louisa and her mother. She had wept so much, that inanition seemed more dangerous for her, than perhaps for any other of the circle. No one can conceive, who has not felt it, how affecting a contest of this kind must appear to me, sensible as I was to the danger that their virtue and generous affection were the prelude only to their common destruction. I said, there was a general contest who should avoid all share in the distribution; but I recollect that the little Marguerite, two years and a half old, exclaimed at first, "I am so hungry, mamma!" But watching, as she carefully did, every thing that passed, she presently laid down her bread upon the table in silence, and almost untouched; and being asked, Why she did so? she replied, in a tone of speaking sensibility, "Thank you, I am not hungry now!"

This scene made an impression on my mind never to be forgotten. It blasted and corrupted all the pulses of my soul. A little before, I had reconciled myself to poverty; I had even brought myself to regard it with cheerfulness. But the sentiment was now reversed. I could endure it, I could steel myself against its attacks; but never from this hour, in the wildest paroxysms of enthusiasm, has it been the topic of my exultation or my panegyric. No change of circumstances, no inundation of wealth, has had the power to obliterate from my recollection what I then saw. A family perishing with hunger; all that is dearest to you in the world sinking under the most dreadful of all the scourges with which this sublunary scene is ever afflicted; no help near; no prospect but of still accumulating distress; a death, the slowest, yet the most certain and the most agonising, that can befall us: no, there is nothing that has power to rend all the strings of the heart like this! From this moment, the whole set of my feelings was changed. Avarice descended, and took possession of my soul. Haunted, as I perpetually was, by images of the plague of famine, nothing appeared to me so valuable as wealth; nothing so desirable as to be placed at the utmost possible distance from want. An appetite of this kind is insatiable; no distance seems sufficiently great; no obstacles, mountains on mountains of gold, appear an inadequate security to bar from us the approach of the monster we dread.

While I speak of the sentiments which in the sequel were generated in my mind by what I now saw, I am suspending my narrative in a crisis at which a family, interesting, amiable and virtuous, is reduced to the lowest state of humiliation and distress.

They are moments like these, that harden the human heart, and fill us with inextinguishable hatred and contempt for our species. They tear off the trappings and decoration of polished society, and show it in all its hideousness. The wanton eye of pampered pride pleases itself with the spectacle of cities and palaces, the stately column and the swelling arch. It observes at hand the busy scene, where all are occupied in the various pursuits of pleasure or industry; and admires the concert, the wide-spreading confederacy, by means of which each after his mode is unconsciously promoting the objects of others. Cheated by the outside of things, we denominate this a vast combination for general benefit. The poor and the famished man contemplates the scene with other thoughts. Unbribed to admire and applaud, he sees in it a confederacy of hostility and general oppression. He sees every man pursuing his selfish ends, regardless of the wants of others. He sees himself contemptuously driven from the circle where the rest of his fellow-citizens are busily and profitably engaged. He lives in the midst of a crowd, without one friend to feel an interest in his welfare. He lives in the midst of plenty, from the participation of which he is driven by brutal menaces and violence. No man who has not been placed in his situation can imagine the sensations, with which, overwhelmed as he is with domestic ruin and despair, he beholds the riot, the prodigality, the idiot ostentation, the senseless expense, with which he is surrounded on every side. What were we to do? Were we to beg along the streets? Were we to in treat for wretched offals at rich men's doors? Alas! this, it was to be feared, even if we stooped to the miserable attempt, instead of satisfying wants for ever new, would only prolong in the bitterness of anguish the fate for which we were reserved!——

An unexpected relief at this time presented itself. While the scanty meal I have mentioned was yet unfinished, a letter was presented me inclosing under its cover a bill of one hundred crowns. The letter was from Bernardin, the faithful servant whom we found it necessary to dismiss three months before, when we quitted our residence in Switzerland. It informed us that, as soon as he had parted from us, he had set out on his return to his native town, next adjacent to my paternal residence; that he found his father had died a short time before, and that, from the sale of his effects, he had reaped an inheritance to triple the amount of the sum he had now forwarded to us. He had heard by accident of the death of our friend in Switzerland, and the character of his successor, and dreaded that the consequences might prove highly injurious to us. He had still some business to settle with the surviving branches of his family, but that would be over in a few weeks; and then, if we would allow him, he would return to his dear master, and afford us every assistance in his power. The little property that had now fallen to him would prevent him from being a burthen; and he would hire a spot of land, and remain near us, if we refused him the consolation of returning to his former employment.

What a reproach was it to me, that, descended from one of the most illustrious families in Europe, the heir of an ample patrimony, and receiving a still larger fortune in marriage, I should, by the total neglect and profligate defiance of the duties incumbent on me, have reduced myself so low as to be indebted to a peasant and a menial for the means of saving my family from instant destruction! This was a deep and fatal wound to the pride of my soul. There was however no alternative, no possibility of rejecting the supply afforded us at so eventful a moment. We determined to use it for the present, and to repay it with the earliest opportunity; and in the following week, in spite of the remonstrances of Marguerite, the yet feeble state of my health, and the penalties annexed to the proceeding, I set off for the canton of Soleure, determined, if possible, to wrest the little staff of my family from the hand that so basely detained it.

I passed through Zurich and a part of the canton of Basle without obstacle; these parts of Switzerland had not suffered from the calamity which had occasioned our exile. In proceeding further, I found it necessary to assume a disguise, and to avoid large towns and frequented roads. I reached at length the well known scene in which I had so lately consumed twelve months of my life; in which I first began to breathe (to breathe, not to be refreshed) from ruin, beggary, and exile. There was no pleasing recollection annexed to this spot; it was a remembrancer of shame, sorrow, and remorse. Yet, such is the power of objects once familiar, revisited after absence, that my eye ran over them with delight, I felt lightened from the weariness of the journey, and found that the recollection of pains past over and subdued was capable of being made a source of gratification. The mountains among which I had wandered, and consumed, as it were, the last dregs of my insanity, surrounded me; the path in which I was travelling led along one of their ridges. I had performed this part of my journey by night; and the first gleams of day now began to streak the horizon. I looked towards the cottage, the distant view of which had so often, in moments of the deepest despair, awakened in my heart the soothings of sympathy and affection. I saw that as yet it remained in its forlorn condition, and had undergone no repair; while the lands around, which had lately experienced the superintendence of Marguerite, had met with more attention, and began to resume the marks of culture. I sighed for the return of those days and that situation, which, while present to me, had passed unheeded and unenjoyed.

I repaired to the house of my late protector, now the residence of monsieur Grimseld. He was a meagre shrivelled figure; and, though scarcely arrived at the middle of human life, exhibited all the marks of a premature old age. I disclosed myself to him, and began warmly to expostulate with him upon the profligacy of his conduct. He changed colour, and betrayed symptoms of confusion, the moment I announced myself. While I pressed him with the barbarity of his conduct, the dreadful effects it had already produced, and the incontestible justice of my claim, he stammered, and began to propose terms of accommodation. During this conversation we were alone. After some time, however, a servant entered the room, and the countenance of the master assumed an expression of satisfaction and confidence. He eagerly seized on the occasion which presented itself, and, instantly changing his tone, called on his servant to assist him in securing a criminal against the state. I at first resisted, but Grimseld perceiving this, applied to his bell with great vehemence, and three other servants made their appearance, whose employment was in the field, but who had now accidentally come into the house for refreshment. I had arms; but I found it impracticable to effect my escape; and I soon felt that, by yielding to the impulse of indignation, and punishing Grimseld on the spot for his perfidy, I might ruin but could not forward the affair in which I was engaged.

I was conducted to prison; and the thoughts produced in me by this sudden reverse were extremely melancholy and discouraging. Grimseld was a man of opulence and power; I was without friends, or the means of procuring friends. The law expressly condemned my return; and what had I not to fear from law, when abetted and inforced by the hand of power? I might be imprisoned for ten years; I might be imprisoned for life. I began earnestly to wish that I had remained with my family, and given up at least all present hopes of redress. It would be a dreadful accumulation of all my calamities, if now at last I and my children were destined to suffer, perhaps to perish, in a state of separation; and the last consolations of the wretched, those of suffering, sympathising, and condoling with each other, were denied us.

Full of these tragical forebodings, I threw myself at first on the floor of my cell in a state little short of the most absolute despair. I exclaimed upon my adverse fortune, which was never weary of persecuting me. I apostrophised, with tender and distracted accents, my wife and children, from whom I now seemed to be cut off by an everlasting divorce. I called upon death to put an end to these tumults and emotions of the soul, which were no longer to be borne.

In a short time however I recovered myself, procured the implements of writing, and drew up, in the strong and impressive language of truth, a memorial to the council of the state. I was next to consider how this was to reach its destination; for there was some danger that it might be intercepted by the vigilance and malignity of my adversary. I desired to speak with the keeper of the prison. He had some recollection of me, and a still more distinct one of my family. He concurred with the general sentiment, in a strong aversion to the character of Grimseld. As I pressed upon him the hardship of my case, and the fatal consequences with which it might be attended, I could perceive that he fully entered into the feeling with which I wished him to be impressed. He blamed my rashness in returning to Switzerland in defiance of the positive prohibition that had been issued; but promised at all events that my paper should be delivered to the president to-morrow morning.

I remained three days without an answer, and these days were to me an eternity. I anticipated every kind of misfortune; I believed that law and malice had succeeded to the subversion of equity. At length however I was delivered from my apprehensions and perplexity, and summoned to appear before the council. It was well for me perhaps that I had to do with a government so simple and moderate as that of Switzerland. I obtained redress. It was referred to an arbitration of neighbours to set a fair price on my property, and then decreed, that if monsieur Grimseld refused the purchase, the sum should be paid me out of the coffers of the state. He was also condemned in a certain fine for the fraud he had attempted to commit. The affair, thus put in train, was soon completed; and I returned with joy, having effected the object of my journey, to my anxious and expecting family. Soon after, we removed to the spot we had chosen on the eastern bank of the lake, where we remained for the six following years in a state of peace and tranquillity.

CHAPTER XI.

It was in the evening of a summer's day in the latter end of the year fifteen hundred and forty-four, that a stranger arrived at my habitation. He was feeble, emaciated, and pale, his forehead full of wrinkles, and his hair and beard as white as snow. Care was written in his face; it was easy to perceive that he had suffered much from distress of mind; yet his eye was still quick and lively, with a strong expression of suspiciousness and anxiety. His garb, which externally consisted of nothing more than a robe of russet brown, with a girdle of the same, was coarse, threadbare, and ragged. He supported his tottering steps with a staff; and, having lost his foreteeth, his speech was indistinct and difficult to be comprehended. His wretched appearance excited my compassion, at the same time that I could easily discern, beneath all its disadvantages, that he was no common beggar or rustic. Ruined and squalid as he appeared, I thought I could perceive traces in his countenance of what had formerly been daring enterprise, profound meditation, and generous humanity.

I saw that he was much fatigued, and I invited him to rest himself upon the bench before the door. I set before him bread and wine, and he partook of both. I asked him his name and his country. He told me that he was a Venetian, and that his name, as nearly as I could collect, was signor Francesco Zampieri. He seemed however averse to speaking, and he requested me to suffer him to pass the night in my habitation. There was nothing singular in the request, a hospitality of this sort being the practice of the neighbourhood; and humanity would have prompted my compliance, if I had not been still more strongly urged by an undefinable curiosity that began to spring up in my bosom. I prepared for him a camp-bed in a summer-house at the end of my garden. As soon as it was ready, he desired to be left alone, that he might seek in rest some relief from the fatigue he had undergone.

He retired early; and therefore, soon after daybreak the next morning, I waited on him to enquire how he had rested. He led me out into the fields; the morning was genial and exhilarating. We proceeded, till we came to a retired spot which had frequently been the scene of my solitary meditations, and there seated ourselves upon a bank. We had been mutually silent during the walk. As soon as we were seated, the stranger began: "You are, I understand, a Frenchman, and your name the count de St. Leon?" I bowed assent.

"St. Leon," said he, "there is something in your countenance and manner that prepossesses me in your favour. The only thing I have left to do in the world is to die; and what I seek at present, is a friend who will take care that I shall be suffered to die in peace. Shall I trust you? Will you be that friend to me?"

I was astonished at this way of commencing his confidence in me; but I did not hesitate to promise that he should not find me deficient in any thing that became a man of humanity and honour.

"You do not, I think, live alone? You have a wife and children."

"I have."

"Yet none of them were at home when I arrived last night. You brought yourself to the summer-house every thing that was necessary for my accommodation."

"I did so. But I have a wife to whom I have been married seventeen years, and with whom I have no reserves. I told her of your arrival; I spoke of your appearance; I mentioned your name."

"It is no matter. She has not seen me. My name is not Zampieri; I am no Venetian."

"Who are you then?"

"That you shall never know. It makes no part of the confidence I design to repose in you. My name shall be buried with me in the grave; nor shall any one who has hitherto known me, know how, at what time, or on what spot of earth, I shall terminate my existence. The cloud of oblivion shall shelter me from all human curiosity. What I require of you is that you pledge your honour, and the faith of a man, that you will never reveal to your wife, your children, or any human being, what you may hereafter know of me, and that no particular that relates to my history shall be disclosed, till at least one hundred years after my decease."

"Upon these conditions I am sorry that I must decline your confidence. My wife is a part of myself; for the last six years at least I have had no thought in which she has not participated; and these have been the most tranquil and happy years of my life. My heart was formed by nature for social ties; habit has confirmed their propensity; and I will not now consent to any thing that shall infringe on the happiness of my soul."

While I spoke, I could perceive that my companion grew disturbed and angry. At length, turning towards me a look of ineffable contempt, he replied—

"Feeble and effeminate mortal! You are neither a knight nor a Frenchman! Or rather, having been both, you have forgotten in inglorious obscurity every thing worthy of either! Was ever gallant action achieved by him who was incapable of separating himself from a woman? Was ever a great discovery prosecuted, or an important benefit conferred upon the human race, by him who was incapable of standing, and thinking, and feeling, alone? Under the usurping and dishonoured name of virtue, you have sunk into a slavery baser than that of the enchantress Alcina. In vain might honour, worth, and immortal renown proffer their favours to him who has made himself the basest of all sublunary things—the puppet of a woman, the plaything of her pleasure, wasting an inglorious life in the gratification of her wishes and the performance of her commands!"

I felt that I was not wholly unmoved at this expostulation. The stranger touched upon the first and foremost passions of my soul; passions the operation of which had long been suspended, but which were by no means extinguished in my bosom. He proceeded:—

"But it is well! Years have passed over my head in vain, and I have not learnt to distinguish a man of honour from a slave. This is only one additional sorrow to those in which my life has been spent. I have wandered through every region of the earth, and have found only disappointment. I have entered the courts of princes; I have accompanied the march of armies; I have pined in the putridity of dungeons. I have tasted every vicissitude of splendour and meanness; five times have I been led to the scaffold, and with difficulty escaped a public execution. Hated by mankind, hunted from the face of the earth, pursued by every atrocious calumny, without a country, without a roof, without a friend; the addition that can be made to such misfortunes scarcely deserves a thought."

While he spoke, curiosity, resistless curiosity, presented itself as a new motive, in aid of the sense of shame which the stranger had just before kindled in my bosom. His manner was inconceivably impressive; his voice, though inarticulate from age, had an irresistible melody and volume of sound, which awed, while it won, the heart. His front appeared open, large, and commanding; and, though he complained, his complaints seemed to be those of conscious dignity and innocence. He went on:—

"Farewell, St. Leon! I go, and you shall see me and hear of me no more. You will repent, when it is too late, the folly of this day's determination. I appear mean and insignificant in your eyes. You think my secrets beneath your curiosity, and my benefits not worth your acceptance. Know that my benefits are such as kings would barter their thrones to purchase, and that my wealth exceeds the wealth of empires. You are degraded from the rank you once held among mankind; your children are destined to live in the inglorious condition of peasants. This day you might have redeemed all your misfortunes, and raised yourself to a station more illustrious than that to which you were born. Farewell! Destiny has marked out you and yours for obscurity and oblivion, and you do well to reject magnificence and distinction when they proffer themselves for your acceptance."

"Stop," cried I, "mysterious stranger! Grant me a moment's leisure to reflect and determine."

He had risen to depart, with a gesture of resolution and contempt. At my exclamation he paused, and again turned himself towards me. My soul was in tumults.

"Answer me, most ambiguous and impenetrable of mortals! What is thy story? and what the secrets, the disclosure of which is pregnant with consequences so extraordinary?"

"Do you recollect the conditions upon which only the disclosure can be made?"

"What can I say? Shall I determine to part with that which for years has constituted the only consolation of my life? Shall I suppress the curiosity which now torments me, and reject the boon you pretend to have the power to confer?"

"I grant you the interval for reflection you demand. I refuse to place further confidence in you, till you have maturely examined yourself, and roused all the energies of your spirit to encounter the task you undertake."

"One word more. You know not, indeed you know not, what a woman you exclude from your confidence. She is more worthy of it than I am. Referring to my own experience and knowledge of the world, I can safely pronounce her the first of her sex, perhaps the first of human beings. Indulge me in this; include her in your confidence; and I am content."

"Be silent! I have made my determination; do you make yours! Know I would not if I could, and cannot if I would, repose the secrets that press upon me in more than a single bosom. It was upon this condition I received the communication; upon this condition only can I impart it. I am resolved; to die is the election of my soul—a consummation for which I impatiently wait. Having determined therefore to withdraw myself from the powers committed to me, I am at liberty to impart them; upon the same condition, and no other, you may one day, if you desire it, seek the relief of confidence."

Having thus spoken, the stranger rose from his seat. It was yet early morning, nor was it likely we should meet any one in our walk. He however employed the precaution of causing me to explore the path, and to see that we should return uninterrupted. We came back to the summer-house. The window-shutters were still closed; the stranger determined they should remain so. When I had come to him as soon as I rose, I had found the door secured; nor had he admitted me, till he recognised my voice, and had ascertained that I was alone. These precautions scarcely excited my attention at the time; but, after the conversation that had just passed, they returned distinctly to my memory.

The remainder of the day which had been opened by this extraordinary scene was passed by me in great anxiety. I ruminated with unceasing wonder and perturbation upon the words of the stranger. Shall I shut upon myself the gate of knowledge and information? Is it not the part of a feeble and effeminate mind to refuse instruction, because he is not at liberty to communicate that instruction to another—to a wife? The stranger professes to be able to raise me to the utmost height of wealth and distinction. Shall I refuse the gift, which in a former instance I forfeited, but for which, though contemplated as at an impracticable distance, my whole soul longs? If there is any thing dishonourable connected with the participation of this wealth, I shall still be at liberty to refuse it. There can be no crime in hearing what this man has to communicate. I shall still, and always, be master of myself; nor can I have any thing personally to fear from a man so feeble, so decrepit, so emaciated. Yet what can be the gifts worthy of acceptance of a man who, while he possesses them, is tired of life, and desires to die? or what the wealth of him who bears about him every external symptom of poverty and desolation?

The conversation I had just held revived in my mind the true feeling of my present situation. The wounds of my soul had been lulled into temporary insensibility; but they were in a state in which the slightest accident was capable of making them bleed afresh, and with all their former violence. I had rather steeled my mind to endure what seemed unavoidable, than reconciled myself to my fate. The youthful passions of my soul, which my early years had written there in characters so deep, were by no means effaced. I could not contemplate the splendour of rank with an impartial eye. I could not think of the alternative of distinction or obscurity for my children with indifference. But, most of all, the moment I had experienced for them of hunger, and impending destruction by famine, had produced an indelible impression. It had destroyed all romance, I had almost said all dignity, in my mind for ever. It had snapped, as by the touch of a red-hot iron, all the finer and more etherialised sinews of my frame. It had planted the sordid love of gold in my heart, there, by its baneful vegetation, to poison every nobler and more salubrious feeling.

When I returned to the house, Marguerite enquired of me respecting the stranger, but my answers were short and embarrassed. She seemed to wonder that he did not come into the house, and partake of some refreshment in the midst of my family. She asked, whether he were indisposed? and whether he did not stand in need of some assistance that she might afford him? Perceiving however that I was desirous of saying as little as possible respecting him, she presently became silent. I could see that she was hurt at my incommunicativeness, yet I could not prevail upon myself to enter into an explanation of the causes of my taciturnity. Ours was a family of love; and I could observe that the children sympathised with their mother, and secretly were surprised at and lamented my reserve. There would have been little in this, in perhaps any other family than ours. But the last six years had been spent by us in such primeval simplicity, that scarcely one of us had a thought but what was known to the rest. Marguerite cherished my frankness and unreserve with peculiar zeal; she remembered with bitterness of soul the periods in which I fostered conceptions only proper to myself—periods of dreadful calamity, or of rooted melancholy and sadness. She could not help regarding the silence into which for the present occasion I relapsed, as a portent of evil augury. Charles, who was now sixteen years of age, recollected the period of our ruined fortunes when he had been alone with me at Paris, and partook of his mother's feelings.

A trifling circumstance, at this time occasioned by the little Marguerite, now eight years of age, rendered the restraint under which I laboured more memorable and striking. She had left a little book of fairy tales, in which she had been reading the day before, in the summer-house. At first she did not recollect what was become of it, and employed herself in searching for it with great assiduity. Of a sudden however she remembered where she had read in it last; and, exclaiming with exultation, "It is in the summer-house!" sprang forward to fetch it. I detained her, and told her there was a sick gentleman there that she would disturb! "Then, dear Julia!" rejoined she, "be so good as to get it for me; you are so quiet and careful, you never disturb any body."

"My love," answered I, "nobody must get it for you. The gentleman chooses to be alone, and will not let any body come to him. You shall have it after dinner."

"Ah, but, papa, I want it now. I put it away, just where the naughty giant had shut up the gentleman in the dungeon, who came to take away the lady. I was obliged to put it away then, because mamma called me to go to bed; but I want so to know what will become of them, you cannot think."

"Well, dear Marguerite, I am sorry you must wait; but you must learn to have patience."

"Do you know, papa, I walked in the garden before breakfast: and so, not thinking of any thing, I came to the summer-house; and I tried to open the door, but I could not. I found it was locked. So I thought Julia was there; and I knocked, and called Julia, but nobody answered. So then I knew Julia was not there, for I was sure she would have opened the door. So I climbed upon the stump of the pear-tree, and tried to look in at the window; but the shutters were shut, and I could not get to see over the top of them. And I walked all round the summer-house, and all the shutters were shut. Papa, I wish you would not let a man get into the summer-house, who shuts all the shutters, and locks the door. You always used to let me go into every room I liked; and, do you know, I think none but bad people lock and bolt themselves up so. It puts mind of the giants with their drawbridges and their pitfalls; I shall be quite afraid of this frightful old man."

This prattle of the child was nothing; yet it increased the embarrassment of my situation, and made the peculiarity of the case more conspicuous. Finding her pertinacious in insisting upon a topic that was disagreeable to me, her mother called her from me, and put her upon some occupation that served to divert her attention. I felt like a person that was guilty of some crime; and this consideration and kindness of my wife, when I seemed to myself to deserve her reproach, had not the power to calm my uneasiness.

These little occurrences appeared like the beginning of a separation of interests, and estrangement of hearts. I tasked myself severely. I summoned the whole force of my mind, that I might strictly consider what it was in which I was about to engage. If this slight and casual hint of a secret is felt by both Marguerite and myself with so much uneasiness and embarrassment, what will be our situation, if I go on to accept the stranger's confidence, and become the depository of an arcanum so important as he represents his to be? He declares himself able to bestow upon me the highest opulence; what will be the feelings of my wife and children when they see my condition suddenly changed from its present humble appearance to splendour and wealth, without being able to assign the source of this extraordinary accession?

It is difficult to conceive a family picture more enviable that than to which I was now continually present, and of which I formed a part. We had been happy on the banks of the Garonne, and we had pictured to ourselves a plan of happiness immediately on our arrival in the city of Constance. But these were little and imperfect, compared with what I now enjoyed. In the first situation my children were infants, and in the second the eldest was but ten years of age. The mother was now thirty-five; and she had lost, in my eyes at least, none of her personal attractions. Her intellectual accomplishments were much greater than ever. Her understanding was matured, her judgment decided, her experience more comprehensive. As she had a greater compass of materials to work upon, her fancy was more playful, her conversation richer, and her reflections more amusing and profound. The matron character she had acquired, had had no other effect on her feelings, than to render them more deep, more true and magnetical. Her disposition was more entirely affectionate than it had been even in the first year of our cohabitation. Her attachment to her children was exemplary, and her vigilance uninterrupted; and, for myself, she was accustomed, in all that related to our mutual love, to enter into my sentiments and inclinations with so just a tone of equality and kindness, that we seemed to be two bodies animated by a single soul. If the mother were improved, the children were still more improved. In their early years we are attached to our offspring, merely because they are ours, and in a way that has led superficial speculators to consider the attachment, less as the necessary operation of a sensible and conscious mind, than as a wise provision of nature for the perpetuation of the species. But as they grow up, the case is different. Our partiality is then confirmed or diminished by qualities visible to an impartial bystander as really as to ourselves. They then cease to be merely the objects of our solicitude, and become our companions, the partners of our sentiments, and the counsellors of our undertakings. Such at least was my case at the present period. Charles, who was now sixteen, was manly beyond his years; while the native fire of his disposition was tempered by adversity, by an humble situation, and by the ardour of filial and fraternal affection. Julia, who was two years younger, became daily more interesting by the mildness of her disposition and the tenderness of her sensibility. Louisa was only twelve; but, as she was extremely notable, and had an uncommonly quick and accurate spirit of imitation, she rendered herself exceedingly useful to her mother. Marguerite, the plaything and amusement of the family, had, as I have said, just completed the eighth year of her age.

One exquisite source of gratification, when it is not a source of uneasiness, to speak from my own experience, which a parent finds in the society of his children, is their individuality. They are not puppets, moved with wires, and to be played on at will. Almost from the hour of their birth they have a will of their own, to be consulted and negotiated with. We may say to them, as Adam to the general mother of mankind, "But now, thou wert flesh of my flesh, and bone of my bone; and, even now, thou standest before me vested in the prerogatives of sentiment and reason; a living being, to be regarded with attention and deference; to be courted, not compelled; susceptible of the various catalogue of human passions; capable of resentment and gratitude, of indignation and love, of perverseness and submission. It is because thou art thus formed that I love thee. I cannot be interested about objects inanimate or brute. I require a somewhat that shall exercise my judgment, and awaken my moral feelings. It is necessary to me to approve myself, and be approved by another. I rejoice to stand before you, at once the defendant and the judge. I rejoice in the restraint to which your independent character subjects me, and it will be my pride to cultivate that independence in your mind. I would negotiate for your affections and confidence, and not be loved by you, but in proportion as I shall have done something to deserve it. I could not congratulate myself upon your correspondence to my wishes, if it had not been in your power to withhold it."

While I indulge this vein of reflection, I seem again to see my family, as they surrounded me in the year fifteen hundred and forty-four; Marguerite the partner of my life, Charles the brother of my cares, the blooming Julia, the sage Louisa, and the playful cadette of the family. How richly furnished, how cheerful, how heart-reviving, appeared to me the apartment in which they were assembled! I dwell upon the image with fond affection and lingering delight. Where are they now? How has all this happiness been maliciously undermined, and irrevocably destroyed! To look back on it, it seems like the idle fabric of a dream. I awake, and find myself alone! Were there really such persons? Where are they dispersed? Whither are they gone? Oh, miserable solitude and desertion, to which I have so long been condemned! I see nothing around me but speechless walls, or human faces that say as little to my heart as the walls themselves! How palsied is my soul! How withered my affections!—But I will not anticipate.

CHAPTER XII.

I carried food to the stranger as occasion required in the course of the day. He seemed indisposed to speak, and we exchanged scarcely more than two or three words. The next morning was the implied time to which the question of his confidence was deferred, and I went to him with the full resolution of refusing it. Whether it were that he discerned this resolution in my countenance, or that, in the interval that elapsed, he had formed a meaner opinion of my character, and thought me unfit for the purposes he intended I should answer, certain it is that he anticipated me. At the same time he magnified the importance of the gifts he had to communicate. He expressed himself astonished at the precipitateness of his yesterday's conduct. It was not till after much trial and long probation that he could choose himself a confidant. I was not at present fit for the character, nor perhaps ever should be. The talent he possessed was one upon which the fate of nations and of the human species might be made to depend. God had given it for the best and highest purposes; and the vessel in which it was deposited must be purified from the alloy of human frailty. It might be abused and applied to the most atrocious designs. It might blind the understanding of the wisest, and corrupt the integrity of the noblest. It might overturn kingdoms, and change the whole order of human society into anarchy and barbarism. It might render its possessor the universal plague or the universal tyrant of mankind.

"Go, St. Leon!" added the stranger, "you are not qualified for so important a trust. You are not yet purged of imbecility and weakness. Though you have passed through much, and had considerable experience, you are yet a child. I had heard your history, and expected to find you a different man. Go; and learn to know yourself for what you are, frivolous and insignificant, worthy to have been born a peasant, and not fitted to adorn the rolls of chivalry, or the rank to which you were destined!"

There was something so impressive in the rebuke and contempt of this venerable sage, that made it impossible to contend with them. Never was there a man more singular, and in whom were united greater apparent contradictions. Observe him in a quiet and unanimated moment, you might almost take him for a common beggar; a poor, miserable wretch, in whom life lingered, and insensate stupidity reigned. But when his soul was touched in any of those points on which it was most alive, he rose at once, and appeared a giant. His voice was the voice of thunder; and, rolling in a rich and sublime swell, it arrested and stilled, while it withered all the nerves of the soul. His eye-beam sat upon your countenance, and seemed to look through you. You wished to escape from its penetrating power, but you had not the strength to move. I began to feel as if it were some mysterious and superior being in human form, and not a mortal, with whom I was concerned.

What a strange and contradictory being is man! I had gone to the summer-house this morning, with a firm resolution to refuse the gifts and the communication of the stranger. I felt as if lightened from a burthen which the whole preceding day had oppressed me, while I formed this resolution: I was cheerful, and conscious of rectitude and strength of mind. How cheaply we prize a gift which we imagine to be already in our power! With what philosophical indifference do we turn it on every side, depreciate its worth, magnify its disadvantages, and then pique ourselves upon the sobriety and justice of the estimate we have made! Thus it was with me in the present transaction; but when I had received the check of the stranger, and saw the proposed benefit removed to a vast and uncertain distance, then it resumed all its charms; then the contrast of wealth and poverty flashed full upon my soul. Before, I had questioned the reality of the stranger's pretensions, and considered whether he might not be an artful impostor; but now all was clearness and certainty: the advantages of wealth passed in full review before my roused imagination. I saw horses, palaces, and their furniture; I saw the splendour of exhibition and the trains of attendants,—objects which had been for ever dear to my puerile imagination; I contemplated the honour, love, obedience, troops of friends, which are so apt to attend upon wealth, when disbursed with a moderate degree of dignity and munificence. When I compared this with my present poverty and desertion, the meanness of our appearance, our daily labours, the danger that an untoward accident might sink us in the deepest distress, and the hopelessness that my son or his posterity should ever rise to that honour and distinction to which they had once been destined, the effect was too powerful.

Another feeling came still further in aid of this: it was the humiliating impression which the stranger had left upon my mind: this seemed to be his great art, if in reality his conduct is to be imputed to art. There is no enemy to virtue so fatal as a sense of degradation. Self-applause is our principal support in every liberal and elevated act of virtue. If this ally can be turned against us; if we can be made to ascribe baseness, effeminacy, want of spirit and adventure, to our virtuous resolutions; we shall then indeed feel ourselves shaken. This was precisely my situation: the figure I made in my own eyes was mean; I was impatient of my degradation; I believed that I had shown myself uxorious and effeminate, at a time that must have roused in me the spirit of a man, if there had been a spark of manly spirit latent in my breast. This impatience co-operated with the temptations of the stranger, and made me anxious to possess what he offered to my acceptance.

I reasoned thus with myself: what excites my scruples is simply the idea of having one single secret from my wife and family. This scruple is created by the singular and unprecedented confidence in which we have been accustomed to live. Other men have their secrets: nor do they find their domestic tranquillity broken by that circumstance. The merchant does not call his wife into consultation upon his ventures; the statesman does not unfold to her his policy and his projects; the warrior does not take her advice upon the plan of his campaign; the poet does not concert with her his flights and his episodes. To other men the domestic scene is the relaxation of their cares; when they enter it, they dismiss the business of the day, and call another cause. I only have concentrated in it the whole of my existence. By this means I have extinguished in myself the true energy of the human character. A man can never be respectable in the eyes of the world or in his own, except so far as he stands by himself and is truly independent. He may have friends; he may have domestic connections; but he must not in these connections lose his individuality. Nothing truly great was ever achieved, that was not executed or planned in solitary seclusion.

But if these reasons are sufficient to prove that the plan I have lately pursued is fundamentally wrong, how much more will the importance of what is proposed by the stranger plead my excuse for deviating from it? How bitterly have I lamented the degradation of my family! Shall I not seize this opportunity of re-installing them in their hereditary honours? I deemed the ruin I had brought upon them irreparable; shall I not embrace the occasion of atoning for my fault? No man despises wealth, who fully understands the advantages it confers. Does it not confer the means of cultivating our powers? Does it not open to us the career of honour, which is shut against the unknown and obscure? Does it not conciliate the prepossessions of mankind, and gain for us an indulgent and liberal construction? Does it not inspire us with graceful confidence, and animate us to generous adventure? The poor man is denied every advantage of education, and wears out his life in labour and ignorance. From offices of trust, from opportunities of distinction, he is ignominiously thrust aside; and though he should sacrifice his life for the public cause, he dies unhonoured and unknown. If by any accident he comes into possession of those qualities which, when discerned and acknowledged, command the applause of mankind, who will listen to him? His appearance is mean; and the fastidious auditor turns from him ere half his words are uttered. He has no equipage and attendants, no one to blow the trumpet before him and proclaim his rank; how can he propose any thing that shall be worthy of attention? Aware of the prepossession of mankind in this respect, he is alarmed and overwhelmed with confusion before he opens his lips. Filled with the conscience of his worth, he anticipates the unmerited contempt that is prepared to oppress him, and his very heart dies within him. Add to these circumstances, the constitution of our nature, the various pleasures of which it is adapted to partake, and how many of these pleasures it is in the power of wealth to procure. Yes; an object like this will sufficiently apologise for me to those for whose sake alone it was estimable in my sight. It is, indeed, nothing but our poverty and the lowness of our station that have thus produced in us an habitual and unreserved communication of sentiments. Wealth would, to a certain degree, destroy our contact, and take off the wonder that we had each our thoughts that were not put into the common stock.

These considerations decided my choice. I was not indeed without some variations of mind, and some compunction of heart for the resolution I had espoused. The longer the stranger remained with me, the more evident it was that there was something mysterious between us; and the unreserved affection and union that had lately reigned under my roof suffered materially the effects of it. The stranger had been led to my cottage, in the first instance, by the entire solitude in which it was placed. There was nothing about which he was so solicitous as concealment; the most atrocious criminal could not be more alarmed at the idea of being discovered. I was unable to account for this; but I was now too anxious for his stay and the promised reward, not to be alert in gratifying all his wishes. The most inviolable secrecy, therefore, was enjoined to the whole family; and the younger branches of it, particularly the little Marguerite, it was necessary to keep almost immured, to prevent the danger of their reporting any thing out of the house, that might be displeasing to the stranger and fatal to my expectations. Upon the whole my situation was eminently an uneasy one. No experiment can be more precarious than that of a half-confidence; and nothing but the sincere affection that was entertained for me could have rendered it successful in this instance. My family felt that they were trusted by me only in points where it was impossible to avoid it, and that I was not therefore properly entitled to their co-operation; I was conscious of ingratitude in making them no return for their fidelity. They kept my secret because they were solicitous to oblige me, not from any conviction that they were conferring on me a benefit; but, on the contrary, suspecting that the object as to which they were blindly assisting me would prove injurious to me as well as to themselves.

The health of the stranger visibly declined; but this was a circumstance which he evidently regarded with complacency. It was the only source of consolation of which he appeared susceptible; his mind was torn with painful remembrances, and agitated with terrible forebodings. He abhorred solitude, and yet found no consolation in society. I could not be much with him; my duty to my family, who were principally supported by my labour, was a call too imperious to be neglected. Even when I was with him, he commonly testified no desire for conversation. "Stay with me," he was accustomed to say; "give me as much of your time as you can; but do not talk." Upon these occasions he would sit sometimes with his arms folded, and with the most melancholy expression imaginable. He would then knit his brows, wring his hands with a sadness that might have excited pity in the hardest breast, or, with both hands closed, the one clasping the other, strike himself impatiently on the forehead. At other times he would rise from his seat, pace the room with hurried and unquiet steps, and then again throw himself on his couch in the greatest agitation. His features were often convulsed with agony. Often have I wiped away the sweat, which would suddenly burst out in large drops on his forehead. At those seasons he would continually mutter words to himself, the sense of which it was impossible for me to collect. I could perceive however that he often repeated the names of Clara!—Henry!—a wife!—a friend! a friend!——and then he would groan as if his heart were bursting. Sometimes, in the midst of these recollections, he would pass the back of his hand over his eyes; and then, looking at it, shaking his head, and biting his under lip, exclaim with a piteous accent, "Dry!—dry!—all the moisture of my frame is perished!" Then, as if recovering himself, he would cry with a startled and terrified voice, "Who is there? St. Leon? Come to me! Let me feel that there is a human being near me! I often call for you; but I find myself alone, deserted, friendless!—friendless!"

At times when his recollection was more complete, he would say, "I know I tire you! Why should I tire you? What gratification can it be to me to occasion emotions of disgust?" Upon these occasions I endeavoured to soothe him, and assured him I found pleasure in administering to his relief. But he replied, "No, no: do not flatter me! It is long since I have heard the voice of flattery! I never loved it! No; I know I am precluded from ever exciting friendship or sympathy! Why am I not dead? Why do I live, a burthen to myself, useful to none? My secret I could almost resolve should die with me; but you have earned, and you shall receive it."

The stranger was not always in this state of extreme anguish, nor always indisposed to converse. He had lucid intervals; and could beguile the sorrow of his heart with social communication. We sometimes talked of various sciences and branches of learning; he appeared to be well informed in them all. His observations were ingenious; his language copious; his illustrations fanciful and picturesque; his manner bold and penetrating. It was easy to observe in him the marks of a vigorous and masculine genius. Sometimes we discussed the events at that time going on in the world. When we discoursed of events that had passed, and persons that had died, more than a century before, the stranger often spoke of them in a manner as if he had been an eye-witness, and directly acquainted with the objects of our discourse. This I ascribed to the vividness of his conceptions, and the animation of his language. He however often checked himself in this peculiarity, and always carefully avoided what could lead to any thing personal to himself. I described to him the scenes of my youth, and related my subsequent history; he on his part was invincibly silent on every circumstance of his country, his family, and his adventures.

The longer I was acquainted with him, the more my curiosity grew. I was restless and impatient to learn something respecting a man who thus wrapped himself up in mystery and reserve. Often I threw out, as it were, a line by which to fathom his secret. I talked of various countries, I mentioned different kinds of calamities and even of crimes, that by some incidental allusion I might discover at unawares his country, his connections, or the nature of his story. When any thing that offered seemed to lead to the desired point, I doubled my questions, and endeavoured to construct them with the skill of a crafty litigant in a court of justice. There were some subjects, the very mention of which gave him uneasiness, and upon which he immediately silenced me; but these were not of themselves enough to afford me a clue, or to furnish materials out of which for me to construct the history of the stranger. He did not always perceive the drift of my questions and snares; but, when he did, he generally became loud, resentful, and furious. There was nothing else that so completely roused his indignation.

"St. Leon!" said he to me one day, "silence this inquisitive temper of yours; check your rash and rude curiosity. The only secret I have that can be of any importance to you, you shall one day know. But my country, my family, my adventures, I have once told you, and I tell you again, you shall never know. That knowledge can be of moment to no one, and it shall never be disclosed. When this heart ceases to beat, that tale shall cease to have a place on the face of the earth. Why should my distresses and disgraces be published to any one? Is it not enough that they have lacerated my bosom, that they have deprived me of friends, that they have visited me with every adversity and every anguish, that they have bowed me down to the earth, that they have made thought, and remembrance, and life itself, a burthen too heavy to be borne? Your present injudicious conduct, if persisted in, will have the effect of driving me from your roof, of turning me once more upon the world, upon that world that I hate, upon that world whose bruises and ill treatment I feel in every fibre of my frame; of exposing me again to fresh persecutions, and causing me to perish miserably in a dungeon, or die upon a scaffold. Spare me, my generous host; I know you are capable of generosity. Indeed I have endured enough to satiate the rage of malice itself. You see what I suffer from the rage and tempest of my own thoughts, even without the assistance of any external foe. Let me die in that degree of tranquillity I am able to attain. I will not trouble you long."

At another time he addressed me in a different style. "You see, St. Leon, that the anguish of mind I endure is such as is ordinarily attributed to the recollection of great crimes; and you have very probably conjectured that in my case it arises from the same source. If you have, I forgive you; but I assure you that you are mistaken. Take from yourself that uneasiness, if it has ever visited you; you are not giving sanctuary to a villain! I am innocent. I can take no crime to my charge. I have suffered more almost than man ever suffered; but I have sinned little. The cause of my uneasiness and prime source of all my misfortunes, I dare not disclose to you. Be contented with the plan of my conduct. I have digested my purpose: I have determined where to speak and where to be silent."

The more I saw of this man, the more strange and unaccountable appeared to me every thing that related to him. Why was he so poor, possessing, as he pretended, inexhaustible wealth? Why was he unhappy, with so great talents and genius, and such various information? Why was he friendless, being, as he solemnly assured me, so perfectly innocent, and of consequence so respectable? That he was an impostor, every thing that I saw of him forbade me to believe. His sorrows were too profound and excruciating, for it to be possible for me to rank them among the actions that a man may play. The greatness of his powers, the dignity of his carriage, the irresistible appearance of sincerity that sparkled in his eye and modulated his voice, fully convinced me that he really was what he pretended to be. I had heard of men who, under the pretence of alchemy, fastened themselves upon persons possessing sums of money; and, beguiling them with a delusive expectation of wealth, reduced them to beggary and ruin. One such person I had had a brief connection with during my residence in the Bordelois, though, finding the incident by no means essential to the progress of my history, I have passed it over, together with many others, in silence. But nothing could be more unlike than that man and the person respecting whom I was now concerned. In reality I possessed at that time, if I may be allowed to say so, a more than common insight into the characters of mankind, so as to be little likely, except under the tyranny of passion, as in the instance of gaming, to be made the prey of imposition. I had studied my species as it exhibits itself in history, and had mixed with it in various scenes and under dissimilar aspects. I had accordingly, in the transaction I have just alluded to, soon detected the plans of the villain who expected to delude me. But what could be the purpose of the stranger in this respect? The pretended alchemist in France had obtained a certain sum of money of me, and demanded more. The stranger never made such a demand of me; and perfectly knew that, even if I had been inclined, I was not able to supply him. The alchemist had amused me with descriptions of various processes for the transmutation of metals, had exhibited his crucibles and retorts, and employed a sort of dramatic coup d'œil for the purpose of awakening my curiosity and stimulating my passions. The stranger had simply stated, in the plainest and most direct manner, that it was in his power to enrich me; but had been silent as to the manner of producing the wealth he promised, and had abstained from every effort to intoxicate my mind. I felt therefore in this instance the effect, that, without being able to solve the difficulties and contrarieties that hung about him, I yet believed his assertions; nor was the inscrutability of his history and his motives capable of shaking my confidence.

One day, during the period of his concealment, certain officers of the bishop of Constance, accompanied by a foreigner in a Neapolitan habit, came to my house, and, as it proved, with the express purpose of searching for the man who had put himself under my protection. Charles and myself were at work in the fields within sight of the lake.

Their appearance first caught the attention of Charles as they approached the shore, and he enquired of me respecting the habit of the foreigner, which was different from any he had been accustomed to see. While we were yet speaking, I observed in them an intention to land within sight of my cottage. This was an uncommon circumstance; our privacy was rarely invaded, and we lived almost as much out of the world as we should have done in the remotest island of the Atlantic ocean. I reasoned in my own mind upon their appearance: they had little resemblance to a party of pleasure; the habit of the officers of justice I was perfectly acquainted with; and the suspicion of the real nature of their errand immediately darted on my thoughts. Without saying a word to Charles on the subject, I hastened with all the speed I could exert to the apartment of the stranger, and acquainted him with what I had seen. He concurred with me in the ideas I had formed, and appeared much shocked at the intelligence. There was however no time to be lost; and, after having for a moment given vent to an anguish which was too powerful to be suppressed, he withdrew as hastily as he could from the summer-house, and betook himself to the woods. He recommended to me to leave him, telling me that he could conceal himself most effectually alone, and observing that it would be necessary for me to meet the officers, and endeavour as much as possible to remove their suspicions.

Accordingly, as soon as he was gone, I threw open the windows of the summer-house, removed the shutters, and took from it as effectually as I could all appearance of having served as a place of concealment. This was a precaution which the stranger had on a former occasion recommended to me. It fortunately happened that Julia and the little Marguerite were gone out together in the fields on the eastern side of my cottage; otherwise infallibly the child by her innocent prattle, and perhaps Julia by the apprehensive sensibility of her temper, would have betrayed our secret, or at least have suggested to the officers a feeling as if, by a longer stay and a more diligent search, they might possibly succeed in the object of their expedition. As it was, I received them at the door, and learned from their own mouths the nature of their errand. Of Charles, whom they had crossed in the fields, they had simply asked whether they were right as to the name of the person who was proprietor of the cottage before them. They described to me with great accuracy the appearance of the stranger, and insisted that he had been an inhabitant of my cottage. They told me, they were well informed that the summer-house in my garden had carefully been shut up for more than a month past, and that some person had been concealed there. I was interested in the distress of the stranger; I was impressed with the dignity of his character; I implicitly confided in his assertions of innocence, and the unjust persecution that he suffered; I was not insensible to the proposed reward, the realising of which probably depended on his safety. But, most of all, I considered my honour as pledged for the protection of the man who had thus cast himself upon my fidelity, and believed that I should be everlastingly disgraced if he suffered any evil through treachery or neglect on my part. I therefore answered confidently to the officers that they were misinformed, and offered to conduct them over every part of my house and demesnes, that they might satisfy themselves by inspection that there was no person concealed any where within my possessions. I should have been better pleased, openly to have defied their interrogatories, and to have asked them whether, allowing their suspicions to be just, they were entitled to believe that I was such a villain as to betray a man who had thrown himself upon my generosity? But though this conduct would have had a greater appearance of gallantry, I believed it would have less of the reality, as it would have strengthened their idea of my participation, and increased the danger of the person I was bound to protect.

They accepted my offer of submitting to their search, and made a strict examination of every place about my habitation in which the stranger could be concealed. Disappointed here, they endeavoured by threats to discover whether I was able to give them any information. To these I calmly answered, that they had mistaken my character; that, though I was a poor man, I had not forgotten that I was noble; that they were already in possession of my spontaneous answer to their enquiries; and that, in no case, and upon no supposition, should tyranny and ill treatment extort from me what I was not in the first instance disposed to give. My wife was present during this conversation, and, I could perceive, felt an alarm for my danger that she would have been incapable of feeling for a danger to herself.

Though I was extremely anxious that these men should be disappointed in the object of their expedition, yet I did not neglect this opportunity of endeavouring to obtain satisfaction for my own curiosity. I remarked at first that the Neapolitan was an inquisitor, and this circumstance had given additional poignancy to the uneasiness of Marguerite. But the accusations of which the inquisition at this time took cognisance were so numerous— the ecclesiastical power continually usurping upon the civil—that I was little assisted in the judgment I was desirous to frame by any inference to be deduced from this circumstance. I questioned directly, with an air as if it were merely in the way of conversation, what was the crime of the man of whom they were in pursuit? and what was the cause forcible enough to induce a Neapolitan inquisitor to follow so decrepit and forlorn an individual as he described, beyond the Alps, and almost to the banks of the Danube? To this he answered roughly, that though he was not able to discover the object of his search, he was by no means convinced that I was not his abettor and accomplice; and that as to his crime, that was not to be named; the welfare of Christendom demanding that the criminal, and the memory of his offences, should be buried together. At the same time he warned me to consider well what I did, before I exposed myself to be overwhelmed by the vengeance of the court of which he was a member. To this I answered haughtily, that I had already condescended to repel his suspicion, and that no other man than an inquisitor would have had the stupidity or the audaciousness to question my veracity. I added, that I was perfectly acquainted with the nature of his court, which was an object of abhorrence to the whole Christian world; but that he was mistaken if he supposed that the detestable nature of its proceedings would enable him to practise every sort of outrage with impunity. The officers withdrew into the little inclosure in front of my cottage, and I overheard them consulting whether, having failed in their principal object, they should carry me a prisoner along with them. The firmness of my manner however had awed them, and the fearlessness I expressed seemed to them to arise from a consciousness of innocence. They at length departed as they came.

I watched them from my cottage as they descended to the shore, and it was with no little pleasure that I perceived them re-embark, and stand off for the opposite side of the lake. This spectacle for a time entirely engaged me, and when I turned from the door I observed that my beloved Marguerite had been in tears. She endeavoured to hide this circumstance from my sight. I took her affectionately by the hand, and, pressing her to my bosom, entreated her not to make herself uneasy.

"Ah, Reginald!" said she, "how can I avoid being uneasy, when I see you exposed to this imminent danger? I thought that, in forfeiting our fortune and our rank, and retiring to this obscure and sequestered situation, we might at least promise ourselves the blessing of the poor—oblivion and security; and that should have consoled me for all I have lost. Who is this man that is thus mysteriously hidden among us? What is the guilt from the punishment of which he thus anxiously withdraws himself? What can be the nature of your connection with such a man? And what will be the issue of so perilous an adventure?"

I hesitated. I knew not what to answer to so earnest an anxiety. I was melted at the distress and the affection of Marguerite. She saw my embarrassment, and proceeded:—

"Mistake me not, my beloved!" said she. "I have no desire to pry into what you are willing to conceal. Forgive the perturbation which has poured itself out in these involuntary questions. I repose an entire confidence in you. I would sooner die than interfere with any object you have at heart. Go on according to the dictates of your own judgment, undisturbed by me. I will not doubt that you have sufficient reasons for what you communicate, and what you suppress. I am grieved indeed at the interruption of our obscure and unambitious tranquillity; but I had resolved not to trouble you with my uneasiness and apprehensions. The incident of this morning has extorted them from me; but I will behave better in future."

This scene was extremely distressing to me. My wife was oppressed with fears, and I had nothing to answer her. The consolations that rose up in my own mind I was prevented from communicating. The more generously she confided in me, the more I felt the ungracious and disagreeable nature of the concealment I practised. I endeavoured however to encourage myself with the idea, that the labour would not be long, and the harvest would prove abundant. I said in my own mind, The worst is now over; the business has been commenced; the shock to my own family has actually occurred; I must go on resolutely, and shut my eyes to the temporarily displeasing circumstances that may be connected with the completing my object.

CHAPTER XIII.

Another source of uneasiness was added to the distraction my mind already endured. The stranger did not appear. It was in the morning that the officers of justice arrived; they departed about noon; and in two hours afterwards I entered the wood in search of my guest. The wood was of some leagues in extent; it was intersected by paths in various directions; it was interspersed with caverns; its growth was of all kinds,—in some places lofty trees that seemed to form a support for the clouds, in others an underwood impenetrable alike to the feet and to the eye. As I entered the wood, I however conceived that the discovery of the stranger, to me who was acquainted with its lurking-places, would be an affair of little toil; his feebleness and decrepitude would not suffer him to proceed to any great distance. In this I was mistaken. I looked carefully on all sides; I examined every recess and corner with which I was acquainted: but I found no trace of the stranger. The scene was so complicated and involved, that even this was a labour of considerable duration. At length I became satisfied that he was not in the nearer division of the wood.

I paused. I felt at once that it was little less than a Herculean task to hunt through the whole of its dimensions. It would probably be of little use to call, and endeavour by that means to discover his retreat. I knew of no name by which he was to be recognised; and, if my own voice was but a slight resource to penetrate this immense labyrinth of foliage, the voice of the stranger, weakened by age, and now probably still more enfeebled by hunger and fatigue, could not be expected to make itself heard. Beside which, as I knew not what the source of information had been to the officers who had just left me, I was unwilling to expose my guest to the danger that might arise from this mode of seeking him. I could not even be sure, though I had seen their boat stand off from the shore, that they might not afterwards land one or more of their party, and be at this very moment within ear-shot of me. I therefore proceeded in anxiety and silence.

My search was no more successful in the part of the wood with which I was little acquainted, than in the part with which I was most familiar. I had already been engaged four hours in the task, and night began to come on. It shut in with heavy clouds, that on all sides appeared deeply loaded with rain. I now began to consider my own situation; and, by comparing circumstances, found that I was at a great distance from my own habitation. There was no direct path by which for me to return. I had proceeded to the right and the left, backward and forward, sometimes by more open paths, and sometimes forcing my way through briars and brushwood, as caprice, or the hope of effecting the object of my search, happened to guide me. It was therefore no easy matter to guess how I was to return, or even, now that the lowering clouds had covered the horizon with one uniform tint, in which direction lay the cottage or the lake. While I stood contemplating what was to be done, I heard the howling of the wolves at a distance; and their howl had that particular melancholy and discomfiting sound which is well known to precede a coming storm. There was no time to be lost, and accordingly I set out. I was less anxious to be at home on my own account, than for the sake of quieting the alarms of my family, to whom I had already occasioned too great a portion of uneasiness.

I had not proceeded far before the rain descended in torrents, intermingled with peals of thunder and sheets of lightning. The thunder, interrupted, as it were, from time to time, with the noise of the wild beasts that inhabited the wood, deafened me, while the excessive and instantaneous brilliancy of the lightning occasioned me an intolerable aching in the organ of sight. It rained incessantly for two hours, and I found myself drenched and fatigued with the wet. During this time my progress was small; and I was ever and anon intercepted by the underwood, and could not without repeated experiments discover the means of proceeding. At length the rain subsided, and seemed to give place to a gloomy and motionless calm. Soon after, I discovered a light at a distance, and advanced towards it. As I approached, I perceived that it proceeded from a set of banditti, to the amount of fourteen or fifteen persons, sitting round a fire in the mouth of a cavern. I was glad to turn my steps another way, and was for some time afraid that the noise I made in occasionally forcing my way through the bushes would alarm them, and cost me my life. I however fortunately escaped their notice. This was in a part of the wood remote from the path I ought to have taken, and near the road to Lindau.

The day began to dawn before I reached my own habitation. The conjecture I had made, when I was unawares upon the point of falling into the hands of the banditti, that the road of Lindau was on the other side of their retreat, was of some service to me as an indication where to find the cottage and the lake. This road skirted the wood on the side nearly opposite to that by which I entered it. The difficulties however I had to encounter were inconceivably great, in endeavouring to preserve my line of direction. After having been compelled four or five times to deviate from the line, it is seldom that a traveller will find himself right in his conjecture as to the direction he is pursuing, unless he has some sensible object as a sort of pole-star by which to govern his route. It happened in this instance that I was more fortunate than I was entitled to expect. I laboured indeed till daybreak without getting out of the labyrinth that inclosed me. But the sun no sooner began to lend an imperfect light, than I recognised certain objects which upon some former occasions I had observed, and perceived that my journey was nearly at an end. I entered my cottage, and found Marguerite alone awake and expecting me.

She had been somewhat uneasy on account of my absence, both from the extreme tempestuousness of the night, and in consequence of the painful sensations the events of the preceding morning had introduced,—events with which it was almost unavoidable for her to imagine that my absence was in some way connected. The period of my insanity in Switzerland might indeed have accustomed her to the irregularity of my motions, but a term of more than six years which had intervened, had produced in her expectations and habits of a different sort. I related to this admirable woman the adventures of the night and the fruitlessness of the search in which I had been engaged; and this openness of communication, unresembling the nature of the intercourse which had lately existed between us, relieved in some degree my burthened heart, and cheered the drooping spirits of Marguerite. She dropped some consolatory and sadly pleasing tears; and her manner seemed to say, though she would not suffer her tongue to give the idea words, How sweet are cordiality and confidence! Oh! do not let our situation, which has deprived us of many other comforts, ever again be robbed of this comfort, which is alone worth all the rest! Though she necessarily felt the presence of the stranger as an evil, the bane of our domestic peace, yet it was impossible for her not to compassionate his fate, and suffer some distress from his strange and abrupt disappearance.

After the conversation which had so eminently served as a relief to our minds, Marguerite left me to repose myself from the extraordinary fatigue I had undergone. But my mind was too much disturbed to suffer me to sink into the arms of forgetfulness. I felt something tragical in the sad destiny of my unfortunate guest. It was but too probable that, in his peculiarly weak state of body, and with his declining health, the being thus exposed for a day and a night to the effects of hunger, of the inclemency of the air, and the tempestuousness of the elements, would put a close to his existence. I was determined soon to recommence my search. But how could I be sure that I should be more fortunate to-day, than the day before? If I found him, it was most likely I should find him either dead or dying. The degree of intercourse that had taken place between us had made him occupy a considerable space in my thoughts. The prospects he had opened to me, the conduct he had induced me to adopt, the painful effects and dissatisfaction of mind which had been produced by that conduct as it respected my family, all combined to give me an interest in his fate. I had seen his talents; I had felt his ascendancy; I had experienced that sort of conflict, which appearances of guilt on the one hand, and asseverations of innocence on the other, are calculated to produce in the thoughts and emotions of a bystander. He was no common man; the expectations and conjectures he excited were of no ordinary sort; and I felt that an army might be destroyed, and a spacious plain covered with the wounded and the dying, without producing greater commotion in my soul.

In the anxious and disturbed state of mind in which I was, the thoughts flow with extraordinary rapidity. It will be found attended with a strange, and, previously to the experiment, incredible mixture of reasoning and passion, of philosophising and fury. I was accordingly conscious at this moment of the truth of the stranger's assertion, that in me he had a protector, not a friend. Friendship is an object of a peculiar sort; the smallest reserve is deadly to it. I may indeed feel the emotions of a friend towards a man who in part conceals from me the thoughts of his heart; but then I must be unconscious of this concealment. The instant I perceive this limitation of confidence, he drops into the class of ordinary men: a divorce is effected between us: our hearts, which grew together, suffer amputation; the arteries are closed; the blood is no longer mutually transfused and confounded. I shall be conscious of all his qualities, for I stand in the place of an impartial umpire. I consider him as a machine capable of so much utility to myself, and so much utility to other men. But I do not regard him as the brother of my soul: I do not feel that my life is bound up in his: I do not feel as if, were he to die, the whole world would be at an end to me, and that my happiness would be buried with him for ever in the darkness of the grave. I am not conscious of those emotions which are the most exquisite and indescribable the human mind can experience; and which, being communicated by a sort of electrical stroke to him who is their object, constitute the solace of all his cares, the alleviator of all his calamities, the only nectar and truest balm of human life. For me, he stands alone in the world, having companions and associates, the connections, as it were, of mercantile selfishness, or casual jollity and good humour, but no friend. It was thus that I thought of the stranger. He obtained from me the compassion due to a human being, and the respect extorted by his qualities, but nothing calculated radically to disturb the equilibrium of the mind. I looked forward to his death with unruffled thoughts and an unmoistened eye. There was one thing indeed that shook me more deeply; the thought of losing the promised reward, and of having exposed myself to the evil of an unquiet and dissatisfied mind in vain.

I rested but a few hours before I set out again upon the search, to which the interposition of the darkness of the preceding night had put an abrupt close. I had the precaution to take with me a slight provision of food and cordials, believing that, if I found the stranger, he would at least be in the greatest need of something reviving and restorative. Charles earnestly intreated to assist me in the search, but upon this I put a peremptory prohibition. It would have been in direct contradiction to what the stranger had most solemnly required of me.

I had already spent several hours in anxiously tracing the wood in every direction; and the period of noon was past, when, approaching an obscure and almost impenetrable thicket, my ear was caught by a low and melancholy sound, which at first I knew not to what I was to ascribe. It however arrested my attention, and caused me to assume an attitude of listening. After the lapse of little more than a minute, the same sound was repeated. I now distinctly perceived that it was the groan of some creature in a very feeble and exhausted state, and immediately suspected that it was the stranger. I went almost round the thicket before I could discern an entrance, and, though I looked with the utmost care, could perceive nothing that the thicket inclosed. The groan was repeated a third time. The long intervals between the groans gave a peculiar melancholy to the effect, and each seemed so much lower than the groan before, that nothing but the ear of anxious attention would have caught it; at the same time that the tone conveyed an idea of stupified, yet vital, anguish. At length I perceived the legs and something of the garb of a man. It was the stranger! He appeared to have crept into the thicket upon his hands and knees. When I forced my way to him, he seemed in the very act of expiring. He was lying on his face, and I raised him a little. His eyes were fixed; his mouth was open; his lips and tongue were parched and dry. I infused a few drops of a cordial into his mouth. For a moment it appeared to produce no sensation, but presently my patient uttered a deep and long-drawn sigh. I repeated my application. As a principal cause of the condition in which I found him was inanition, the stimulant I administered produced a powerful effect. He moved his hands, shuddered, turned his eyes languidly upon me, and, having appeared to recognise me, shut them hastily again. I moved him slowly and softly into a freer air, and bathed his temples with one of the liquids I had about me. By this time he looked up, and then suddenly round him with a wild and hurried air. He spoke not however; he was speechless. In about a quarter of an hour he relapsed into convulsions, in which it seemed probable he would expire. They lasted a considerable time, and he then sunk into a state of insensibility. I thought he was dead. Thus circumstanced, it was some relief to my humanity to have found him yet alive, and to have received his parting breath. But in a moment his secret and his promises recurred to me with inexpressible anguish, and I inwardly reproached him for having deferred his communication so long, as now to preclude its ever being made. I cannot describe the keenness, the burning and intolerable bitterness, of my sensation. Keen it may well be supposed to have been, from its having so instantaneously and forcibly recurred at a time when other objects seemed to press upon my senses. No one who has not felt what it is to fall in a moment from hope, or, as I should rather say, from assured possession of what his soul most loved and desired, into black and interminable despair, can imagine what was then the state of my mind. The body of my patient slided from my nerveless arms; I lifted up the eyes of rage and phrensy, as if to curse the Author of my being; and then fell helpless and immoveable by the side of the stranger.

I felt him move; I heard him sigh. I lifted up my head, and perceived stronger marks of life and sense about him than had yet displayed themselves. I threw my arms about him; I pressed him to my heart. The emphatical gesture I used seemed to have a sort of magnetical force to rouse his dying powers. With a little assistance from me he sat upright. My assiduity produced wonders: it fortunately happened that this thicket was but a half a mile from my habitation, and indeed was one of the spots which I had searched without success the day before. About the hour of sunset, partly by leading, and partly by supporting him, I restored my guest to his former apartment.

He remained speechless, or nearly so. He vented his sensations in sighs, in inward and inarticulate sounds; and even when he arrived at the power of making himself understood by words, it was only by monosyllables and half sentences that he conveyed to me his meaning. I now gave up my time almost entirely to an assiduous attendance on the stranger. Every day I expected to be his last; every day was more or less interspersed with symptoms that seemed to menace his instant dissolution. During all this time I remained in the anxious suspense of contending hope and fear. Was it probable that he would ever recover strength enough to confer on me the legacy he had announced? The particulars of his secret I knew not; but, judging from what I had heard of the pretences and pursuits of alchemy, it was natural to suppose that he had a process to communicate, which would require on his part considerable accuracy of recollection, as well as the power of delivering himself in a methodical and orderly discourse.

I was fortunate enough however to perceive, after a tormenting and tedious crisis, that he appeared to be in a progress of convalescence, and that his strength both of body and mind were recruited daily. After the lapse of a fortnight from the adventure of the wood, he one evening addressed me in the following manner:—

"St. Leon, I have been to blame. I have put you to a sufficient trial; I have received from you every assistance and kindness that my situation demanded; I have imposed on you much trouble and anxiety; I have excited your expectations by announcing to you in part what it was in my power to bestow; and I have finally risked the defrauding your hopes and your humanity of their just reward. Do me the justice however to remember, that I had no presentiment of the event which has so inauspiciously come between you and your hopes. Fool that I was, I imagined I had suffered enough, and that, as I had obtained a longer respite from external persecution than I almost ever experienced, I should be permitted to spend the short remainder of my days uninterrupted! I now however look back upon this last assault with complacency. It has cut off something from the last remnant of a life to the close of which I look forward with inexpressible longing; at the same time that I am still in prospect of obtaining the final wish of my heart—the stealing out of the world unperceived, and thus in some measure eluding the last malice of my enemies. After my death I have but one injunction to leave with you—the injunction of Hercules to Philoctetes—that no inducement may move you to betray to mortal man the place in which you shall have deposited my ashes. Bury them in a spot which I will describe to you: it is not far, and is only recommended to me by its almost inaccessible situation: and that once done, speak of me and, if possible, think of me no more. Never on any account mention me or allude to me; never describe me, or relate the manner of our meeting, or the adventure which has at length brought on the desired close of my existence.

"Believe me, in the feeble and helpless condition in which I have spent the last fortnight, your wishes and expectations have been uppermost in my mind, and there is nothing I have felt with so much compunction as the danger of leaving them unsatisfied. To you perhaps I at present appear to be rapidly recovering, I feel the dart of death in my vitals; I know I shall not live four days. It is necessary therefore that I should finish without delay all that remains for me to finish. I will devote this night to the arranging my thoughts and putting in order what I have to communicate, that no mistake or omission may have part in a transaction so important. Come to me to-morrow morning; I will be prepared for you."

As soon as I heard this discourse, and provided the stranger with every thing he could want during the night, I withdrew. My heart was big with expectation; my thoughts all night were wild and tumultuous. When the hour of assignation arrived, I hastened along the garden to the summer-house, conscious that upon that hour depended all the colour of my future life. Since the stranger had been in his present dangerous condition, the door was not bolted; it was only locked: the key was in my possession, and remained night and day attached to my person. I opened the door; I panted and was breathless.

I immediately saw that the stranger had undergone some great alteration for the worse. He had suffered a sort of paralytic affection. He lifted up his face as I entered; it was paler than I had ever seen it. He shook his head mournfully, and intimated by signs the disappointment which this morning must witness. He was speechless. "Fate! fate!" exclaimed I in an agony of despair, "am I to be for ever baffled? Is the prize so much longed for and so ardently expected at last to escape me?"—It is not to be imagined how much these successive, endless disappointments increased my impatience, and magnified in my eyes the donation I sought.

The whole of this and the following day the stranger remained speechless. The third day, in the morning, he murmured many sounds, but in a manner so excessively inarticulate, that I was not able to understand one word in six that he said. I recollected his prediction that he should die on the fourth day. The fever of my soul was at its height. Mortal sinews and fibres could sustain no more. If the stranger had died thus, it is most probable that I should have thrown myself in anguish and rage upon his corpse, and have expired in the same hour.

In the evening of the third day I visited him again. He had thrown his robe around him, and was sitting on the side of his couch. The evening sun shot his last beams over the window-shutters. There were about eight inches between the shutter and the top of the window; and some branches of vines, with their grapes already ripe, broke the uniformity of the light. The side of the couch faced the west, and the beams played upon the old man's countenance. I had never seen it so serene. The light, already softened by the decline of day, gave it a peculiar animation: and a smile that seemed to betoken renovation and the youth of angels sat upon it. He beckoned me to approach. I placed myself beside him on the couch; he took my hand in his, and leaned his face towards me.

"I shall never witness the light of the setting sun again!" were the first words he uttered. I immediately perceived that he spoke more collectedly, and with better articulation than at any time since the paralytic stroke. Still however it was no easy matter to develop his words. But I wound up every faculty of my frame to catch them; and, assisted as I was by the habit of listening to his speech for many weeks, which during the whole of that time had never been distinct, I was successful enough to make out his entire discourse.

It continued, though with various interruptions, for more than half an hour. He explained with wonderful accuracy the whole of his secrets, and the process with which they were connected. My soul was roused to the utmost stretch of attention and astonishment. His secrets, as I have already announced in the commencement of this history, consisted of two principal particulars; the art of multiplying gold, and the power of living for ever. The detail of these secrets I omit; into that I am forbidden to enter. My design in writing this narrative, I have said, is not to teach the art of which I am in possession, but to describe the adventures it produced to me.

The more I listened, the more my astonishment grew. I looked at the old man before me; I observed the wretchedness of his appearance, the meanness of his attire, his apparent old age, his extreme feebleness, the characters of approaching death that were written on his countenance. After what I had just heard, I surveyed these things with a sensation of novelty, as if I had never remarked them in him before. I said to myself, Is this the man that possesses mines of wealth inexhaustible, and the capacity of living for ever?

Observing that he had finished his discourse, I addressed to him these words, by a sort of uncontrollable impulse, and with all the vehemence of unsated and insuppressible curiosity.

"Tell me, I adjure you by the living God, what use have you made of these extraordinary gifts? and with what events has that use been attended?"

As I spoke thus, the countenance of the old man underwent a surprising change. Its serenity vanished; his eyes rolled with an expression of agony; and he answered me thus:—

"Be silent, St. Leon! How often must I tell you that no single incident of my story shall ever be repeated! Have I no claim upon your forbearance? Can you be barbarous and inhuman enough to disturb my last scene with these bitter recollections?"—I was silent.

This is all that is material that passed at our interview.

The stranger died the next day, and was buried according to his instructions.

CHAPTER XIV.

From the moment of my last interview with the stranger I was another creature. My thoughts incessantly rolled upon his communications. They filled me with astonishment and joy, almost to bursting. I was unable to contain myself; I was unable to remain in any posture or any place. I could scarcely command myself sufficiently to perform the last duties to his body in the manner he had directed. I paced with eager step the sands of the lake; I climbed the neighbouring hills, and then descended with inconceivable rapidity to the vales below; I traced with fierce impatience the endless mazes of the wood in which I so hardly recovered my bewildered guest. The uninterruptedness and celerity of bodily motion seemed to communicate some ease to my swelling heart.

Yet there was one thing I wanted. I wanted some friendly bosom into which to pour out my feelings, and thus by participation to render my transports balsamic and tolerable. But this was for ever denied me. No human ear must ever be astonished with the story of my endowments and my privileges. I may whisper it to the woods and the waters, but not in the face of man. Not only am I bound to suppress the knowledge of the important secret I possess, but even the feelings, the ruminations, the visions, that are for ever floating in my soul. It is but a vain and frivolous distinction upon which I act, when I commit to this paper my history, and not the science which is its corner-stone. The reason why the science may not be divulged is obvious. Exhaustless wealth, if communicated to all men, would be but an exhaustless heap of pebbles and dust; and nature will not admit her everlasting laws to be so abrogated, as they would be by rendering the whole race of sublunary man immortal. But I am bound, as far as possible, not only to hide my secrets, but to conceal that I have any to hide. Senseless paper! be thou at least my confidant! To thee I may impart what my soul spurns the task to suppress. The human mind insatiably thirsts for a confidant and a friend. It is no matter that these pages shall never be surveyed by other eyes than mine. They afford at least the semblance of communication and the unburthening of the mind; and I will press the illusion fondly and for ever to my heart.

To return to the explanation of my feelings immediately after receiving possession of my grand acquisition; for, without that explanation, the spirit and meaning of my subsequent narrative will scarcely be sufficiently apprehended.

"Happy, happy, happy man!" exclaimed I, in the midst of my wanderings and reveries. "Wealth! thy power Is unbounded and inconceivable. All men bow down to thee; the most stubborn will is by thee rendered pliant as wax; all obstacles are melted down and dissolved by the ardour of thy beams! The man that possesses thee, finds every path level before him, and every creature burning to anticipate his wishes: but if these are the advantages that wealth imparts to such as possess only those scanty portions which states and nations allow to the richest, how enviable must his condition be, whose wealth is literally exhaustless and infinite! He possesses really the blessing, which priestcraft and superstition have lyingly pronounced upon the charitable: he may give away the revenues of princes, and not be the poorer. He possesses the attribute which we are accustomed to ascribe to the Creator of the universe: he may say to a man, 'Be rich,' and he is rich. He can bestow with equal facility the smallest gifts and the greatest. Palaces, as if they were the native exhalations of the soil, rise out of the earth at his bidding. He holds the fate of nations and of the world in his hand. He can remove forests, and level mountains, drain marshes, extend canals, turn the course of rivers, and shut up the sea with doors. He can assign to every individual in a nation the task he pleases, can improve agriculture, and establish manufactures, can found schools, and hospitals, and infirmaries, and universities. He can study the genius of every man, and enable every man to pursue the bent of his mind. Poets and philosophers will be fostered, the sublimest flights of genius be produced, and the most admirable discoveries effected, under his auspicious patronage. The whole world are his servants, and he, if his temper be noble and upright, will be the servant of the whole world. Nay, it cannot happen otherwise. He has as few temptations to obliquity as omnipotence itself. Weakness and want are the parents of vice. But he possesses every thing; he cannot better his situation; no man can come into rivalship or competition with him. I thank God, I have known the extremes of poverty, and therefore am properly qualified to enjoy my present happiness. I have felt a reverse of fortune, driving me in one instance to insanity, in another instance threatening to destroy me, my wife, and children together, with the plague of hunger. My heart has been racked with never-dying remorse; because, by my guilt and folly, my children have been deprived of the distinction and rank to which they were born, and plunged in remediless obscurity. Heaven has seen my sufferings, and at length has graciously said, 'It is enough.' Because I have endured more than man ever endured from the privation of fortune, God in his justice has reserved for me this secret of the transmutation of metals. I can never again fall into that wretchedness, by which my understanding was subverted, and my heart was broken."

From this part of the legacy of the stranger, my mind reverted to the other. I surveyed my limbs, all the joints and articulations of my frame, with curiosity and astonishment. "What!" exclaimed I, "these limbs, this complicated but brittle frame, shall last for ever! No disease shall attack it; no pain shall seize it; death shall withhold from it for ever his abhorred grasp! Perpetual vigour, perpetual activity, perpetual youth, shall take up their abode with me! Time shall generate in me no decay, shall not add a wrinkle to my brow, or convert a hair of my head to grey! This body was formed to die; this edifice to crumble into dust; the principles of corruption and mortality are mixed up in every atom of my frame. But for me the laws of nature are suspended; the eternal wheels of the universe roll backward; I am destined to be triumphant over fate and time!

"Months, years, cycles, centuries! To me all these are but as indivisible moments. I shall never become old; I shall always be, as it were, in the porch and infancy of existence; no lapse of years shall subtract any thing from my future duration. I was born under Louis the Twelfth; the life of Francis the First now threatens a speedy termination; he will be gathered to his fathers, and Henry his son will succeed him. But what are princes and kings and generations of men to me? I shall become familiar with the rise and fall of empires; in a little while the very name of France, my country, will perish from the face of the earth, and men will dispute about the situation of Paris, as they dispute about the site of ancient Nineveh and Babylon and Troy. Yet I shall still be young. I shall take my most distant posterity by the hand; I shall accompany them in their career; and, when they are worn out and exhausted, shall shut up the tomb over them, and set forward."

There was something however in this part of my speculation that did not entirely please me. Methought the race of mankind looked too insignificant in my eyes. I felt a degree of uneasiness at the immeasurable distance that was put between me and the rest of my species. I found myself alone in the world. Must I for ever live without a companion, a friend, any one with whom I can associate upon equal terms, with whom I can have a community of sensations, and feelings, and hopes, and desires, and fears? I experienced something, less than a wish, yet a something very capable of damping my joy, that I also were subject to mortality. I could have been well content to be partaker with a race of immortals, but I was not satisfied to be single in this respect. I was not pleased to recollect how trivial would appear to me those concerns of a few years, about which the passions of men are so eagerly occupied. I did not like the deadness of heart that seemed to threaten me. I began to be afraid of vacancy and torpor, and that my life would become too uniformly quiet. Nor did it sufficiently console me to recollect that, as one set of friends died off the stage, another race would arise to be substituted in their stead. I felt that human affections and passions are not made of this transferable stuff, and that we can love nothing truly, unless, we devote ourselves to it heart and soul, and our life is, as it, were, bound up in the object of our attachment.

It was worse when I recollected my wife and my children. When I considered for the first time that they were now in a manner nothing to me, I felt a sensation that might be said to mount to anguish. How can a man attach himself to any thing, when he comes to consider it as the mere plaything and amusement of the moment! In this statement however I am not accurate. Habit is more potent than any theoretical speculation. Past times had attached me deeply, irrevocably, to all the members of my family. But I felt that I should survive them all. They would die one by one, and leave me alone. I should drop into their graves the still renewing tear of anguish. In that tomb would my heart be buried. Never, never, through the countless ages of eternity, should I form another attachment. In the happy age of delusion, happy and auspicious at least to the cultivation of the passions, when I felt that I also was a mortal, I was capable of a community of sentiments and a going forth of the heart. But how could I, an immortal, hope ever hereafter to feel a serious, an elevating and expansive passion for the ephemeron of an hour!

As the first tumult of my thoughts subsided, I began, as is usual with persons whose minds are turned loose in the search of visionary happiness, to picture to myself, more steadily and with greater minuteness, the objects I would resolve early to accomplish. I would in the first place return to France, my adored country, the residence of my ancestors, whose annals they had adorned, whose plains had witnessed their heroic feats, and whose earth enclosed their ashes. To France I was endeared by every tie that binds the human heart; her language had been the prattle of my infancy; her national manners and temper were twined with the fibres of my constitution, and could not be rooted out; I felt that every Frenchman that lived was my brother. Banishment had only caused these prejudices to strike their tendrils deeper in my heart. I knew not that I should finally limit my abode to France. A man who, like Melchisedec, is "without end of life," may well consider himself as being also, like him, "without father, without mother, and without descent." But at all events I would first fix my children, who did not participate in my privileges, in their native soil. I would reside there myself, at least till they were fully disposed of, and till the admirable partner of the last seventeen years of my life had resigned her breath. I would immediately repurchase the property of my ancestors, which had been so distressfully resigned. The exile should return from his seven years' banishment in triumph and splendour. I would return to the court of my old patron and friend, the gallant Francis, and present to him my boy, the future representative of my family, now one year older than I had been at the field of the Cloth of Gold. Though an exile from my country, I had not been an inattentive witness of her fortunes. The year fifteen hundred and forty-four was a remarkable and interesting year in the history of France. The endless animosities of Francis and the emperor had broken out with new fury about two years before. In the spring of the present year, the count d'Anguien had won a battle in Piedmont, in which ten thousand imperialists were left dead upon the field, and which might be considered as having at length effaced the defeat of Pavia, in the same part of the world nineteen years before. The moment it had been announced that a battle was resolved on, the young nobility of France, with their characteristic ardour, had hurried to the scene, and the court of Paris was, in an instant as it were, turned into a desert. On the other hand, the emperor and the king of England had concerted for the same season a formidable plan of attack against our northern frontier. With an army of twenty-five thousand men respectively, the one on the side of Champagne, and the other of Picardy, they agreed to advance directly into the heart of the kingdom, and to unite their forces in the neighbourhood of Paris. The last intelligence that had reached me was, that Château Thierry, about twenty leagues from the metropolis, was in the hands of the emperor, and that the inhabitants of the capital, filled with consternation, were seeking their safety by flight in every direction. These circumstances had passed idly by me, and left little impression, so long as I considered myself as an obscure peasant cut off for ever from the bosom of my country. But, vested with the extraordinary powers now intrusted to me, the case was altered. I felt even a greater interest in my sovereign, now pressed down with disease and calamity, yet retaining the original alacrity and confidence of his soul, than I had done, when I saw him in all the pride of youth, and all the splendour of prosperity. I was anxious that Charles should now enter into his service; and I determined once again to assume the cuirass and the falchion, that I might be the instructor of his youth, and his pattern in feats of war. I resolved that my shepherd-boy, bred in obscurity among woods and mountains, should burst with sudden splendour upon his countrymen, and prove in the field his noble blood and generous strain. I also proposed to myself, both out of sympathy for my king, and to give greater éclat to my son's entrance into life, to replenish with my treasures the empty coffers of France, and thus to furnish what at this period seemed to be the main spring upon which the fortune of war depended. With the advantages I could afford him, the career of Charles could not fail to be rapid and illustrious, and he would undoubtedly obtain the staff of constable of France, the possessor of which, Montmorency, was now in disgrace. I would marry my daughters to such of the young nobility as I should find most distinguished in talents and spotless in character. When, by the death of her I most loved, my affections should be weaned from my country, and the scenes to which I had been accustomed were rendered painful and distressing, I would then set out upon my travels. I would travel with such splendour and profusion of expense (for this, though mortified in me by a reverse of many years' duration, continued to be the foible of my heart) as should supersede the necessity of letters of recommendation, and secure me a favourable reception wherever I appeared. I might spend a life, in a manner, in every country that was fortunate enough to allure my stay, spreading improvements, dispensing blessings, and causing all distress and calamity to vanish from before me.

CHAPTER XV.

My mind was occupied in these and similar reveries for several weeks after the death of the stranger. My wife and children had hoped, after that event, that I should have returned to the habits which had pervaded the last six years of my existence, and which they had felt so eminently productive of gratification and delight. In this hope they found themselves deceived. My domestic character was, for the present at least, wholly destroyed. I had a subject of contemplation that did not admit of a partaker, and from this subject I could not withdraw my thoughts, so much as for an instant. I had no pleasure but in that retirement, where I could be unseen and unheard by any human eye or ear. If at any time I was compelled to join the domestic circle, I despatched the occasion that brought me there as speedily as possible; and even while I remained in it, was silent and absent, engrossed with my own contemplations, and heedless and unobservant of every thing around me.

My abstraction was not however so entire as to prevent me from sometimes stealing, in a sort of momentary interregnum of thought, in that pause where the mind rests upon the chain already passed over, and seems passively to wait for the sequel, a glance at my family. I looked at them without knowing what it was that I did, and without the intention to notice what I saw. Yet, even in this state of mental abstraction, visible objects will sometimes succeed in making their impression. I perceived that my wife and children suffered from my behaviour. I remarked a general air of disconsolateness, and a mild unexpostulating submission, to what nevertheless the heart deeply deplored. They did not presume to interrupt me; they did not by prying and inquisitive speeches attempt to extort from me the secret of the alteration they saw; but it was manifest they conceived some great and radical calamity had poisoned the heart of our domestic joy.

It was these symptoms thus remarked by me, that first roused me from the inebriation of my new condition. I was compelled to suspect that, while I revelled in visions of future enjoyment, I was inflicting severe and unmerited pains on those I loved. It was necessary, if I valued their happiness, that I should descend from the clouds of speculation and fancy, and enter upon the world of realities.

But here I first found a difficulty to which, during the reign of my intoxication, I had been utterly insensible. I was rich; I could raise my family, as far as the power of money extended,—money, which may in some sense be styled the empress of the world,—to what heights I pleased. I had hitherto committed the fault, so common to projectors, of looking only to ultimate objects and great resting places, and neglecting to consider the steps between. This was an omission of high importance. Every thing in the world is conducted by gradual process. This seems to be the great principle of harmony in the universe. Nothing is abrupt; one thing is so blended and softened into another, that it is impossible to say where the former ends and the latter begins.

This remark is fully applicable to the situation which was now before me. Yesterday I was poor; to-day I was possessor of treasures inexhaustible. How was this alteration to be announced? To dissipate the revenues of princes, to purchase immense estates, to launch into costly establishments, are tasks to which the most vulgar mind is equal. But no man stands alone in the world, without all trace of what he has been, and with no one near, that thinks himself entitled to scrutinise his proceedings and his condition. Least of all was this my case. I was bound to certain other persons by the most sacred obligations; I could not separate myself from them; I could not render myself a mere enigma in their eyes; though, in the language of the world, the head of my family, they were my natural censors and judges. I was accountable to them for my conduct; it was my duty, paramount to all other duties, to stand as a fair, upright, and honourable character in their estimation.

If these remarks be true taken in a general view, they are much more so when applied to my particular case. There are men who live in the midst of their families like an eastern despot surrounded with his subjects. They are something too sacred to be approached; their conduct is not to be reasoned upon; the amount of their receipts and disbursements is not to be inspected; their resources are unknown; no one must say to them, What dost thou? or, why hast thou thus conducted thyself? Even these persons will not escape the tax to which all men are liable. They cannot kill the general spirit of enquiry; the mystery in which they wrap themselves will often serve as an additional stimulus; they will finally encounter the judgment and verdict of all. For myself, I had lived in the midst of my family upon a system of paternal and amicable commerce. I had suffered too deeply from a momentary season of separation and mystery, not to have been induced to renounce it decisively and for ever.

Firm, however, as I had imagined my renunciation to have been, I was now thrown back upon what I had most avoided. I had a secret source of advantage, the effects of which were to be participated by those I loved, while the spring was to remain for ever unknown. What I most sought upon this occasion, was, that my family should share my good fortune, and at the same time be prevented from so much as suspecting that there was any thing mysterious connected with it. To effect this, I presently conceived that it would be necessary to sacrifice the sudden and instantaneous prosperity I had proposed to myself, and introduce the reverse of our condition by slow, and, as far as possible, insensible degrees.

One thing on which I determined, preparatory to the other measures I had in view, was to remove from my present habitation, and take up my residence for a time in the city of Constance. In the cottage of the mountains it was impossible to make any material alteration in my establishment. My property was of the narrowest extent; nor would it be easily practicable in a country, the inhabitants of which were accustomed to a humble allotment, considerably to enlarge it. My house was frugal, if not mean; and, unless it were first pulled down and built over again, the idea of introducing servants, equipage, or splendour into it, would be absurd. My design was not to make a long abode where I now was; but, as soon as my family should be sufficiently prepared for the transition, to return to my native country. I believed in the mean time, that, in the capital of the bishopric, where my name was scarcely remembered by a single individual, I should be more at liberty to proceed as circumstances suggested, than in my present rural situation, where every neighbour regarded himself as vested with a sort of inquisitorial power over all around him.

To account for this measure to my family, I felt it incumbent on me to confess to them a certain pecuniary acquisition. The story that most readily suggested itself, was that of the stranger having left behind him a certain sum of which he made a donation to me. This, though in the plain and direct sense of the terms it were false, yet in its spirit bore a certain resemblance to the truth; and, with that resemblance, in spite of the rigid adherence to veracity, that first ornament of a gentleman, that most essential prerequisite to the regard and affection of others, which I had hitherto maintained, I was induced to content myself. What could I do? I was compelled to account for appearances; I was forbidden by the most solemn injunctions to unfold the truth. I should indeed have felt little complacence in the disclosure; I should have been reluctant to announce a circumstance which, as I began to feel, introduced a permanent difference and separation between me and my family.

The sum at which I fixed the legacy of the stranger was three thousand crowns. I was not inattentive to the future; I should have been glad, by my present account, to have furnished a more ample solution for circumstances which might occur hereafter. But some regard was due to probability. An unknown, a solitary man, broken with age, who arrived on foot, and who declined all aid and attendance, must not be represented as possessing mines of treasure.

It was some time before I could prevail on myself to break my story to the inhabitants of my cottage. As the time approached when I was to bid an everlasting farewell to rural obscurity and a humble station, they seemed to adorn themselves in new charms. I was like the son of a king, who had hitherto been told by his attendants that he was a mere villager, and who, while his youthful imagination is dazzled by the splendour that awaits him, yet looks back with a wistful eye upon his mirthful sports, his former companions, and the simple charms of her who first obtained his guileless love. I announced my acquisition and my purpose with a faltering tongue and a beating heart.

I could perceive that my tale produced few emotions of pleasure in those who heard it. Julia and her mother, especially, were warmly attached to their retirement; and the scenes which had witnessed so many pleasurable incidents and emotions. Chagrin, in spite of themselves, made a transient abode upon their countenances; but the unresisting mildness of the one, and the considerate attachment of the other, prevented, for the present, their sensations from breaking out into words. The feelings, however, that they consigned to silence, did not entirely escape the notice of the lively little Marguerite. She sympathised with them, probably without being aware that they were sad. She came towards me, and, with much anxiety in her enquiring face, asked why we must go away from the cottage? If I had got some money I might go to the town, and buy sweetmeats, and ribands, and new clothes, and a hundred more pretty things, and bring them home. For her part, she should be better pleased to put on her finery, and make her feast in the pretty old summer-house, now she was again permitted to go and play in it, than in a palace all stuck over with emeralds and rubies. Her mother wiped away a tear at the innocent speech of her darling, kissed her, and bid her go and feed the hen and her chickens. Charles was the only one in whom I could observe any pleasure at my intelligence. He was not as yet skilful enough to calculate the advantages that three thousand crowns could purchase. But I could see joy sparkle in his eyes, as I announced my intention of bidding adieu to retirement, and taking up my rest in the capital of the district. His veins swelled with the blood of his ancestors; his mind was inured to the contemplation of their prowess. Already sixteen years of age, he had secretly burned to go forth into the world, to behold the manners of his species, and to establish for himself a claim to some rank in their estimation. He had pined in thought at the mediocrity of our circumstances, and the apparent impossibility of emerging; for he regarded the duty of contributing his labour to the subsistence of the family, as the first of all obligations; and the more the bent of his spirit struggled against it, the more resolutely he set himself to comply.

The rest of the family were no sooner retired, than Marguerite, finding in what I had just announced to all, an occasion from the use of which she could not excuse herself, took this opportunity of unburthening the grief which had long been accumulating in her mind.

"St. Leon," said she, "listen kindly to what I am going to say to you, and assure yourself that I am actuated by no spleen, resentment, or ill-humour, but by the truest affection. I perceive I have lost, in your apprehension, the right of advising you. I am no longer the partner of your counsels; I am no longer the confident of your thoughts. You communicate nothing but what you cannot suppress; and that you communicate to your whole family assembled. Heaven knows how dear to me is every individual of that family! but my love for them does not hide from me what is due to myself. I know that a husband, who felt as a husband ought, and, give me leave to say, as I have deserved you should feel towards me, could not act as you have acted to-night.

"You must excuse my reminding you of some things which you seem to have forgotten. I would not mention them, if they had not been forgotten when they ought to have been remembered. I have lived seventeen years with you; my whole study had been your advantage and pleasure. Have you any thing to reproach me with? Point out to me, if in any thing I could have added to your pleasure, and have neglected it! What I have done, has not been the ceremonious discharge of a duty; it has been the pure emanation of an attachment that knew no bounds. I have passed with you through good fortune and ill fortune. When we were rich, I entered with my whole heart into your pleasures, because they were yours. When we were poor, I endured every hardship without a murmur; I watched by you, I consoled you, I reconciled you to yourself. I do not mean to make a merit of all this: no! Reginald! I could not have acted otherwise if I would.

"Do me the justice to recollect, that I have not been a complaining or irritable companion. In all our adversities, in the loss of fortune, and the bitter consequences of that loss, I never uttered a reproachful word. What poverty, sorrow, hunger and famine never extorted from me, you have at length wrung from my bleeding heart. St. Leon! I have known your bosom-thoughts. In no former instance has your affection or your confidence been alienated from me; and that consoled me for all the rest. But now, for three months, the case has been entirely altered. You have during all that time been busy, pensive, and agitated; but I have been as much a stranger to your meditations as if I had never been accustomed to be their depository. You have not scrupled to inflict a wound upon me that no subsequent change will ever be able to cicatrise. Nor indeed do I see any likelihood of a change. You announce our removal to Constance; what we are to do next, with what views, or for what purpose, I am ignorant.

"I have made my election. My heart is formed for affection, and must always feel an uneasy void and desolation without it. If you had thus robbed me of your attachment in an early period of our intercourse, I know not upon what extremity my disappointment and anguish might have driven me. They are harder to bear now; but I submit. It is too late either for relief or remedy. What remains of my powers and my strength I owe to my children. I will not seduce them from their father. They may be benefited by his purse or his understanding, though, like me, they should be deprived of his affection. You may be their friend when I am no more. I feel that this will not last long. I feel that the main link that bound me to existence cannot be snapped, and thus snapped by unkindness worse than death, without promising soon to put a period to my miseries. I shall be your victim in death, after having devoted my life to you, in a way in which few women were ever devoted to their husbands.

"But this is not what I purposed chiefly to say. This is what my situation and my feelings have unwillingly wrung from me. Though you have injured me in the tenderest point, I still recollect what you were to me. I still feel deeply interested in your welfare, and the fair fame you are to transmit to your children. I entreat you then to reflect deeply, before you proceed further. You seem to me to stand upon a precipice; nor do the alteration that has taken place in your manners, and the revolution of your heart, lead me to augur favourably of the plans you have formed. What is this stranger? Whence came he? Why did he hide himself, and why was he pursued by the officers of justice? Had he no relations? Was his bequest of the sum he had about him his own act, and who is the witness to its deliberateness or its freedom? You must not think that the world is inattentive to the actions of men or their circumstances; if it were, the fame we prize would be an empty bauble. No, sir, a fair fame can only be secured by unequivocal proceedings. What will, what can, be thought of your giving shelter to an unknown, a man accused of crimes, a man never beheld even by an individual of your own family, and upon the strength of whose alleged bequest you are about to change the whole mode of your life?

"Nor, Reginald, must you think me credulous enough to imagine that you have now disclosed the whole or the precise truth. Three thousand crowns is not a sum sufficient to account for what you propose, for the long agitation of your thoughts, or for the change of character you have sustained. You must either be totally deprived of rational judgment, or there must be something behind, that you have not communicated. What do you purpose in going to reside in the midst of a city foreign to the manners of a Frenchman, distracted with internal broils, and embittered to us by the recollection of the extremities we personally suffered in it? Is your ambition sunk so low, that it can be gratified by such a transition? No; you mean more than you have announced; you mean something you are unwilling to declare. Consider that meaning well! Put me out of the question! I am nothing, and no longer desire to be any thing. But do not involve yourself in indelible disgrace, or entail upon your memory the curses of your children!"

What a distress was mine, who, in return to so generous and noble an expostulation, could impart no confidence, and indulge no sincerity! I felt a misery, of which, till this hour, I had been unable to form a conception. Fool that I was, I had imagined that, when endowed with the bequests of the stranger, no further evil could approach me! I had, in my visionary mood, created castles and palaces, and expatiated in the most distant futurity! and here I was, stopped and disappointed at the threshold, in the very first step of my proceedings. What I could however I did; I poured forth to Marguerite, not the secrets of my understanding, but the overpowering emotions of my soul.

"Best, most adorable of women!" cried I, "how you rend my heart with the nobleness of your remonstrances! Never was man blessed with a partner so accomplished and exemplary as I have been! Do you think your merits can ever be obliterated from my memory? Do you think the feelings of gratitude and admiration can ever be weakened in my bosom, or that the strength and singleness of my attachment can suffer decay? Bear me witness, Heaven! I know no creature on the face of the earth that can enter into competition with you; there is not the thing in nature that I prize in comparison. I love you a thousand times better than myself, and would die with joy to purchase your ease and satisfaction. I can never repay the benefits you have conferred on me; I can never rise to an equality with you.

"What anguish then do you inflict upon me, when you talk of becoming the victim of my unkindness? Believe you I can endure, after having dissipated your patrimony and drawn you with me into exile, after having experienced from you a tenderness such as man never in any other instance obtained from woman, to entertain the idea of embittering the remainder of your life, and shortening your existence? I should regard myself as the most execrable of monsters. I could not live under the recollection of so unheard-of a guilt. If you would not have me abhor myself and curse existence, live, confide in me, and be happy!

"Oh, Marguerite! how wretched and pitiable is my situation! Make some allowance for me! I have a secret that I would give worlds to utter, but dare not. Do not imagine that there is, or can be, any decay in my affection! Confide in me! Allow to necessity, what never, never could be the result of choice! In all things else, you shall know my inmost heart, as you possess the boundless and unalterable affections of my soul."

Marguerite was somewhat, but not wholly, soothed by the earnestness of my protestations. She saw, for the prescience of the heart is never deceived, that a blow was given to the entireness of our affection, from which it would never recover. She felt, for in truth and delicacy of sentiment she was much my superior, that the reserve, in which I persisted, and for which I deprecated excuse, might be sufficiently consistent with a vulgar attachment, but would totally change the nature of ours. She was aware that it related to no ordinary point, that it formed the pole-star of my conduct, that it must present itself afresh from day to day, and that in its operation it amounted to a divorce of the heart. She submitted however, and endeavoured to appear cheerful. Though she felt the worm of sorrow gnawing her vitals, she was unwilling to occasion me an uneasiness it was in her power to withhold. She was struck with the consistency and determination of my resistance, and expostulated no more.

We went to Constance. We bade adieu to the scene of a six years' happiness, such as the earth has seldom witnessed. I alone had occasioned some imperfection in that happiness. There were times indeed when, sitting in affectionate communion with my wife, and surrounded by my children, my sensations had been as delicious as the state of human existence ever had to boast. I felt my heart expand; I was conscious to the unreserved union that subsisted among us; I felt myself identified with all that I loved, and all for whom my heart was anxious. But the curse entailed upon me from the earliest period to which my memory can reach, operated even in the cottage of the lake. I was not formed to enjoy a scene of pastoral simplicity. Ambition still haunted me; an uneasiness, scarcely defined in its object, from time to time recurred to my mind. If I thought I wanted nothing for myself, I deemed a career of honour due to my children. Again, when I regarded honour as an empty phantom, and persuaded myself that all conditions of life were intrinsically equal, I recollected the fearful scene where hunger and destruction had hung over us in Constance, and in imagination often pictured to myself that scene as on the point of being renewed. The sword of the demon, famine, seemed to my disturbed apprehension to be suspended over us by a hair. Such had been the draught of bitterness that occasionally detracted from this most enviable, as in retrospect I am willing to denominate it, period of my existence.

We quitted our rural retreat, and took up our abode in a prosperous mercantile city. I hired commodious apartments in one of the grand squares, not far from the spot where the fairs are usually held. Undoubtedly there was nothing in this residence very congenial to the bent of my disposition, or the projects that fermented in my mind. I had merely chosen it by way of interval, and to soften the transition from what I had been, to what I purposed to be. In the multitude of irresolute thoughts with which I laboured, the small distance of Constance from the cottage of the lake, made me feel as if the removal thither was one of the gentlest and most moderate measures to which I could have recourse.

I had never been less happy and at peace with myself than I was now. From general society and the ordinary intercourse of acquaintance I had long been estranged, and it was in vain that I endeavoured to return to habits of that sort. The society which the city of Constance afforded had few charms for me. It had no pretensions to the politeness, the elegance, the learning or the genius, an intercourse with which had once been familiar to me. It scarcely contained within its walls any but such as were occupied in merchandise or manufacture. The attention of its inhabitants were divided between these objects, and the encroachments which were making upon the ancient religion by the Confession of Augsburg and the dogmas of Calvin. The majority of the inhabitants were protestants; and, a few years before, they had expelled their bishop and the canons of their cathedral. Having however miscarried in a religious war into which they had entered, these dignitaries had been reinstalled in their functions and emoluments. The situation thus produced was an unnatural one; and a storm was evidently brewing more violent than any which the city had yet sustained. The gloomy temper and melancholy austerity of the reformers were as little congenial to my temper, as the sordid ignorance and selfishness of the trading spirit of the community.

I therefore lived in a state of seclusion. I endeavoured to seek amusement in such novelties and occupations as might present themselves to a person disengaged from the general vortex. But, if the distinguished sphere in which I had once moved disqualified me for taking an interest in these puerilities, the anticipations in which I indulged of the future disqualified me still more. My domestic scene too no longer afforded me the consolation and relief I had been accustomed to derive from it. Marguerite exerted herself to appear cheerful and contented; but it was an exertion. I began to fear that the arrow of disappointment had indeed struck her to the heart. I was anxiously occupied in considering what I was to do next. I hoped that our next step might operate to revive her gaiety, and by additional splendour amuse her solicitude. I began to fear that I had taken a wrong method, and entered the career of a better fortune with too much caution and timidity. At all events I felt that we no longer lived together as we had done. There was no more opening of the heart between us, no more infantine guilelessness and sincerity, no more of that unapprehensive exposure of every thought of the soul, that adds the purest zest to the pleasures of domestic life. We stood in awe of each other; each was to the other in some degree an intrusive and unwelcome spy upon what was secretly passing in the mind. There may be persons who regard this as an evil very capable of being endured; but they must be such as never knew the domestic joys I once experienced. The fall from one of these conditions of life to the other was too bitter.

CHAPTER XVI.

Anxious to divert my thoughts from what I hoped was only a temporary evil, I determined, accompanied by Charles, to make a tour of some of the cities of Germany. Dresden was the capital to which I was most desirous of conducting him. Maurice, duke of Saxony, who held his court there, and who was now only twenty-three years of age, was incomparably the most accomplished prince of the empire. Desirous as I was that my only son should fill a distinguished career, I thought I could not better prepare him for the theatre of his native country, than by thus initiating him beforehand in scenes of distinction and greatness.

He was delighted with his tour. We had not proceeded many leagues from Constance, before, indulging in the bent of my mind, I laid aside the humbleness of our appearance, and the obscure style in which we travelled; and having procured a numerous cavalcade of horses and servants, I set forward with considerable magnificence. We passed through Munich, Ratisbon, and Prague. At Munich we found the court of the elector palatine; the diet of the empire was sitting at Ratisbon, when we arrived at that city. Charles had been almost entirely a stranger to every thing princely and magnificent from the time he was nine years of age; and he was now exactly at that period of human life when external appearances are apt to make the strongest impression. To him every thing that occurred seemed like transportation into a new world. The figure we made procured us, as strangers, unquestioned admission into every circle. We mixed with princes, ourselves in garb and figure confounded with those we saw. I had lived too much and too long in the most splendid society, to find difficulty in resuming the unembarrassed and courtly manners which I had for years laid aside; and Charles might be said to see his father in a new character. Novelty prompted his admiration; he was intoxicated with wonder. His disposition had always led him to bold and adventurous conceptions; nothing less than an imperious sense of duty could have restrained him from quitting our cottage, and casting himself upon the world in search of honour and distinction. His generous heart had beat to burst away from the obscurity of his station; and it was with impatience and discontent that he looked forward to the life of a swain. Yet he knew not how to break through the obstacles that confined him. It was therefore with transports of pleasure that he saw them vanishing as of themselves, and the career of glory opening, as if by enchantment, to his eager steps.

The court of Dresden was infinitely more delightful to him than the court of Munich, or the imperial display at Ratisbon. Here Charles saw a young prince in the flower of his age, whose talents and spirit rendered him the universal object of attention and adoration. He remarked, in the fire of his eyes, the vivacity of his gestures, and the grandeur of his port, something inexpressibly different from those princes, of whom it is necessary that their rank should be announced to you by some extrinsic circumstance, that you may not mistake them for a merchant's clerk or a city magistrate. The sentiment that he breathed, as it were instinctively, as we returned from the first time of our seeing duke Maurice, was, "At twenty-three years of age may I, in appearance, accomplishments, and spirit, resemble this man!"

Here I was desirous of making a longer stay than at the cities through which we had previously passed, and of procuring for my son some personal intercourse with this great ornament of the age. I judged this to be the more easy, as, in our first visit to the palace, I had perceived some French noblemen of the Protestant persuasion, who had resorted to the duke's court in search of employment. They appeared not to know me; but that was little to be wondered at, considering that I had been seven years absent from my country, and that the calamities by which I had been overtaken more than once during that period, might be supposed to have produced a greater effect upon me than the mere lapse of years would have done. Among the rest I remarked Gaspar de Coligny, who was only twenty-one years of age at the time I quitted France, and had then been remarked as one of the most promising young men his country had to boast. His stay here was expected to be short; his hopes in his own country, from the greatness of his connections, were of the highest class; and he had only come to Dresden at the earnest invitation of duke Maurice, who entertained an ardent affection for him. My heart led me towards him; policy concurred in dictating the application, as, if I were fortunate enough to gain his favour, my son could not have a friend better qualified either to form his character or forward his advancement.

I wrote to Coligny to announce my request to him, and in a few hours after the delivery of my letter that young nobleman came in person to wait on me. He informed me that he had done so, because he had something of delicacy to mention, which he did not choose to trust to the intermission of a third person, and upon which, as he hoped I could remove his scruple, he did not like even to bestow the formality of putting it on paper.

"I am a gentleman of France," said Coligny; "you will excuse my frankness. I am a gentleman of France; you will not wonder at the niceness of my honour. Mixing in society, I do not pretend minutely to investigate the character of every person with whom I converse; but what you ask of me obliges me to consult my understanding, and enquire into facts. I cannot consent to vouch for any man's character to another, till I have paid some attention to the ground upon which that character rests.

"I remember the count de St. Leon with pleasure and advantage at the court of my own sovereign. Every one admired his accomplishments, his gallantry, and his learning; every one spoke of him with respect. Unfortunate circumstances, as we all understood, deprived you of your patrimony; that is nothing to me; I respect a nobleman in misfortune, as much as when he is surrounded with wealth and splendour. You retired into voluntary exile; I heard, with great grief, of some subsequent calamities that have overtaken you. But, here in Saxony, I see you resuming all your former splendour, and coming forward with the magnificence of a prince. Other of your countrymen have remarked it, as well as myself, and feel themselves at a loss to account for what they see.

"Excuse me, count! by your application to me, you oblige me to speak freely. I dare say you can clear up the difficulty, and account for this second revolution in your fortune, upon which I shall then be the first to congratulate you. I cannot suspect a man, with your high descent and the illustrious character you formerly maintained, of any thing dishonourable. But you have not sufficiently considered the account we all owe to one another, and the clearness of proceeding we are obliged to maintain, not only to our own hearts, but in the face of the world. The present occasion is, I trust, fortunate for you; and, when you have assisted me in complying with the rules by which every honourable man governs himself, I shall be eager to publish your justification, and render you all the service in my power."

I was ready to burst with astonishment and vexation during this representation of Coligny. I could feel my colour change from pale to red, and from red to pale. I could only answer with suffocation and inward rage, that I was much obliged to him; I would consider what he said; I would acquaint him with my justification; and, whenever it was made, he might be assured it should be an ample one.—I was cautious as to what I uttered; I could not immediately foresee what it was eligible, or what it was possible, to do; and I was resolved that I would not, by an idle or hasty expression, preclude myself, in a matter of so much moment, from the benefits of future deliberation. If what I had just heard had come from any other person, I should probably have despised it; but I felt at once that Gaspar de Coligny might be considered, in a case of this sort, as the representative of all that was most honourable and illustrious in my native country.— Finding that I was indisposed to any further communication on the subject, he took a polite leave, and departed.

I was no sooner alone than I felt myself overwhelmed with mortification and shame. I had rejoiced in the bequests of the stranger, because I regarded them as the means of restoring me to splendour, and replacing my children in the situation to which they were entitled by their birth. Was that which I had regarded as the instrument of their glory, to become the medium of their ignominy and disgrace? I had suffered all other misfortunes, but the whisper of dishonour had never been breathed against me. I was a son of honour, descended of a race of heroes, and cradled in the lap of glory and fame. When we quitted Paris in the year 1537, my incomparable wife had set to sale our entire property, resolved that, though driven into exile, we would not leave it in the power of the meanest individual to controvert the sacred attention we yielded to every just obligation. Since that time I had declined from the splendour of rank to the humble situation of a rustic, cultivating my little property with my own hands; nay, I had even, for a short time, hired myself as a labourer in the garden of the bishop of Constance. But the same disdain of every thing disgraceful had followed me to my cottage and my truckle bed, which I had originally learned in the halls of chivalry and the castle of my ancestors. Accordingly I had uniformly retained the same honourable character and spotless fame. St. Leon, the virtuous cottager, had in nothing blemished the name of St. Leon, surrounded with glory in the siege of Pavia. Often, and with pride, had I pointed out this circumstance to my son, adding, Wherever fortune calls you, for whatever scenes you may be reserved, remember that your father was unfortunate, but that through life he never acted a deed nor conceived a thought, that should stain your manly cheeks with the blush of shame! I stand before you a culprit, as having robbed you of your patrimony, but I have preserved for you entire the inheritance of our honour!

This had been the first lesson imprinted upon my infant mind. All other possessions I had ever held cheap and worthless in comparison with that of an illustrious name. My indignation at the attack it now sustained was boundless. The more I thought, the more intolerable it appeared. I was impatient and furious, like a lion struggling in the toils. I could with joy have trampled under my feet whoever aspersed me. I could have wantoned in blood, and defied my adversaries to mortal combat. Alas, all my fury was useless here! It was no tale whispered in the dark that I had to contend with; it was the commentary of the world upon incontestable facts. Though a hecatomb of souls should be sacrificed at the shrine of my blasted name, the facts would still remain, the mystery still require to be solved. Coligny, the virtuous Coligny, had made no observations on the circumstances he mentioned; he merely proposed a difficulty, and waited my answer.

I was called upon to exercise the whole of my deliberative powers as to the reply which was to be returned, or the conduct to be held, upon the question of Coligny. Every thing I most valued was now at issue; and a false step taken under the present circumstances could never be retrieved. I had another sort of party to deal with here, than when I had told Marguerite the tale of the stranger and his legacy. Nothing would pass now, but what bore an open, fair, and unequivocal appearance. I must vent no assertion that could not bear to be sifted to the bottom, and that did not fully accord with all the vouchers with which it could be collated. I had written to Marguerite, immediately after launching into the expense with which our tour had been attended, that I had received an unexpected acquisition from the death of a relation of my own family in France. I knew that the story of the three thousand crowns would no longer account for the style in which I was proceeding, and this fabrication suggested itself upon the spur of the moment. I hated to think of the difficulties in the way of explanation in which I was involved; I abhorred the system of falsehood I was driven to practise. It did not occur to me at the time, infatuated as I was! that I should have occasion to account for this accession of wealth to any one out of my own family. Marguerite, I well knew, had no correspondence in France, nor therefore any obvious means of verifying or refuting this second deception. But such a story could not be told to noblemen of France, without being instantly liable to be compared with known facts, and eventually investigated upon the spot where the scene was laid. Marguerite herself, I well knew, had listened with incredulity to the explanation I had made, and the alleged legacy of the stranger; what could I expect from indifferent hearers? They might not all possess her good sense and sagacity in judging; but they were destitute of that personal kindness and partiality which were calculated to induce her to credit whatever I affirmed. Most men have a malignant pleasure in the detection of specious pretences, in humbling the importunate superiority that obscures their claims, and removing the rival who might otherwise acquire the prize of which they are in pursuit.

My mind was still torn and distracted with these contemplations, when in the afternoon of the same day on which I had received the visit of Coligny, my attention was suddenly roused by the abrupt entrance of my son into the chamber where I was sitting. He opened the door with a hurried action as he entered, and, having closed it impetuously after him, advanced directly towards me. He then stopped himself; and, turning from me, I could perceive a rush of crimson in his face like that of a man suffocated. A passion of tears succeeded that shook his frame, and sufficiently proved that his feelings had sustained some extraordinary shock. My whole soul was alarmed at what I saw; and, following him as he retired to the other side of the room, in the gentlest accents I endeavoured to soothe him, while I enquired with earnestness and trepidation into the cause of his grief.

CHAPTER XVII.

He repelled me. "Sit down, sir, sit down! Do not follow me, I beg of you; but sit down!"

His manner was earnest and emphatical. Mechanically and without knowing what I did, I obeyed his direction. He came towards me.

"I have no time," added he, "for qualifying and form. Tell me! am I the son of a man of honour or a villain?"

He saw I was shocked at the unexpected rudeness of his question.

"Forgive me, my father! I have always been affectionate and dutiful; I have ever looked up to you as my model and my oracle. But I have been insulted! It never was one of your lessons to teach me to bear an insult!"

"Is it," replied I, with the sternness that the character of a father will seldom fail to inspire under such circumstances, "because you have been insulted, that you think yourself authorised to come home and insult him to whom you owe nothing but respect and reverence?"

"Stop, sir! Before you claim my reverence, you must show your title to it, and wipe off the aspersions under which you at present labour."

"Insolent, presumptuous boy! Know that I am not by you to be instructed in my duty, and will not answer so rude a questioner! The down as yet scarcely shades your school-boy's cheek; and have you so forgotten the decencies of life as to scoff your father?"—His eye brightened as I spoke.

"You are right, sir. It gives me pleasure to see your blood rise in return to my passion. Your accent is the accent of innocence. But, indeed! the more innocent and noble you shall prove yourself, the more readily will you forgive my indignation."

"I cannot tell. My temper does not fit me to bear the rudeness of a son. Nor do I think that such behaviour as this can be any credit to you, whatever may have been the provocation. Tell me however what is the insult that has thus deeply shaken you?"

"I went this afternoon to the tennis-court near the river, and played several games with the young count Luitmann. While we were playing, came in the chevalier Dupont, my countryman. The insolence of his nature is a subject of general remark; and he has, though I know not for what reason, conceived a particular animosity to me. A trifling dispute arose between us. We gradually warmed. He threatened to turn me out of the court; I resented the insult; and he passionately answered, that the son of an adventurer and a sharper had no business there, and he would take care I should never be admitted again. I attempted to strike him, but was prevented; and presently learned that the sudden and unexplained way in which we have emerged from poverty was the ground of his aspersion. As I gained time, and reflected more distinctly upon what was alleged, I felt that personal violence could never remove an accusation of this sort. I saw too, though, intoxicated as I had idly been with the unwonted splendour to which I was introduced, I had not adverted to it at the time, that the case was of a nature that required explanation. I had been accustomed to reverence and an implicit faith in the wisdom and rectitude of my parents, and therefore encountered in silent submission the revolution of our fortune. But this neutrality will suffice no longer.

"To you, sir, I resort for explanation. Send me back to the insolent youth and his companions, with a plain and unanswerable tale, that may put to silence for ever these brutal scoffs and reproaches. Let it be seen this night which of the two has most fully merited to be thrust out of honourable society. I trust I have not so demeaned myself but that our mutual companions will join to compel this unmannered boor to retract his aspersions."

"Charles, you are too warm and impetuous!"—

"Too warm, sir! when I hear my father loaded with the foulest appellations?"

"You are young and ill qualified to terminate in the proper way a business of this serious aspect: leave it to me!"

115

"Excuse me, my father! Though the names I have repeated were bestowed upon you, it was against me that the insult was employed. I must return immediately, and obtain justice. This is a moment that must in some degree fix my character for fortitude and determination, and I cannot withdraw from the duty it imposes. Only tell me what I have to say. Furnish me with a direct and unambiguous explanation of what Dupont has objected to us, and I undertake for the rest."

"I see, my son, that you are moved, and I will trust you!"

He seized my hand, he gazed earnestly in my face, he seemed prepared to devour every word I should utter.

"Gaspar de Coligny, the flower of the French nobility, has been with me this morning. He has stated to me in an ingenuous and friendly way the same difficulty with which Dupont has so brutally taunted you. I was meditating and arranging my answer but now, when you entered the room."

As I uttered these words, Charles let go my hand, and withdrew his eyes, with evident tokens of disappointment and chagrin. He paused for a few moments, and then resumed:—

"Why do you tell me of meditation and arrangement! Why did you send away Coligny unanswered, or why baffle and evade the earnestness of my enquiries? I know not all the sources of wealth; but I cannot doubt that the medium through which wealth has honourably flowed may, without effort and premeditation, easily be explained. A just and a brave man acts fearlessly and with explicitness; he does not shun, but court, the scrutiny of mankind; he lives in the face of day, and the whole world confesses the clearness of his spirit and the rectitude of his conduct.

"Sir, I have just set my foot on the threshold of life. There is one lesson you have taught me, which I swear never to forget,—to hold life and all its pleasures cheap, in comparison with an honourable fame. My soul burns with the love of distinction. I am impatient to burst away from the goal, and commence the illustrious career. I feel that I have a hand and a heart capable of executing the purposes that my soul conceives. Uninured to dishonour, or to any thing that should control the passion of my bosom, think, sir, what are my emotions at what has just occurred!

"I was bred in obscurity and a humble station. I owed this disadvantage, you tell me, to your error. I forgave you; I was content; I felt that it was incumbent on me by my sword and my own exertions to hew my way to distinction. You have since exchanged the lowness of our situation for riches and splendour. At this revolution I felt no displeasure; I was well satisfied to start upon more advantageous terms in the race I determined to run. But, sir, whence came these riches? Riches and poverty are comparatively indifferent to me; but I was not born to be a mark for shame to point her finger at. A little while ago you were poor; you were the author of your own poverty; you dissipated your paternal estate. Did I reproach you? No; you were poor, but not dishonoured! I attended your couch in sickness; I exerted my manual labour to support you in affliction. I honoured you for your affection to my mother; I listened with transport to the history of your youth; I was convinced I should never blush to call Reginald de St. Leon my father. I believed that lessons of honour, so impressive as those you instilled into my infant mind, could never flow but from an honourable spirit. Oh, if there is any thing equivocal or ignoble in the riches we have displayed, restore me, instantly restore me, to unblemished and virtuous poverty!"

I was astonished at the firmness and manliness of spirit that Charles upon this occasion discovered. I could scarcely believe that these were the thoughts and words of a youth under seventeen years of age. I felt that every thing illustrious and excellent might be augured of one who, at these immature years, manifested so lofty and generous a soul. I could have pressed him in my arms, have indulged my emotions in sobs and tears of transport, and congratulated myself that I was father to so worthy a son. But his temper and manners awed, and held me at a distance. This was one consequence of the legacies of the stranger!

"Charles!" said I, "your virtues extort my confidence. For the world a tale must be prepared that shall serve to elude its curiosity and its malice. But to you I confess, there is a mystery annexed to the acquisition of this wealth that can never be explained."

He stood aghast at my words. "Am I to believe my ears? A tale prepared? A mystery never to be explained? I adjure you by all that you love, and all that you hold sacred———!"

His voice was drowned in a sudden gush of tears. With an action of earnestness and deprecation, he took hold of my hand.

"No, sir, no artful tale, no disguise, no hypocrisy!———" As he spoke, his voice suddenly changed, his accent became clear and determined.—"Will you consent this very hour to quit the court of Dresden, and to resign fully and without reserve this accursed wealth, for the acquisition of which you refuse to account?"

"Whence," replied I, "have you the insolence to make such a proposal?———No, I will not!"

"Then I swear by the omnipresent and eternal God, you shall never see or hear of me more!"

I perceived that this was no time for the assertion of paternal authority. I saw that the poor boy was strangely and deeply moved, and I endeavoured to soothe him. I felt that the whole course of his education had inspired him with an uncontrollable and independent spirit, and that it was too late to endeavour to repress it.

"My dear Charles," said I, "what is come to you? When I listen to a language like this from your lips, I scarcely know you for my son. This impertinent Dupont has put you quite beside yourself. Another time we will talk over the matter calmly; and depend upon it, every thing shall be made out to your satisfaction."

"Do not imagine, sir, that my self-possession is not perfect and complete. I know what I do, and my resolution is unalterable. If you have any explanation to give, give it now. If you will yield to my proposal, declare your assent, and I am again your son. But to bear the insults of my fellows unanswered, or to live beneath the consciousness of an artful and fictitious tale, no consideration on earth shall induce me. I love you, sir; I cannot forget your lessons or your virtues. I love my mother and my sisters; no words can tell how dearly and how much. But my resolution is taken; I separate myself from you all and for ever. Nothing in my mind can come in competition with a life of unblemished honour."

"And are you such a novice, as to need the being told that honour is a prize altogether out of the reach of an unknown and desolate wanderer, such as you propose to become? My wealth, boy, is unlimited, and can buy silence from the malicious, and shouts and applause from all the world. A golden key unlocks the career of glory, which the mean and the pennyless are never allowed to enter."

"I am not such a novice, as not to have heard the language of vice, though I never expected to hear it from a father. Poverty with integrity shall content me. The restless eagerness of my spirit is so great, that I will trust to its suggestions, and hope to surmount the obstacles of external appearance. If I am disappointed in this, and destined to perish unheard of and unremembered, at least I will escape reproach. I will neither be charged with the deeds, nor give utterance to the maxims, of dishonour."

"Charles," replied I, "be not the calumniator of your father! I swear to you by every thing that is sacred; and you know my integrity; never did the breath of falsehood pollute these lips;———"

He passionately interrupted me. "Did the stranger bequeath you three thousand crowns? Have you lately received an unexpected acquisition by the death of a near relation in France?"

I was silent. This was not a moment for trifling and equivocation.

"Oh, my father, how is your character changed and subverted? You say true. For sixteen years I never heard a breath of falsehood from your lips; I trusted you as I would the oracles of eternal truth. But it is past! A few short months have polluted and defaced a whole life of integrity! In how many obscurities and fabulous inconsistencies have you entangled yourself? Nor is it the least of the calamities under which my heart sickens at this moment, that I am reduced to hold language like this to a father!"

What misery was mine, to hear myself thus arraigned by my own son, and to be unable to utter one word in reply to his accusations! To be thus triumphed over by a stripling; and to feel the most cruel degradation, in the manifestation of an excellence that ought to have swelled my heart with gratulation and transport! I had recollected my habitual feelings for near forty years of existence; I had dropped from my memory my recent disgrace, and dared to appeal to my acknowledged veracity; when this retort from my son came to plunge me tenfold deeper in a sea of shame. He proceeded:—

"I am no longer your son! I am compelled to disclaim all affinity with you! But this is not all. By your dishonour you have cut me off from the whole line of my ancestors. I cannot claim affinity with them, without acknowledging my relation to you. You have extinguished abruptly an illustrious house. The sun of St. Leon is set for ever! Standing as I do a candidate for honourable fame, I must henceforth stand by myself, as if a man could be author of his own existence, and must expect no aid, no favour, no prepossession, from any earthly consideration, save what I am, and what I shall perform."

"My son," replied I, "you cut me to the heart. Such is the virtue you display, that I must confess myself never to have been worthy of you, and I begin to fear I am now less worthy of you than ever. Yet you must suffer me to finish what I was about to say when you so passionately interrupted me. I swear then, by every thing that is sacred, that I am innocent. Whatever interpretation the world may put upon my sudden wealth, there is no shadow of dishonesty or guilt connected with its acquisition. The circumstances of the story are such that they must never be disclosed; I am bound to secrecy by the most inviolable obligations, and this has led me to utter a forged and inconsistent tale. But my conscience has nothing with which to reproach me. If then, Charles, my son, once my friend, my best and dearest consolation!"—I pressed his hand, and my voice faltered as I spoke,—"if you are resolute to separate yourself from me, at least take this recollection with you wherever you go,—Whatever may be my external estimation, I am not the slave of vice, your father is not a villain!"

"Alas, my father!" rejoined Charles, mournfully, "what am I to believe? What secret can be involved in so strange a reverse of fortune, that is not dishonourable? You have given utterance to different fictions on the subject, fictions that you now confess to be such; how am I to be convinced that what you say at this moment is not dictated more by a regard for my tranquillity, than by the simplicity of conscious truth? If I believe you, I am afraid my credit will be the offspring rather of inclination, than of probability. And indeed, if I believe you, what avails it? The world will not believe. Your character is blasted; your honour is destroyed; and, unless I separate myself from you, and disown your name, I shall be involved in the same disgrace."

Saying thus, he left me, and in about half an hour returned. His return I had not foreseen; I had made no use of his absence. My mind was overcome, my understanding was stupified, by a situation and events I had so little expected. I had stood, unmoved, leaning against the wall, from the instant of his departure. I seemed rooted to the spot, incapable of calling up my fortitude, or arranging my ideas. My eyes had rolled,—my brow was knit,—I had bit my lips and my tongue with agony. From time to time I had muttered a few words,—"My son! my son!—wealth! wealth!—my wife!—my son!" but they were incoherent and without meaning.

Charles re-entered the apartment where the preceding conversation had passed, and the noise he made in entering roused me. He had his hat in his hand, which he threw from him, and exclaimed with an accent of dejection and anguish, "My father!—farewell!"

"Cruel, cruel boy! can you persist in your harsh and calamitous resolution? If you have no affection for me, yet think of your mother and your sisters!"

Seek not, sir, to turn me from my purpose! The struggle against it in my own bosom has been sufficiently severe; but it must be executed."—His voice, as he spoke, was inward, stifled, and broken with the weight of his feelings.

"Then—farewell!" I replied. "Yet take with you some provision for your long and perilous adventure. Name the sum you will accept, and, whatever is its amount, it shall instantly be yours."

"I will have nothing. It is this wealth, with whose splendour I was at first child enough to be dazzled, that has destroyed us. My fingers shall not be contaminated with an atom of it. What is to be my fate, as yet, I know not. But I am young, and strong, and enterprising, and courageous. The lessons of honour and nobility live in my bosom. Though my instructor is lost, his instructions shall not be vain!

"Once more farewell! From my heart I thank you for your protestations of innocence. Never will I part with this last consolation, to believe them. I have recollected the manner in which they were uttered; it was the manner of truth. If there be any evidence of a contrary tendency, that I will forget. Though to the world I shall be without father and without relatives, I will still retain this sacred consolation for my hours of retirement and solitude, that my ancestors were honourable, and my father, in spite of all presumptions to the contrary,—was innocent.

"How hard it is to quit for ever a family of love and affection, as ours has been! Bear witness for me, how deeply, I sympathised with you at Paris, in Switzerland, in Constance! Though now you dissolve the tie between us, yet, till now, never had a son greater reason for gratitude to a father. You and my mother have made me what I am; and that I may preserve what you have made me, I now cast myself upon an untried world. The recollection of what I found you in the past period of my life, shall be for ever cherished in my memory!

"I quit my mother and my sisters without leave-taking or adieu. It will be a fruitless and painful addition to what each party must learn to bear. Dear, excellent, peerless protector and companions of my early years! my wishes are yours, my prayers shall for ever be poured out for you! You, sir, who rob them of a son and a brother, be careful to make up to them a loss, which I doubt not they will account grievous! I can do nothing for them. I can throw myself into the arms of poverty; it is my duty. But, in doing so, I must separate myself from them, assuredly innocent, and worthy of more and greater benefits than I could ever confer on them!—Farewell!"

Saying this, he threw himself into my arms, and I felt the agonies of a parting embrace.

CHAPTER XVIII.

For some time I could not believe him departed. When I retired to rest, I felt the want of Charles to press my hand, and wish me refreshing slumbers; and I passed on, sad and solitary, to my chamber. When I came next morning into the breakfasting room, Charles was not there, to greet me with looks of affection and duty; and the gilding and ornaments of the apartment were to me no less disconsolate than the damps and sootiness of a dungeon.

I hoped he would return. I knew how tenderly he was attached to his mother and his sisters; I was fully convinced that the affection for me which had been the perpetual habit of his mind, could not be entirely eradicated from his heart. I mentioned him not in my letters to Constance; the pen lingered, my hand trembled, when I thought of him; I could neither pretend that he was with me, nor announce the catastrophe of his absence. But I opened the letters of Marguerite with still increasing impatience. Finding that he did not return to me, I hoped that some alteration of the extraordinary resolution he had formed, would lead him to Constance. In vain I hoped! There reached me, by no conveyance, from no quarter, tidings of my son!

How surprising an event! A youth, not seventeen years of age, forming and executing in the same instant the purpose of flying from his parents and his family! Deserting all his hopes, all his attachments, all his fortune! Refusing the smallest particle of assistance or provision in his entrance upon the wide scene of the world! Oh, Charles! exclaimed I, you are indeed an extraordinary and admirable youth! But are you fortified against all the temptations of the world and all its hardships? Do your tender years qualify you to struggle with its unkindness, its indifference, and its insults? In how few quarters is merit ever treated with the attention and benevolence it deserves! How often is it reduced to tremble with indignation, at the scoffs and brutality to which it is exposed, and at the sight of folly and vice exalted in its stead, and appointed its despot and its master! My son, my son! what will be your fate? Is your unseasoned frame reserved to perish by hunger, in barren deserts and beneath inclement skies? Will you not in some hour of bitter disappointment and unpitied loneliness, lay yourself down in despair and die? Will you not be made the slave of some capricious tyrant for bread? Generous as is your nature, will it be eternally proof against reiterated temptation? Upon what a world are you turned adrift! a world of which you know as little, as the poor affrighted soul of a dying man knows, when launching into the mysterious, impenetrable abyss of eternity! Unnatural father, to have reduced my only son to this cruel alternative! I should with a less aching and agonising heart have accompanied his senseless remains to the grave. Dreadful as that parting is, there at least the anxious mind of the survivor has rest. There are no thoughts and devices in the silence of the tomb. There all our prospects end, and we are no longer sensible to pain, to persecution, to insult, and to agony. But Charles, thus departed, wandering on the face of the globe, without protector, adviser or resource, no lapse of years can put a close upon my anxiety for him! If I am in ease and prosperity, I cannot relish them, for my exposed and living son may be at that moment in the depth of misery! If I am myself oppressed and suffering, the thought of what may be his fate will form a dreadful addition to all my other calamities! What am I to say of him upon my return to Constance? If he had died, this was a natural casualty; and, whatever grief it might occasion, time no doubt would mollify and abate it. But what account can now be rendered of him to his disconsolate mother and terrified sisters? How can I lift up my head in their presence, or meet the glance of their reproachful eyes!

The idea had occurred to me, in the instant of Charles's departure, and immediately after his exit, of detaining or bringing him back by force. He was by his extreme youth, according to the maxims of the world, still in a state of guardianship, and unqualified to be the chooser of his own actions. But to this mode of proceeding, however deeply I felt the catastrophe which had taken place, I could never consent. It was in utter hostility to the lessons of chivalry and honour, with which I had been familiarised from my earliest infancy. There might be cases, in which this restraint laid by a father upon his child would be salutary. But the idea which had occasioned the secession of Charles, was decisive in this instance. What right had I to chain him to dishonour? The whole bent of his education had been, to impress him with the feelings by which he was now actuated. If I detained him for a short time, was there any vigilance on earth that could finally prevent him from executing a purpose upon which his whole soul was resolved? Or, suppose there were, must not the consequence be to break his spirit, to deprive him of all manliness and energy, and to render him the mere drooping and soulless shadow of that conspicuous hero I had been anxious to make him? It might be said indeed, that this was the determination of a boy, formed in an hour, and that, if I detained him only long enough for deliberation and revisal, he would of his own accord retract so desperate a project. But I felt that it was a resolution formed to endure, and was built upon principles that could not change so long as an atom of his mind remained. No; I was rather disposed to say, however grievous was the wound he inflicted on me, Go, my son! Act upon the dictates of your choice, as I have acted on mine! I admire your resolution, though I cannot imitate it. Your purpose is lofty and godlike; and he that harbours it, was not born to be a slave. Be free; and may every power propitious to generosity and virtue smooth your path through life, and smile upon your desires!

The anguish I felt for having lost my son, and in this painful and reproachful manner, was not diminished to me either by society or amusement. I dared not go out of my house. I saw no one but my own attendants. I had not the courage to meet the aspect of a human creature. I knew not how far persons in Dresden might have heard the injurious reports which occasioned the flight of my son, or even have been acquainted with the nature of that flight. I had promised to see Coligny again; but, alas! the affair which had at first led me to wish to see him, was now at an end. I had no heart to seek him; nor indeed did I know what story I was to tell him, or how I was to remove the suspicions he had urged against me. The machine of human life, though constituted of a thousand parts, is in all its parts regularly and systematically connected; nor is it easy to insert an additional member, the spuriousness of which an accurate observation will not readily detect. How was I to assign a source of my wealth different from the true, which would not be liable to investigation, and, when investigated, would not be seen to be counterfeit? This indeed is the prime source of individual security in human affairs, that whatever any man does, may be subjected to examination, and whatever does not admit of being satisfactorily accounted for, exposes him whom it concerns to the most injurious suspicions. This law of our nature, so salutary in its general operation, was the first source of all my misfortunes.

I began now seriously to consider what judgment I was to pass upon the bequests of the stranger. Were they to be regarded as a benefit or a misfortune? Ought they to be classed with the poisoned robe of Nessus, which, being sent as a token of affection, was found, in the experiment, to eat into the flesh and burn up the vitals of him that wore it? Should I from this instant reject their use, and, returning to the modes of life established among my fellow men, content myself with the affection of those with whom I had intercourse, though poverty and hardships mingled with the balm?

The experiment I had made of these extraordinary gifts was a short one; but how contrary were all the results I had arrived at, from those I looked for? When the stranger had appeared six months before at the cottage of the lake, he had found me a poor man indeed, but rich in the confidence, and happy in the security and content, of every member of my family. I lived in the bosom of nature, surrounded with the luxuriance of its gifts and the sublimity of its features, which the romantic elevation of my soul particularly fitted me to relish. In my domestic scene I beheld the golden age renewed, the simplicity of pastoral life without its grossness, a situation remote from cities and courts, from traffic and hypocrisy, yet not unadorned with taste, imagination, and knowledge. Never was a family more united in sentiments and affection. Now all this beauteous scene was defaced! All was silence, suspicion, and reserve. The one party dared not be ingenuous, and the other felt that all the paradise of attachment was dwindled to an empty name. No questions were asked; for no honest answer was given or expected. Though corporeally we might sit in the same apartment, in mind a gulf, wide, impassable, and tremendous, gaped between us. My wife pined in speechless grief, and, it was to be feared, had sustained a mortal blow. My son, my only son, a youth of such promise that I would not have exchanged him for empires, had disappeared, and, as he had solemnly protested, for ever. My heart was childless: my bosom was bereaved of its dearest hope. It was for him principally that I had accepted, that I had rejoiced in the gifts of the stranger. My darling vision was to see him clothed in the harness, surrounded with the insignia, of a hero. There was nothing I so earnestly desired as that his merits, graced with the favours of fortune, might cause him to stand confessed the first subject of France; a situation more enviable than that of its monarch, since he who holds it is raised by deeds, and the other only by birth; and if less respected by interested courtiers, is certain to be more honoured by the impartial voice of history. But, if I felt thus desolate and heartbroken for the loss of my son, what would be the sentiments of his mother, more susceptible to feel, and, in her present weakness of spirits, less vigorous to bear, than myself, when the dreadful tidings should be communicated to her?

Yet I could not resolve to renounce donations which I had so dearly appropriated. I held it to be a base and cowardly to surrender gifts so invaluable, upon so insufficient an experiment. He, I thought, must be a man of ignoble and grovelling spirit, who could easily be prevailed on to part with unbounded wealth and immortal life. I had but just entered the vast field that was opened to me. It was of the nature of all great undertakings to be attended with difficulties and obstacles in the commencement, to present a face calculated to discourage the man that is infirm of purpose. But it became my descent, my character and pretensions, to show myself serene in the midst of storms. Perseverance and constancy are the virtues of a man. Affairs of this extensive compass often prove in the issue the reverse of what they seemed in the outset. The tempest might be expected to disperse, difficulties to unravel themselves, and unlooked-for concurrences to arise. All opposition and hostile appearance give way before him who goes calmly onward, and scorns to be dismayed.

CHAPTER XIX.

It was thus that I spurred myself to persist in the path upon which I had entered. Having remained some time at Dresden, flattering myself with the hope that Charles might yet join me before I quitted that city, I began to think of once more turning my steps towards the residence of my family. This was no cheerful thought; but upon what was I to determine? I had a wife whom I ardently loved, and three daughters the darlings of my heart. Because I had lost a beloved son was I to estrange myself from these? I already felt most painfully the detachment and widowhood to which I was reduced, and I clung with imperious affection to what remained of my race. The meeting I purposed must be a melancholy one; but, in the sorrows of the heart there is a purer and nobler gratification than in the most tumultuous pleasures where affection is silent. I looked forward indeed to scenes of endless variety and attraction, but in the mean time what seemed first to demand my attention was the beloved circle I had left behind in the city of Constance.

I retraced, upon the present occasion, the route I had lately pursued with my son. How different were now my sensations! My heart was then indeed painfully impressed with the variance and dissolution of confidence that had arisen between me and his mother. It was perhaps principally for the sake of banishing this impression that I had had recourse to the splendour of equipage and attendance which was first assumed upon the journey from Constance to Dresden. Nor, frivolous as this expedient may appear in the unattractive dispassionateness of narrative, had it been by any means weak of effect at the time it was employed. When Charles was once mounted on his proud and impatient steed, and decorated in rich and costly attire, I felt, as it were, the sluggishness of my imagination roused; I surveyed his shape and his countenance with inexpressible complacence; and already anticipated the period when he was to become the favourite of his sovereign and his country's pride. Now I returned with the same retinue; but the place that had been occupied by my son was empty. I sought him with frantic and restless gaze; I figured him to my disturbed and furious imagination, till the sensations and phantoms of my brain became intolerable; I raved and imprecated curses on myself. I endeavoured to divert my thoughts by observing the scenes that passed before me. They talked to me of Charles; they had been pointed out by each to each, and had been the subject of our mutual comment. Though Charles was endowed with a high relish for the beauties of nature, and, in our little retreat on the borders of the lake, had lived in the midst of them, he had seen little of the variety of her features; and the journey we made through the heart of Germany had furnished him with continual food for admiration and delight. Nor did the scenes I beheld merely remind me of the sensations they produced in Charles; they led me through a wider field. I recollected long conversations and digressive excursions which had been started by the impression they made. I recollected many passages and occurrences to which they had not the slightest reference, but which, having arisen while they constituted the visible scene, were forcibly revived by its re-appearance. Thus, from various causes, my lost and lamented son was not a moment out of my thoughts during the journey. While I continued at Dresden, I seemed daily to expect his return; but no sooner did I quit that city than despair took possession of my heart.

Thus, anxious and distressed, I arrived at Prague, and soon after at Ratisbon. I travelled slowly, because, though I was desirous of returning to Constance, I anticipated my arrival there with little complacence. As I drew nearer to my family, I felt more distinctly the impossibility of presenting myself before them, without first endeavouring to take off the shock they would sustain at seeing me return without my son. I therefore resolved to send forward a servant from Ratisbon, whom I directed to make all practicable speed, as I designed to wait for an answer he should bring me at the city of

Munich. To attempt to write to Marguerite on this subject was a severe trial to me. The whole however that I proposed to myself was, to remove the surprise which would be occasioned by seeing me alone, and to anticipate questions that it would be impossible for me to hear without anguish of mind and perturbation of countenance. I therefore took care to express myself in such terms as should lead Marguerite to believe that I had voluntarily left her son in Saxony, and that in no very long time he would rejoin his family. I trusted to subsequent events to unfold the painful catastrophe, and could not prevail on myself to shock her maternal feelings so much as I must necessarily do, if I informed her of the whole at once. Charles had not been mentioned but in ordinary terms and the accustomed language of affection, in the letters I had recently received from Constance; and I was therefore convinced that he had neither gone to that place, nor had conveyed thither any account of his proceedings.

The answer I received from Marguerite by my messenger was as follows:—

"Your absence has been long and critical, and the welfare of your daughters seems to require that we should rejoin each other as speedily as may be. Whether we should meet here or at any other place you must determine. It is, however, right I should inform you that, during your absence, rumour has been busy with your reputation. What the extent or importance of the ill reports circulated of you may be, I am scarcely competent to judge. We have lived in uniform privacy, and it is natural to suppose that the portion of censure that has reached us is but a small part of what really exists. The mode in which you have proceeded, and the extraordinary figure you have made in a progress through Germany, have given weight to these insinuations. But it is not my intention to comment on what you have done.

"You appear to design that I should understand you have left my son behind you in Saxony. Poor Charles! I had a letter from him three weeks ago, in which he informs me of what has happened, and apologises in the most pathetic terms for any seeming want of regard to me in his conduct, at the very moment that his heart bleeds for my fate. I did not think it necessary to communicate this circumstance to you. I have done with complaining. Now that I have fallen into the worst and most unlooked-for misfortunes, I have a gratification that I do not choose to part with, in shutting up my sorrows in my own breast.

"Oh, Charles! my son, my idol! What is become of you? For what calamities are you reserved? He tells me it is necessary that I should never see or hear of him again. Never—I—his mother!—Reginald, there are some wounds that we may endeavour to forgive; but they leave a sentiment in the heart, the demonstrations of which may perhaps be restrained, but which it is not in nature wholly to subdue. If I did but know where to find or to write to my poor boy, I would take my girls with me, and partake his honest and honourable poverty, and never again join the shadow of him who was my husband. Forgive me, Reginald! I did not intend to say this. If I should prove unable to control the impatience of my grief, do not inflict the punishment of my offence on your innocent daughters!

"As to your fiction of voluntarily leaving him behind for further improvement, it corresponds with every thing you have lately attempted to make me believe. I no longer expect truth from you. For seventeen years I had a husband. Well, well! I ought not perhaps to repine. I have had my share of the happiness which the present life is calculated to afford.

"Reginald! I have not long to live. When I tell you this, I am not giving way to melancholy presentiment. I will exert myself for the benefit of my girls. They will have a grievous loss in me; and for their sake I will live as long as I can. But I feel that you have struck me to the heart. My nights are sleepless; my flesh is wasted; my appetite is entirely gone. You will presently be able to judge whether I am deceiving myself. The prospect for these poor creatures, who are at present all my care, is a dismal one. I know not for what they are reserved; but I can hope for nothing good. When I am dead, remember, and be a father to them. I ask nothing for myself; I have no longer any concern with life; but, if my dying request can have weight with you, make up to them the duty you have broken to me. By all out past loves, by the cordiality and confidence in which we have so long lived, by the singleness and sincerity of our affection, by the pure delights, so seldom experienced in married life, that have attended our union, I conjure you listen to me and obey me in this."

If I were deeply distressed for the loss of my son, if I looked forward with a mingled sensation of eagerness and alarm to the approaching interview with my family, it may easily be imagined that this letter formed a heavy addition to my mental anguish. I confess I thought it a cruel one. Marguerite might well suppose, that the departure of Charles was a circumstance I must strongly feel; and she should not have thus aggravated the recent wounds of paternal grief. Some allowance, however, was to be made for a mother. When we are ourselves racked with intolerable pain, that certainly is not the time at which we can rationally be expected to exert the nicest and most vigilant consideration for another. Add to which, she was innocent of the calamities she suffered, and could not but know that I was their sole author. But, whatever may be decided as to the propriety of the letter, its effect upon my mind was eminently salutary. I instantly determined on the conduct it became me to pursue.

I lost not a moment. From Dresden to Munich I had advanced with slow and unwilling steps; from Munich to Constance I proceeded as rapidly as the modes of travelling and the nature of the roads would permit. I left my retinue at the gates of the town, and flew instantly to the apartments of my family. I hastened up stairs, and, as I entered the sitting-room, I saw the first and most exemplary of matrons surrounded by her blooming daughters. I instantly perceived a great alteration in her appearance. Her look was dejected; her form emaciated; her countenance sickly and pale. She lifted up her eyes as I entered, but immediately dropped them again, without any discernible expression, either of congratulation or resentment. I embraced my children with undescribable emotion; I said within myself, the love and affection I had reserved for Charles shall be divided among you, and added to the share you each possess of my heart! Having saluted them in turn, I addressed myself to Marguerite, telling her that I must have some conversation with her instantly. My manner was earnest: she led the way into another apartment.

I felt my heart overflowing at my tongue.

"I am come to you," cried I, "a repenting prodigal. Take me and mould me at your pleasure!"

She looked up. She was struck with the honest fervour of my expression. She answered in almost forgotten terms, and with a peculiar fulness of meaning, "My husband!"—It seemed as if the best years and the best emotions of our life were suddenly renewed.

"Most adorable of women!" I continued: "do you think I can bear that you should die, and I your murderer? No man in any age or climate of the world ever owed so much to a human creature as I owe to you; no woman was ever so ardently loved! no woman ever so much deserved to be loved! If you were to die, I should never know peace again. If you were to die the victim of any miscalculation of mine, I should be the blackest of criminals!"

"Reginald!" replied she, "I am afraid I have been wrong. I am afraid I have written harshly to you. You have a feeling heart, and I have been too severe. Forgive me! it was the effect of love. Affection cannot view with a tranquil eye the faults of the object beloved."

"Let them be forgotten! Let the last six months be blotted from our memory, be as though they had never existed!"

She looked at me. Her look seemed to say, though she would not give the sentiment words, that can never be; the loss of Charles, and certain other calamities of that period, are irretrievable!

"I resign myself into your hands! I have been guilty; I have had secrets; meditations engendered and shut up in my own bosom; but it shall be so no more! The tide of affection kept back from its natural channel, now flows with double impetuousness. Never did I love you, not when you first came a virgin to my arms, not on the banks of the Garonne, not in the cottage of the lake, so fervently, so entirely, as I love you now! Be my director; do with me as you please! I have never been either wise or virtuous but when I have been implicitly guided by you!

"I have wealth; I am forbidden by the most solemn obligations to discover the source of that wealth. This only I may not communicate; in all things else govern me despotically! Shall I resign it all? Shall I return to the cottage of the lake? Shall I go, a houseless and helpless wanderer, to the farthest quarter of the globe? Speak the word only, and it shall be done! I prefer your affection, your cordial regard, in the most obscure and meanest retreat, to all that wealth can purchase or kings can give!"

"Reginald, I thank you! I acknowledge in your present language and earnestness the object of my first and only love. This return to your true character gives me all the pleasure I am now capable of receiving. But it is too late My son is lost; that cannot be retrieved. Your reputation is blasted; I am sorry you are returned hither; Constance is in arms against you, and I will not answer for the consequence. For myself; I grieve to tell you so; I am ashamed of my weakness; but—my heart is broken! I loved you so entirely, that I was not able to bear any suspension of our confidence. I had passed with you through all other misfortunes, and the firmness of my temper was not shaken. For this one misfortune, that seemed the entire dissolution of our attachment, I was not prepared.

I feel, every morning as I rise, the warnings of my decease. My nights are sleepless; my appetite is gone from me."

"Oh, Marguerite, talk not thus; distract me not with the most fatal of images! Our confidence shall return; all the causes of your malady shall be removed! With the causes, the symptoms, depend on it, will disappear. Your youth, your tranquillity, your happiness, shall be renewed! Oh, no, you shall not die! We will yet live to love and peace!"

"Flatter not yourself with vain hopes, my love! I feel something wrong within me, which is rapidly wearing my body to decay. Reconcile your mind to what very soon must happen! Prepare yourself for being the only parent to your remaining offspring! I have composed my spirit, and calmly wait my fate. You have now administered to me the only consolation I aspired to, by this return to your true character, which affords me a sanguine hope that you will faithfully discharge the duty to your offspring, which, when I am gone, will be doubly urgent on you."

I was grieved to see that the mind of Marguerite was so deeply impressed with the notion that she had but a short time to live. I could not bear to imagine for a moment that her prognostic was just. The thought seemed capable of driving me to distraction. I however conceived that the best thing that could be done for the present, was to turn the conversation to some other topic.

"Well, well, my love!" I answered. "There are some things that are immediately pressing. Direct me, direct a husband so amply convinced of your discretion, what I am to do at present! Shall I instantly annihilate all that has made this unfortunate breach between us; shall I resign my wealth, from whatever source derived? Whither shall we go? Shall we return to the cottage of the lake? Shall we retreat into some distant part of the world?"

"How can you expect me," said Marguerite, faintly smiling, "to advise you respecting the disposal of a wealth, of the amount of which I am uninformed, and the source of which is invisible? But I guess your secret. The stranger who died your guest was in possession of the philosopher's stone, and he has bequeathed to you his discovery. I have heard of this art, though I confess I was not much inclined to credit it. I do not ask you to confirm my conjecture: I do not wish that you should violate my engagements into which you have entered. But, upon putting circumstances together, which I have been inevitably compelled to do, I apprehend it can be nothing else. I am astonished that a conjecture so obvious should have offered itself to my mind so late.

"If your wealth is of any other nature, ample as it apparently is, it is a natural question to ask, to whom is it to be resigned? The ordinary wealth of the world is something real and substantial, and can neither be created nor dissipated with a breath. But if your wealth be of the kind I have named, let me ask, is it possible to resign it? A secret is a thing with which we may choose whether we will become acquainted; but, once known, we cannot become unacquainted with it at pleasure. Your wealth, upon my supposition, will always be at your beck; and it is perhaps beyond the strength of human nature to refuse, under some circumstances, at least in some emergencies, to use the wealth which is within our reach.

"It has been our mutual misfortune that such an engine has been put into your hands. It has been your fault to make an indiscreet use of it. Gladly would I return to the tranquil and unsuspected poverty of the cottage of the lake. But that is impossible. You have lost your son; you have lost your honest fame; the life of your Marguerite is undermined and perishing. If it were possible for us to return to our former situation and our former peace, still, my Reginald! forgive me if I say, I doubt the inflexibleness of your resolution. The gift of unbounded wealth, if you possess it, and, with wealth, apparently at least, distinction and greatness, is too powerful a temptation. Nor, though I should trust your resistance, could I be pleased in a husband with the possession of these extraordinary powers. It sets too great a distance between the parties. It destroys that communion of spirit which is the soul of the marriage-tie. A consort should be a human being and an equal. But to this equality and simple humanity it is no longer in your power to return.

"Circumstanced then as we now are, the marriage union, you must allow me to say, irreparably dissolved, your son lost, your fair fame destroyed, your orphan daughters to be provided for, I know not if I should advise you to forget the prerogative that has been bought for you at so dreadful a price. Beside, if I am not mistaken, there are great trials in reserve for you. I am afraid your present situation is extremely critical. I am afraid the suspicions you have excited will cost you dear. At all events I believe it to be but a necessary precaution that we should fly from Constance. I have nothing therefore to recommend to you on the subject of wealth, but discretion. I shall not long live to be your adviser. I shall always regard the donation you have received, you cannot wonder that I should so regard it, as one of the most fearful calamities to which a human being can be exposed. If you had used your prerogative with discretion, you might perhaps, though I confess I do not see how, have escaped the obloquy of the world. Into your domestic scene, where the interest is more lively, and the watch upon you more unremitted, it must have introduced alienation and distrust. As it is, I see you surrounded with dangers of a thousand denominations. Police has its eyes upon you; superstition will regard you as the familiar of demons; avarice will turn upon you a regard of jealousy and insatiable appetite. If I could recover from the weakness that at present besets me, and continue to live, I foresee more and severer trials, both at home and abroad, than any I have yet sustained; and I am almost thankful to that Providence which has decreed to take me away from the evil to come.

"One thing further let me add. I will speak it, not in the character of a censor, but a friend. It must ever be right and useful, that a man should be undeceived in any erroneous estimate he may make of himself. I have loved you much; I found in you many good qualities; my imagination decorated you in the virtues that you had not; but you have removed the veil. An adept and an alchemist is a low character. When I married you, I supposed myself united to a nobleman, a knight, and a soldier, a man who would have revolted with disdain from every thing that was poor-spirited and base. I lived with you long and happily. I saw faults; I saw imbecilities. I did not see them with indifference; but I endeavoured, and with a degree of success, to forget and to forgive them; they did not contaminate and corrupt the vitals of honour. At length you have completely reversed the scene. For a soldier you present me with a projector and a chemist, a cold-blooded mortal, raking in the ashes of a crucible for a selfish and solitary advantage. Here is an end of all genuine dignity, and the truest generosity of soul. You cannot be ingenuous; for all your dealings are secrecy and darkness. You cannot have a friend; for the mortal lives not that can sympathise with your thoughts and emotions. A generous spirit, Reginald, delights to live upon equal terms with his associates and fellows. He would disdain, when offered to him, excessive and clandestine advantages. Equality is the soul of real and cordial society. A man of rank indeed does not live upon equal terms with the whole of his species; but his heart also can exult, for he has his equals. How unhappy the wretch, the monster rather let me say, who is without an equal; who looks through the world, and in the world cannot find a brother; who is endowed with attributes which no living being participates with him; and who is therefore cut off for ever from all cordiality and confidence, can never unbend himself, but lives the solitary, joyless tenant of a prison, the materials of which are emeralds and rubies! How unhappy this wretch! How weak and ignoble the man that voluntarily accepts these laws of existence!"

In the advice of Marguerite I saw that sound wisdom and discernment, by which in all the periods of our connection she had been so eminently characterised. With her views of the future I was not disposed to accord. I regarded them as obscured and discoloured by the unfortunate state of her health. I could not indeed refuse to believe that the prerogative I had received had been the parent of much domestic unhappiness. Willingly would I have resigned all that I had derived from the stranger, to be replaced in the situation in which his pernicious legacies had found me. He had robbed me of my son; he had destroyed my domestic peace; he had undermined the tranquillity and health of the partner of my life. These calamities pressed with a heavy and intolerable weight at my heart. But, if, as Marguerite affirmed, they were irretrievable, or if they could once be removed, and the domestic advantages I had heretofore enjoyed be restored, I was not disposed to fear those external mischiefs which Marguerite so feelingly predicted. I could not believe that I should have such a league of foreign enemies to encounter, nor could I easily image to myself any external evils which it was not in the power of gold to remedy. These considerations I urged to my beloved partner, and by enforcing them endeavoured to remove those gloomy apprehensions, from the prevalence of which I feared much injury to her health. There was another circumstance I was led particularly to insist on; I mean the nature of the secret intrusted to me.

"I admire your discernment and ingenuity, Marguerite," said I, "in your conjecture respecting the source of my wealth. I admire your delicacy in not pressing me to decide upon the truth of your conjecture. This only I must be permitted to say on that subject. It is a secret; and you will perceive that the same reasons, whatever they are, which make that secret obligatory on me, require that it should be respected by you. The same evils that my own indiscretion may draw on me, I shall be equally exposed to by any error or miscalculation of yours. I have therefore most earnestly and solemnly to conjure you, whatever misfortunes may hereafter befall me, in whatever perilous situation I may be involved, that you will never utter a syllable on this subject; and that, as I am the selected depository of this secret, and alone know with certainty what is its nature, you will trust our prosperity in this point to me."—Marguerite engaged to conduct herself as I desired.

The night which succeeded this explanation, was particularly soothing and grateful to me. I was relieved from a great and oppressive burthen. I was conscious of that particular species of pleasure which arises from the resolute discharge of an heroic duty. The peace I felt within shed its gay and reviving beams upon all around me. Reconciled to myself, I was filled with sanguine and agreeable visions of the future. My mind obstinately rejected all dark and hateful presages. I had intrusted myself and the direction of my conduct, as far as it was possible, to that better pilot, under whose guidance, if I had not avoided the rocks and quicksands of life, I had at least escaped with little comparative injury. I felt therefore as if my domestic enjoyments were restored, and the pleasures of my better years were about to run over again their auspicious career. Not so Marguerite. She was mild, gentle, and soothing. Displeasure and resentment towards me were banished from her mind. She endeavoured to conquer her melancholy, and to forget the wounds that had been so fatal to her hopes. But her endeavours were fruitless. A fixed dejection clung to her heart: nor could the generous sweetness that pervaded her manners hide from me entirely what was passing in her bosom.

During this interval we had talked over the plan of our future operations. Marguerite was exceedingly urgent with me to quit Constance; nor did I, though not impressed with her presentiments, feel any reluctance to that change of scene, which, I believed, would materially contribute to the serenity of her mind and the restoration of her health. We determined on some of the cities of Italy as the next place of our residence, and, fixed, if possible, to set out some time in the next day or the day after. The plan of proceeding to France, which had lately been a favourite with me, was a favourite no longer. That had been the project of cheerful and wanton prosperity. It had had for its object the re-establishment of my family honours, and the elevation of my son. Now my son was lost, my wife was oppressed with languor and disease, my house was overwhelmed with sorrow. This was no time for wantonness and triumph. If I could ever hope to resume the plans my frolic fancy had sketched, an interval at least of soberer hue must first be suffered to elapse.

My mind at this time sustained a revolution sufficiently remarkable, but of which the urgency of events that immediately succeeded prevented me from ever ascertaining whether it would have proved temporary or permanent. When I first received the donation of the stranger, my thoughts, as I have already said, were in a state of enthusiastic transport; and, amidst the golden visions in which my fancy revelled, I became in a considerable degree alienated from domestic sentiments and pleasures. If I still loved my wife and children, it was the love of habit rather than sympathy; more an anxiety for their prosperous success in the world, than an earnest craving for their presence and intercourse. This state of intoxication and rapture had now subsided. The events of the few last weeks had sobered my thoughts. Having lost my son, and being threatened with the loss of his mother, I was roused to a sense of their value. The influx of wealth and supernatural gifts had grown familiar to my mind, and now only occupied the back-ground of the picture. I was once more a man, and I hoped to partake of the privileges and advantages of a man. The fate reserved for these hopes will speedily be seen.

Some readers will perhaps ask me why, anxious as I was for the life of Marguerite, and visible as was the decline of her health, I did not administer to her of the elixir of immortality which was one of my peculiar endowments. Such readers I have only to remind, that the pivot upon which the history I am composing turns, is a mystery. If they will not accept of my communication upon my own terms, they must lay aside my book. I am engaged in relating the incidents of my life; I have no intention to furnish the remotest hint respecting the science of which I am the depository. That science affords abundant reasons why the elixir in question might not, or rather could not, be imbibed by any other than an adept.

CHAPTER XX.

The morning after my return to my family, as I sat surrounded with my girls, and endeavouring to make myself their playmate and companion, certain officers of justice belonging to the supreme tribunal of the city entered my apartment. They were sent, as they informed me, to conduct me to prison. My blood at this intelligence mounted into my face.

"To prison?" cried I—"wherefore?—what have I done?—I am no citizen of your state. What is the charge against me? Lead me not to prison: lead me to your chief magistrate!"

"You will be called up for examination, when his honour is at leisure to hear you: in the mean time you must go to prison."

"Do those who sent you know that I am a native and a gentleman of France? They will be made to repent this insolence. Upon what pretence do they dare to act thus?"

"You will please not to talk of insolence to us. If you do not demean yourself quietly——"

"Silence, fellow!" answered I fiercely. "Lead the way!"

By this time the children, astonished at a scene so alarming and unintelligible to them, began to express their terror in various ways. Julia, who was ready to faint, occupied the attention of her mother. The little Marguerite clung round my knees, and expressed her emotions by shrieks and cries. To see her father about to be torn from her by four strangers, the peculiarity of whose garb of office aggravated the rudeness of their countenances and the peremptoriness of their behaviour, was a spectacle which the affectionateness of her nature was unable to endure.

"I will go with you presently," said I to the officers. "See, how you have terrified the children!"

"Nay, sir, if you will behave civilly, and make it worth our while, we do not desire to hurry you."

I was stung with the brutal assurance with which they thus set the liberty of a few moments at a price to me. But I checked my impatience. I felt that it would be both foolish and degrading to enter into contention with such wretches. I turned from them proudly, and took my child in my arms.

"I will not be long gone, my love!" said I. "These people have made a mistake, and I shall soon be able to rectify it."

"I fancy not," muttered one of them surlily.

"They shall not take you away, papa; that they shall not! I will hold you, and will not let you go!"

"You are a good girl, Marguerite! But I know best what is proper, and you must not think to control me. The men will not do me any harm, child; they dare not. Perhaps I shall be back to dinner, and mamma will then tell me how good you have been."

As I spoke, she looked steadfastly in my face; and then, flinging her arms round my neck, cried, "Good-by, papa!" and burst into a flood of tears.

I embraced the other children and their mother; and, saying to the latter significantly, "Fear nothing; you know I have nothing to fear!"—departed with my conductors.

The way to the citadel lay through the market-place. The scene was already crowded; and I had the mortification to be led along as a criminal, in the midst of a thousand gazing eyes and enquiring tongues. New as every thing connected with my present situation was to me, I had not anticipated this vexation. I was stung with shame and impatience. "To my dungeon!" said I to my conductors sternly. "If you had shown yourself better humoured," cried the most brutal of them, "we would have led you round by the back way."

The master of the prison was somewhat less a savage than his officers. He knew my person, and had heard of my wealth. "Does monsieur choose the best apartment?" said he. "Any where that I can be alone!" answered I hastily. He hesitated a moment. I looked in his face: "Oh, yes, you will be paid!" He bowed, and showed me to a room.

I shut the door as he retired. What had happened to me was of little importance in itself. The impertinence of bailiffs and thief-takers is of no more real moment than the stinging of a gnat. But I was so utterly unacquainted with scenes of this nature! The pride of rank that swelled within me made every appearance of restraint galling to my sense. From the instant I was able to write, man, no one, except in the voluntary compact of military service, had ever said to me, Go there! or, Do this! And now, was I to be directed by the very refuse of the species? Was I to learn the prudence of not replying to their insults? Was I to purchase, at a stipulated price, their patience and forbearance?—I request the reader to pardon me for troubling him with my noviciate feelings: I soon learned to understand the world—the world of a prison—better!

But, what was of more importance, I was apprehended as a criminal: I had been dragged a prisoner of justice through the streets of Constance; I was, by and by, to be subjected to the interrogatories of the municipal tribunal. I could scarcely credit my senses, that such an indignity had happened to the blood of St. Leon. It is true, I was innocent. I was conscious, whatever might be my imprudences and offences towards my own family, that I had done nothing to merit the animadversion of public justice. But this was of no consequence. Nothing, in my opinion, could wipe away the disgrace of being interrogated, examined! of having for an instant imputed to me the possibility of being a criminal! I writhed under this dishonour, and felt it as a severer attack than the question, which was comparatively of ceremony and etiquette, that had oppressed me in my residence at Dresden.

The next day, when I was brought up for examination, I had expected to be the complainant, in demanding redress for the injury I had sustained. But I was mistaken.

I entered the room haughtily, and with the air of a man that felt himself aggrieved. Of this however the magistrate took no notice. "Do you know, sir," said I, "that I am a citizen and a gentleman of France? Are you acquainted with the treatment I have experienced? Have you lent your authority to that treatment?"

"Wait a few minutes," replied he with an imperious tone, "and I shall be at leisure to attend to you."

I was silent. After the interval of nearly a quarter of an hour, he resumed—

"You call yourself the count de St. Leon!"

"I do."

"Perhaps, sir, you are uninformed of the purity with which justice is administered in the city within whose jurisdiction you now stand. Our state is a small one, and its magistrates are therefore enabled to discharge the office of a parent, not only to its proper citizens, but to all strangers that place themselves under its protection."

"I remember, sir, that seven years ago, I and my wife and four children, sick and unfriended, were upon the point of perishing with hunger within the walls of this city!"— The fact I mentioned was wholly foreign to the point with which I was at present concerned; but the parading arrogance of the man brought it forcibly to my memory, and wrung it from my lips.

"Monsieur le comte," replied he, "you are petulant. It is not the office of a state to feed the souls it contains; it could not do that without making them slaves. Its proper concern is to maintain them in that security and freedom of action, which may best enable them to support themselves."

I suppressed the emotions which the tone of this speech excited. I was unwilling to enter into contention with a man whom I regarded as inexpressibly my inferior.

"Is it," cried I sternly, "a part of the justice you boast of, to drag a man of rank and a stranger from his home, without any intimation of the cause of his being so treated, and then, instead of investigating immediately the charge against him, to send him to prison unheard? I disdain to mention the behaviour of your officers: those things naturally grow out of the abuses practised by their superiors."

"The mode of our proceeding," replied he, "depends upon the seriousness of the crime imputed. If a man of distinction labours under a slight accusation only, we then treat him with all proper forbearance and respect. But, when he is suspected of a crime of more than ordinary magnitude, that alters the case. The man who has ceased to respect himself, must look for no respect from others."

I was for a moment thunderstruck and speechless. At length fiercely I cried, "Produce my accusers!"

"That is not the mode of proceeding in Constance. I have certain questions to propound to you. When you have answered them, we shall see what is to be done next."

"Carry me before the prince-bishop of your city! If I am to be examined further, let it be by your sovereign!"

"The prince-bishop, moved by the state of our affairs in matters of religion, has been prevailed on to delegate his juridical authority. I am the person to whom the cognisance of your business belongs; and at certain times, aided by my assessors, have the power of life and death within this city. You have had every indulgence to which you are entitled, and it will be your wisdom to be no further refractory."

"Propose your questions!"

"A person, apparently greatly advanced in years, arrived in the autumn of last year at a miserable farm you at that time cultivated, called the Cottage of the Lake. It is to him that my questions will principally relate."

I stood aghast. The words of the magistrate were most unwelcome sounds. I remembered that the stranger had said to me, "When I am once buried, speak of me, and, if possible, think of me no more." I replied with eagerness and alarm—

"Of that person I have nothing to say. Spare your questions: I have no answer to return you!"

"What was his name?"

"I know not."

"His country?"

"I cannot inform you."

"It is understood that he died, or in some manner disappeared, while under your protection. Yet in the registers of the church there is no notice of that event. If he died, no application was made for the rites of religion to him dying, or to his body when his spirit had deserted it. You are required to answer, what became of him or his remains?"

"I have already told you, that from me you will obtain no information."

"One question more, sir. Seven years ago, you tell me, you and your family were perishing with hunger. Soon after, you removed from obscure lodgings in this city to the cottage of the lake, and seemed to be laudably employed in earning for yourself a scanty livelihood with the labour of your hands. But within the last six months the scene is wholly changed. You appear to have suddenly grown rich, and here, and in other parts of Germany, have actually disbursed considerable sums. Whence comes this change?"

The train of questions thus proposed to me, impelled me to a serious reply.

"Monsieur le juge," said I, "I am a stranger, a native of France, and a man of rank in my own country. I have paid your state the compliment of choosing it for my residence. I have expended my industry, I expend my wealth among you. I have comported myself as a peaceable inhabitant. No action of my life has brought scandal upon your state, or disturbed the peace and tranquillity of your affairs. I cannot collect from any thing you have said, that I have any accuser, or that any charge has been alleged against me. Till that happens, I cannot fall under your animadversion. I am a man of generous birth and honourable sentiments. To myself and my own conscience only am I accountable for my expenditure and my income. I disdain to answer to any tribunal on earth an enquiry of this sort. And now, sir, in conclusion, what I demand of you is, first, my liberty; and secondly, an ample reparation for the interruption I have sustained, and the insults to which I have causelessly been exposed."

"You are mistaken, sir," said the magistrate. "What you mention may be the rule of administering justice in some states. They may decide, if they think proper, that some open act, apparently of a criminal description, must be alleged against a man, before he can become an object of animadversion to the state. But in Constance, as I have already told you, the government assumes to act the part of a parent to its subjects. I sit here, not merely to investigate and examine definite acts, but as a censor morum; and I should violate the oath of my office, if I did not lend a vigilant attention to the behaviour and conduct of every one within my jurisdiction. The city of Constance requires that nothing immoral, licentious, or of suspicious character, shall be transacted within its walls. Your proceedings have escaped notice too long; much longer than they would have done but for your late absence. In cases where what is committed is merely immoral or licentious, we content ourselves with sending the offender out of our walls. But your case is of a complicated nature. It has scandalised all the inhabitants of our virtuous and religious city. Unless you answer my enquiries, and give a clear and satisfactory account of your wealth, I am bound to believe that there is something in the business that will not bear the light. The coincidence of times obliges me to connect the disappearance of your guest, and the sudden growth of your fortune. This connection gives rise to the most alarming suspicions. I have therefore to inform you that, unless you honourably clear up these suspicions by the most ample communication, my duty directs me to remand you to prison, and to assure you that you will not be liberated thence till you have satisfied the whole of my interrogatories."

"Think deliberately," answered I, "of your decision before you form it. Your prisons I despise; but I will not suffer my reputation and my honour to be trifled with. I came before you willingly, though I could easily have avoided doing so; because I was eager to clear my fame. I expected accusers, and I knew I could confound accusation. But what is this that you call justice? You put together circumstances in your own mind: you form conjectures; and then, without information, accuser, or oath, without the semblance of guilt, you condemn me to prison, and expect to extort from me confession. In defect of articles of charge I disdain to answer: the only return a man of honour should make to loose conjectures and random calumnies is silence. I am descended from a race of heroes, knights of the cross, and champions of France; and their blood has not degenerated in my veins. I feel myself animated by the soul of honour, and incapable of crime. I know my innocence, and I rest upon it with confidence. Your vulgar citizens, habituated to none but the groveling notions of traffic and barter, are not the peers of St. Leon, nor able to comprehend the views and sentiments by which he is guided."

"You are mighty well-spoken, monsieur St. Leon," replied the magistrate, "and your words are big and sounding; but we know that the devil can assume the form of an angel, and that the most infamous and profligate character can pronounce with emphasis sentiments of the purest virtue. You are pleased to decide that the presumptions against you are nothing but calumnies. Is it nothing that, having received a stranger and retained him with you for months, you endeavoured to conceal this fact, and never suffered him to be seen by a human creature? Is his final disappearance nothing? Is it nothing that, supposing him to be dead, as he probably is, you denied to his remains the rites of funeral, and refuse to tell what is become of the body? Is it nothing that, upon the death of this stranger, you, who were before in a state almost of penury, suddenly appear to be possessed of unbounded riches? Where is the will of this stranger? In what archives have you deposited the declaration of his wealth? Let me tell you, sir, that these presumptions, which you call nothing, form a body of circumstantial evidence that, in many countries, would have led you to the scaffold as a murderer. But the laws of Constance, which you audaciously revile, are the mildest in the universe. Here we never put a man to death but on his own confession. We simply condemn him to perpetual imprisonment, or until he makes a declaration of his guilt. You refuse to declare the name or country of the man whom you are suspected of murdering, and then have the assurance to boast that no private accuser rises against you. No, sir, we know there can be no private accuser, where the connections of the party can be successfully concealed. But shall this concealment, which is an aggravation of the murder, prove its security? In conclusion, you boast of your blood and heroic sentiments, and rail at our citizens as shopkeepers and merchants. Let me tell you, sir, shopkeepers and merchants though we are, we should scorn to conduct ourselves in the obscure and suspicious manner that you have done. And, now I have taken the trouble to refute your flimsy pretences, which it was wholly unnecessary for me to do, I have done with you. You know your destination, unless you are prepared immediately to give a satisfactory account of yourself and your proceedings."

Finding it impossible to make on this man the impression I desired, I declined entering into further parley; and, telling him that I should convey a representation of my case to my native sovereign, and did not doubt soon to make him feel the rashness of his proceeding, I withdrew, in the custody of the officers who had conducted me to the scene of audience. I was, I confess, struck with the coincidence of circumstances, which the magistrate had placed in a fight equally unexpected and forcible, and which I now saw calculated to subject me to the most injurious suspicions. I was not disposed in the smallest degree to yield to the attack, but I felt a desire to act deliberately and with caution. The whole of what I had heard was utterly unforeseen, and it was with peculiar anguish that I became aware of this new consequence of the stranger's pernicious donation. This was a consequence that no resignation, no abjuration of his bequests could cure; and that must be stood up to with manly courage, if any hope were entertained of averting it.

CHAPTER XXI.

The appearance of wealth that accompanied me had by this time made its impression upon my keepers; and one of them now informed me, that monsieur Monluc, an agent of the court of France, who was making a tour of several of the German states by order of his sovereign, had arrived the night before at the city of Constance. There was no representative of my country regularly resident here, and I immediately felt the presence of Monluc to be the most fortunate event that could have occurred for effecting my honourable deliverance. Selfishness and avarice, it may be thought, would rather have impelled the persons who had me in custody to conceal from me a circumstance calculated to deprive them of an advantageous prey. But in those groveling souls from whom riches never fail to extort homage, however strange it may seem, the homage often appears disinterested. They pay it by a sort of irresistible instinct; and, admiring what they covet, at an awful distance, with difficulty assume the courage to pollute their worship with ideas of calculation and gain.

I immediately addressed a memorial to this gallant soldier, with whose person indeed I was unacquainted, but the fame of whose spirit and enterprise had not failed to have reached me. I represented to him that I was a Frenchman of family and distinction; that I had been seized upon and was retained in prison by the magistrates here, without accuser or the hope of a trial; that I had not been guilty of the shadow of a crime; and that I knew the benignity and courage of my sovereign would never permit a subject of France to languish under calumny and oppression in a foreign country. I added, that he would do an acceptable service to king Francis, to whom I had the honour to be known, by interfering in my favour; and therefore entreated him to obtain for me immediate justice and deliverance. Monluc returned me an answer by the bearer of my memorial, assuring me that he would lose no time in enquiring into the merits of my case, and that I might depend upon receiving every assistance from him that a man of honour could desire.

The warmth and frankness of this answer filled me with hope, for there was no deliverance from my present situation that I could contemplate with satisfaction, but such a one as should be accompanied with reparation and éclat. Three days however elapsed before I heard again from the French envoy. On the morning of the fourth he announced his intention of visiting me; and, about an hour after, arrived at the prison. His appearance was striking. He was tall, slender, and well made, with a freedom of carriage, not derived from the polish of courts, but which appeared to flow from the manliness and active energies of his mind. His hair and complexion were dark; the former, though he was still young, rather scantily shaded a high and ample forehead. His features were expressive of the sanguine and adust temper of his mind; and, though his eye was animated, his countenance, as he entered, struck me as particularly solemn.

"You are the count de St. Leon?" said he.

"I am."

"You sent me a memorial a few days ago complaining of the tribunal of this city: I am afraid, sir, I can do nothing for you."

My countenance fell as he spoke; I gasped for breath. I had conceived a most favourable anticipation as he entered, and my disappointment was particularly cruel. I had said in my heart, This is the very man to rescue my injured fame.

"I see, sir, you are disappointed," resumed he. "I have not given up the affair: if I had, this visit, which I design as a mark of attention, would be an insult. The moment I received your memorial, I paid the utmost regard to it. If the affair had been as you represented it, I know I could not do any thing more acceptable to my sovereign than interfere in your behalf. I have spent the whole interval in investigating the case. I have seen the magistrate who committed you; I have visited the spot where your crime is alleged to have been perpetrated; I have had an interview with your wife."

"Well, sir," cried I, alarmed and impatient—"well, sir, and the result?"

"Appearances are uncommonly strong against you: they can scarcely be stronger. But you have a right to be heard; it is for the sake of discharging that last act of justice that you see me this morning."

"Great God!" exclaimed I, overwhelmed with chagrin, "is if possible that my countryman, the man to whom I was proud and happy to appeal, the gallant Monluc, should believe me a murderer? I swear by every thing that is sacred, by the blood of him that died for me on the cross, and by my eternal salvation, that I am as innocent as the child unborn!"

"I am glad to hear you express yourself with this emphasis and fervour. I cannot but say that to my own feelings it has great weight. But I must not suffer myself as a man, and still less in the public capacity in which I stand, to be overcome and confounded by your asseverations. There is a connected and most unfavourable story against you: this it is incumbent on you to clear up."

"And you say, you have seen my wife?" I was distracted and overwhelmed by Monluc's way of putting the question. I was divided between my anxiety to be justified, and the solemn mystery of the affair to which his enquiries led; and I probably spoke thus from an unconscious desire to gain time.

"Yes, that is another presumption in your favour. Madame de St. Leon is perhaps the most striking and extraordinary woman I ever saw. Of the husband of such a woman, especially when he appears to be the object of her attachment, I should be always inclined to think well. Madame de St. Leon pleaded for you with earnestness and affection. But, amidst all her ardour, I could perceive that she felt there was something mysterious and unpleasant in the affair, that she was unable to develope."

As Monluc spoke, I saw that I had failed in one of the main anchors of my hope. I thought that no one could have talked with my beloved Marguerite, and have left her with the opinion that I was a murderer. How did this happen? Was she lukewarm and unfaithful in my vindication?

"What she," continued my countryman, "I could see, was not only unable to explain, but did not fully understand, it is you alone can clear; the concealment of the stranger, his disappearance, what became of the body, and your own sudden transition from poverty to wealth."

I was by this time fully sensible of the nature of my situation. I summoned my fortitude; I felt that I had no longer any hope but in the dignity of innocence.

"You call on me for explanation," replied I. "Can you not conceive, gallant Monluc, that I may be able to resolve your doubts, and yet that I will not? Explanation is not the business of a man of honour. He cannot stoop to it. He will win the applause and approbation of mankind, if won, in silence. He will hold on the even course of a generous spirit, and turn neither to the right nor to the left, to court the suffrage, or deprecate the condemnation of a giddy multitude. Such, my brave countryman, have been the maxims of my past life; such will be the maxims of my future."

"I admire," answered Monluc, "at least the gallantry of these sentiments, though I may be inclined to doubt their prudence. But, if such is your determination, permit me to say, you have no concern with me. He who resolutely withholds explanation, must arm himself with patience, and either wait the operation of time, or rest satisfied with the consciousness of his innocence."

"And is that all? Will there not be some noble spirits, who, separating themselves from the herd, will judge of him by what they feel in their own breasts, and be drawn to him with an irresistible impulse? Was it not natural that I should expect Monluc to be one of these? It would be hard indeed, if he who disdains to temporise with popularity, and to vindicate himself from the ungenerous constructions of sordid minds, should not by that very proceeding secure the friendship and sympathy of those, whose friendship it will be most grateful to him to possess."

"The friends of an innocent man, whom a combination of circumstances has exposed to the most painful suspicions, must always be few. He can scarcely expect the acquittal and sympathy of a stranger. I must know, I must have felt and observed in a man a thousand virtues, before I can be entitled to treat accumulated presumptions against him as nothing."

"And thus then are to end my hopes in Monluc? He does not feel that I am innocent? He does not recognise in me the countenance, the voice, the turn of thought, of a brother, a man no less incapable than himself of every thing disgraceful and ignominious? Be it so! I will, as you advise me, rest upon the consciousness of my innocence. A Frenchman, the descendant of illustrious ancestors, long an exile, long the victim of adversity, but at all times conscious of the purity of my sentiments and the integrity of my conduct, I will not suffer myself to be overwhelmed with this last desertion, this ultimate refusal of justice!"

"Count de St. Leon! your appeal is full of energy. In whatever way I decide, it will leave an unpleasant sensation in my breast. Let us suppose that, as a private man, I could take you to my arms, and dismiss every unfavourable appearance from my mind. You must remember that I am here in a public character, and that only in a public character am I capable of affording you assistance. Thus situated, I am bound to resist the impulses of a romantic and irregular confidence, and to do nothing of which I shall not be able to render a clear and intelligible account.

"Let us not part thus! It is not the vindication of your character to the world, with which we are at present concerned. It is only necessary that you should furnish a sufficient ground to justify me to myself for interfering in your behalf. Explain to me the particulars of your case, in confidence if you will, but fully and without reserve. I will not abuse your confidence. I will make no use of your communication, but such as you shall yourself approve. Only enable me to have a reason for acting, that is not merely capable of being felt, but that I may know is in its own nature capable of being stated to another. It is upon me that you call to take certain measures; you must enable me to judge of their propriety.

"You are mistaken when you suppose the appearances against you to be slight. It is not a slight circumstance, that you profess to be ignorant of, or have refused to disclose, the country, the connections, and even the name of the stranger whom you so anxiously concealed. The disappearance of his body is still more extraordinary. What intelligible motive, except a guilty one, can I assign for that? But your sudden wealth immediately after this disappearance, is especially material. It is a broad and glaring fact, that men cannot shut their eyes on, if they would. The chain and combination of events, that proceeds systematically from link to link, is the criterion of guilt and the protector of reputation. Your case, as it now stands, is scarcely to be termed equivocal: upon the supposition of your criminality all is plain and easy to be accounted for; upon any other supposition it appears an inscrutable mystery. Place but the balance even; present to me an exposition of these facts, that shall make your innocence not less probable than your guilt; and, as I feel myself interested for you and your family, and as the presumption, when matters are doubtful, ought always to be on the favourable side, I consent to be your friend!"

"How unfortunate," I exclaimed, "am I doomed to be! Your proposal is liberal and generous; but I must refuse it! My story is an unhappy one: particulars have been reposed in my fidelity, which I am not at liberty to communicate, but which, if communicated, you would not regard as dishonourable. I may be made the martyr of infamy, and the abhorrence of my species; I can endure adversity and anguish; I can die; but that which you demand from me never can be confided to any mortal ear!"

"As you please," rejoined Monluc. "The secrets of a dead man, to be preserved after his death, and that to the ruin of him who is their depository, must, I believe, be villanous secrets; and the secret of a villain no one is bound to observe. You must further give me leave to tell you, that, whatever a high-strained sense of honour might dictate in that point, the fortune you possess is your own affair, and to dissipate or not the mystery which hangs upon that is wholly at your discretion. But I have already advanced as far, perhaps further, than circumstances or propriety could justify, and there can now be no more parley between us."

"Monluc," cried I, "I submit! However harsh your decision is as towards me, however painful and unfortunate its consequences, I will admit it to be that which duty prescribes to you. I struggle, I contend, no further. One thing only I would willingly obtain of you, that you would interpose your influence to obtain for me the society and intercourse of my family. The transaction of this day will then be remembered by me with respect towards you, and a melancholy regret that I could not entitle myself to your esteem. I shall recollect with pleasure that I owe something to the generosity of Monluc."

"Incredible pertinacity!" exclaimed my visitor, with a voice of perplexity and astonishment. "What am I to conceive of you? Under what appearance shall I consider you in the records of my memory? Your silence is the indication of guilt, and in that indication I ought to acquiesce. Yet the fortitude of your manner, and something, I know not what, of emotion, that your manner produces in my own bosom, would fain persuade me you are innocent. Why will you leave me a prey to this contention of thought? If all men, constituted as I am, were to feel in you, as it were, the magnetism of innocence, shame, the simple inference of understanding, and the general sense of mankind, would oblige them to treat you as guilty. What I can however, be assured I will cheerfully do for you. I cannot deliver you from prison, but I will not fail to obtain the mitigation you ask. Farewell!"

Such was the issue of my interview with Monluc. It was clear that my reputation was wounded beyond the power of remedy. While the question had only been of a magistrate, haughty, supercilious, insolent and unfeeling, I flattered myself that the harshness of the conclusions that were drawn, might be ascribed to the depravity of his character. But Monluc was the reverse of this man. He was not less generous and heroic than the magistrate was gross and illiberal. His desire to relieve me was not less apparent than the magistrate's eagerness to oppress. Yet his conclusion was the same, and was felt by me so much the more bitterly, in proportion to the humanity, the kindness, the intrepidity, and the virtue, of the man from whom it flowed. Virtue and vice, barbarism and refinement, were equally engaged in the concert against me, and there was no chance I should triumph in a contention with so many enemies.

I might now be said to have reached the end of my adventure: I had closed one grand experiment upon the donation of the stranger. What had it produced to me? Not one atom of the benefits I anticipated; not a particle of those advantages which a little while ago had made the intoxications of my waking dreams. Its fruits had been distasteful and loathsome. Whether I looked to my person, my family, or my fame, I had felt in all the miserable effects of this treacherous and delusive gift. My person was shut up in prison; and I was now to make an experiment whether, by clandestine and secret proceedings, wealth could restore to me the liberty of which wealth had deprived me. My family was blasted; my wife was struck to the heart, and no mortal skill could restore the wound she had suffered; my son was gone unaided into voluntary exile, that he might shun the contagion of my follies; what was I to do with the poor remains of my house, forlorn, dejected, and wretched? The wound my good name had received, was of the most decisive species. When I first encountered contumely at Dresden, and was called on for explanation by Coligny, the difficulties of my condition struck anguish to my soul. But what were they, compared with what had now overtaken me? I was charged with robbery and murder, with every thing that combines the whole species against the perpetrator, and determines them, without sense of compunction, to extirpate him from the face of the earth. Perhaps it was only by the courtesy of the laws of this state, that I was permitted my choice between an ignominious death and perpetual imprisonment. I might possibly indeed escape from my confinement; I might pass into a distant country; I might be fortunate enough to cut off all connection between my past and my future life, and thus enter upon a new career. But this to a man of honourable mind is a miserable expedient. With what feelings does he recollect, that there is a spot where his name is abhorred, where a story is told against him to excite the wonder of the ignorant, and the torpid feelings of the sluggish soul, a story to darken with new infamy the records of guilt, and to infect the imagination of the solitary man with nameless horrors? To be the theme of such a tale, is no common evil. No matter how far the man to whom it relates, shall remove from the detested spot; the spot itself with all its chain of circumstances, will often recur; the voices that repulsed and humbled him will ring in his ear; the degraded figure he made will rise for ever fresh to his imagination. He cannot ascend to any free and lofty sentiment; he cannot attain the healthful tone of unblemished virtue; wherever he goes, he carries the arrow of disgrace in his bosom, and, when he would erect his head on high, it reminds him of the past, and stings him to the heart.

If the consciousness of all this would have been painful to any other man, what was it to me, who had been brought up from my infancy in the opinion that fame was the first of all human possessions, and to whom honour and an unimpeached integrity had ever been more necessary than my daily food, or than the life which that food supported? What would I not have given could I have returned to the situation in which the inauspicious arrival of the stranger had found me? But that was impossible. If all that I had recently passed through could but have proved a dream, if I could have awakened and freed myself from the phantoms of this horrible vision, how happy beyond all names of happiness should I by such an event have been made! What a lesson would it have taught me of the emptiness and futility of human wishes! What a sovereign contempt would it have impressed upon me for wealth and all its train of ostentation! How profound a feeling of contentment with humble circumstances and a narrow station would it have produced in my mind! Alas, the conception of those advantages and that peace was the illusion, and not the evils I had sustained, and from which I could not escape!

CHAPTER XXII.

Meanwhile it was necessary that I should make the best of the present circumstances. My heart was wounded; my spirit was in a manner broken; but not so utterly withered and destroyed as to make me rest supine in perpetual imprisonment. I felt with equal conviction and pungency that my character and my happiness had sustained the deepest injuries; but I felt it incumbent on me to collect and improve the fragments that remained. For some days indeed after the conference with Monluc, I was sunk in the deepest dejection. But, as that dejection subsided, I began to turn a steady attention upon the future. I recollected that an eternal and inexhaustible gift deserved to be made the subject of more than one experiment, before a decision was formed upon its merits. I shall become wiser, said I, as I go forward. Experience, however bitter, will teach me sagacity and discrimination. My next experiment shall be made with more prudence and a soberer gradation. I will remove to some distant country, where the disadvantages of my past adventures shall not follow me. I will take a new name. I shall then enjoy the benefit of a tyro just entering a scene, to all the personages of which he is wholly unknown. I shall be like a serpent that has stripped its tarnished and wrinkled skin, and comes forth in all the gloss and sleekness of youth. Surely, in an unknown land, with the prejudice of wealth in my favour, and no prejudices against me, I shall know how to conduct myself so as to obtain honour and respect. It is impossible that inexhaustible wealth and immortal youth, gifts so earnestly coveted by every creature that lives, gifts which if I were known to possess, my whole species from the mere impulses of envy would probably combine to murder me, as not able to endure the sight of one so elevated above his brethren,—it is impossible that such gifts should not be pregnant with variety of joy.

Marguerite greatly contributed to raise me from the dejection, into which my imprisonment and the conference of Monluc had sunk me. She was my better genius. I had been so accustomed to receive consolation from her lips in the most trying circumstances, that now the very sound of her voice was able to smooth my wrinkled brow, and calm my agitated spirit. I listened as to the sound of an angelic lyre; I was all ear; I drank in the accents of her tongue; and, in the dear delight, my cares were hushed, and my sorrows at an end. She talked to me of her daughters, whom she represented as about to have no protector but their father; she urged me to watch over them, and to take such steps as should most conduce to their future virtue and happiness; she pointed out the practicability of escape, and recommended to me to fly to some distant country: the dreams of future prosperity from the gifts of the stranger were not hers; they were all my own. It was inexpressibly affecting at this time to receive consolation from her, who had no consolation in her own breast, who had bid farewell to all the gay attractions of the world, and talked familiarly of her death as a thing certain to happen in no very long time. She had lost the purest gratifications of the domestic scene; she had lost her son; her heart was broken; yet with her dying accents she sought to dispel retrospect, and inspire cheerfulness, in the breast of her husband.

The reader may perhaps imagine that I was something too sanguine, when, surrounded with jailors and all the precautions of a prison, I planned the nature and scene of my next residence exactly as if I had been a person at large. But I took it for granted that the power of money I possessed would easily unlock to me the gates of my captivity. I believed that, upon the lowest calculation, personal liberty was clearly included among the gifts of the stranger. Impressed with this opinion, I fixed upon a negro, a servant of the prison, and who had the keys of my apartment, as the subject of my pecuniary experiment. The idea of applying to him had perhaps first occurred to me, from the mere circumstance of my seeing him more frequently than any other attendant of the prison. When I thought further of the matter, I judged, from the meanness of his rank and his apparent poverty, that I could not have chosen better. So far as related to the sum to be paid as the price of my liberty, it was indeed indifferent to me, whether it were large or small. I had however suffered so much from the inconsiderate lavishing of wealth, that I had no inclination on the present occasion to make ostentation of more than was necessary. But, what was of most importance to me, I was desirous that my first experiment should be a successful one. Though not unaware of the power of gold, I conceived that, among persons of middling rank and easier circumstances, there might be varieties of disposition, and I might be mistaken in my choice. Some might have the whim of integrity, or might place a sturdy sort of pride in showing that they were content with what they had, and were too high for a bribe. There might be persons who, though of plebeian rank, might value reputation as much as ever I had done, and be of opinion that no advance of station could compensate for the name or the consciousness of dishonour. These distinctions may seem an idle and superfluous refinement, when it is considered that I had the power of raising my bribe to the level of any man's honesty or pride, be it as great as it might; and it may be thought that my offer might be so increased as to be too dazzling for mortal firmness to resist. Be that as it will, I am merely stating the reflections that passed through my mind, not entering into their vindication.

Taking the first opportunity then of accosting this man when he was alone with me, I addressed him thus:—

"My good friend, are not you poor?"

"Yes, sir."

"Would not you readily do me a kindness?"

"If my master give me leave, I will."

"You mistake me. Would you be my friend?"

"I do not know what you mean, sir. I have been used to call the man I love my friend. If you mean that, you know I cannot choose whether I will be a man's friend; it comes of itself."

"Can I not make you my friend?"

"That is, make me love you?"

I was surprised at the propriety of his answers. I am unable at this distance of time to recall the defects of his language: and I disdain the mimic toil of inventing a jargon for him suitable to the lowness of his condition: the sense of what he said I faithfully report. I had before been struck with a certain correctness of thinking in him; but I now examined his countenance more attentively than I had ever before done, and thought I could distinctly trace in it the indications of a sound understanding and an excellent heart.

"I do not know, sir," continued he. "If I see that you are a good man, I believe I shall love you. But if it happened that you were good and generous to me, I am sure I should love you very much."

"You are very poor?"

"So they tell me. I never had more than a shilling or two at a time in my life."

"It is a very sad thing to be poor?"

"Why, yes, so I have heard, sir. But, for my own part, I am always merry and gay."

"My good fellow, I will make you rich."

"Thank you, sir! But what good will that do me?"

"You are a servant: I will make you a master of servants."

"Now, that I should not like at all. I am merry, because I am light-hearted. If I had money, and property to take care of, and servants to direct, I am afraid they would make me grave and suspicious, and in every respect unlike what you see me."

"Is it possible you should be pleased with your present situation, under the orders of one man in a house, and obliged to play the tyrant to the rest?"

"Why, as you say, sir, there may be more agreeable situations than the life of a jail. But, as to being under orders, I have no objection to that. I never knew any other condition, and therefore I am contented. It is not pleasant indeed to have a master who is always scolding and dissatisfied; but the gentleman I serve at present is reasonable; I know how to content him, and, when I have done that, he leaves me to please myself. You offer me money: now, sir, that is not what I call being generous; I count nothing for much, except when a man shows me has bowels, and convinces me that he thinks justice due even to a negro. I dare say however you designed it for generosity, and expected something from me in return. Tell me what it is you want, and whatever I can do with propriety, you may depend on it I will."

"Do you approve of a man's being deprived of his liberty?"

"Will you please to tell me what you mean by liberty? You offered me just now what you called liberty and independence; and I am content to be a servant."

"Would you be pleased, instead of being a turnkey, to have the key turned on yourself?"

"That I should not. I understand the disagreeableness of that well enough, for when I first entered this place, it was as a prisoner."

"If then, my good fellow, you were convinced that I was a man disposed to be generous to you in your own way, and to deserve your attachment and love, surely you would not refuse to deliver me from a situation which you have yourself felt to be so disagreeable and calamitous."

"I understand you now, sir. I have already a master with whom I am satisfied, and I do not wish to change my service. When I was a prisoner, he found out that I was innocent; he got me cleared, and gave me employment. I am put here for the express purpose of seeing the prisoners in safe custody. That is the contract between me and my master. When I took the keys, by that action I pledged myself to be faithful to my trust; and the nobleness of my master's behaviour to me in removing me from being a prisoner to be a free servant, is a double bond upon my fidelity. I would sooner consent to be torn limb from limb, than fail in what is expected from me. You may be generous to a harmless stranger; you have most reason to be generous to a man you love; but, if you would heap benefits upon me merely because I proved myself a villain, I can only say it would be disgraceful to be the object of your favour."

Thus saying, he quitted me, and withdrew from further parley. The conversation in which we had engaged, though I had had considerable experience in the world, was altogether new to me, and overwhelmed me with astonishment. I found in this trial, that the power of money was subject to limitations, of which previously I had not been in the slightest degree aware. I thought that nothing but the most extraordinary degree of resolution and self-denial could enable a man to resist its enticements; and I had even been told, though I did not believe, that every man had his price, and a bribe capable of indefinite augmentation must be in all cases victorious. Yet here was a poor creature utterly exempt from its operation. He had no sense of those attractions, which so often degrade the best, and convert virtue into the most shameless profligacy. It cost him no effort to be honest, and he uttered sentiments that would have given lustre to the most heroic character, without any consciousness of their greatness. What I had seen, led me also to reflect on another singularity I discerned in him. In the midst of the admirable, I had almost said the sublime, integrity he discovered, (for is it not a criterion of the sublime to be great without an effort?) he was destitute of knowledge, of intellectual cultivation, and all those exquisite sensations that most distinguish the man from the brute. He passed on quietly in the road of ordinary life, and thought not of the ambition to be wise or great, to be honoured by thousands, or a benefactor to ages yet unborn. Kings might have confessed their inferiority to this man. But is he to be regarded as the model of what a human creature should be wished to be? Oh, no!

But the most memorable feeling impressed upon me by this conversation, was a conviction of what I had been backward to confess, that knaves were the persons to whose assistance and concert I must look, and that I must be upon my guard against an honest man. No one was qualified to be my coadjutor, till he had proved himself unworthy of all just and honourable society. The friend I must seek, was a man whose very soul melted at a bribe, whom money would seduce to perpetrate whatever his judgment most abhorred. Honour and integrity in the most refined and the rudest state, Monluc and the negro, both refused. It is impossible to conceive a sensation more painful and humiliating, than was this conviction to my mind.

I was not long at leisure for these reflections. In a few minutes the master of the prison entered my apartment, and with him the negro whom I had endeavoured to prevail on to assist in restoring me to liberty. The master began to reproach me in very harsh terms for attempting to seduce his servant from his duty, and asked me what sort of enjoyment or satisfaction a man could have in life, if he could not depend upon the people he put into his employment? To this I answered with sternness, "that I should hold no debate about right and wrong with a jailor; that he might depend upon it I would leave no stone unturned to set myself free, and, what was more, that I would be free; and that, for his part, it was his business to keep me if he could, but not to insult me." I therefore insisted upon his quitting the room.

"What use," replied the fellow, "do you think now there is in putting yourself in a passion? If I have not a right to speak to you, I know what I have a right to do, put you in the strong room, and load you with irons."

I turned my back upon him. "And how came you," said I to the negro, "to go and betray me? I should have expected better things of you. If you refused to serve me, at least you needed not have endeavoured to hurt me."

"I did nothing but my duty, sir. I have no wish to hurt you: but it is my business, not merely to take care of my master's interests myself, but to see that they are not injured by any body else. If he was not put on his guard, you might have been more successful with the next turnkey you endeavoured to bribe."

"You will find it more to your interest, monsieur," interposed the jailor, "to talk to me than to my servant. You are determined to be free, you say. If that is the case, and it is to happen, who has so good a right to benefit by your resolution as I have?"

My eyes were opened in a moment. I saw that the knave whose rigour and sternness could not hold out against the warmth of a bribe, the friend of whose assistance I was in want, stood before me.

"I do not wonder," proceeded he, "that you preferred applying to one of my servants. Their honesty must be expected to be had at a cheaper market. But, for my part, I am determined that no man shall ever pass these walls, without my being the richer. If then your escape is a thing that must happen, let us see what you can afford to give me for it."

"Dear master," interposed the negro, "you surely will not listen to the gentleman's offer. When I refused to betray my trust, it is impossible you should consent to betray yours!"

"Hold your tongue, blockhead!" said the other. "Do not you see that monsieur is determined to escape? I know he is rich. Though you have refused a bribe, I am sure that all your fellows will not. The thing will happen sooner or later in spite of every thing I can do; and there can be no harm in my helping to bring about, what it is impossible I should prevent."

A morality like this seems exactly in its place in the breast of a jailor. We had already made some progress in adjusting the terms of our contract, when the keeper of the prison interposed:—

"But, monsieur, you will please to remark, that this is an affair which will be attended with difficulty. Whatever passes between you and me must be a secret. Your escape will be a thing open and notorious, and you must have a confederate, that I may not bear the blame of it. You must therefore take my black here along with you, that his flight may cause all the blame to fall upon him."

"O, pray, master," said the negro, "do not part with me! I love you, and will do any thing in the world, if you will let me stay. You saved my life for aught I know, and made a man of me again; you cannot think what good it does me to serve a master that has been so kind to me!"

"Get you gone!" replied his owner. "You are of no use to me; you are not fit for a jail; you are so simple, I cannot tell what to do with you!"

"Indeed I do not like to go with this gentleman; it will break my heart. He said he would be generous and kind to me, if I turned a villain; I shall never be able, and shall never desire to earn his kindness: but you rewarded me because I was innocent. He said he would make a master of me; and I am better as I am; I had much rather be a servant."

The difficulties of this poor fellow were soon silenced by the peremptoriness of his master. The jailor told him that he would do him a great service, by thus giving his master an opportunity of representing him as the traitor; and, with this consideration, the negro dried his tears, and with a reluctant heart consented to accompany me. Thus were his exemplary fidelity and affection rewarded! So little do some men seem capable of feeling the value of attachment! The character of the master was a singular one. The meanness and mercenariness of his spirit were unredeemed by a single virtue. He was avarice personified. But he had found or imagined an interest in taking this negro, who had been want only thrown into prison by a former tyrant, for his servant; and this the poor fellow, in the simplicity of his heart, had mistaken for an act of exalted generosity. His avarice had swallowed up all his other passions; and his servants had neither impatience nor insolence to encounter from him: weighed therefore in the balance of the negro's experience, he appeared a miracle of mildness and benevolence.

Our bargain was at length concluded; and, the next time Marguerite came to visit me, I announced to her the success of my negotiation. Before we parted, we sent for the jailor, and discussed with him the road I should take. My purpose was to pass into Italy; and Marguerite undertook by midnight to have every thing prepared to convey us to the foot of the mountains. This point being adjusted, the keeper of the prison left us; and, tenderly embracing Marguerite, I besought her to congratulate me upon the recovery of my liberty. She had heard however of the infamous nature of the charge against me, and, though she yielded it no credit, I could easily perceive that it rendered yet heavier the depression under which she laboured. She returned my embrace; the tears stole down her cheeks; but she was silent. I endeavoured to divert her thoughts and re-animate her spirits, by hinting at the new scenes before us, and the distant country to which we were about to remove; but in vain. "I will not reproach you, Reginald!" said she; "I will not desert my duty while I have power to perform it; you may depend upon my doing every thing I am able both for the children and yourself!"

She left me in a very melancholy frame of mind. I had not expected to see her thus languid and disconsolate; and upon the eve of my liberation, I felt it like caprice. Incomparable woman! She was incapable of giving intentional pain: but, with her exquisitely susceptible mind, she was unable to support the dreadful reverse in which I had involved her, or even at times to assume the gestures of cheerfulness and tranquillity; gestures that, at the best, but ill disguised the grief within!

I was busily reflecting on what had just occurred, when the keeper of the prison re-entered my apartment. "I am come, monsieur," said he, "to take my leave of you. As I do not at all intend to lose my place, it is not proper that I should see you any more. You understand me?"

Two days had already elapsed since the conclusion of our contract, and I had provided myself for this and such other demands as seemed likely to be immediately impending. I should have preferred indeed to have delayed this payment till the moment of my departure: but what the jailor suggested appeared reasonable; and I could not assign, even to my own mind, any cause why I should be reluctant to comply with it. I paid to this wretch the price of his villany.

I now began to count the hours, and eagerly to anticipate the arrival of midnight. Though the moment of my liberty was so near, I yet contemplated with unspeakable loathing the scene of my confinement, which was associated with the deepest disgrace and the blackest charges that are incident to a human creature. I felt as if, in proportion as I removed from the hated spot, I should at least shake off a part of the burthen that oppressed me, and grow comparatively young again.

Time was far from moving indeed with the rapidity my impatience required; but the hour of appointment at last was near, and I expected every moment the faithful negro to appear, and announce to me my freedom. The cathedral bell now sounded twelve; I heard the noise of steps along the gallery; and presently a key was applied to the door of my apartment. It opened; and three persons, whom I knew for servants of the prison, entered.

"Come, sir," said one of them; "you must follow me."

"Where is my friend the negro?" said I.

"Ask no questions; speak never a word; but come."

It was strange that the master of the prison, whose temper was so full of anxiety and caution, should unnecessarily trust three of his people, who might easily have been kept ignorant of this hazardous secret! This circumstance however did not strike me at first so strongly as it ought to have done. I had perfect confidence in his fidelity to his profligate bargain, and expected every moment to meet the negro who was to be my guide. My conductors led me by a way which I soon perceived did not lead to the ordinary entrance of the prison.

"Where are we going?" said I.

"Hold your tongue, or you will spoil all;" replied one of them roughly.

I bethought me that there might be an objection to the dismissing me by the public gate; I recollected to have heard that there were several subterranean outlets to the citadel;

I judged from the words I had just heard that my conductors were acquainted with the plan that had been formed; and for all these reasons I proceeded with tolerable ease and security. I was not much longer however permitted to doubt. I was conducted to one of the dungeons of the prison, and told that there I was to remain. At first I remonstrated loudly, and told them "that I had been promised my liberty, and not a treatment like this."

"We know that, sir," replied they, "and that is the reason you are brought here. It is our business to teach you that the greatest offence that can be committed by a man in prison is to attempt to escape."

The shock and surprise that so unexpected an issue to my adventure produced, rendered me outrageous. I was no longer able to control my fury; and, without knowing what I proposed, I knocked down two of my attendants before they had an opportunity to secure me, and rushed up the flight of steps by which we had descended. The third however contrived to intercept me; and, while we struggled, the other two came to his assistance. They loaded me with fetters and chained me to the wall. I was then left in utter darkness.

I felt myself sore with the bruises I had received in the contest; but what was infinitely worse, I found the expectations of freedom I had so confidently entertained, baffled and disappointed. Marguerite and my children were at this moment waiting for me to join them. They would probably wait hour after hour in vain. To what cause would they attribute my failing of my appointment? To what cause was I myself to attribute my miscarriage? My hopes in this instance had been in the utmost degree sanguine; what was I to count upon for the future? Was money useless in every instance in which mankind agreed to think its power unquestionable? What was the source of the present catastrophe and the harsh treatment I endured? Was the keeper of the prison discovered, and dismissed from his office? Had the negro gone and given information against him? I formed a thousand conjectures as to what might have happened; but I was unable to rest in any.

I had remained about twelve hours in this situation, full of angry and disconsolate thoughts, when the principal jailor entered my dungeon. I looked at him with astonishment; the cloud vanished from my understanding, and I began to comprehend the solution of the enigma.

"Are you at large?" cried I, with indignation: "why then am I here?"

"You are here by my orders."

"Execrable villain!" said I. "Did you not promise me my freedom? Have you not received the price of it? How dare you show yourself in my presence?" As I spoke, I shook my chains, I clenched my fists, I trembled with resentment and rage.

"If you are not perfectly quiet and reasonable," said he, "I shall leave you to your fate and return no more."

Nothing is more singular in a state of great mental effervescence, than the rapidity with which our ideas succeed each other. At such times we seem to think more in minutes than at other times in hours. I felt how miserable a slave a man is, the moment he falls completely into the power of another. The wretch who stood before me was more vacant of human affections than any one I ever saw. Yet I was his creature, to be moulded as he pleased. A thousand injuries he could inflict upon me, for which neither the institutions of society nor the extraordinary endowments I derived from the stranger could afford a remedy. He might so torture my mind and baffle my wishes, as to kill in me every spark of lofty adventure and generous pride. My liberty might, for aught I knew, be for years at his disposal. I felt however that my best course was to regard him with contempt, and use him as I would a spade or a file, to execute my purposes, without suffering him to awaken my passions. I immediately grew more calm, and he perceived the revolution of my sentiments.

"You seem to wonder," continued he, "that I did not keep my engagement with you? I pride myself upon being superior to the prejudices, by which other men are frightened, like children with a bugbear. I have therefore no rule but my interest: and I did not see how my interest bound me to keep my engagement with you."

"And what became of the countess?"

"I neither know nor care. I suppose she stayed all night under the walls; I knew she durst not disturb the prison."

I felt I had still emotions to suppress. I curbed my tongue, but they showed themselves in my eyes.

"How do you intend to dispose of me?"

"Keep you in close custody. I have got your thousand pounds; the next thing for me to take care of is, that I do not lose my place."

"And for what purpose do you come to me now?"

"Why to tell you a secret, I have not quite determined what conduct to pursue, and therefore I came here that I might have a better opportunity of judging."

"Are you not afraid that I should inform the government how you have cheated me?"

"You inform! Have not I got you under lock and key? I warrant you, I will take care what goes out of these walls to the government."

"The countess has a licence to visit me."

"What care I for that? I can keep her at bay as long as I will. She will not easily go to the government; and she is not such a fool as not to know, that to lodge a complaint against me, is not the way to procure the liberty of a man condemned to perpetual imprisonment. I can at any time trump up a story of your attempting to corrupt the turnkeys, and be sure, when I do, I will not want for proofs. That will cover any thing I can do to annoy you, and answer any accusation you can make against me. Do you think that the word of a jailor will not be taken, before that of the murderer he has in custody?"

"I can bring your own servants as witnesses, three of whom assaulted me last night."

"Dunce, do you think I trusted them with my secret? They have nothing to tell, and apprehend nothing but a plot between you and my black, who has been put into the penitentiary for his offence. He is my only confident; and I trust him, because his stupidity answers to me for his faith."

"Suppose I were to double the bribe for which you sold me my liberty, what security should I have that you would abide by your bargain?"

"Oh, if you were to do that, it would alter the case."

"Might you not then detain the money, and defy me, as you have done now?"

"Suppose that a thing which might happen: can you help yourself? can you do better?"

I saw there was no remedy, and I was constrained to allow the success of this twofold perfidy. It was with an ill grace, and an attempt at sullenness and indifference, that the jailor accepted my proposal. The second thousand however had irresistible charms; and, in spite of himself, the sensation that made his heart dance, relaxed his muscles, and played about his mouth. He was puzzled what to think of me. The facility with which I produced the sums he demanded, with less apparent effort than they might have come from a duke or a sovereign prince, startled and staggered him. He had still his qualms, and evidently doubted whether he should not raise his price a third time. I saw no safety but in pertinacity and firmness, and had the good fortune ultimately to check his doubtful, half-formed experiments.

I was led by the accidents which have just been related, into further and deeper reflections on the power of money, as well as on the nature of the situation in which I found myself placed by the legacy of the stranger. My present experiment had been made upon a subject apparently the most favourable that could have been devised, upon a man whose breast the love of gold occupied without a rival: yet with this man I very hardly succeeded. I was not indeed so blinded by the present dejection of my spirit and sickness of my heart, as to imagine that I had not a secure game with this base-minded wretch, if I consented to play it. I had only to enlarge my bribe, to change it from the limited sum of two thousand pounds to the more brilliant offer of two thousand per annum, and no doubt I might have led him with me to the extremity of the globe. However he might have demurred, however he might have doubted, however curiosity, whetted even to agony by the goadings of avarice, might have prompted him to an incessant enquiry within himself as to the solution of my character and my powers, his grasping spirit would infallibly have chained his tongue, and been surety for his fidelity. But I could not yet prevail upon myself to endow such groveling and noxious propensities with so rich a reward. I considered, in the language of the stranger, that the talent I possessed was of the most momentous nature, and bestowed by the governor of the universe for the highest purposes; and I should have held myself unjustifiable in enriching by its means, however urgent the necessity might appear, the most worthless of mankind.

The sentiments of my tyrant varied every hour; he was fickle, anxious, and undetermined; harassed with the double fear of losing the sum already obtained, and of not securing the whole of what was capable of being acquired. He parted with me at last with all the pangs of a lover, who witnesses the ceremony of his mistress's taking the monastic veil, and being sundered from him for ever. I was his Fortunatus's purse, and this was the last day he was to enjoy the use of it; I was to him as the buried treasure of some long-forgotten hoarder, and he feared he should quit his digging before he had carried off every thing that the field concealed. At length however he began to apprehend that he had urged the refinement of an unprincipled avarice as far as it would go; and therefore in a few days, the negro being already discharged from his penance, he suffered us to escape together.

CHAPTER XXIII.

Having rejoined the remainder of my family, we set out together for the plains of Italy. My first interview with Marguerite after my return from Dresden had been melancholy. But our situation was now such as to give additional anguish to her serious thoughts. She had then regarded me as ambiguous, mysterious, and impenetrable, qualities from which the frankness of her nature spontaneously revolted; she saw in me the destroyer of her son, the idol of her heart; she believed me an alchymist, a character which she viewed as base, degrading, and insensible; she had heard that rumour had been busy with my fame. But now she saw in me a man of blasted reputation, arraigned and imprisoned for robbery and murder. She did not credit these imputations. But did the ingenuous and noble-minded Marguerite de Damville ever think to find herself allied to a being thus loaded with the world's abhorrence; that she should be compelled to honour with the sacred name of husband a fugitive, a prison-breaker, and an outlaw? If I had suffered these things in the defence of my children, my religion, or my country, the case would have been widely different. If, while encountering the contempt of men, I had carried within me the glorious feeling, that what they regarded as my disgrace was indeed my immortal honour, Marguerite de Damville, beyond all women, was prepared to despise their senseless blame, and proudly to demand her share in such a dishonour.

I know there are men who will listen with fretful impatience to a detail of such sorrows as hers, and who will cry out, "If we must be distressed, give us more substantial and genuine sources of distress!" They will regard the dejection of Marguerite as an idle wilfulness of grief, better entitled to aversion than to sympathy; and will tell me that nothing but the most deplorable blindness could have prevented her from discerning the happiness of her condition; that she had the world before her, a rich, a brave, and an enterprising husband, with a lovely family of children; that they could move from country to country, and from climate to climate, carrying with them the means of luxury, indulgence, homage, and usefulness. To such moralisers I write not. For those who are incapable of sympathising with the delicate sensations of Marguerite, I am as little qualified to enter into their feelings as they into mine. In the sequel of the story however it is not impossible they may meet with their gratification. I am hastening to events corporeal and palpable. I and my family did wander from country to country, and from climate to climate. With what resulting success will speedily be seen.

Our destination at the present moment led us through the territory of the Grisons, and over a limb of the Rhetian Alps, to Como, Milan, Piacenza, Parma, and Pisa, in the neighbourhood of which latter city we resolved to take up our immediate residence. In this passage we met with few adventures that merit to be recorded in my history. One however seems entitled to a place, both as it tends to display the singular worth of a dumb and unpretending brute, and as it is in some sort connected with the fortunes I encountered in the Pisan territory. It occurred in our journey over the Alps.

One evening, in the wildest and most desolate part of the mountain, after having lodged my family in an inn, I wandered forth to take a survey of the neighbouring scenery. It was moonlight; our travel of the day had been short, and had left on me no impression of fatigue; while the romantic appearance of every thing around, tempted me to extend my excursion further than I had originally purposed. Stories of robberies and murders in the vicinity had been repeated to us, and Marguerite had employed the precaution of desiring Hector, such was the name which the caprice of his former masters had bestowed on my faithful negro, to follow my steps and hold me in sight. No anticipations of danger however disturbed my contemplations. I resigned myself, as all my life I had been accustomed to do, to the impressions of the moment, and sought to shut out memory and the world from all my thoughts. The scene was inexpressibly beautiful; the silence was uninterrupted and awful. The splendour of the moon gave a sober and silvery tint to every thing by which its light was caught; soft white clouds were scattered in the deep azure of the sky; the shades were of a blackness and profundity that could not be surpassed. Every thing was calculated to soothe and subdue the mind, to inspire a grand and expansive tranquillity. The enthusiasm it spoke occupied every channel of my heart. I stood still. It seemed as if motion would have jarred and broken the spell that seized me; I yielded with eager transport to the sentiment that shrowded and enveloped me in its ample embrace.

I had remained motionless for above half an hour, when a sudden and eager sound burst upon my ear. It seemed to be the shriek of some human creature in distress. It was repeated several times. My first impulse was to fly to the spot from which the sound appeared to proceed. Meanwhile Hector came up to me, and endeavoured to detain me by violence. His first principle was obedience to every just and lawful command; and the errand upon which he was commissioned, was to preserve me from the approach of danger. He represented to me the stories of banditti we had recently heard. He told me that we should too probably fall in with a numerous party of these desperadoes, against whom all our efforts, either for ourselves or for those I was desirous to succour, would be nugatory. What would become of my children? what would become of his mistress, if my rashness were succeeded by a fatal event? While he was thus speaking, and exerting himself to detain me, the cries ceased. I believed they were those of a person assassinated. I conceived that I should be the vilest of poltroons if I suffered any consideration to prevent me from endeavouring to afford to this unfortunate the relief in my power.

I had not advanced far, before I perceived coming towards us, in the same direction from which the sound had reached my ear, a dog, entirely black, and of uncommon stature and strength. He was alone. Having caught sight of us, he increased his pace, and had no sooner reached the spot on which we stood, than he seized the flap of my coat, and pulled it with considerable violence. I was somewhat alarmed at his size and action, the latter of which I apprehended to have a hostile design; and, having shaken him off, I put myself in a posture of defence with a cane that I carried in my hand. Undeterred however by my gesture, he returned to the attack, only pulling with something less exertion of strength than he had done before. More accurate attention convinced me that he had no intention to injure me, and I withheld the action of Hector, who had raised his hand to strike in defence of his master. I suffered him to guide me; and, after a considerable circuit which the nature of the road obliged us to take, he led me to a spot where I found a man lying on the ground, and weltering in his blood, but with no person near, to whom to impute the violence he had sustained.

His blood flowed copiously from two or three different wounds, one of them in particular near his left breast; and my first care was to stop the effusion. For this purpose we stripped him of his clothes, and tore his linen into bandages. When we found him, he was insensible; but the anguish of binding his wounds revived him a little, though only enough to extort from him sighs and groans. This accomplished, I dismissed Hector to the inn to procure something in the nature of a litter, by which he might more easily be conveyed within reach of effectual assistance.

I was now left for six hours with no other companions than the wounded gentleman and his dog, upon the very spot upon which he had just before sustained so ferocious a treatment, probably from the hands of banditti. They might every moment be expected to return. This was no agreeable notion to a person circumstanced as I was. I was compelled to feel that a man possessed of boundless and illimitable wealth, and of the power of repelling old age and disease, did not in these advantages possess every thing. Notwithstanding the disappointments and mortifications I had sustained, I was yet attached to life: and though the bequests of the stranger had hitherto produced to me nothing but evil, I still looked, with almost puerile eagerness and beating of heart, for the time when I might spread out the whole extent of my treasures without parsimony or the dread of reverse. During the interval which I employed in these reflections, the wounded man was for the most part in a state of insensibility, and constantly speechless. I expected his death every moment, and I perceived, as I thought with certainty, that there was no hope of his recovery. While we had dressed his wounds, the dog had watched our motions with the most restless attention, and, now that it was over, he came and licked my hands, and laid himself down at my feet. The least motion however, so much as a rustling among the leaves, startled him: he rose, looked round, and seemed to enquire into the cause of the disturbance; but he abstained from barking and every kind of noise; whether it were that he was conscious of the advantage of quiet to a person in his master's condition, or that he had the sense to know, in the situation in which we were placed, that whatever produced alarm, might eventually expose us to undiscovered danger.

It was broad daylight before Hector re-appeared, and several other persons in his company. Hector was not of a temper to have receded from any thing he undertook, and the authority of Marguerite had in this instance seconded his remonstrances with the surly and inactive peasants of the place. I had at this time only one other male servant; but, when Hector returned, he brought with him a crazy kind of litter, and a recruit of four mountaineers. The wounded man still lived, and was conveyed alive to the place at which

I had taken up my lodging. He survived three days; and, during the whole of that period, the dog could neither be moved by force, nor prevailed on by entreaties, to quit the apartment of his master. Before his death my unfortunate guest recovered the power of speech. He told me that his name was Andrea Filosanto, and, which struck me as somewhat extraordinary, that he was of Pisa, the very place at which I purposed to take up my abode. He had a brother resident in that city, and had himself been about to marry a very beautiful and accomplished young lady, an heiress, of the house of Carracciuoli in Pisa. Previously to his marriage, he resolved to make a visit to his mother, who had espoused to her second husband a French nobleman of Languedoc. He had travelled accompanied only by one servant, contrary to the persuasions both of his brother and the family of his intended bride; but that servant, though he had been a very short time in his employment, was active, ingenious, and obliging, and had established himself strongly in the favour of his master. Signor Filosanto had taken with him a sum of money, the produce of one year's income of the dower of his mother; and it was but too probable that the richness of the charge he bore, had been fatal to the life of the bearer. His servant had disappeared from his side not a quarter of an hour before his being attacked by the banditti; and various concurring circumstances seemed to fix on this servant the accusation of being an accomplice with the murderers. Having heard from the unfortunate sufferer the tale of treachery of his human attendant, I related to him the extraordinary example of fidelity and attachment shown by his dog. The master was struck with the story I told, and called the dog to him upon his bed. The poor animal first leaped up upon the foot of the bed, and then warily and with great caution crawled to his master's face. Filosanto embraced the dog, who by his manner showed himself fully sensible of the purport of the action. That very evening, having requested me to convey his remains to the tomb of his ancestors at Pisa, the master expired. The dog in dumb and constant grief watched by the corpse, and followed the vehicle in which it was conveyed to Pisa. After the funeral, he made the choice, from which he could not be diverted, of living with me, and not with the brother and relations of his master, to whom he was almost wholly a stranger, but who would gladly have received him. One of the advantages I derived from this adventure, was the friendship and protection of the Filosanti and Carracciuoli, two of the most powerful families in Pisa.

I have not yet finished the history of my dog. A few months after our establishment in the Pisan territory, the valet of the deceased had the audacity to appear in that city. He believed himself to be entirely unknown there, his master having taken him into his service during his residence as a student in the university of Bologna; and having ordered him, previously to his projected tour into France, to stay behind and settle his debts and other affairs at that place. He found however an adversary in Pisa that in all his anticipations had never occurred to his thoughts. The dog saw him at a distance in the street, ran towards him with incredible swiftness, and fell upon him with savage violence and ferocity. The man was not extricated from his grip, till he had been severely and dangerously wounded. Thus assailed, all the terrors of superstition and an accusing conscience seized on this devoted villain; he owned who he was, and confessed that he had made one among the assassins and plunderers of his master, visible probably to the dog, though unseen by the unfortunate Filosanto. He declared, that he knew not what motive had brought him to Pisa, that he seemed to himself under the guidance of an impulse which he had not power to resist, and that he rejoiced that Providence had thus conducted him to the expiation of his guilt. He was brought to his trial, and suffered death for his crime.

Charon, such was the name by which my dog was distinguished, showed himself in all his actions worthy of the character for attachment and sagacity which he had in these instances acquired. He was therefore the favourite of my whole family, and particularly of Hector. But his own partiality was with the nicest discrimination reserved for me. The ruling passion of his preceding master had been the sports of the field, and his leading singularity an uncommon familiarity and friendship towards his brute attendants. By this conduct he had won the affections, and perhaps awakened the understanding and virtues, of the faithful Charon. I own my weakness. I could not resist the assiduities and regard of this generous brute; and, though I had never before conceived any extraordinary partiality for creatures of his species, his sagacity and nobleness of nature took a strong hold of my affection. I admired his form and agility as he bounded and gamboled before me upon the plain. In the midst of his gayest frolics he was all attention, and the least sign I made him would instantly divert his exertions to a different pursuit. He was accustomed to salute me with honest, undesigning homage every morning as I came from my chamber, and I should have missed his presence with heaviness of heart upon this plain and homely occasion. He was the associate of my solitary walks, and my companion when pensive meditations induced me to withdraw from all human society. I became accustomed at such periods to observe him by my side, and should have felt that all was not right if he were not there. I was interested in his health, his well-being and his enjoyments; and, if any calamity befell him, was prepared to feel it more severely than a wise man is sometimes willing to confess.—It would scarcely be necessary to add to this simple history of my faithful Charon, the circumstance of his having saved the life of a beautiful little boy of ten years old, who had unluckily slipped into the Arno, and whom he seized by his garments and drew to the shore, had it not some connection with what I shall speedily have occasion to relate.

CHAPTER XXIV.

To return to the thread of my narrative, which in stating these particulars I have in some points anticipated.—I sat down, as I have already said, in the environs of the city of Pisa. Marguerite, as well as myself, had a powerful attachment to the retirement of rural life, and I judged it equally eligible for the health and intellectual improvement of my daughters. I accordingly purchased a small domain, delightfully situated, but of simple appearance, on the banks of the Arno. Here I proposed to remain during the indisposition of my wife, which I flattered myself retirement, tranquillity, attention and kindness, would in no long time be able to cure. To this object I resolved to devote my exertions. Well did she merit this return from me, who had restored me in the guilty ruin of my fortunes, and raised me from the abyss of insanity. Odious and detestable in the utmost degree should I have appeared in my own eyes, if I could have neglected any means I was able to devise, to heal a mischief of which my own precipitation, selfishness, and folly were the only causes. Every little, continual, nameless care I exerted, was as a drop of healing balm to the burning fever and remorse of my conscience. Nothing indeed could eradicate my distemper; I felt the ever-living worm of perpetrated guilt gnawing at my heart. But my solicitudes for Marguerite, at least during the moments they were in action, mitigated my anguish; and this transitory relief, however insignificant it may appear in the eyes of others, I cherished beyond the wealth of kingdoms.

Marguerite and myself appeared at this time to have changed characters. She was languid, indisposed in body and mind, her thoughts gloomy, her hopes blasted, her wishes bankrupt. Still however she maintained her superiority to what I had been in a similar condition. She endeavoured to make the best of what yet remained to her, though she declined the vain attempt of forgetting what she had lost. She hung over her daughters with inexpressible endearment. She consoled them; she reasoned with them; she endeavoured to steel their minds for whatever ill might be yet in store. She cultivated their understandings; she breathed into them mingled sentiments of resignation and energy. There was in her conversation with them a striking tone of celestial and divine. Her eloquence was copious; her manner rich, unaffected, and flowing; her speech simple, free from exaggeration and turbulence, but mild, affectionate, and winning. It sank deep into the hearts of her hearers, and seemed to give a new turn to their tempers and disposition. It rendered the character of Julia at once more distinctive, and yet more chastised; it inspired an unwonted mildness and sensibility to that of Louisa; and rendered the cadette of the family unusually grave, thoughtful, and sedate.

But upon me were devolved the more active occupations of our establishment. Marguerite had formerly been, I was now, the steward. Every kind of superintendence, from which the distinction of sex did not unavoidably exclude me, was resigned to me by the lovely victim of my indiscretions. Marguerite had been my nurse, I was now ambitious to be hers. I made myself the schoolmaster of my children; Marguerite confined her communications to general topics and the culture of the heart. I initiated them in music, drawing, geography, several different languages of Europe, and in every accomplishment that I believed would be really ornamental or improving to them. I might, it is true, have hired different masters to instruct them in each of these branches, and it is not impossible that they might then have been better taught, though I was myself no incompetent preceptor. But I had an honest artifice for my guide in the plan I adopted: I was desirous of removing out of the sight of my wife every thing that might remind her of the fatal legacy, the effects of which she was induced so bitterly to deplore. In some particulars I may affirm of myself that I was now a better and a kinder husband, than I had been in the days of our gayest prosperity, or the scene of our infant loves. I studied with assiduity the temper of Marguerite; I watched her looks; I endeavoured to anticipate her every wish. I meditated with care the plan of life, which her simple and feeling heart, if solely consulted, would have led her originally to have chosen; and I copied out in the whole arrangement of our household the idea painted in my mind. Far from us were now the ostentation and pomp of the family-château on the banks of the Garonne. We lived now, not to awaken admiration and envy in the bosom of guests and spectators: we lived for ourselves. Every thing was elegant; every thing was tasteful; but not an article found its place in our residence, that did not rest its claim to be there upon a plea of usefulness. Though, by the nature of my situation, I was superior to all restraint from a consideration of expense, yet our competent board and orderly habitation approached nearer in their appearance to the honest plainness of a rustic, than to the sumptuousness of hereditary nobility. A table set out with striking propriety and neatness was preferred to the richness of plate and the splendour of porcelain and lustres. I was anxious that Marguerite should forget the change of our situation and the extent of my resources. The objects of my present pursuit were obscurity and content. That Marguerite might forget my acquisition, I was studious to appear to have forgotten it myself. If a stranger had entered our habitation, and surveyed our economy, he would have judged that our revenues amounted to a decent competence, and that we disbursed them with a judicious discretion. Nothing was to be seen that would have betrayed the possessor of the powder of projection.

We had no guests. We cultivated no acquaintance. We were formed to suffice to each other within our little circle; and, but for the importunate recurrence of disquieting reflections, we should have done so. To look at the exterior of our household, it might have been thought that we had arrived at that sweet forgetfulness of anxious care, that delicious leisure and unbroken retreat, which have in all ages been the theme of panegyric to poets and philosophers. But it was not so. Our reciprocal relations were changed; and the hope of the house of St. Leon was no longer in the midst of us, to cheer, to enlighten, and to warm our bosoms.

A life of leisure is often an active and a busy life. The grand, I might almost say the single, object of present attention to me, was the restoration of the health and tranquillity of Marguerite. For that I watched with unwearied assiduity. Subordinate to this occupation were the different arts and accomplishments in which I instructed my daughters. Yet neither the former nor the latter of these engagements filled up all the time of a mind so restless and rapid as mine was. Intervals occurred, in which my attentions to Marguerite would have been, not soothing, but troublesome, and in which I could no longer impart a lesson to my daughters, without relaxing and weakening the spring of progression in their minds. These intervals I sometimes dedicated to chemistry and the operations of natural magic. The more effectually to hide these pursuits from the eye of Marguerite, I occupied, unknown to her, a sort of grotto, buried almost from human observation in a hollow on the banks of the river, and which was connected, by a winding path and a concealed subterranean passage, with the garden of my own habitation. The secrets of the stranger had given me a particular relish for this kind of pursuit. There are habits of the mind and modes of occupying the attention, in which, when once we have engaged, there seems a sort of physical impossibility of ever withdrawing ourselves. This was my case in the present instance. My habit was of no long standing. But no reading of my story, no mere power of language and words, can enable a bystander to imagine how deep it was sunk into my heart, how inextricably it was twisted with all the fibres of my bosom. That he may in some degree enter into my situation, I entreat the reader to consider what are the most imperious passions of the human mind. They have rudely been described to be wealth, power, and pleasurable sensation. How alluring to every one of us are the visionary conceptions of the mind respecting these most potent excitements! But mine were no visions. I had grasped them in my hand, and known their reality. I had felt that the wealth of the whole world was at my disposal, and that I held my life by a tenure independent and imperial. These are not of the class of conceptions that fade and perish from the mind. We cannot wake from them as from a dream, and forget that ever such things were. They had changed the whole constitution of my nature. It would have required a miracle, greater than all the consecrated legends of our church record, to have restored me to what I formerly was. If then I could have resolved never henceforth to use the gifts I had received, I yet firmly believe that I never could have refrained from the composition and decomposition of simples, and from experiments on the nature of substances, chemical and metallic. I was however far from having formed any such resolution as that I have named. My present forbearance to bring forth the secret treasure of my powers was purely an accommodation to the unhappy condition of my wife; and I felt it as a meritorious exertion thus to postpone the use of the faculties I possessed. In the mean time the amusement I sought, that I regarded as properly and entirely my own, consisted in these experiments. While I was busied with my crucible, I was able more vividly to present to myself my seeming superiority to the rest of my species. I used the employments of my grotto, as a sort of starting-post from which to set forth in a series of intoxicating reveries; not to mention that to improve in the facility of my secret operations might become a valuable subsidiary to the pursuits of my future life.

I took occasionally as my companion at these periods the negro of the prison of Constance. I found him sufficiently adapted for my purpose; his innocence and implicit obedience to whomever he served, rendering me secure that he would anticipate nothing, that he would conjecture nothing, that he would rest in what he saw, that I might almost exhibit my whole process under his eye, without once awakening the busy fiend of curiosity in a mind to which science had never unveiled her charms. He was formed to be a pure, passive machine in the hands of his employer, only with this singular difference from the lifeless machine of the engineer or mechanical inventor, that he was susceptible of attachment and affection, as well as of a certain species of contentment and a certain species of goodness and virtue.

A feature of my individual character which has already frequently presented itself to the attention of the reader is the love of admiration and spontaneous deference. I am at this moment ashamed of my vices and my follies; but it must be recollected, in the first place, that they are human, and in the second that I am writing, not their vindication, but their history. In the midst of my experiments and chemical lucubrations, I could not help sometimes ostentatiously exhibiting to Hector the wonders of my art, and those extraordinary effects which have in all ages drawn upon the more eminent operators of natural magic the reproach of being necromancers and conjurers. This I did, partly perhaps that my attendant might learn to look up to me with a kind of nameless respect and awe, but partly also that I might divert myself with the simplicity of his nature, and the gaping and motionless astonishment with which he viewed my performances. If I had not done this, or digressed into idle and ostentatious experiments, he would otherwise have seen enough, in the operations in which his assistance, if not absolutely necessary, was extremely convenient, to have induced a person, so void of the meanest European information, to regard me as assisted by and in league with invisible powers.

The prejudice against me, with which this poor fellow had been impressed at the commencement of our intercourse did not long hold out, in his ingenuous mind, against the more favourable sentiments which my present situation and mode of living were calculated to inspire. The specimens he had hitherto seen of European society were of the most unfavourable kind. His first master was a wretch of brutal disposition, ferocious and insolent; disdaining to reason himself, and impatient of remonstrance in others. This man had exercised the temper of his humble and honest attendant with every variety of savage caprice; and, having tired the restlessness of his own gloomy tyranny, without being able to exhaust the modest and unexampled patience of his servant, had finished by throwing him into gaol, upon a wanton and groundless charge of dishonesty. This, which was intended as a further exercise of tyranny, deserved to be hailed by the poor sufferer as a period of jubilee and deliverance. His innocence, as I have already related, was speedily recognised by his new task-master, who accordingly exerted himself to obtain justice for the friendless victim; and from a reputed thief proposed to elevate him to the rank of a turnkey. Hector had neither kindred nor patron to assist him; the outcast of a gaol, he must again have entered the world with a blasted character. Thus circumstanced, and influenced beside by gratitude to the unlooked-for liberality of his deliverer, he willingly accepted the situation proposed to him. With his new master, who, not less unprincipled, was less tyrannical than his predecessor, the humbleness of his hopes taught him to be contented. Yet in the bosom of the gaoler all his fidelity and regard could not enable him to detect one positive virtue; and, within the walls of the prison, there had existed nothing that could by any possibility cherish and refresh the human heart.

The scene presented to Hector's observation in our little retreat, on the banks of the Arno, was of a very different nature. To his frank and affectionate spirit, it appeared a perfect paradise. He had yet scarcely been acquainted with any but the refuse of mankind, from the infection of whose vices his unapprehensive and invincible simplicity had been his only safeguard; and he was now suddenly introduced to the presence and intercourse of the most perfect of her sex. He loved her as a benefactor, and he worshipped her as a god. There is no receipt for begetting affection in others, so infallible as a warm and susceptible heart. Hector accordingly soon became in a remarkable degree the favourite of my daughters. His temper was naturally cheerful and gay; and, warmed by their encouragement, it became a thousand times more so. When he had completed the occupations of the day, the lightness of his spirit would prompt him to sing and dance for ever. He exhibited the whole circle of his sportive games for their amusement. The infantine innocence of his understanding remarkably adapted him to be the butt of their little waggeries and mischiefs. Whatever tricks were played upon him, were however tempered by the forbearance and regard his worth demanded; while the obstreperous cheerfulness with which he would second their mirth, when most ignorant of its occasion, gave uncommon zest to the amusement, and furnished eternal provocation to the prolonging and varying its features.

Let not the fastidious reader complain of the inconsistency of this part of my picture, or censure the levity of my daughters. I am not writing a tragedy, but a history. Sad grief and melancholy cannot, and ought not, for ever to reign in the human face or the human heart. No daughters ever loved a mother more entirely, more fervently, than Marguerite was loved by her children. They were unwearied in their attention to her: often was their pillow watered with tears, occasioned by the sad presentiment of the loss they were destined to sustain. But the human mind, particularly in the season of youth, has an unconquerable principle of elasticity in its frame. The bow cannot be kept for ever on the stretch; and, when the whole soul appears to be bent down by calamity to the grave, it will often surprisingly recover its vigour and renew its strength. The ingenuous nature of these poor girls led them indeed occasionally to reproach themselves with these moments of cheerfulness as with a crime. But it was no crime. None but the uncharitably rigorous and morose will charge it upon them as a crime. It interfered with no duty; it diminished no affection; it had no tendency to harden their hearts. It was a tax they paid to the imperfectness of our nature; it was a tribute of gratitude to that God who, while he deals out to us the most terrible calamities, fails not to mix with the copious draught some solitary drops of beneficence. Julia alone, whose temper was constitutionally serious and soft, entered little into these sports, of which her youngest sister was the eternal leader and untired partaker. Yet even upon the grave countenance of Julia they would sometimes provoke an unwilling smile, which upon her countenance sat with uncommon lustre.

The hilarity and loveliness which Hector found in the midst of my family instigated and increased the attachment he began to feel for myself. He could not believe that the father of such daughters, and the chosen husband of such a consort, could be destitute of a title to be loved. He reasoned in his own way upon the attempt I had made to corrupt his fidelity, an attack which he never thoroughly digested. I have reason to believe that his attendance upon my chemical processes, and the wonders I occasionally showed to excite his astonishment, did not tend to elevate me in his good opinion. But he could not avoid witnessing in me many of the virtues of a good husband and a good father, and these, so new to his observation, strongly impressed him in my favour. The regularity of my habits and the mildness of my carriage were also calculated to win his affection and esteem. Never had the poor fellow's affections been so forcibly called out as they were in his new situation; and he would cheerfully have stretched out his neck to the assassin's knife, to have warded off impending evil from the meanest of us.

Prosperity and ease have often been found the parents of wishes and inclinations unfelt before. Adversity is the season of sober thought, calls home the erratic mind, and teaches us to be cheaply satisfied. But the man who has many gratifications is apt to wander in imagination from daily and familiar joys, and confidently to reach after things yet untried. Such was the situation of Hector: Hector was in love. Our sweet and simple mansion was distant scarcely more than two hundred yards from a characteristic Italian village. The maid of a little albergo in this place had caught his inexperienced heart. He had been invited by some peasants to a moonlight festivity on the lawn of the albergo; and, though I should have been better pleased that my servants should decline this sort of amusement, I could not have the heart to deny him. It was, so far as I knew, the first and the last time that Hector had ever resorted to it. But I was deceived. Hector had proved the gayest and most amusing of the whole circle. His cheerfulness was inexhaustible, and his mirth in the utmost degree harmless and good humoured. He had played a thousand antics, and danced with an agility that knew no end. In a word, the accomplishments of Hector, in spite of the jetty hue that stained his face, had won the heart, or roused the coquetry, of the plump and rosy bar-maid. The overtures she made and the lures she threw out were too glaring to escape the notice even of the modest Hector. He felt himself flattered, such is human nature, at suddenly becoming an object of admiration and preference to a woman, whom his imagination, stimulated by her visible partiality, attired in a hundred charms. He owned himself hers, in all fair and honest fealty, to the world's end.

Love taught Hector a lesson which he had never learned before. In nature he was frank, and, as far as fidelity to his master permitted it, wore his heart as naked as his face. Love taught him dissimulation. A vulgar footman or clown is as forward as the most empty beau, in boasting of the triumphs he has gained over the female heart, and in sacrificing the reputation of those who have loved him at the shrine of his vanity. Not such was Hector. He shut Up his new sensations and reveries as a sacred deposit in his bosom. Nature worked within him, and he would have been ashamed to speak, and distressed to hear, of emotions, now felt, till now never experienced. His artless and ingenuous temper in this one particular assumed the guise of cunning. Never did he tell his love in the ear of any indifferent auditor; assiduously did he avoid pronouncing even the name of her to whom he was attached. In any other case he would have announced to me his inclinations, and previously demanded my leave of absence for his excursions. But love seemed to him imperiously to command privacy, and he employed every imaginable precaution to prevent me and all human beings from knowing whither he went, or that he was absent at all.

In one of his visits to his fair donzella, he happened incautiously to drop some very remote hint of the scenes in which he had just been engaged with me in my secret grotto. The curiosity of the girl was strongly roused; she questioned him further. He started, and was terrified to recollect what he had said. I had strictly enjoined him secrecy towards every member of my family: my precaution had extended no further; for, as I have said, I scarcely knew that he had the most casual intercourse with any person beyond my own roof. But Hector naturally dreaded that what I was so earnest to conceal from every one in my house he would be highly to blame to communicate to a stranger. He therefore peremptorily refused, and with many signs of distress, to say another word on the subject.

The donzella, piqued at his resistance, had recourse to female arts. She was cruel; she uttered words of sharp displeasure and disdain; she knew that a person who refused her such a trifle could not have an atom of regard for her; she commanded him never to see her more. Unsuccessful in these expedients, she had recourse to expedients of a different sort. She wept; she called him base, false-hearted and unkind; she saw he was determined to be the death of her; she was seized with strong fits of sobbing and hysterical affection. In the midst of all this he was as unmoved as a rock of marble. He interpreted every thing that passed in its most literal form; he felt more severely her unkindness, and sympathised more truly in her distress, than perhaps any human creature would have done. But no further could she gain upon him. The confidence of his master was in question, and he would sooner have died upon the rack, than run the slightest risk of betraying it.

From these arts she descended to arts more congenial to the habits of her life. She summoned all her skill to perplex him with cunning and insidious questions. From her questions he ought to have fled; but of this Hector was incapable. He was distressed by her severity, he grieved for the unintentional pain he had caused her. All these circumstances melted his heart; and he could not resolve upon any thing that was not considerate and respectful towards her. As the framing of artful questions was the stronghold of the donzella, and she might have challenged in this article the most hoary practitioner of the quibbling bar, so it was exactly the weakest side upon which poor Hector could be attacked. His simplicity yielded him up a defenceless prey to the assailant; least of all human undertakings was he capable of detecting the various faces of a doubtful question, and of guarding himself against the traps of an insidious foe. It was not till the fourth interview from Hector's original hint, that the donzella had recourse to this species of attack; and she did not withdraw her forces, till she had extorted from him all he knew.

When Hector found that all his guards were baffled and put to flight, he had then recourse to the only expedient that remained, conjuring her by every thing sacred and every thing tremendous, not to betray a trust she had so ungenerously obtained from him. She readily promised every thing he desired. Soothed by her compliance, he determined not to mention to me the lapse of which he had been guilty. It would in his opinion have been little less than treason, to suspect his Dulcinea of indiscretion or frailty. In the breast of this miracle of nature was not his loyalty as secure as it could be even in his own? Why then should he betray the secret of his love, which had never yet been confided even to the senseless air? Why should he subject himself to the inconceivable anguish and confusion, of owning, where my interests, or where my wishes were concerned, that he had been found tripping and imperfect? Why should he inflict a pain, or cause in me a fear, which he knew, and he only could know, was groundless? Thus it happened that I had one more confident of what I purposed should be secret, than I was myself in the smallest degree advertised of.

The consequences of this indiscretion of my servant were not slow in rendering themselves visible. The donzella was by no means so scrupulous or delicate in her sentiments, as my humble, but faithful, attendant. As she had given her company to Hector, she had had an opportunity of observing in him such integrity and goodness of heart, as could not fail to extort the esteem of any human being. She really honoured him; she was unwilling to give him any cause of uneasiness. But she had another lover; perhaps she had more. The laws of chastity she regarded as prejudices, and believed they were never formed for persons in her situation in society. She was of opinion that the more lovers she had, provided she satisfied them all, the more completely did she improve the talents with which Heaven had endowed her. Few women have any secrets for the man they admit to their embraces. In an hour of amorous dalliance she communicated to Agostino, the ostler, all that she knew of the conjurations and spells of Monsieur Boismorand, such was the name I had assumed upon my entrance into Italy. Her communication was probably attended with cautions, imitated from those with which Hector had so industriously loaded the donzella in the preceding example. Perhaps the illustrissimo Agostino had another mistress, with whom he thought it would be unjust to practise greater reserves than the donzella had done with him. Be that as it will, the rumours which were whispered to my prejudice speedily got air; and, it may be, were repeated with the greater avidity, on account of the mystery that attended them, and the injunctions of secrecy with which they were accompanied.

CHAPTER XXV.

Italy may be considered as the very focus and parent of superstitious credulity. The materials which Hector had furnished, after all the interrogations of the donzella, were slight compared with the superstructure which was presently erected on them. My grotto was said to be the appropriated haunt where a thousand devils held their infernal sabbath. The terrified imagination of the rustics, listening with a temper horribly distracted between curiosity and alarm, created to itself fictitious howlings and shrieks, and saw pale and sulphureous flames dancing upon the surface of the stream. Poor Hector was early the victim of their cruel and untamed ignorance; they believed that the peculiarity of his complexion rendered him a singularly agreeable intercessor between me and my infernal familiars. The colour of Charon was similar to that of my confidential attendant; and he, like Hector, fell under the calumnious misconstructions of the affrighted villagers. Conspicuously noble, affectionate and useful as he was, the jaundiced eye of superstition metamorphosed him into a devil. The storms of thunder and lightning to which the climate in which I resided is particularly subject acquired new terror from the ill fame which now pursued the name of Monsieur Boismorand. At those times the shapeless form of monsters vomiting smoke and flames were visible to the neighbourhood, sometimes scudding along the blue tops of the distant hills, and at others, with audaciousness incredible, brushing even at the elbow of the almost lifeless clowns and dairy-maids, and then suddenly dissolving into air, their place no longer marked but by the noisome and deadly stench they left behind. All the misfortunes of the district were imputed to me, the mortality of cattle, the convulsions and death of children, and the pale and lingering decay of persons recently advanced to an age of puberty. Innocent and blameless was my conduct to all around us; often was I forward and eager for the relief of the poor and afflicted; never was I the author of the slightest inconvenience or prejudice to any. Yet nothing merely human could be hated in the degree in which I was hated; few were daring and intrepid enough to repeat the very name I bore; and, when it was inadvertently pronounced, it produced through the whole extent of the astonished circle an involuntary and supernatural shudder.

Agostino, the first lover who had made an impression on the heart of Hector's donzella, was, as I afterwards found, a fellow of a gloomy and ferocious disposition, a true Italian spadaccino, determined that none should perpetrate an affront against him with impunity, but should expiate, in some refined and cruel vengeance, the levity by which they had been so unfortunate as to give birth to his hatred. He by no means relished or approved the liberal and good-humoured sentiments of the donzella; often had they inflicted on him the darkest torments of jealousy; nor had he failed, at least in one preceding instance, to make his rival the victim of his resentment. The donzella however went on in her career; she was light of heart, gay in temper, and careless of consequences. She had always hitherto succeeded, by playful blandishments, or more serious demonstrations of contrition, in mollifying the temper of her brute; and every pardon she received operated with her as a new permission to offend. She did not sufficiently consider that she was thus continually raising to a higher pitch the frenzy of his malice. Hector in the mean time was utterly unconscious and ignorant of the perilous situation in which he stood; while, to the apprehension of Agostino, the giving him a negro for a rival, whom his pride regarded as belonging to an inferior species of beings, and his devout ignorance likened to the leader of the infernal squadrons, was the last and most intolerable insult.

His malice was ingenious and subtle. He disdained the vulgar revenge of stabbing his antagonist in the dark, and supposing that his enmity could be gorged by a blow. When the venom of his nature was thoroughly put in motion, nothing could restore it to quietness and tranquillity but some mighty stroke, to excite the wonder of every bystander, and that should leave behind it a track of desolation, never to be filled up again and erased. He heard therefore with unsated appetite and eager joy the tale of necromancy and infernal machination repeated to him from Hector by the donzella. The impression which the narrative produced upon him was a mixed sentiment of transport at the apprehension of such an instrument of vengeance and of palpitating hatred; superstition teaching him to believe and to view with abhorrence that which he desired to render tenfold more an object of faith and aversion to his neighbours. He struck an auspicious and august alliance between his revenge and his religion; his religion exciting him to exterminate that, the destruction of which would produce inexpressible gratification to his revenge. The darkness of his spirit led him to proceed with double caution and vigilance in his correspondence with the donzella. He discovered nothing to her of the dark project which was engendering in his mind; and only betrayed so much of his superstitious feelings and fears as, by giving new emotion, might stimulate her to gratify his curiosity and her own by a detection of further particulars. He was assiduous in the underhand and sinister propagation of the tale, to which he did not fail to give his own colouring and affix his own feelings. He was desirous that the train should be laid in silence, and that the explosion he designed should be free from all pre-signification of the event. Thus an individual, of whose animosity I had no apprehension, and the meanness of whose appearance would probably have made me neglect all precaution against him, gave method and direction to an evil, of which however, upon a review, I am not inclined to doubt I should have been the victim, if the enmity and industry of this individual had been wholly withdrawn.

The mischief was long in preparation, before I received in any way the slightest intimation of the predicament in which I stood. The first circumstance at all calculated to excite alarm in my mind, was the singular manner in which I found myself regarded, if I entered any of the neighbouring villages, or met the rustics and their dames, as I strayed along the roads or the fields. They fled my approach, deserted the streets, and carefully shut themselves up in their houses, till I had passed. Where it was impossible to avoid me, they bowed themselves to the earth in the most submissive guise before me, while the most lively terror was painted in their countenances, dreading lest they should excite the resentment of a tremendous and inexorable foe. These tokens however were far from inspiring me with a conception of the truth. They perplexed, they astonished, they distressed me. Sore as I was with my recent afflictions, my mind was but too fully prepared for anticipations of evil. I had suffered from suspicions, I had suffered from calumnious imputations, I had suffered from the malignant effects of popular rumour. Had I yielded my confidence to any person but such a one as Hector, it is probable my suspicions would have turned on that side. But my reliance on him was not less than that which Alexander the Great yielded to Philip the physician: I knew his rectitude, his simplicity, his fidelity, and the singleness of his heart; and I could not harbour the shadow of a doubt respecting him. My reliance was of that entire and perfect sort, which did not express itself by a recollection of the physical possibility and an acquittal founded in deliberation, but by a total vacancy of doubt, or of retrospect that way directed, just such as the state of my mind would have appeared, if the thing had been naturally impossible.

I was not however ignorant and raw enough to be deceived by the exterior of homage I have described; I sufficiently knew that what I beheld was the offspring of hatred. To feel one's self hated is in all instances a painful and humiliating state of the human mind. To me it was especially so. I was not formed to retaliate this species of injury; I could not hate in my turn. I was formed to love. I could not look upon my species with dark and gloomy contemplations; I was prompt to admire their virtues, and perhaps even too prompt to extenuate their errors. It may, I believe, be laid down as a rule, that they who cannot hate can least endure to be made objects of hatred. Fettered however as I now was, by the tenderest consideration for the health and tranquillity of Marguerite, I thought it best to temporise and submit in silence. My principal anxiety was to hide these symptoms from the notice of my family. This I could not completely effect; some of them were too glaring and obtrusive, entirely to escape the observation of my daughters in their walks. But the filial forbearance they felt towards their mother led them implicitly and without any concerted plan to concur with me in my exertions for her quiet.

The animosity of Agostino was restless and inextinguishable. His plans did not terminate in exciting against me a secret and covered abhorrence; they aimed at nothing less than my utter destruction. The next exertion of the conspiracy which was engendering against me was of a tragical nature.

It happened one night, after all my family was retired to rest, and I was myself sunk into a slumber, that I was suddenly alarmed at the report of a musket, which seemed to be fired almost under the window of my chamber. This was a very singular circumstance, and calculated to convey an impression of danger. I leaped from my bed, and ran to the window. The night was extremely dark, and every thing seemed perfectly quiet. Presently I discerned a glimmering light, like that of a lantern, which however appeared to be gradually retiring to a greater distance. I was not thus satisfied, but determined to hasten down stairs, and investigate the cause of the disturbance. Marguerite, who had heard the firing of the musket as well as myself, now called me to her, and entreated me not to expose myself to unnecessary danger. In compliance with her remonstrances I promised, though unwillingly, not to go out into the court or upon the lawn, but to content myself with examining the state of every part of the house. When I came to the staircase and the hall, I found that the alarm had communicated to almost every person in the family, who presently assembled round me. We patroled the house, but found every thing in the situation in which it had been left, and nowhere any appearance of violence. I opened several of the windows, but all was darkness and silence. Having thus far satisfied myself, I listened with a degree of amusement to the conjectures and sage remarks of several of the servants, a rank of society who may usually be found to derive a degree of enjoyment from incidents of this sort, which, for the moment, strikingly tend to level all artificial distinctions, and confer on every one the liberty of uttering his reflections without apprehension or constraint. I did not however feel myself entirely easy; the circumstance which had just occurred, combined with the forebodings which had lately impressed me, had filled me with undefinable terror and alarm. Hector would willingly have gone over the grounds contiguous to the house, to see if he could discover any thing that related to or could explain the incident; but I had promised Marguerite that I would search no further, and the temper of my mind would not suffer me to expose another to a danger, which I abstained from encountering in my own person. It was more than an hour before the conclave in which we were assembled broke up, and every one retired, fatigued with attention, and prepared to fall into the soundest sleep. My dreams were uneasy and disturbed; my mind was in a tumult of imaginary calamities; and I passed the greater part of the night in a state of singular anxiety.

In the morning I was scarcely sunk into a refreshing slumber, before I was suddenly roused from sleep by a repetition of shrieks of astonishment and distress. I put on my clothes as quickly as I could, and hastened towards the spot from which the sounds appeared to proceed. The first object I beheld was the little boy of ten years' old, whom Charon had a short time before dragged out of the river, stretched along upon the lifeless body of this faithful and generous animal. The musket, the report of which had alarmed us the night before, had no doubt been aimed against Charon, and the greater part of its contents appeared to be lodged in his body. As no further sound had succeeded the firing, he had probably been killed on the spot. He was at a small distance from the house, near a private footpath, where he had been found in the morning by the lad whose life he had recently preserved. The poor boy had not at first understood what had happened to his benefactor, but only thought him asleep, and, prompted by affection for the generous creature, had quietly sat down by him till he should awake. He had not sat long however, before he discerned about him the marks of blood. He put his hand to the wound; the animal stirred not. He passed to his head; he saw his eyes fiery and starting, and his lips distorted. He endeavoured to awake him, as one would awake a human being to whom some mischief had happened of which he was not aware. All his efforts were fruitless. He found his body motionless, and his joints stiff in death. The apprehension of what had occurred then suddenly flashed on his mind. He burst out into shrieks of astonishment and anguish. Hector was the first person who caught the sound, and hastened to the spot; I immediately followed. The poor negro, who, in the innocence of his heart was uninitiated in the proud distinctions by which civilised man is taught to place so vast a barrier between the human nature and the brute, was struck speechless with sorrow and amazement. He recognised the dead being before him for his fellow-creature. He recollected in him his friend, his companion, his intimate acquaintance, between whom and himself there had for some time passed an uninterrupted reciprocation of acts of kindness and assistance.

A morose and fastidious reader perhaps will ask me why I lay so great a stress upon so petty and insignificant an incident as the death of a dog. It might have been little to other persons; it was not little to us. Let the reader recollect his ingenuity in procuring aid for his dying master, his gratitude to the person by whom that aid was afforded, and his unconquerable antipathy to his master's murderer. These are not common traits. There are many men whose premature fate has been the most unrelentingly avenged, that in moral and useful qualities could not have stood the comparison with my generous Charon. It surely was no common cause for regret, that a creature who had distinguished himself by a conduct so peculiarly admirable, should have encountered so premature and unmerited a fate. His conduct the reader may in some degree comprehend and appreciate; but I should in vain attempt to delineate those admirable qualities in this faithful domestic, which do not fall within the province of narrative, and which to have justly appreciated you must have been personally and familiarly acquainted with him. Beside, ours was a family of love. As we were affectionately attached to each other, so we never admitted a servant under our roof, who did not prove himself by his conduct utterly unworthy, to whom we did not extend a share of that friendship and affection, which seemed to be the right of every one that dwelt in our family. Feeling does not stay to calculate with weights and a balance the importance and magnitude of every object that excites it; it flows impetuously from the heart, without consulting the cooler responses of the understanding.

There was another circumstance which rendered the catastrophe of this generous animal of great moment to us. It was a clear proof that there was somewhere a strong animosity at work against his master. It was impossible he could himself have provoked his fate. Never was a creature more gentle and inoffensive. Though his bulk was great, and his strength uncommon, the energies he possessed were always employed in acts of justice and beneficence, never in acts of aggression. But if a hatred were at work so busy and fierce as to prompt an action like this, how were we to estimate it? What was its source, and whither did it tend? These were very interesting and serious considerations. We however dwelt for some time longer in the centre of general antipathy and abhorrence, without being able in the smallest degree to explain to ourselves what we saw. As we knew not in what we had offended, we were unable to atone for our fault, or even to guard ourselves against the repetition of it; nor were we by any means prepared to comprehend the extent of our danger. Happily Marguerite, whose health was now in a rapid decline, was least exposed to the observation of this new mischief; though she felt enough of it to confirm her in the sentiment, that she had nothing fortunate and happy to look forward to in the small remainder of her existence. There was indeed one idea perpetually present to her, which rendered the impression of ordinary occurrences extremely feeble upon her mind:—Charles, Charles, wandering alone in the world, unknowing and unknown, without a friend, a relative, a counsellor, or a protector, without money and without a name! This melancholy image followed her wherever she went, haunted her nightly in her dreams, attended her in all her occupations, filled all her intervals of leisure; and, though she laid it down as a law to herself never to repeat his beloved name in my presence, she could think of nothing else.

CHAPTER XXVI.

It was no long time after the death of Charon, that Hector came home one evening in a state of the most violent anxiety and trepidation. He burst upon me in my study, where I was sitting alone, buried in one of those deep reveries which, especially since the legacy of the stranger, had been among the most frequent habits of my mind. His perturbation was such as to render it impossible for him to impose on himself the smallest degree of caution and restraint. The noise he made in entering the apartment startled me. I looked up, and perceived his features swelled, his face bruised, and his garments disfigured with blood.

"For heaven's sake, Hector," exclaimed I, "what is the matter?"

He answered not. He advanced towards the upper end of the room, he took down a pistol, one of those which I always kept loaded in my apartment, he came towards me, he fell upon his knees, he tendered the pistol to my acceptance.

"Hector!" cried I, "what am I to understand? what is the meaning of this?"

"Kill me, dear master! For Christ's sake I entreat you to kill me!"

I took the pistol from his hand; it pointed towards the floor.

"And will you not kill me?" in a mournful accent exclaimed he.

"What have you done, that deserves that I should kill you?"

"Kill me! only kill me! pray kill me!" He spread out his hands towards me with a gesture of intreaty.

"Hector, what means this agitation? what has happened? You terrify me beyond expression."

"Must I speak?" replied he. "Must I be the accuser of my guilty self?" He burst into an agony of tears.

"Would I were dead! Would I had been torn into a thousand pieces, before this had happened! Indeed, sir, I am innocent! I thought no harm! Indeed it is not my fault!"

"What have you done? Whence come these bruises and this wound?"

"It is all my fault! It is all my doing,—nobody else! Why will you not kill me?"

"Hector, I cannot bear this uncertainty. Recollect yourself! Be pacified! and tell your story!"

"Will you forgive me?"

"Forgive you what? What have you done to deserve my anger?"

"No, no, I do not wish to be forgiven! I only wish you to abhor, to detest, to curse and to kill me!"

"This is beyond all patience."

"I never loved any body but you, and my mistress, and my dear young ladies. I never did any body else the least atom of mischief; and now my folly will be the ruin of you all!"

"Pardon me, sir! I will torment you no longer. I will get the better of myself, and tell you all that has happened."

He then informed me, though with many breaks and passionate interruptions, of what he had just discovered, my evil repute as a necromancer, the many strange and terrible stories that were circulated of me, the antipathy universally entertained against me, the active ferociousness with which this antipathy was accompanied, and the consequences that he feared would result. He ascribed the whole to his own imprudence, and to the particulars which the superior cunning of the donzella, in spite of his invincible refusal to acquaint her with a single circumstance, had wrung from him. Hector had collected several of these particulars accidentally from a neighbouring rustic, and had been vehement in my defence. While they were eager in debate, others had joined them, but Hector had found them all opponents, not one a supporter. Irritated with the contest, and the opprobrious language heaped upon himself and his master, Hector had been provoked to strike the most insolent of the disputants. Immediately several had fallen upon him at once, and it was owing to the uncommon strength and dexterity he possessed, that he had escaped alive out of their hands. Beside innumerable blows with fist, foot, and stick, he had received two or three stabs in different parts of the body, from the knives with which the Italian is too much accustomed to assail his adversary. It was easy to see that the gallant and generous defence of Hector had considerably augmented the danger of my situation. They dismissed him with a thousand execrations against both him and myself, and vows that they would signalise their vengeance by setting fire to my house. Having related his story, Hector concluded with again earnestly conjuring me to kill him, that so he might expiate the imprudence and folly by which he had made himself the author of my calamity.

The excessiveness of the poor fellow's distress excited me to employ every effort to pacify his mind. "Hector," said I, "you have been very imprudent, but I foresee no such consequences as your terrified imagination has led you to forebode. The idle threats of clowns in the midst of their brawls are entitled to little regard. I am not so weak and infirm of soul as to be moved from my tranquillity by their senseless prate. I entertain no doubt of your fidelity and affection. I am not angry with you. The fault you have been guilty of, arose from no defect of vigilance or attachment. You did what you could, and where you failed, it was only in that to which your powers were not commensurate. You have done well and wisely now, in acquainting me with particulars and the whole extent of the danger: doubt not but I will employ such precautions and be so awake to my situation, as to forestall the possibility of mischief."

Thus I endeavoured to assuage honest Hector's perturbation, but with no adequate effect. He hung his head in sorrow, and refused to be comforted. Shame and terror assailed him together, and he knew not how to support their united pressure. He intreated me not to lull myself in fancied security, and fall blindfold on my ruin. He entreated me not to forgive him. My clemency and forbearance served only to make him regard with greater horror the crime of which he had been guilty. If however I refused to punish him, and by penance or death to lighten the remorse that hung upon his heart, he would at least devote himself in opposition to the evil he had created, and die rather than it should touch a hair of our heads. This idea he seemed to view with some complacency; but the pleasure it gave was a glimmering and momentary light; he could not remain in any place for an instant; he wrung his hands with anguish, and exhibited every feature of the deepest despair. I examined his bruises and wounds, the latter of which, though attended with a copious effusion of blood, did not appear to be dangerous. I warned him to be guilty of no further indiscretion, to betray nothing of what had happened to any one of my family, and to engage in no further controversies and broils in my vindication.

Though I endeavoured to make light of what I heard in compassion to the distress of my servant, yet, when I came to reconsider the subject in solitude, it by no means appeared to me in a light and trivial point of view. One part of Hector's story had related to the death of Charon, who, I now found, had owed his fate to the superstition of my uncultivated neighbours. I had always entertained a formidable idea of the character of an Italian populace, whom I regarded as more suspicious, sanguinary, and violent than any other race of men in the world. I deplored my fate that exposed me to their rage. I deplored my folly that had admitted any confidant into my individual pursuits, though my confidence had been so limited, and its receiver so trustworthy, that I could not have imagined any evil would have resulted. I determined that I would not expose myself to the risk of such sinister consequences, as in my opinion might in my present situation easily overtake me. I grieved for the tender health and the doubtful state of mind of my beloved Marguerite, which alone opposed themselves to the adoption of an immediate change of scene. In the state of her health I had been grievously disappointed. I had looked for amendment; I found decay. The decay however was gradual, almost imperceptible; from time to time I had even flattered myself that the progress was in an opposite direction; but the delusion was soon banished. Another difficulty arose in addition to the rest; Marguerite appeared pregnant; a circumstance that now first presented itself after a cessation of ten years.

The morning after the accident and disclosure of Hector I went to Pisa, determined to consult with the marchese Filosanto, elder brother of the unfortunate Andrea, who was probably more accurately acquainted with the Italian character than myself, and understood the shades of that character, as they were modified in the particular territory in which I resided. The marchese was a man universally admired for subtlety of reasoning, vigorousness of comprehension, and refinement of taste. In the structure of his mind he was scarcely an Italian. He had resided several years in England, and was the intimate friend of Henry Howard earl of Surrey, who some time after fell a victim to the jealous tyranny of his native sovereign, king Henry the Eighth. The marchese was frank, generous and disinterested, and possessed more fully the affections of every one within the circle of his friendship than any other man I ever knew. He was of a sanguine temper, always contemplating the world on its brightest side; and, from the generosity of his own heart, incapable of crediting a distant danger, or of discerning the storm in the embryo cloud where it was silently engendering.

In the conference we held, I was influenced too implicitly by my consciousness of his integrity and the gigantic powers of his mind, and did not sufficiently advert to those peculiarities in his temper which I have now described. The external facts with which the narrative of Hector had furnished me I fully detailed to him; as to my particular pursuits, I contented myself with stating that I indulged freely in the study of chemistry, and was of those persons, ordinarily accounted visionaries, who amused themselves with the expectation of finding the philosopher's stone. Having heard my story to an end, the marchese ridiculed my apprehensions. He saw nothing in the facts that alarmed me, but a cowardly superstition whose utmost flight reached no higher than the shooting a dog, and a squabble between a boisterous rustic, and a servant too acutely sensitive for the reputation of his master. He assured me that the days of such superstition as I contemplated were long since past, and that his countrymen less deserved the imputation than any others, as, living at the very centre and source of catholic imposition, they saw deeper into the mystery, and were not exposed to the advantage which distance possesses for augmenting our reverence. He expatiated with great eloquence on the vice of a suspicious temper. A spirit of alarm and continual apprehension, like the jealousy of lovers, he said, made the meat it fed on. It brooded over plots that had no existence but in the wanderings of a disturbed imagination. It was continually interrupting the quiet of its owner, and the tranquillity of society; and, for the sake of avoiding imaginary evils, often plunged into such as were real. He advised me to go home and be contented. He recommended to me to clear up the clouds of my mind, and cultivate a light heart, a cheerful temper, and a generous confidence in the honest sympathies of mankind. In fine, he bade me continue my pursuits, avoid éclat, and trust in his sagacity that no ill consequences would ensue.

The remonstrances of the marchese Filosanto led me to suspect that I had been idly credulous. I had too easily participated the feelings and apprehensions of a poor uninstructed negro, and had suffered the secret griefs that brooded in my heart, to discolour my perceptions, and aggravate the features of circumstances in themselves trifling or indifferent. I began to be half ashamed of the gloominess of my conceptions. I could not, alas! follow the advice of the marchese as to the cheerfulness of my heart; but I could exert myself to prevent my present melancholy from disfiguring to me every thing I saw. The influence exercised over my conceptions by persons of eminent intellect has always been great. Not that the judgment I formed of the powers of my own mind was peculiarly humble; but I reasoned thus. Perhaps the person I consult is as well informed in the subject under consideration as I am, in that case his decision is as fully entitled to attention as my own; and thus, without cowardly self-contempt on my part, the general balance of the argument was materially altered. Perhaps, without being on the whole my superior, he may be more competent to this particular question. In either case my idea of its merits became perceptibly modified. I never listened to the sentiments of a man of talents when they differed from my own, unless where he was evidently visionary and irrational, without being shaken as to the credit due to my own view of the subject.

Such then was the effect produced on me by the marchese's expostulation. I shook off my apprehensions, and laughed at my fears. I was ashamed of the want of gallantry that had possessed me, when I meditated flight from so trivial a menace. I concluded that dangers, particularly such as arise from the irrational passions of a capricious multitude, were increased when symptoms of apprehension discovered themselves, and abated, when received with neglect or repelled with a magnanimous serenity.

CHAPTER XXVII.

Meanwhile the unrelenting Agostino was fixed in his purpose and incessant in his machinations. He believed that the destructive mine was now sufficiently prepared, and that he might proceed in all surety to the ultimate explosion. He apprehended that he had advanced too far to retract, that the death of Charon and the assault upon Hector were calculated sufficiently to announce what was to follow, and that it would be injudicious and idle to grant me much respite for reflection. The passions of his associates were wrought up to a frenzy of horror, and needed only a bold and artful director to urge them to any point of fury and destruction.

Implicitly as I had confided in the decision of the marchese, I had speedily reason to know that it was the dictate of too sanguine and presumptuous a spirit. On my return from his palace, and, on several subsequent occasions, I found the manners of the populace altered respecting me. They no longer viewed me with a sort of reverential awe, or fled my approach. They insulted me with their eyes, they muttered curses upon me in a voice sufficiently audible to be understood, they broke forth in gestures of abhorrence and derision. They regarded me with looks of ferocious hatred; and when I had passed them, their murmurs gradually swelled into shouts of triumphant contumely. These symptoms however were progressive; each day became more odious and intolerable than the last. They who have never been placed in a situation like mine, will never be able to do justice to my grievance. They will perhaps say, that the calamity I now endured was a trifling one, and that a weak mind only can be elevated by the acclamations and huzzas of the multitude, or depressed by their hisses and scorn. I did not, and I could not, feel it so. There is no pleasure more congenial to the human heart, than the approbation and affection of our fellows. I call heaven to witness that I could mount the scaffold, surrounded with an innumerable multitude to applaud my fortitude, and to feel as it were on their own neck the blow that ended me, and count it a festival. But I cannot bear to be surrounded with tokens of abhorrence and scorn. I cannot bear to look round me through an extended circle, and see the impatience of despite in every face. Man was not born to live alone. He is linked to his brethren by a thousand ties; and, when those ties are broken, he ceases from all genuine existence. Their complacence is a food more invigorating than ambrosia; their aversion is a torment worse than that of the damned. While I write, I seem again to hear resounding in my ears the hootings and clamours of these infatuated peasants. When heard indeed, they went to my heart, and sat there colder than the aspic's venom: they rose to my throat with a sensation bitterer than wormwood. They unstrung all my muscles and nerves. I could not stay; I could not fly. I wished myself buried deep in the centre of the earth. I felt something worse, more revolting, more opposite to all the prejudices and propensities of the soul, than annihilation. I have known in various situations and conditions of human life, what it was to be distressed, to be dejected, to be miserable; but never in any other situation have I felt a misery so concentrated, so gnawing and insufferable.

I began however, like the critics I am figuring to myself, to despise the pusillanimity of my submission, and to believe that, if I would only make a stand and turn round upon my enemy, I should subdue him. This resolution I could with difficulty have taken in the moment of attack; it was formed in an interval of retrospect and reflection. Having formed it, the contempt I should have felt for myself would have been too exquisite, if I had failed to put it in execution. I was not long at a loss for an opportunity. In one of my walks I found myself pursued by a numerous populace with a peculiar degree of inveteracy. I yielded for some time, till I came to a place that appeared convenient for the purpose of haranguing them. It was a bench, placed upon a rising ground and sheltered behind by a thicket, which had been erected for the purpose of commanding a neighbouring prospect. I stopped; I stepped upon the bench; I waved my hand towards the multitude. They perceived my purpose with some degree of confusion and surprise; they drew nearer. "Do not listen to him! Do not hear a word he has to say!" cried some of them. "Oh, hear him! hear him!" exclaimed others. I obtained an audience.

"What is the cause," said I, "of all this hatred and persecution?"

"Because you are a wizard, a necromancer, a dealer in the black art; because you are in league with hell, and have sold yourself to the devil!" answered twenty voices at once.

"Hear me," replied I, "and I will convince you of my innocence: but hear me in silence, and do not interrupt me."

"For myself, I have no belief in the existence of such an art."

This remark produced a general groan.

"Why should I have sold myself to the foe of mankind? What could he give me, that should compensate me for consigning myself over to him for ever hereafter? The power of exhibiting strange and extraordinary tricks. What a pitiful recompence? But, if I had bought this power at so dear a price, should I hide it? Should I not take every opportunity of exciting your reverence and astonishment? Who has seen me perform any wonderful feat? I live quietly among you, and give no cause of offence to any. I live retired in the midst of my family. I form no party or connections. I do not intrude into any of your affairs, political or private. I do not even enter into conferences with any of you, unless induced by the apparent occasion of doing some good and benevolent action.

"Quit then this ungenerous persecution! Do not turn the fury of your resentment upon a harmless stranger! You are Italians, the most polished and ingenious people on the face of the earth: the most glorious monuments of art, in building, in statuary, and in painting, are to be found in the midst of you: ancient Italy governed the world by her arms; modern Italy governs the world through the medium of that pure and sublime religion of which Providence has graciously made her the repository. Do not stain the glory of this character! Show yourselves worthy of the honour with which your name is heard in every corner of the habitable world!"

While I was yet speaking, a large clot of mud reached me, and struck me on the face and the upper part of my breast. I calmly endeavoured to free myself from its effects with my handkerchief; and, looking round me, demanded, in the sacred spirit of conscious innocence, "How have I deserved this treatment?"

Thus far I had been heard with a doubtful sentiment of murmur and approbation, and I began to feel that I was rather gaining ground upon my audience. But this new insult seemed to turn the tide of popular impression in an instant.

"Villain, renegado, accursed of God!" I heard from every side; "did not you bewitch my cow? did not you enchant my child? have not you killed my daughter? Down with him! exterminate him! do not suffer him to live!"

I continued my efforts to be heard. It was a critical moment, a last experiment upon the power of firmness and innocence to control the madness of infuriated superstition. It was in vain. I was deafened with the noise that assailed me. It was no longer shouts and clamours of disapprobation. It was the roaring of tigers, and the shriek of cannibals. Sticks, stones, and every kind of missile weapon that offered itself, fell in showers around me. It seemed a sort of miracle that I escaped instant destruction. I eluded their pursuit: after some time I ventured to return to my own house. I had in the interval terrified myself with the idea that, having missed my person, they might have hurried thither, and executed some terrible vengeance on my helpless family. I found them however in safety: the mob had for this time contented itself to disperse without further mischief.

As soon as it was dark, I hastened to Pisa, and related what had just occurred to my friend the marchese. He was surprised; but he still adhered to his opinion. He had never supposed, he told me, that a noisy and clamorous mob was a proper subject upon which to make experiment of the energy of truth; and he laughed at my attempt to reason them out of their superstition. But they meant nothing by all that had passed. It was the mere foam and fury of a moment, poured out with vehemence, and then dissipated in air. A certain set of politicians had for their particular ends represented a mob as a terrific and formidable engine: alas! they were rather to be pitied than condemned. There was no malice in their hearts. They were in reality a mere material machine, led on without reflection, and, when they had committed a momentary ravage, astonished themselves the most at the injury they had perpetrated. They were as light and variable as a feather, driven with every breath; and nothing could argue greater obliquity of intellect than to suppose, because they were in a certain temper and sentiment to-day, that they would be found in a similar temper and sentiment to-morrow. The marchese however wished, he said, to relieve me from the apprehension of this imaginary danger, and therefore offered me the whole suite of his servants for the defence of my house. He added that, among his friends and retainers in the city of Pisa, he did not doubt in an hour's time to be able to raise a troop of four hundred men; and, whatever power of that sort he possessed, he assured me was wholly at my service. I was not convinced by the marchese's arguments, but I declined his offer. I could not bear to think that blood should be spilled, and the lives of these poor ignorant wretches sacrificed, for the preservation of a thing so worthless in my eyes as the local property I possessed. I therefore told the marchese, that I might perhaps wait yet a day or two longer before I formed my resolution; but that, the instant I saw one fresh symptom of the hostility of the villagers, I was determined to take my family with me, and remove far beyond the reach both of their terrors and their hatred.

I staid two hours with the marchese, and then set out to my own house. The way I took was by a private road, open only to the neighbouring gentry, but of which my servant carried the key. It led along the higher ground, and commanded a view of the common highway. Considerably before I reached my own habitation, I was struck with the appearance of persons passing, in considerable numbers, and in a tumultuous manner, along the public road. Some of them were armed with clubs, and others with torches. Their march however led, not towards my house, but in an opposite direction. I mended my pace, terrified with a sort of vague apprehension of what might have happened, though I did not disguise to myself that what I saw was not precisely that which I might have expected to see, if they had been returned from demolishing my property, and burning my house.

When I arrived, I found indeed that no mischief had been actually committed, but that I was indebted for the preservation of my house, and perhaps for the lives of my wife and children, to the sagacity and presence of mind of Bernardin, the servant of my early years. My residence had been the object against which the march of the populace had been directed. Bernardin, perceiving their intentions, had with great difficulty prevailed upon Hector to keep out of sight. Nothing could be more adverse to the feelings and inclination of my faithful negro; but, Bernardin having convinced him that his appearance would only exasperate the rage of the assailants, and that perhaps every thing of importance to his master's service and happiness depended at present upon his concealment, Hector yielded to his representations. This accomplished, Bernardin next assembled the gardener and one or two labourers in my employment, who happened to be at hand; and, having furnished them with fire-arms, stationed them at different windows, in the front of the house. With these preparations, when the mob arrived he resolutely told them that he would fire on the first person that attempted to break in. They were staggered: furious as they appeared the moment before, this threat held them in awe. They paraded two or three times round the house, clattering their arms, and pouring out vehement execrations; and then withdrew, solemnly promising that they would return the following night, and level the house with the ground.

I no longer yielded the smallest degree of credit to the unsuspicious and confiding philosophy of the marchese Filosanto. I sent off my wife and children before daybreak for Lucca, determined to take shipping at the first convenient port, and pass over into Spain. I was little solicitous, for reasons with which the reader is already acquainted, about my property and moveables: I had no motive to induce me to fetter and clog my retreat, at this hour of peril and terror, with a single article of rarity and price. My furniture indeed was not splendid, but it was handsome and valuable; and the indifference with which I resigned the whole to the mercy of chance, was a matter of some surprise to the persons around me. My servants offered to defend my possessions, at the peril of their lives; but I peremptorily forbade it. I would not even consent to their taking away certain articles, by way of appropriating them to their personal use. I believed that if I admitted a single act of that sort, I should find it no easy matter to set limits to their avidity; and, as I had determined to take none of my present servants with me, the negro and Bernardin excepted, I feared that the apparent possession of a single article that had been mine might hereafter mark its proprietor a victim to the senseless rage of blindfold superstition. I could easily make up to these honest and faithful dependants the injury they might sustain from the seeming severity of this order. I determined to shut up my house, with all its present contents, as Joshua, the captain of the Jews, drew a line of separation round the profane possessions of Achan; and to leave the villagers, if so it seemed good to them, to make of the whole a burnt-offering, to propitiate the wrath of their avenging divinity.

The directions I issued being unhesitating and peremptory, met with a ready submission from all my other domestics: Hector only, the mild and complying Hector, of whom obedience had hitherto appeared to constitute the very soul, met my commands with a resolute refusal. The present distressed appearance of my fortunes seemed to have worked the poor fellow's mind to a paroxysm of insanity. He considered himself as the sole author of my calamity. He reviled himself in the bitterest terms of compunction and abhorrence. The language which the agony of his soul forced from his lips, was such as could not fail to impress upon my other servants a conviction of the justice of the imputations that were now brought against us. This however was of little importance. I must at all events have been contented to leave behind me, in my present neighbourhood, a name loaded with the execrations of religious fanaticism. Hector imprecated upon himself a thousand curses, if, so long as he continued to live, the populace should lay hands upon a straw of my property. He would not move so much as an inch from the defence of my house. He would either, by preserving it, expiate in some degree the mischief in which he had involved me, or fall and be crushed to death in the midst of its ruins. Arguments and expostulations were useless here: his mind was worked up to too high a tone, to be susceptible of the patience necessary for hearing or understanding any reasoning that was addressed to him. Authority itself was of no avail: for the first and the last time he threw off the character of a servant, and appeared obstinate, self-willed, and ungovernable. It was only by direct violence that he could be forced from the spot. I gave him in charge, with the most strict orders not to suffer him to escape from their custody, to two of his fellows.

This business being despatched, I went, at the invitation of the marchese, to a small cottage he possessed at no great distance from my own house. Its situation was so private and retired, that few persons knew or could perceive that there was any building on the spot. Here therefore I could remain in the most perfect safety. I felt myself unaccountably impelled to stay and witness the catastrophe of the tragedy. I should not have been satisfied to continue in uncertainty as to what it would prove. After all that had passed, like the marchese, I should have been apt to accuse myself of cowardice, and a mind soured and degenerate, if the mob had not put their threats in execution. The marchese himself was well pleased with my determination in this respect. He was not yet convinced that I had not painted to myself a danger, which had no adequate counterpart in the world of realities.

I had not long to wait. The night had no sooner spread an even-coloured and almost impervious veil over the world, than the marchese, as if moved by a secret impulse to witness what he yet refused to believe, came to me at the cottage. He had scarcely arrived, when he heard the confused murmurs and turbulence of the populace; for we were near enough to distinguish almost every thing. As they did not meet with the defence of the preceding evening, the work they had undertaken was presently despatched. We saw the flames ascend. We recognised the shouts of infernal joy with which they witnessed the catastrophe. When the marchese beheld what, till seen, he would never admit to be possible, he burst out into a sort of transport of misanthropy. He exclaimed that no innocence, and no merit, could defend a man from the unrelenting antipathy of his fellows. He saw that there was a principle in the human mind destined to be eternally at war with improvement and science. No sooner did a man devote himself to the pursuit of discoveries which, if ascertained, would prove the highest benefit to his species, than his whole species became armed against him. The midnight oil was held to be the signal of infernal machinations. The paleness of study and the furrows of thought were adjudged to be the tokens of diabolical alliance. He saw, in the transactions of that night, a pledge of the eternal triumph of ignorance over wisdom. Above all, he regretted that his countrymen, his dear Italians, should for ever blot their honour and their character by such savage outrages. Though myself the principal sufferer, I was obliged to perform the part of the comforter and consoler, and endeavour to calm the transport of agony that seized upon the susceptible Filosanto. He was astonished, shocked, and beside himself: I viewed the whole with the gloomy firmness of a desperate resolution.

The worst event of this detested evening remains yet unrecorded. Even now I tremble, while I attempt to commit the story to my harmless paper. So far as related to the mere destruction of my property, I looked on with a philosophical indifference. I had no reason, and I disdained to regret the loss of that which I had it in my power to repair in a moment. I thought I had taken care that no human life should be risqued upon this critical occasion. But I was mistaken. I learned the next morning with anguish inexpressible that Hector, the negro of the prison of Constance, was no more. He had eluded the vigilance of his keepers. No sooner was he at liberty, then he hastened, unknown to every one, to die, as he had declared he would, in the defence of my house. The mob had burst into the house; they seized him alive. They dragged him out in the midst of them; they insulted over him, as the special favourite of the infernal king. They inflicted on him every species of mockery and of torture; they killed him joint by joint, and limb by limb.——The pen drops from my lifeless hand.

What right had I to make this man the victim of my idle and unhallowed pursuits? What has the art and multiplication of gold in it, that should compensate the destruction of so ingenuous, so simple-hearted, so noble a creature? If I had myself fallen into the hands of the populace, it had been well: I was a criminal, worthy of every retribution they could inflict upon me! Some men perhaps will ask, why I lamented so bitterly over so uncultivated and uninformed an individual as this negro. There was however something so truly tragical in the fate to which this creature in his generosity and remorse devoted himself, that I believe for the moment I felt a sharper pang in it, than in the strange and extraordinary loss of my only son, or perhaps in the premature death of my beloved Marguerite.

CHAPTER XXVIII.

Before the dawn of the succeeding morning I turned my face towards Lucca. I beheld the last cloud of mingling smoke and flame ascend from the ashes of my villa. The blaze sunk, its materials were nearly consumed, and it yielded an uncertain and fitful light only, when I withdrew from being any longer the melancholy and heart-wounded spectator of the ruin. I took an everlasting leave of the marchese. I had been introduced to him under a friendly aspect, as the man who had had courage to perform the last offices of humanity to his unfortunate brother; and he had conceived a warm affection for me. The painful nature of the catastrophe he had witnessed melted his heart, and he earnestly pressed me to draw upon him for any supplies I wanted, or rather to receive from him a sum equivalent to the damage the superstition of his countrymen had inflicted on me. This I positively refused; but I found it impossible to silence his importunity, till I submitted to the duplicity of promising that, if I found myself reduced to any necessity, I would not fail to apply to him. It was in the very moment of our separation that intelligence was brought me of the fate of Hector. The reader may imagine with how heavy a heart I set out on my journey.

Lucca is about seventeen miles from the city of Pisa; from the place where I had spent the greater part of this memorable night it was twenty. The marchese made me promise to take a serpentine and circuitous route, the more completely to elude the possibility of future danger. An adventure occurred to me in this passage, with the relation of which I will not interrupt my narrative, which prevented me from arriving at Lucca till the noon of the following day. Suffice it to say, that it was of such a nature, that, impatient as I was under my present extraordinary circumstances to rejoin my family, I should have held myself destitute of every atom of humanity, if I had not submitted to this short delay.

Short as it was, I found, when I reached Lucca, that my evil genius had been busy to accumulate for me new misfortunes. Marguerite and her daughters were wholly unknown in this place; and the intelligence of the Pisan riot having reached Lucca in the course of the day, it was related to my wife, as to a hearer unconcerned, with all its horrid circumstances and the calamitous fate of our generous Hector, by the hostess of the inn. The rapidity of events, during the last part of our residence in the Pisan territory, was such as to have obliged me to say little of the effect they produced upon Marguerite. But the reader can scarcely be so inadvertent and unreflecting, as not easily to imagine to himself that she felt them in the highest degree painful and overwhelming. This last blow was too much. Marguerite had been some months pregnant. She was immediately seized with the pains of labour, and delivered of a dead child. The first intelligence communicated to me upon my arrival was that my wife was dying.

Lucca however did not witness the period of her existence. After having continued for several days upon the very extremity, as it were, between life and death, she grew perceptibly better; and in a week more, though in a very feeble state, it became apparent that her case was not a rapid one. We agreed to proceed upon our Spanish voyage. It appeared not improbable that the sea-air might be found beneficial, and the experiment was warmly recommended by her physicians. They were not however aware of the whole extent of her disorder. During the voyage her crisis returned with such malignant symptoms, as scarcely to permit us the hope she would reach the land alive. We debarked at Barcelona on the 14th of April 1546.

We had no sooner taken up our abode in this city than, fully aware of the state of her disease, she assembled her daughters, and poured forth to them without restraint that flood of affection, that ardent spirit of love, by which she was distinguished and elevated above every creature that lived. Her mind was clear, her intellectual powers were complete and entire. The enthusiasm with which she now expressed herself was not of that inconsiderate nature which should tend to make them feel with greater acuteness the loss they were about to sustain. It was bright, unclouded and serene. It was the eloquence as of a disembodied spirit, freed from the perturbation and alloy of human passions. She reminded them that they were sisters, and exhorted each to fulfil the duties of a sister and a mother to the other two. If wise and good, they would be happy in each other, and their little association would be a school, preparing them for the more genuine and venerable duties for which nature had destined them. Her views of all human things were altered by her present situation on the brink of the grave. Our reserves and misunderstandings had wrung her heart; but she forgave me. Things which had lately appeared of the highest magnitude and moment, faded in the distance, and mingled with the vulgar crowd of human concerns which was now retiring from her view: she must again return, she said, to life, before she could again feel the passions and the interests of this petty scene. For the sake of her daughters she had lately desired to live. She was now reconciled and content to die. She had formed the chain and link of connection between me and my girls; perhaps it was better that we should burst our fetters and be free. On the fourth day after our arrival at Barcelona Marguerite expired.

There is nothing in the vast variety of objects which this wretched world presents to our view so dreadful and distressing as the sight of one we have loved, but who is now no more. I saw, these eyes beheld, the lifeless corse of Marguerite. Great God of heaven! what is man? and of what are we made? Within that petty frame resided for years all that we worship, for there resided all that we know and can conceive of excellence. That heart is now still. Within the whole extent of that frame there exists no thought, no feeling, no virtue. It remains no longer, but to mock my sense and scoff at my sorrow, to rend my bosom with a woe, complicated, matchless and inexpressible. The cheek is pale and livid; the eyes are sunk and circled with blackness. Corruption and ruin have already seized their prey and turned it into horror. Draw, for heaven's sake, draw the pall over those lifeless features! Bury, bury them deep in the bowels of the earth! Let not my imagination follow them into the chambers of the grave, and dwell amidst pestilential damps and all the series of destruction! Let me recollect all that Marguerite was as she lived, her numerous accomplishments, her unparalleled virtues,—ay, in all the magnitude and wealth of their detail,—for that is a divine and celestial madness: but let me not recollect her as I saw her on the bier, lest I become raving and blaspheme!

I have no power to talk of the situation in which I was now placed, and the reader must therefore explain it for himself,—if he can. I never loved but once; I never loved but Marguerite. All other affection is stillness and ice compared with this. This is the great crisis of my history, the gap between life and death, the gulf that cut me off for ever from every thing that deserves the name of human. Such was the legacy of the stranger! my son an exile, myself publicly arraigned as a murderer, the unmerited and tragical death of Hector, the premature and self-deriving loss of the better half of my soul! Who would have believed that this envenomed gift would, in less than two years, have thus dreadfully changed the face of my affairs, and destroyed every thing that composed the happiness of my life?

After some delay in this wretched and ill-omened town of Barcelona (such it has ever since appeared to my thoughts), we proceeded to Madrid. The reader will give me credit, when I tell him that, however eager I had lately felt to exhibit my magnificence and my wealth, I had no such eagerness now. I speak no more of the character of Marguerite; I attempt not to compose her panegyric. The story of her life is the best record of her virtues. Her defects, if defects she had, drew their pedigree from rectitude of sentiment and perception, from the most generous sensibility, from a heart pervaded and leavened with tenderness. A simple stone in the western aisle of the great church at Barcelona records her personal and her family name, with this single addition, the preserver of her family in poverty and ruin, the victim of her disconsolate and repentant husband's unhallowed wealth.

But, dismissing for ever, and henceforth consigning to unviolated silence her excellencies, could I avoid feeling that I could never again form a similar, or indeed any real union, so long as I existed? Being now indeed more than forty years of age, having spent near twenty of that forty in a most enviable wedlock, and being blessed with a sufficiently numerous offspring, it may be thought perhaps I might be contented. But, without discussing the propriety of such a maxim as it relates to the species in general, it must be recollected in my case that my youth was to be recommenced by a perpetual series of renewals. I never gave credit to that axiom of a sickly sensibility, that it is a sacrilege, in him who has been engaged in one cordial and happy union, ever to turn his thoughts to another. Much more reasonable than this is the Indian doctrine, that the survivor ought to leap into the flames, and perish upon the funeral pyre of the deceased. While we live, it is one of our most imperious duties to seek our happiness. He that dedicates his days to an endless sorrow is the worst and most degraded of suicides. It is an important question in the economy of human life, up to what age we should allow ourselves to contract engagements to a wife and a probable offspring: but, separately from this consideration, I should hold that in many cases he who entered into a second marriage, by that action yielded a pure and honourable homage to the manes of the first. But from genuine marriage I was henceforth for ever debarred. An immortal can form no true and real attachment to the insect of an hour.

Mourning, a depressing and speechless regret, was yet the inmate of our house. Grief does not commonly lay a strong and invincible hold of us in the morning of our days; and, though the temper of Julia was perhaps at her age the most tender and susceptible I ever knew, even she, who was now in her seventeenth year, reaped the benefit of that elasticity which in early life is the portion of humanity. Nothing material occurred to us in the first three months of our residence in Madrid. It was impossible for any one to be surrounded with a more lovely and blooming family than I was.

Yet from happiness I was immeasurably distant. Exclusively of my recent and in every sense irreparable loss, my mind was full of dark and gloomy forebodings. I feared not for myself, but I had an unconquerable alarm and apprehension for my children. My youngest was but ten years of age; the eldest was not seventeen. Sweet, tender blossoms, that the cruelty and hardness of mankind might so easily blight, and that required a concurrence of favourable circumstances to ripen into all they were capable of becoming! When I recollected what had happened in the course of the last two years, I could not flatter myself that our misfortunes were at an end, or that I had not, to speak moderately, many fierce trials yet to encounter. I seemed, like the far-famed tree of Java, to be destined to shelter only to destroy, and to prove a deadly poison to whatever sought its refuge under my protecting branches. In this melancholy frame of mind the last words of my adored Marguerite passed and repassed ten thousand times through my recollection. "She had formed the chain and link of connection between me and my girls; perhaps it was better that we should burst our fetters and be free."

Whatever she had said was sacred to the present temper of my imagination: her last behest I would have died to execute. The idea contained in the sentence I have just repeated was ambiguous and obscure, rather hinted, than expressed. But was it worthy of the less attention, because its author, with her usual gentleness and sweetness, had modestly suggested an advice, instead, which she was well entitled to have done, of prescribing a will? I determined to part with my children, that I might no longer be to them a source of corroding misery and affliction. I believed that the cloud that now oppressed me was transitory. I seemed pursued for the present by a malignant genius; but a man, endowed as I was with unbounded wealth and immortal vigour, cannot easily be reduced to despair. When the tide of my prosperity should unfold its rich and ample current, I might easily communicate of its bounty to my daughters. If I parted with them now, I did not lose them as I had perhaps lost their brother for ever. I could turn to a particular point, and say, "There lies my soul!" I could cast my eye upon a projection of the globe, and put my finger upon their residence. Wherever I wandered, whether I were plunged in a dungeon or mounted a throne, my heart, like the mariner's needle, would tremble towards that point as its cynosure. I had still something to love, something to pant for, something to dream about, and be happy.

Having ruminated insatiably upon the last expressions of Marguerite, having formed my commentary, and fixed my predilection, I recollected a person, then a young woman upon my paternal estate, for whom my wife had conceived a remarkable friendship. She was the daughter of a peasant, her birth had been low, and her education confined. But she had taste, she had discretion, she had integrity, I think I may add, she had genius. As Marguerite had discovered her merits, and distinguished her from her equals, she had been of great use to this extraordinary rustic in unfolding her mind, and guiding her propensities. This was not so much a matter of deliberate and meditated purpose in la dame du seigneur; it rose out of the circumstances of their situation. They were almost of an age; and Marguerite frequently invited her to be the associate of her studies and amusements. Mariana, that was her name, did not perhaps resemble my wife considerably in her features, but her stature was the same, her complexion and the colour of her hair. The similarity in carriage and gesture, Mariana having never had an opportunity of contemplating the accomplishments she admired in any one but madame de St. Leon, was still more striking. There were points indeed in which no human creature could compare with Marguerite, the expressive and flexible tone of her voice, and those cadences, which sprung from, and communicated to every susceptible hearer, the divinest sensibility. One of the unhappy consequences of our exile from the Bordelois was the misfortunes of Mariana. Her father had fallen to decay. To relieve his distress she had contracted a marriage, not of sentiment and predilection, but with a man who had promised her that her father should never come to want. This marriage had been unhappy. The husband was a prodigal and a profligate. A period of seven years however delivered her from her Egyptian bondage. She had but lately become a widow; and the prudence and integrity of her conduct had rendered this alliance, which to many women would have proved a rock of destruction, an additional source of honour and respect. Mariana, at the death of her husband, had no children; she had buried her father; she was consequently entirely alone.

It was this woman I fixed upon as the protector of my daughters. I was better pleased with the meanness of her extraction, than I should have been with one of the high-born descendants of the houses of St. Leon or Damville, had it been my fortune to have had in the female line any near relations on either side. My daughters were no longer children; they were singularly prudent, considerate, and unimpeachable in their conduct and propensities. They wanted a protector in the eye of the world; it was desirable for them that they should have an adviser; but I should have been grieved and mortified to give them a dictator.

I wrote to Mariana Chabot, communicating my project, and requesting her to give us the meeting at St. Lizier on the frontiers of France. She was delighted with the office I tendered to her acceptance, and readily consented to every thing I required. I conducted my daughters to the place of rendezvous without imparting to them the design by which I was actuated; I believed that they would of their own motion conceive a partiality for the friend of their mother. I was not deceived in my prognostic; the meeting was an interesting one. The eyes of Mariana overflowed at meeting, after so long an interval, the husband and progeny of the dearest and most revered friend she had ever known; the mourning we wore reminded her how lately her incomparable patroness had been committed to the grave. My girls were struck with the resemblance of Mariana to their mother. Accident had prevented us from cultivating almost any intimate connections out of our own family from the period of our exile; my girls had therefore never met with a person who approached in any degree so near their mother in accomplishments, in skill, in turn of thinking and opinion. Mariana came up to my warmest hopes as a protector and companion for my children; her unhappy marriage, by concentrating her thoughts and expectations in herself, had perhaps rendered her more exemplary in carriage, and more elevated in sentiment, than she would ever have been without it.

At St. Lizier I passed myself for monsieur Valmier, the guardian of the orphan heiresses of St. Leon. It fortunately happened that my paternal estate was at this time upon sale. I determined to become the purchaser, and to settle my girls in the scene of their nativity. I procured an agent, and despatched him with an ample commission for that purpose. Having adjusted this point, I resolved to make a tour with my daughters, through Languedoc, Dauphiné, and the provinces usually known by the denomination of the south of France. I wished to familiarise them to the society of madame Chabot, and to assist them in discerning her merits under a variety of points of view. I asked them whether they would not be delighted to obtain her as a companion, who might assist and conduct them in such points as only a woman of understanding and experience is competent to. They, every one of them, listened to the idea with pleasure.

At length I received the information that the purchase of St. Leon was completed, and I proceeded to the critical disclosure that my daughters were on the point of being separated from their father. They listened to the communication with astonishment and terror. They had entered successively into the feelings of their deceased mother, and I am well persuaded felt a less ardent attachment to my person than they had done at the cottage of the lake of Constance. But, culpable and criminal as I had been, I was not destitute of every virtue, and they could not extinguish in themselves the respect they had so long entertained for me. Habit has a resistless empire over the human mind; and, when we reflect with how much reluctance we consent to the removal of a tree or a hedge, to the sight of which we have been accustomed, it will not be wondered at that my daughters could not calmly think of so complete a separation from their father. The impression of their mother's death was yet green, and to lose me, was to become orphans a second time. But I had fully meditated my plan, and was peremptory. That I might withhold from them no advantage it was in my power to confer, I gave them Bernardin for their superintending bailiff and steward of their property. Our parting was not less painful and melancholy, than its occasion was extraordinary and its mode uncommon. It took place at the town of Montauban.

I saw my dear children set forward on their journey, and I knew not that I should ever behold them more. I was determined never again to see them to their injury; and I could not take to myself the consolation,—on such a day, in such a month, or even after such a lapse of years, I will again have the joy to embrace them. In a little while they were out of sight, and I was alone. The reader will perhaps agree with me, that no man had more exquisitely enjoyed the dearest ties of society than I had, and that perhaps few men were ever better formed to enjoy them. This complete and dreadful separation, this stroke that seemed to cut me off abruptly from every thing most valuable that the earth contains, was not the result of any of the ordinary necessities of human life. Still less was it the dictate of alienation or indifference. No; it was the pure effect of love, of a love so strong, complete, and uncontrollable, as inflexibly to refuse every thing that could be injurious to its objects. I own I could not thus have parted with Marguerite. Her idea was mingled with the vital springs of my existence; and scarcely any power less resistless than death could have made me consent to pass an entire day without her society. But then it is to be considered, that my daughters were in the morning of life; their hopes were untarnished, their prospects not obscured by a single cloud; and that the crime would probably have been greater, obstinately to have made them the partners of my misfortunes and disgrace. There are persons who will regard this passage in my history as culpable, and the testimony of a cold and unsusceptible heart. I contemplate it, even at this distance of time, as the noblest and most virtuous effort of my life; and a thousand circumstances have occurred since, to induce me to congratulate myself that I had the courage to achieve my purpose.

CHAPTER XXIX.

Nineteen years had now elapsed from the day that had witnessed my union with Marguerite de Damville. In all that time I had never been alone. Alone in a certain sense indeed I had stood at Paris in the period that had led to my exile, and at Soleure in that which immediately succeeded it. In each case I was solitary, and my solitude was unhappy. But my unhappiness was then in a certain sense spontaneous; my solitude was a luxury in which I felt myself impelled to indulge. He that has experienced both, will readily acknowledge the extreme difference between the misery we embrace and the misery from which we shrink with abhorrence and loathing. I relinquished in the former instances my dearest connections, my proper post and situation; but I felt that I could return to the one and resume the other at pleasure. I repeat it therefore, Then I had not been alone, and now I was alone. The same motive, which in this instance made me cut myself off from my daughters that I might not be the cause of their misery, forbad me to be the parent of a future offspring upon whom I might entail similar misfortune. Tell me then, was I not alone? I recollected the words of the stranger, wrung from him by the excess of his misery at the summer-house of the lake, "Alone—alone!—friendless—friendless!" I began to penetrate the enigma of his history.

I fixed my daughters with an ample revenue in the château of St. Leon; I repurchased for them all my paternal property. I waited some time at Montauban to hear of the event of my project, and their final settlement. I learned with pleasure that they found their situation peaceful, easy, and reputable; I enjoined them that they should speak and think of me as dead. I led them to suppose, when I left Montauban, that I should set out upon an extensive tour, that I should traverse the Indus and the Ganges, and penetrate into the furthest extremities of the East. How uncommon, how pitiable a fate! I became prematurely dead to my country and my race, because I was destined never to die! The first sensation I derived from their prosperity, as I have already said, was pleasure: my second was that which the devil might have felt, when he entered paradise for the seduction of our first parents. I contemplated with some degree of malignant envy a happiness of which it was little probable I should ever partake. Let me not be censured for this: let any man put himself in my situation, and say, whether the pleasure he feels at contemplating the separated happiness of those he loves be not a mingled sensation? With heavy heart I sought again the road of Madrid.

Though my spirits underwent an extreme depression, I determined not to desert myself or the advantages I had purchased at so inestimable a price. I exerted myself to shake off my lethargy, and rouse the faculties of my soul. I refused to give way to omens of evil portent, and resolved to see what might yet be made of my endowments. There is no misfortune that has not in it some slight mixture of good. My being now alone, and detached from every relative tie, left me at liberty to pursue my projects with a bolder enterprise. The mistake of which I accused myself in the former instance, was the entering too precipitately into the exercise of the gifts of the stranger, before I had properly measured my strength, and investigated the use and application of my tools. I had suffered sufficiently from the past uncertainty and irresoluteness of my march. I determined, as far as human precaution could secure its ends, to encounter no more misfortunes, to subject myself to no further miscarriages, but to take care that henceforth the tide of my pursuits should move smoothly onward. I dedicated the six months immediately succeeding my separation from my daughters, to the joint contemplation of morals and natural philosophy. I was resolved to ascertain the simplest mode of manufacturing wealth, the wisest methods for lulling the suspicions and controlling the passions of mankind, and the true science of the use of riches. Alas! I had in the sequel frequent occasions to confess, that, though I had fortuitously entered into possession of the leading secrets of natural magic, I was a mere tyro in the science of man, at least in the degree in which the exercise of these secrets required the possession of it.

Nothing material occurred to interrupt the occupations of the winter. My apathy—intellectual activity, palsy of the heart,—went evenly forward. I made no acquaintance; I was a mere spectator of the busy scenes that passed around me. I was resolved not to entangle myself with rashly formed connections; and it will commonly be found, that he, whose contemplations are principally employed upon some secret and guarded hoard of reflection, has little propensity to communicate upon idle and indifferent matters.

A slight incident indeed disturbed me for a few days during this interval; but it passed away, and for the present I thought of it no more. During the festival of Christmas it happened that I felt an inclination to be the spectator of a celebrated bull-fight, that was exhibited before the emperor and his court. For the most part I was studious of privacy; I therefore felt the less scruple in indulging this unusual caprice. At the commencement of the spectacle, I was attentive only to the exhibition. I was delighted with the form and beauty of the animals, with the freedom and grandeur of their motion, with the terrible energy of their assault and repulse. It was not long, however, before my eye was transiently caught by an individual, who sat in a gallery at no great distance, and who seemed to view me attentively. His figure bespoke some degree of refinement; but his eye was fiery, malicious, and savage. Presently however I turned again towards the area, and thought of him no more. Some time after by mere accident I looked towards the same gallery, and observed this man still in an attitude to examine me. It seemed as if he had not removed his eyes from me during the whole interval. This was repeated three or four times. Without knowing why, I became anxious and uneasy. I had a confused feeling that I had seen the man before, but whether in France, Switzerland, or Italy, I could not tell. I experienced that sort of disagreeable sensation from looking at his face, which arises in the mind from an association of the object present, with some mischief or suffering that was contemporary with its being perceived in a preceding instance. I am now persuaded that this man was one of the multitude to whom I had addressed myself from the bench on the hill a short time before my flight from Pisa, and that he was among the most eager to interrupt and molest me. But he was apparently a Spaniard by birth, and I could not at this time develope the mystery that hung about his features. Finding that I could neither rid myself of his curious and watchful observation, nor of the disturbance it gave me, I withdrew from the gallery where I had hitherto been sitting, and removed to another gallery on the opposite side of the area. About half an hour after, looking accidentally round, I saw this very man at my elbow. I then accosted him with the enquiry, "Do you know me, sir?" to which he immediately returned, with a pure Castilian accent, "No, señor!" He then began to be more reserved in his attention to me, without however entirely withdrawing it.

As soon as the entertainment was over, I went away, and saw no more of my Spaniard. I began to tax myself with pusillanimity in suffering so insignificant an incident to disturb me. A few days after however I suddenly lighted upon him in the street. He was talking to three or four of his countrymen, and in the progress of his discourse frequently pointed to me. I could now perceive something particularly hostile and ferocious in his countenance. The first impulse I felt was, that I would no longer suffer the unquietness and anxiety the sight of him produced in me, but would go up to him, and force him to an explanation. I believed however that, in the temper he indicated, this could not be done without involving myself in a quarrel; and I thought it wiser to endeavour to conquer in silence an unreasonable sensation. I therefore passed on; he immediately broke from his company, and attempted to follow me. This I determined not to endure. I laid my hand on my sword with a peremptory look, and waved to him to desist. His countenance then assumed an air of diabolical malignity, he shook his head furiously, and turned down another street. A strange sort of animosity this, between two persons utter strangers to each other, and which had as yet not deigned to express itself by a word! But such is the world! We hate we know not why. We are ready to cut each other's throats, because we do not like the turn of a feature, or the adjustment of a sword-knot. Prejudice, party, difference of countries, difference of religions, and a thousand wild chimeras of fanaticism or superstition, are continually arming us against a man, of whose virtues and qualities we are ignorant, and into whose benevolent or evil intentions we disdain to enquire.

I saw this Spaniard but once more. It was as I was on the point of entering the house, a part of which I occupied. I was particularly mortified at this circumstance. It was plain the man entertained, for whatever reason, a determined animosity against me; and I was grieved to furnish him with that advantage for injuring me, which consisted in being acquainted with the place of my residence. I would have turned away and gone down the street; but I had too fully marked my design of entering the house, before I reconnoitered my enemy. The displeasure I felt was so unaccountably great, that it was with difficulty my courage got the better of it; and I determined not to change the place of my abode. In a short time however, as I have already said, I thought of this incident no more. That it should have disturbed and unhinged me, in the degree that it had done, even for a moment, was a thing I could not account for. Had the calamities in which the legacy of the stranger involved me, converted me in so short a time, from a knight and a soldier, into a character of that morbid timidity, as to tremble at every shadow? Or, is there in some human countenances a fascination, a sort of mysterious sympathy and presentiment, that makes us cower and quail whenever we meet their eye-beams?

Several weeks now passed away, and I had nearly forgotten all the circumstances of this seemingly foolish story, when, in a little excursion I chanced to make from Madrid to a place about twelve miles distant, I was overtaken upon the road by a cavalier of respectable appearance, who presently took occasion to enter into conversation with me. He explained to me several of the objects that presented themselves on either side, told the names of the different nobility and grandees who occupied the villas we saw, and sometimes entered into the particulars of their history. I at first gave little encouragement to this communicative traveller; but there was something so polite in his manner, and intelligent in his discourse, that I could not prevail upon myself to treat him with rudeness or disrespect. After having talked for some time upon indifferent topics, he led to the general state of literature in Europe. Few subjects could appear less dangerous than this, as there were few upon which I felt myself better qualified to converse. By degrees I threw off some of my original reserve, and I found my companion well informed and ingenious, lively in his manner, and pertinent in his remarks.

By this time the unknown, having discovered that I had only come from Madrid for a day's relaxation, invited himself to dine with me at my inn. I departed from my established system of conduct on this occasion, and admitted his overture. After dinner he gave me some account of himself and his family, and seemed to expect from me a similar explicitness. I was less pleased with him in this particular, than I had been with his frank and undesigning conversation on the road. Strictly speaking however the expectation implied was only a breach of politeness; I had no reason to suppose that he foresaw it to be particularly offensive to me. Observing my backwardness, he immediately changed the subject. Presently he remarked, that by my physiognomy and accent he perceived I was a Frenchman, and asked me if I had known Cornelius Agrippa, who died about twelve years before at Grenoble. I answered in the negative. The unknown then entered into a warm eulogium of the talents of Agrippa, inveighed against the illiberal treatment he had experienced in consequence of his supposed proficiency in magic, and spoke with great asperity of the priests and inquisitors who had been his persecutors. I became attentive, watchful, and suspicious. He went on to expatiate upon the praises of the art magic, which nothing, he said, but the jealousy of churchmen had brought into disrepute; affirmed that it had been treated with respect, and counted illustrious, by the ancients, in the instance of Pythagoras, Apollonius Tyaneus, and others; and expressed a great desire to become a student of the art himself. This kind of discourse made me repent that I had been drawn in so far as to sit down with this unknown, and admit him as my companion of the day. During the whole time he was the principal speaker. Sometimes he paused, with a seeming desire to hear my sentiments. But I had now formed my resolution, and gave him no encouragement. Presently after I called for my horse. I should have observed, that his servant who followed him engaged in conversation with mine, at the same time that the dialogue began between their masters. Seeing me about to depart, the unknown motioned as if to accompany me. Upon this I became serious.

"Señor caballero," said I, "I have now had the pleasure of your company to dinner: I am going home, and have the honour to bid you farewell. It is neither my disposition, nor the habit of the grave and dignified nation among whom I at present reside, to form permanent acquaintances upon casual rencounters: you will not therefore think I violate the hospitality for which I am indebted to them, if I intimate to you my desire to return alone."

All this I said with the grave and formal tone becoming a Spaniard, and the unknown had nothing to reply. It was evident however that my dryness chagrined him; and he even muttered words of resentment between his teeth. I could observe now a degree of hostility and fury in his countenance, which remarkably contrasted with the pliancy and oblingingness of his preceding demeanour. I took no notice however of these circumstances, and rode away. I have since had sufficient reasons to convince me that these two persons, whose story, but for that explanation, may appear to the reader exceedingly frivolous, were the one an informer, and the other a spy of the holy inquisition. The man who had seen me at Pisa had his imagination terrified and his superstition set in arms by all that he had heard of me in that place; and thought he could not perform a more meritorious work, than by giving intelligence to the fathers what sort of person had taken refuge in the metropolis of this most Catholic kingdom. It was with this view he had watched me, and at length, by an accident he deemed peculiarly fortunate, lodged me in my proper habitation. Having given in his denunciation, my travelling companion was next fastened on me by the contrivance and zeal of the fathers inquisitors. He was a familiar of the holy office; and it is well known that persons of the fairest prospects and most polite education in Spain are led by their religious impressions to place a pride in performing menial and even perfidious offices in the service of the inquisition. The kind of dishonour I put upon him in parting, though of a nature he could not openly resent, I fear conspired with his zeal for God's and the church's honour, to induce him to relate a story concerning me, more modelled by the bitterness of his personal feelings, than distinguished by a regard to truth.

Such was the snare, woven and drawing close round me on all sides for my destruction. I was made uneasy by the rencounter of the traveller, but by no means aware of the whole extent of the mischief that impended over me. When I came to retrace, point by point, the discourse he had held, I could not conceive that the turn it had taken originated in accident. I perceived, with no little grief of heart and concern, that I was known. It was however necessary that I should reflect maturely upon the conduct to be pursued by me. I ought not gratuitously to expose myself to danger. But then, on the other hand, it is a point of general wisdom, and was particularly incumbent in my extraordinary circumstances, not to suffer vigilance to degenerate into restless anxiety. It would be easy for me, if I were not strictly on my guard, continually to find food for suspicion, and to surround myself with imaginary plots and dangers. This was a vice that I was willing enough to pity in others; but there was no character that I more cordially disdained for myself. There was none more pointedly in opposition to that gallant, generous, confiding spirit, which had distinguished those military heroes of my native soil, who had been the exclusive object of my earliest admiration, and whom, in my present dejected and deserted situation, I still desired to resemble. When I came to reflect, I easily perceived that this vice was particularly allied to a life of solitude; and that he who is cut off from the genuine and happy connections of husband, father, and friend, is of all men most liable, in their absence, to conjure up for himself the unnatural intercourses and reciprocations of hostility. It was thus that I artificially reconciled myself to my situation, and obstinately closed my eyes upon those equivocal demonstrations of danger which from time to time were presented to my view.

CHAPTER XXX.

Such was the state of my mind, when it happened, one gloomy evening in the latter end of March, that my valet announced to me three gentlemen who were come to visit me. It was strange: I had no visitors; I indulged no relaxation but that of the street, and of public places. Do you know who they are? said I. I accidentally looked up, and saw paleness and terror written in his countenance. He had not however time to reply, before they burst into the room. They were alguazils of the inquisition. They told me their errand was to conduct me to the holy office.

I submitted, and accompanied them. It was already dark. They put me into a litter with the curtains drawn, and then arranged themselves in silence, one on each side, while one brought up the rear. I was taken by surprise: nothing could be further from my expectation than such an event. As we passed along, I ruminated with myself on the line of conduct it was incumbent on me to pursue. To make an immediate experiment of the fidelity of my guides was a doubtful attempt. If, for want of time and the opportunity of a tranquil hearing, I miscarried with them, the trial would be converted into evidence against me. If I succeeded, I had then to escape out of Spain, in the centre of which I now was, from the hostility of a tribunal, which was said to surpass all the tribunals on the face of the earth in activity and vigilance. I knew of nothing that the fathers of the inquisition could have against me. I had lived in the most entire seclusion; and I could defy any one to report a single action of mine, since I had entered Spain, to my prejudice. I had been wholly occupied with melancholy reflections on the past, and solitary inventions and devices which I purposed to bring forward for the future. I determined not to live for ever the slave of fear. I believed that the best method for defeating a danger, in many cases, was undauntedly to encounter it; and I did not imagine that I could have a more favourable opportunity for that purpose than the present. I had heard much indeed of the terrors of the inquisition; but a generous and liberal spirit lends no very attentive ear to horrors, the trite and vulgar rumour of which only has reached him. I disdained to be blown down with a breath. I believed that the inquisition itself would not venture to proceed criminally against a man against whom nothing criminal had been alleged. In every event, I believed it would never be too late to have recourse to my peculiar prerogatives.

Upon entering the prison of the inquisition I was first conducted to a solitary cell. It is not my intention to treat of those particulars of the holy office which are already to be found in innumerable publications. I have no pleasure in reviving the images of this sojourn of horrors. I know it is unreasonable to despise a man for the miseries and wretchedness he has endured; but I know that such is the human heart, and I will not expose myself to be scoffed at and trampled upon for my misfortunes. I found myself under the necessity, while in the inquisition, of submitting to that most profligate of all impositions, an oath of secrecy as to what I had seen, and what I had suffered; and, whatever may be the strict morality of such an obligation, I will not ambitiously thrust myself forward in violation of it. I will restrict the story I have to relate to the peculiarities that characterised my case, and enter as little as possible into the general policy of this frontier intrenchment of the Christian faith.

When I was brought up to be interrogated, I was assailed with innumerable questions, the obvious purport of which was, as much as possible, to extort from me evidence of every kind that might be injurious to my cause. The object of the inquisition is to defend our holy mother, the church, from whatever might defile her sanctity and whiteness. Every thing that calls into question the truth of her doctrines, that pollutes and turns from their original purpose any of her ordinances, or that implies commerce and league with the invisible enemy of saints, it is its peculiar province to investigate. The fathers are therefore particularly cautious that they may not, by confining their questions too much to a single object, preclude themselves from the chance of discovering danger under all the forms it may assume. It is presumed that he who is a corrupt member of the church of Christ in one point is unsound and unfaithful in others.

The inquisitor who examined me, first demanded, whether I were informed for what cause I was brought before that tribunal? Whether I did not find myself able to conjecture the nature of my offence? Whether I did not know the sort of crimes for which men were detained in that prison? He then desired me to recollect myself, and consider, whether I were not conscious of offence against the holy Catholic church? Whether I had never asserted or maintained any doctrines contrary to what mother church asserts and maintains? Whether I had never, to my knowledge, defiled any of the ordinances of God, or applied things sacred to unholy and profane purposes? Whether I had never invocated the devil? Whether I had never held any commerce, or entered into any league, with the enemy of saints? Whether I had never performed, or sought to perform, preternatural and miraculous acts by unholy means? Whether I had never vexed, or sought to vex, those against whom I had enmity, by secret and forbidden arts? Whether I had never resided in countries the inhabitants of which were heretics, and whether I had never listened to their discourses and arguments? Whether, when I inhabited such countries, I had never assisted at the celebration of divine ordinances performed by heretics, or in a form which holy church disapproves or condemns?

Finding that he could gain nothing upon me by these general interrogatories, the inquisitor next descended to particulars. He enquired concerning the incidents of my Pisan story, which, having first assured myself from the train of his questions that some representation of that unfortunate affair had reached his ear, I willingly related, to the same extent that I had previously done to the marchese Filosanto.

He then proceeded to a great number of questions, the source of which is to be traced to the commonly received notions respecting sorcerers and necromancers. They were so artfully contrived, and so large in their scope, that it was not easy to guess whether they related to any particular accusation alleged against me, or were formed entirely on general principles. Yet some of them were so minute, so connected, and arranged so perfectly in series, that I could not but believe they were an echo of the calumnies invented against me at Pisa, of which, however, as I had never collected any regular and detailed account, I could not accurately trace the influence on the present occasion.

The inquisitor demanded of me, Whether I had never seen or held conversation with any supernatural being, or the spirit of a man departed? Whether I had never practised diabolical arts to raise the dead? Whether I had never had a familiar in the form of some insect, domestic animal, or reptile? He was particularly subtle and copious in his questions respecting the history of my unfortunate dog, endeavouring to surprise me in some slip or contradiction in what I affirmed on the subject. He asked, Whether I had never assumed a form different from my real one, either a different age and appearance, or a different species of animal? Whether I had never, by the agency of my demon, inflicted sickness, convulsion-fits, or death? Whether I had never caused the mortality of cattle? Whether I had not the power of being in two places at once? Whether I had never been seen riding through the air? Whether I had never been wounded in my absence, by a blow aimed at my astral spirit or apparition? Whether I had never possessed books of conjuration or the art magic? Whether it had never happened to me that an indifferent person, indiscreetly perusing a spell or incantation in my possession, had been maimed or killed by the spirits he had undesignedly evoked?

A further object particularly pursued in my interrogatory, was the detection of my property; and the questions constructed for this purpose were uncommonly artful and multiplied. The inquisitor told me that the holy office was, by the nature of its institution, the guardian and administrator of every person that fell under its animadversion. Shut up, he said, as I must be, during the pendency of my cause, and separated from the rest of mankind, I was wholly incapable of superintending my worldly affairs, which, unless they were properly looked into, might in the interval be materially injured. I ought therefore implicitly and without reserve to refer myself in this point to the care of the fathers. If my innocence were established, as he hoped, and earnestly prayed to the mother of God, and the saints of Jesus, might ultimately happen, I should find the holy office a faithful and qualified steward. If, on the contrary, I should be proved a heretic and an alien to the Most High, I ought then to rejoice in the beneficent interference of the fathers, who, by dedicating my wealth to consecrated purposes, would mitigate in the eye of the just Judge of heaven and earth the duration or fierceness of my punishments in a future world. The inquisitor had apparently heard various reports of my riches, and was inexpressibly chagrined that he should be found so unskilful a member of his profession, as not to be able to extort from me a full confession on that head. After having employed every artifice of menace and terror, after having endeavoured to soothe and cajole me by blandishments and persuasion, and finding all his expedients fruitless, he poured upon me the full storm of his indignation. He said, it was apparent that I was dealing disingenuously and fraudulently with the delegated guardians of religion; it was impossible that the expenditure I was well known more or less to have incurred could be supported without considerable funds; and my evident duplicity and concealment in this point must be regarded as a full confirmation of every crime my accusers had alleged against me.

In the course of my examinations, the inquisitor who questioned me gave himself the trouble of entering into a full vindication of the tribunal of which he was a member. He said, that every thing that was valuable to mankind, not only in a future state, but also in the present, depended upon preserving in full vigour and strength the sacred institutions of the Christian faith; and that those who were endowed with powers sufficient for that purpose would be in the highest degree inexcusable in the sight of God, if they did not vigilantly and inflexibly maintain the exertion of those powers. It was an egregious mistake of self-willed and opinionated men, to suppose that the maintenance of our holy religion was sufficiently provided for by the clearness of its evidence. It was no less dangerous, to pretend that the stability and duration of the church of Christ might be confided to the providence of God. Providence acts by human means; and it was presumptuous for those who neglected the means to trust that they should nevertheless see the end adequately secured. Why had Providence thought proper to generate an alliance between church and state, and to place the powers and authority of human society in the hands of the adherents of the Christian faith? Magistrates and governments were thus made the vicars of Heaven, and great would be their condemnation if they neglected the trust reposed in them. The great adversary of mankind was incessantly watchful for the destruction of souls; and, while he spread abroad his delusions, it was folly to imagine that evidence alone was powerful enough to counteract them. What judges were the great mass of mankind of the integrity and validity of evidence? The jest of the scorner was ever at hand to turn into ridicule the most sacred mysteries. The opposers of our holy faith were indefatigable in their industry, and as anxious in their exertions to deprive their fellow-men of every comfort and hope, as if infidelity, which was the curse of the human species, were the greatest blessing that could be conferred on them. The devil was a hard task-master, and granted no vacation, night or day, to those who enlisted themselves in the support of his cause. It might answer well enough the purpose of the vain-glorious theorist, to suppose that man was a rational animal; but they who had regarded human society with an observing eye knew that it was otherwise. Delusion would ever be too hard for evidence, and the grossest falsehoods prove victorious over the most sacred truths, if what was illiberally and maliciously styled persecution were not brought in aid of the cause of religion. The passions of mankind were on the side of falsehood; man, unrestrained by law, was a wild, ferocious, and most pernicious beast, and, were it not for the wholesome curb of authority, would speedily throw off all ties and limitations, human and divine. Nothing could more clearly prove, that the heretical followers of Luther and Calvin, who had lately sprung up for the plague of mankind, whatever they might pretend, were in reality the determined enemies of all revelation, than their continual demand, that the cause should be tried by discussion, and that every man should be defended in the exercise of his private judgment. They could not but know,—every man not totally robbed of all power of discernment must know,— that, if this demand were once granted, it would prove a blow at the root of every sentiment of religion. The inquisition therefore was the most salutary institution that had ever been devised; and the future welfare of mankind wholly depended upon the maintenance of its powers and its maxims. By a moderate and judicious exhibition of terror, it superseded the necessity of innumerable punishments. The inquisition was not capricious and uncertain in its policy; it acted under the direction of immutable laws; it held a tender, but a firm rein upon the extravagances and madness of mankind. Nothing was more notorious, than that a regular and systematical proceeding was both more effectual and more generous than one that was fickle. He defied the whole history of the world to produce an example of so merciful a tribunal. The great end of its policy was the reclaiming of sinners and the multiplication of penitents, who, after a gentle and salutary discipline, were again by holy church received into her bosom; and even when they delivered the finally impenitent to the flames, it was to the flames of a purifying fire, which by destroying the flesh redeemed or diminished the punishments of a future world. He knew that an outcry had been artfully raised against the proceedings of the holy office. But it was easy to see that its enemies, under the pretence of compassion for its victims, concealed an inveterate animosity against property, religion, and civil society. The anabaptists had thrown off the mask, and discovered their true designs; and the rest were only more plausible and specious, in proportion as they were more timid. The present was the most important crisis that ever occurred in the history of the world. There was a spirit at work, that aimed at dissolving all the bonds of civil society, and converting mankind into beasts and savages. Who had not heard of the levellers, millenarians, and fifth-monarchy-men, who, under the specious guise of disinterestedness and an universal love of mankind, had nothing in view but the most sacrilegious and unprincipled depredations? It was true that the preachers of these doctrines were utterly contemptible both for numbers and talent: but it would be found a short-sighted policy, to overlook these desperate assailants on account of the poorness and meanness of their qualifications. For his own part he did not hesitate to say, that human society would owe its preservation, if it were preserved, to the merciful yet vigorous proceedings of the court of inquisition. The misrepresentations that were invidiously made of the present firm and vigilant system of policy would be heard for a day, and then universally abandoned. Posterity, he was well assured, would do full justice to the sagacity and soundness of the conduct of this calumniated and much injured institution.

The reader will forgive me if the panegyric thus elaborately pronounced by the inquisitor who examined me, upon the court of which he was a member, had not all the weight with my mind at the moment I heard it which he will probably ascribe to it in the calmness of the closet. It is so difficult to be impartial in our own cause! The candid mind will no doubt make a large allowance for the unhappy situation in which I now stood, and the bitter and galling thoughts that preyed upon my memory. But, if I am chargeable with temporary injustice in the judgment I then passed on the arguments of the inquisitor, I flatter myself that I have been able, after the interval that has elapsed, to give a true and adequate statement of them.

Beside these reasonings on the necessity of a wholesome restraint on the privileges of speaking and writing, the father in another of my examinations condescended to delineate to me the mysteries of the world of spirits. He reminded me that in the first grand rebellion upon record, that of the fallen angels, of which he considered the present defection under Luther and Calvin as in some measure a counterpart, a third of the host of heaven had been thrust out of the celestial mansions. These accursed spirits had since been permitted to pursue their machinations on the face of our earth. "The devil, like a roaring lion, goeth about, seeking whom he may devour." The oracles of the heathens, the temptations of Job and of our Saviour, and the demoniacs of sacred writ, were examples of the extensive power which Heaven had thought fit to allow him. Men of a sceptical and feeble understanding had been tempted to doubt whether this was consistent with the wisdom and goodness of God. But, though it was in vain for us to pretend to fathom the depth of the divine mysteries, there were certain reasons that were sufficiently obvious to every ingenuous mind. There were persons in all ages of the world, who, like the Sadducees in the time of our blessed Saviour, were inclined to affirm "that there was no resurrection, neither angel, nor spirit;" and God permitted the lying wonders of infernal agents the more completely to confound the unbelief of his enemies. He who witnessed the wonderful operations of witchcraft, or saw the ghost of a man departed, could not doubt of the interference of invisible agents in the concerns of our nether world; and, if there were devils and apparitions, it would be to the last degree unreasonable to deny the existence of God, or the miracles of Christ. These were to be received as the grounds of the divine permission of sorcerers, necromancers, and witches. But the rules of the divine conduct were not to constitute the rules of ours. He might permit the agency of invisible malice, because he saw things upon an unlimited scale, his judgments were infallible, and he could say to Beelzebub himself, "Thus far shalt thou go, and no further." Those to whose care was intrusted the welfare of mankind here or hereafter were bound as far as possible to oppose themselves to the empire of Satan. His power was given him only for a time, and, if not strictly restrained of God and the powers ordained of God, it would over-run every thing, and replunge all this beautiful scene of creation in its original chaos. There was an endless and eternal war between God and the devil, and the governors of the church were Heaven's field-officers and pioneers for carrying it on. Of all the crimes, he added, to which the depravity of human nature had given birth, the most astonishing and the most horrible was that of diabolical commerce. That human creatures should be so far infatuated, as to enter into league with the declared enemy of souls, and for the possession of a short-lived and precarious power to sign away their spirits to eternal damnation, was so extraordinary as to have been wholly unworthy of credit, were it not supported by evidence as strong and irresistible as that of the miracles of Jesus Christ himself. The persons who thus voluntarily made themselves accursed before God deserved to be regarded with alienation and horror by the whole human race. Every man that saw them was bound by his baptismal engagements to destroy them; and whoever administered to them the smallest portion of food, drink, or comfort, thereby rendered himself a party to their guilt. The inquisition especially had declared against this race of men eternal war, and considered their crime as more complicated, audacious, and pestilential, than any other branch of heresy. Having, for his own part, no doubt that I was one of these noxious and enormous reprobates, he exhorted me to make a voluntary confession of my evil deeds, and, by submitting readily to the tortures and punishments of this world, endeavour to free myself, if it were yet possible, from those of the world to come.

These discourses of the inquisitor were variously interspersed through the three examinations to which I was subjected a short time after I became an inhabitant of the holy house. On my part I endeavoured to the best of my power to repel the imputations cast upon me, to establish my innocence, and to confound the severity of my oppressors. I told the inquisitor, whatever might be the force of his arguments respecting heresy and dealings with the devil, they were nothing to me. I was no Lutheran, no anabaptist, no necromancer, no underminer of the faith of others, or ally of the prince of the infernal regions. I proudly and earnestly demanded to be confronted with my accusers. I asked my examiner in his turn, What sort of justice that was, which pretended to proceed capitally against its prisoners upon secret and unavowed accusations? He endeavoured to stop me.

He told me that I was not brought there to arraign the methods and practices of their court; that it did not become a prisoner put upon his defence to insult his judges; that this contumacy could not be regarded but as an aggravation of my guilt; and that I was bound strictly and simply to answer the interrogatories that were proposed to me. The rebuke of the inquisitor was unavailing. My spirit was wrought to too high a pitch to be thus restrained; I was too firmly resolved to give the utmost force of mind and truth to the topics of my just defence. It is the practice of the inquisition for the prisoner to sit during his examination. I started upon my feet.

"The mode of your proceeding," cried I, "is the mockery of a trial. From your fatal bar no man can go forth acquitted. How is a story to be refuted, when hardly and with difficulty you suffer your prisoner to collect the slightest fragments of it? If I would detect a calumny, is it not requisite that I should be acquainted with its history, and know its authors and propagators? Then I may perhaps be able to confound their forgeries, to show the groundlessness of their allegations, to expose the baseness of their purposes and the profligacy of their characters. I am informed of nothing; yet I am bid, first to be my own accuser, and then to answer the accusations of others. It is only by following a falsehood through all its doublings that it can be effectually destroyed. You bid me unravel a web, and will not suffer me to touch it with one of my fingers. The defence of the purest innocence is often difficult, sometimes impossible, against the artfulness of a malicious tale, or the fortuitous concurrence of unfavourable appearances. But you strip innocence of those consecrated weapons by which only it can be defended. Give to an accusation the particulars with which what really happens must always be attended, give to it the circumstances of place and of time, lay aside the ambiguity and generalities in which you shelter yourselves, and then, perhaps then only, it can be victoriously repelled. You ask me a thousand various and artfully constructed questions. What sort of a man do you imagine me to be? I am not a fool, that I should be inveigled; I am not a boy, that I should be menaced into confessions. Cease your base and unprincipled arts! I will furnish no materials against myself. If you know anything against me, avow it! Propose it, and I will answer. Think not to patch up a miserable accusation out of the words which inadvertence or weariness may cause me to utter. Shame on your institution! May infamy overtake the system of your proceedings! That religion which is supported by such means is viler than atheism. That civilisation which has its basis in despotism, is more worthless and hateful than the state of savages running wild in their woods.

"Do you not perceive that the language I am now holding to you is the exclusive privilege of conscious innocence? The indignation I express is no artificial rage, studiously contrived to overbear accusation. You have it, as it flows spontaneously to my tongue, warm from the promptings of an honest heart. If I could have consulted a friend, it is probable he would have dissuaded me from my present demeanour as impolitic. If I were governed by the dictates of an ordinary prudence, I should have displayed less ardour, less resentment. But I am willing to try whether shame cannot yet be lighted up even in the cheek of an inquisitor."

The father who examined me, having in vain endeavoured to check the current of my invective, changed his manner, and assumed a tone diametrically the reverse of mine. He professed that he felt much compassion and interest for my misfortune, and should deem himself happy if he could be the instrument of my deliverance. The language I had uttered was highly indecorous, and such as seemed in itself to call for a rigorous penance. But he should not think himself worthy the name of a man, if he did not make suitable allowance for the bitter and extravagant sentiments, that would occasionally find their way into the mind of one in my unfortunate situation. So circumstanced, men would often mistake their friends for their enemies. I regarded the inquisition as my enemy: it was in reality my firm and disinterested friend; zealously watchful for my body, my soul, and my estate. Other courts had other maxims of proceeding, because their motives of action were different; and it was but just that they should furnish their prisoners with a defence against their frailty. But the breast of an inquisitor was accessible to no sentiment but that of love; a burning love of God; love of the church; love of the prisoner, who might be wrongfully accused; love of the penitent, whom he reconciled to our common mother, the church; love even of the incorrigible heretic whose body he burned for the good of his soul. The inquisitor did not discover to the prisoner the evidence adduced against him; that was between God and the inquisitor's conscience. But the suppression which was thus practised rendered him doubly scrupulous and sceptical as to the evidence he received; he sifted it with a severity that the prisoner would in vain endeavour to imitate; and the rules of evidence in that court were so guarded, punctilious, and minute, as to render any mistake in its proceedings altogether impossible. For a man to be once a prisoner of the court of inquisition, by a salutary prejudice which prevailed through the catholic world, rendered him for ever infamous. This was another cause of the extreme wariness and caution, with which that court was accustomed to proceed. They first listened to the accuser, who was obliged to give in his information on oath. They then instituted a secret enquiry against the party accused; and, till they had collected abundant ground for their proceeding, they did not venture to touch a hair of his head. They elaborately classed all the different degrees of evidence into half proof, full proof, proof less than half, and proof less than full. When these things were duly considered, it would appear certain that no court that had at any time existed on earth, had ever been so tender in its proceedings, so pure in its incitements, and so every way superior to the attacks of calumny and malice, as the court of inquisition.

With respect to myself in particular, he said, they had not apprehended me and put me upon my defence, without previously assembling a large body of miscellaneous and circumstantial evidence. The evidence they had drawn from myself was negative only, but it was strong: the obscurity that hung about my person, who I was, and whence I came; and the obscurity that hung about my fortune, a great visible expenditure in Spain or in Italy, and no visible means. These were not the signatures and tokens of innocence. They tended strongly to confirm the accusation under which I laboured. Yet so tender was the inquisition in its proceeding, and so chary of its reputation, that upon these accumulated proofs and presumptions, they were not prepared to pronounce against me. They would hear me again and again. They would give me time to recollect myself, and for this purpose they would order for me a coarse and scanty fare, and a solitary cell. I might depend upon it my contumacy should be overcome. The fundamental principle of their proceedings was borrowed from that humane and compassionate maxim of the old Roman law, De vita hominis nulla cunctatio est longa; and I should accordingly find them free from all precipitation and impatience, and ready to indulge me with a residence, however long, in their prisons, till my case had been sifted to the bottom.

CHAPTER XXXI.

The indulgence thus ostentatiously proclaimed by the father-inquisitor was not exactly to my taste. Finding that all the energy of mind I could apply to my defence was vain, I determined to have recourse to a different mode of proceeding. I received three admonitions, as they call them, the substance of which I have already recited, in the course of the first ten days of my confinement, and I then for some time heard of the inquisitor no more. I understood that it was frequently the practice, after three admonitions, not to bring up the prisoner for further hearing during a whole year; and it appeared sufficiently probable from the last words addressed to me by my judge, that this policy was intended to be employed in my case. Without further delay therefore I resolved to recur to the expedient in the use of which my power was unbounded, and by a brilliant offer at once to subdue the scruples, and secure the fidelity, of the person or persons upon whom my safe custody might be found to depend. All that was necessary was to convince the party to whom I should propose the assisting me, of the reality of my powers; and then to put carte blanche into his hands, or rather to ascertain at once the extent of his hopes and demands, and by a spirited and peremptory conduct to yield them all. In the period which, immediately previous to my present imprisonment, I had devoted to the meditation of my future plans and the review of my past, I had severely accused myself of half measures, and had determined to abjure all hesitation and irresoluteness for the time to come. It is not indeed to be wondered at, that, possessing a power so utterly remote from common ideas and conceptions, and which, speaking from experience, I do not hesitate to affirm no mere effort of imagination is adequate to represent, I should have acted below the prerogatives and demands of my situation. This mistake I would make no more. I would overwhelm opposition by the splendour of my proceedings, and confound scruples by the dignity and princely magnificence of my appearance. Unshackled as I was with connections, and risking no one's happiness but my own, I proposed to compel the human species to view me from an awful distance, and to oblige every one that approached me to feel his inferiority. It would be to the last degree disgraceful and contemptible in me, being raised so far above my peers in my privileges, if I were to fall below the ordinary standard of a gallant man in the decision and firmness of my system of conduct. Decision and firmness were the principles to be exercised by me now; dignity and magnificence must await their turn hereafter.

It was not long before I embraced an opportunity of speaking to the man who waited on me with my daily allotment of provisions, and I designed as shortly as possible to proceed to that species of argument, in which I principally confided to engage him in my cause. But he did not suffer me to utter a sentence before with a very expressive gesture he interrupted me. I had remarked already the silence which seemed for ever to pervade this dismal abode; but I had not ascribed importance enough to this circumstance, to suppose that it could materially interfere with the project I had formed. I now perceived the countenance of my attendant to be overspread with terror and alarm. He put his hand upon my mouth, and by his attitude seemed earnestly to insist upon my conforming to the rules of the prison. I was not however to be thus diverted from my purpose. I seized his hands, and began again to pursue the discourse I had meditated. This proceeding on my part induced him to break the silence he had hitherto preserved. He told me that if I did not instantly set him at liberty, he would alarm the prison. I loosed his hands. I then by every gesture I could devise endeavoured to prevail on him to approach me, to suffer me to confer with him in the lowest whisper, and assured him that he should have no reason to repent his compliance. I might as well have addressed myself to the walls that inclosed me. He would not stay an instant; he would yield in nothing. He burst from me abruptly, and, closing the door of my cell, left me in solitude and darkness.

In the evening of the day of this attempt the keeper of the prison entered my apartment. When he appeared, I began to flatter myself that in this man I should find a better subject for my purpose than in the poor turnkey who had given me so unfavourable a prognostic of my success. I lost no time in saying to him that I had something important to communicate; but he peremptorily commanded me to be silent, and listen to what he was about to say to me. He told me that I had already been complained against for speech, and I was now repeating my offence. He advised me to ponder well the consequences of what I was doing. The orders of the inquisition were rigorous and inflexible. The cells were not so substantially separated but that a voice might be heard from one to the other; yet it had happened more than once, that a husband and wife, a father and child, had for years been lodged next to each other, without the smallest suspicion on either part of the proximity of their situation. He was astonished at the pertinacity of my behaviour. There was no government on the face of the earth, he would venture to say, that had subjects more obedient, more dutiful and exemplary than the holy inquisition. Not a murmur was ever heard; not a discontent ever expressed. All was humbleness, thankfulness, and gratitude. He recommended to me to conform myself to my situation, and let him hear no further complaints of me. He had no sooner finished his harangue, than he left me as abruptly as his servant had done. It is not possible to impart any adequate image of the inflexibility of his features, or the stern composure of his demeanour.

I now saw my situation in a different point of view. Bribery was of no use, where all intercourse was denied. Great God! into what position was I got? In the midst of a great and populous city, at this time perhaps the metropolis of the world, I heard occasionally from beyond the limits of my prison the hum of busy throngs, or the shouts of a tumultuous populace. Yet I was myself in the deepest solitude. Like the wretched mariners I have somewhere read of, shipwrecked upon a desert shore, I might remain encaged, till I lost all recollection of European language, and all acquaintance with the sound of my own voice. A jailor from time to time entered my apartment; but to me he was simply a moving and breathing statue, his features never moulded into the expression of a meaning, nor his mouth opened for the utterance of a sound. From the first I had been struck with the extreme and death-like silence that characterised the place of my confinement; but my mind was occupied with other thoughts, and I had not adverted to the cause of the phenomenon. I had then felt little inclination to the converse of a jailor; my natural disposition was somewhat singular for a Frenchman, and inclined to taciturnity: I had resolved to make a fair and ample trial of the power of a just defence, where my innocence was so complete and I was entirely disengaged from those unfavourable appearances which had constituted my misfortune at Constance; and I even rejoiced, that a silence, which I regarded as casual and individual, delivered me from all fear of impertinence in my attendant. With how different a temper do we contemplate an incident which, we persuade ourselves, continues to operate only because we want inclination to remove it; and an incident which is violently imposed, and to which, with the utmost exertion of our strength, we cannot succeed to impart the slightest shock! The external object is the same; its picture in the intellectual sensorium how unlike! What a profound and inconceivable refinement in the art of tyranny is this silence! The jailor might well tell me, that beneath his roofs there was neither complaint nor murmur, that the very soul of its inhabitants was subdued, and that they suffered the most unheard of oppressions without astonishment or indignation. This is the peculiar prerogative of despotism: it produces many symptoms of the same general appearance as those which are derived from liberty and justice. There are no remonstrances; there is no impatience or violence; there is a calm, a fatal and accursed tranquillity that pervades the whole. The spectator enters, and for a time misinterprets every object he sees; he perceives human bodies standing or moving around him; and it is with the utmost surprise, if he has leisure and opportunity to observe a little further, that he finds at last the things he sees to be the mere shades of men, cold, inert, glaring bodies, which the heaven-born soul has long since deserted. Wonderful, I hesitate not to affirm, is the genuine and direct power of such a situation as that in which I was now placed, upon the human imagination. What was it then to me, to whom speech was not merely one of those things, misnamed indulgences, misnamed luxuries, upon which the desirableness and the health of human existence depend; but who had looked to it as the only and the assured means of my rescue from this scene of horrors! I intreat the reader to pardon me, when I confess, that the operation of the discovery I made was so overwhelming and apparently desperate, that it was some weeks, I might say months, before my mind recovered its wonted bias and activity.

It was towards the close of the period I have named, that a new incident, concurring with that familiarity which serves in some measure to disarm every mischief of its sting, restored and re-awakened my mind. I had vegetated now for some time, if the metaphor can with propriety be applied to existence in a noxious and empoisoned air, by which all vegetation would have been undermined, and which the vital principle in man is scarcely competent to surmount; and in all this period had encountered nothing from without, nor received any intimation, that could in the slightest degree interrupt the progressive destruction and waste of the soul. One day, at the customary hour of my being attended by my warder, I was surprised to see him bring with him a visiter to my cell. The unknown was a man with grey hairs and a silver beard: though once tall, he now stooped considerably, and supported himself with a staff: his dress was simple and neat, and his whole appearance prepossessing. A sweet serenity was diffused over his countenance; yet there were occasionally a fire, and a contemplative grasp of thought, expressed in his eyes, which sufficiently proved to me that his serenity was not the result of vacancy. All this I discerned by the faint and uncertain light of a small lamp which the warder had brought with him, and placed upon my table. The introduction was performed in silence, and the warder left us alone. The unknown beckoned me to be seated, for the first emotion of surprise at the entrance of a stranger had caused me to start on my feet; and, opening a folding stool he had received from my attendant, he placed himself beside me.

He then addressed me in a low voice, and told me, that the humanity of the fathers of the inquisition had given him permission to visit me, and that, if I would be so obliging, in conformity to the regulations of the prison, as to lower my voice to the standard of his, we were at liberty to confer together. He hoped the conference would be some relief to my solitude, if not lead to my complete liberation. He then unfolded to me his story. He told me that he, like myself, had been committed to the prisons of the inquisition upon an accusation of sorcery. Having advanced thus far, he stopped. He talked miscellaneously and digressively of wizards and their familiars, of possessions and demons, of charms, spells, talismans and incantations, even of the elixir vitæ and the philosopher's stone. Sometimes in the progress of this discourse I could perceive him observing me with the utmost narrowness, as if he would dive into my soul; and again, particularly when he caught a glance of suspicion in my eye, with infinite address changing his attitude and tone, and assuming a surprising air of ingenuousness and gaiety. In a word he was a consummate actor. It was evident, whether his designs were hostile or friendly, that his purpose was to make himself master of my secret. I asked him whether the accusation of sorcery which had been preferred against him, were well founded or a calumny. He evaded that question, and was only influenced by it to talk more copiously and fluently on other topics, with the apparent design of making me forget the enquiry I had made. He avoided anticipation, lest he should miscalculate and take wrong ground in my affair; and, though superficially he seemed communicative, I found that he scarcely told me respecting himself any one thing definite and clear. He celebrated the clemency of the fathers of the inquisition. He said, they seemed to regard themselves as the adoptive parents of those they held in their custody, and were anxious solely for the restoration of souls. In their exterior they were austere, and had unfortunately contracted a forbidding manner; but he had soon found, upon a closer inspection of their character, that the only way to deal successfully with them was to repose in them a perfect confidence. This panegyric was not resorted to till he had exhausted the various topics by which he had hoped himself to extort my secret from me. I asked him, whether the effect of his reposing confidence had been an abjuration of sorcery, and reconciliation to the church? But this question experienced the fate of every other that I addressed to him. He only told me generally, that he had every reason to be satisfied with, and to speak well of, the treatment he had experienced in the house of the inquisition. He possessed, or rather, as I believed, affected, a character of thoughtless garrulity and loquacity, well adapted to cover the strange deviations and abrupt transitions that marked his discourse. It was certainly singularly contrasted with that close and penetrating air which from time to time I remarked in him.

The reader may deem it surprising and unaccountable; but certain it is I took uncommon delight in this man's company. I pressed him earnestly to repeat his visits, and would scarcely suffer him to depart, till he had promised to come to me again the next day or the day after. Yet I looked on him as my mortal enemy, and had no doubt that he was one of the infamous wretches, employed by the policy of the inquisition, and well known beneath those hated roofs by the appellation of moscas. Various reasons may be assigned for my conduct in this particular. Let it first be remembered that I was alone, and for months had not heard the sound of my own voice. No incident marked my days; no object arrested my attention. A dull, heavy, pestilential, soul-depressing monotony formed the history of my life. If in this situation I had been visited by a mouse or a rat, I should indefatigably have sought to get within reach of it, I should have put it to my bosom, and have felt with exultation the beat of an animal pulse, the warmth of animal life pressing responsively on my heart. With what eager appetite I should have mixed in scenes of calamity and cruelty, intolerable to any other eye, glad for myself that even upon such terms I could escape the frostbound winter of the soul! How I should have rejoiced, like king Richard of England, to see four grim and death-dealing assassins enter my cell, like him to struggle and wrestle and contend with my murderers, though, as in his case, wounds and a fatal end should be the result! Thus feeling then, it is little wonderful that I should have hailed with pleasure the visit of the mosca.

But this was not all. While I conferred with, or rather listened to my visitor, that pride and self complacency, which I suspect to be the main, or at least the indispensable, ingredient of all our pleasures, revived in my heart. I believed that he was set upon me by these insatiable bloodsuckers of the inquisition, that he might ensnare me with his questions, and treacherously inveigle me to the faggot and the stake. I felt a last, lambent intimation of pride within me, when my heart whispered me, "This man shall not attain his ends." I secretly defied his arts, and amused myself with baffling his most cunning devices. I had now some one with whom to measure myself. The comparison, I own, for a descendant of the counts of St. Leon, was a humble one; but it is not permitted a prisoner in the jails of the inquisition to be fastidious in his pleasures. This man I played with at my ease, and laughed at his stratagems. I therefore felt that I was his superior, and, which was a sensation I had not lately been accustomed to, that I was somebody. These feelings recommended to me his visits.

But what was much more material, I looked further, and proposed an ultimate end to this occurrence. Let it be recollected what was my unhappiness, when I found myself, if I may be allowed the expression, suddenly deprived of speech, and then it will easily be understood how sincerely I rejoiced to have this faculty restored to me. Speech, as I have already said, I had regarded as the only and assured means of my deliverance from this scene of horrors. I therefore doubted not that from this miserable tool of my oppressors I would obtain my enlargement. I stood firmly on my guard. I permitted him to run out the whole length of his own project without interruption. By this delay I should better understand his character, and finally seize it with a more decisive grasp. Thus purposing, I allowed three or four visits to pass before I opened to the mosca my own proposal. I designed unexpectedly to turn the tables upon him, to surprise and finish with him at once. I knew not that all this precaution was necessary, but I played for too deep a stake, not to be anxious to omit nothing, which hereafter in retrospect I might reproach myself that I had omitted.

The time was at length come, at which I judged it convenient to execute what I had planned in my mind. I began with an attempt to mortify and humble my guest in his own eyes, that he might lose the pride to make the smallest resistance to my proposal.

"Do you think, my good sir," cried I, "that I have not perfectly understood your intentions all this while? You have pretended to be my friend, and to come to me for my good. I know that every secret I reposed in your fidelity, every word that I might unguardedly have dropped, every look and gesture that could have been interpreted to my disadvantage, would have been instantly reported to the fathers of the inquisition. Why, what a poor and miserable fool must you have imagined me to be! How came you into my cell? Had you a secret key by which you found your way hither unknown? Could you ever have come into my apartment, if you had not been employed? You fawn upon me, and are the tame and passive agent of my merciless destroyers! Shame on such base and perfidious proceedings! Is this religion, that you should flatter and cajole and lie to a man, purely that you may have the gratification at last of burning him alive? If you or your masters can make out any thing to my disadvantage, let them make it out in the way of fair and open trial, by the production of direct evidence, and calling on me for my defence. They style themselves the champions of Christendom and ornaments of our holy faith; they pretend to an extraordinary degree of sanctity, and would have all men bow down in mute reverence and astonishment at their godliness; and yet they have recourse to means so base, that the most profligate and abandoned tyrant upon record would have disdained to employ them. But, base as are the judges and assessors of the court in whose prison I stand, even they scorn the meanness of the perfidious task in which you have engaged."

The vehemence I put into the suppressed and under-tone with which I delivered these reproaches, seemed to produce no emotion in my guest. He dropped his staff upon his shoulder; he meekly folded his arms upon his bosom, and answered, that he had long since learned to bear every contumely for the cause of God and the Redeemer: they were heaven-directed chastisements, which his manifold sins and iniquities had amply deserved.

"Hypocrite!" replied I, "would you make me believe that a conscientious motive can prompt such conduct as yours, can mould your features into a treacherous expression of kindness, and fill your mouth with lies and deceptions innumerable?"

"No proceedings," rejoined he, with an unaltered air, "are base, that God and his church prescribe. I take up the cross with cheerfulness, and glory in my shame. The more ignominious in the eyes of an unregenerate world is my conduct, the more entire and implicit does it prove my obedience to be."

My heart swelled within me as he talked. I could lend no attention to such despicable cant, and was ashamed to see the most profligate conduct assuming to itself the pretensions to an extraordinary degree of sanctity and disinterestedness.

"Come, come," said I, "dissembler; I know that nothing could buy a man to so loathsome an office but money. You are some galley-slave, some wretch, who by your complicated crimes have forfeited your life to the community, and are now permitted to earn a miserable existence by lying in wait for the unfortunate, and engaging in arts at which humanity shudders. I take you upon your own terms; you are the man I want. Assist me to escape; go with me to some safer and less cruel country; I will reward you to the extent of your wishes. Give me your hand; an estate of six thousand pistoles per annum, without further condition, waits your acceptance. I invoke all the powers, sacred to truth and punishers of deceit, to witness, that I have ability to make good the whole of what I promise."

While I spoke, I could perceive an extraordinary revolution taking place in my guest. The meekness and tranquillity of his countenance subsided; his eye became animated and alive. I hailed the auspicious omen; I urged my proposal with all the impetuosity I could exert and all the arguments I could devise. At length I paused. I looked again at the countenance of the mosca; I was less pleased than before. The expression did not seem to be that of assent and congratulation; it was rather of horror and alarm.

"St. Jago, and all the saints and angels of heaven, protect me!" exclaimed he. "What do I hear? A full confession of guilt! And art thou then the confederate of the prince of the powers of darkness? If we were not here, in the holy house of inquisition, I should die at this moment with fear that the roof would fall and crush us together. I should expect hell to swallow me alive, for being found in thy unhallowed society." He trembled with every expression of the sincerest terror and aversion.

"'Thy money perish with thee,' thou second Elymas, like him 'full of all subtlety and mischief, child of the devil, enemy of all righteousness!' Blasted be thy offers! Have I for this devoted myself to the service of God, assiduously sought out the basest and vilest offices of that service, and loaded myself with ignominy here, that I might obtain a crown of glory hereafter? and am I now to be assaulted with the worst of Satan's temptations? Even so, Lord, if such be thy will! Oh, poor, miserable, deluded victim of the arch-deceiver of mankind, what has the devil done for thee? He has persuaded thee that thou art rich; and thou wantest every joy and every necessary of life. He has promised to be thy friend; and he brings thee to the faggot and flames in this world, as an earnest of thy eternal damnation hereafter."

My visitor had no sooner thus poured out the tumult and agitation of his soul, than he left me abruptly, and I saw him no more.

Such was the event of my attempt to bribe the officers of the inquisition. In my first experiment I could not even obtain a hearing; in what followed, my proposals were rejected with all the transports of religious abhorrence. What I offered indeed, however dazzling in the statement, had not in fact the nature of a temptation. He to whom I addressed it gave no credit to my assertions; he thought that I was the mere drivelling dupe of him he called the arch-deceiver of mankind, or that my money, when possessed, would soon change its figure, and from seeming pieces of solid coin be converted into pieces of horn or of shells. Even if he had not apprehended such a metamorphosis, he would yet have regarded every doubloon he received as the price of his continual adversity here, and damnation hereafter. I gained nothing favourable for my situation by the trial I had made, but I added a new chapter to my knowledge of human nature. I found, that to be a knave, it was not necessary to be an infidel: I corrected the too hasty conclusion which I had adopted with the rest of my contemporaries, that he whose conduct was infamous, must inevitably be destitute of religious impressions and belief; and I became satisfied that a man, while he practised every vice that can disgrace human nature, might imagine he was doing God service.

Enough of the interior of the prison of the inquisition. I remained a tenant of this wretched mansion twelve years. Though the wretch who had been placed upon me as a spy, was, from my proposal to him, satisfied of my guilt, his superiors were not so. They found nothing in what he reported definitive as to the nature of my unlawful practices, and they could extort from me no further confession. They therefore adhered to their favourite maxim, to avoid the precipitate mistakes of other tribunals, and to allow their prisoner full time to develop his guilt, or, as they pretended, to establish his innocence. Perhaps too the temper of the prince who now filled the Spanish throne, contributed to my safety. They could not content themselves with a less punishment for so obstinate and incorrigible a heretic, than that of the flames; but, during the reign of the emperor Charles, this species of punishment for heresy was rarely inflicted, and only one or two contumacious, at intervals, were delivered over to the executioner at a time. The institution whose victim I had become, looked for a richer and more abundant harvest from the well-known piety and zeal of his successor.

I pass over the rest of the years of my tedious imprisonment They had in them a sad and death-like uniformity. What surprising or agreeable adventures can be expected from a man closed up within the four walls of a dungeon? Yet it is not altogether the uniformity of this period that determines me not to dwell upon and expand it. Twelve years cannot pass in the life of man without many memorable incidents and occurrences. He that should be buried alive in the deepest cavern of the earth, if he were not an idiot, or incapable of the task of narration, and could subsist twelve years in that situation, could tell of things that occurred to him, that might fill the busy man of the world with thoughts and speculation almost to bursting. I might unfold the secrets of my prison-house, but that I will not. I refuse the consequences of that story both to my readers and myself. I have no inclination to drive the most delicate or susceptible of my readers mad with horrors. I could convince such, if such there are, who suppose my faculties were altogether benumbed or dead, that it was not so. I did indeed pass days, perhaps weeks, in a condition of that sort. But at other times my mind was roused, and became busy, restless, impatient, and inventive. There was no mode of escape that I did not ruminate upon or attempt; not to mention that, though my body was restrained, my mind occasionally soared to the furthest regions of the empyrean, or plunged into the deepest of the recesses in which nature conceals her operations. All systems of philosophising became familiar to me. I revolved every different fable that has been constructed respecting the invisible powers that superintend the events of the boundless universe; and I fearlessly traced out and developed the boldest conjectures and assertions of demonism or atheism. As the humour of the moment led me, I derived misery or consolation from each of these systems in their turn.—But memory, bitter memory, unperceived by its lord, is seizing my pen, and running away with my narrative. Enough, enough of the interior of the prison of the inquisition!

CHAPTER XXXII.

Philip the Second, king of Spain, succeeded to the throne of that monarchy about the close of the year 1555; but his affairs in England and the Netherlands long withheld him from visiting his beloved country, and he did not reach its shores, after a seven years' absence, till the twenty-ninth of August, 1559. It may be thought that a public event of this sort could be little interesting to me, a forgotten prisoner, immured in the dungeons of the inquisition. The fact was otherwise. The king was desirous of distinguishing his arrival on his native soil by some splendid exhibition or memorable event, that should at once express his piety to God, and conduce to the felicity of his people: and he could think of nothing that so signally united these characters as an Auto de Fé. The Lutheran heresy, which in the course of forty years had spread its poison so widely in the different countries of Europe, had not failed to scatter a few of its noxious seeds even in this, the purest and most Catholic of all its divisions. But Philip had early proclaimed his hostility against this innovation; and, prostrating himself before the image of his Saviour, had earnestly besought the divine majesty, "that he might never suffer himself to be, or to be called, the lord of those in any corner of the globe, who should deny Him the Lord." Previously to his arrival in Spain, directions had been given, and arrangements made, respecting the pious and solemn exhibition he demanded. Formerly those who by the fathers of the inquisition had been delivered over to the secular arm, had been executed in the different places where their crimes had been committed, or their trials been held: but now it was proposed that all those throughout the kingdom, who were found properly qualified to satisfy by their deaths the sublime taste of the royal saint, should be divided into two troops, and sent, the one to Seville, long the capital of an illustrious monarchy, and the other to Valladolid, which had the honour to be the birthplace of the present sovereign. The troop destined to feed the flames at Seville was composed of fifty persons, many of them distinguished for their rank, their talents, or their virtues. The troop to be escorted to Valladolid, of which I was a member, amounted only to thirty: but to compensate this deficiency, Philip himself had signified his gracious intention to be present, together with the heir apparent and his whole court, at that exhibition. The Spanish nation, rejoicing in the approach of a monarch who was born among them, whose manners and temper happily accorded with theirs, and whom they believed about to fix his perpetual residence in their land, expected him with all the longings of the most ardent attachment. We, the unhappy victims of pious and inquisitorial tyranny, also expected him. Our hearts did not pant with a less beating quickness; though our anxiety arose from emotions of a different nature.

Valladolid is distant from the metropolis eighty-four miles. We had already been some weeks prepared for this journey, and piously directed to hold ourselves in readiness to take our part in the solemn national sacrifice. We waited however to receive a previous notice of the day on which the monarch would enter the place of his birth, since so great was his royal zeal for the cause of religion and civil society, that he would not consent to be absent from any part of the spectacle; and accordingly it was not allowed us to enter the scene of our final destination, till the king of Spain and the Indies should be already on the spot, and prepared to receive us. The auto da fé performed at Seville had the precedence of ours: it took place on the twenty-fourth of September; and we were indulged with an accurate account of it, and were present at a public reading of the record of the act, in the chapel of our prison, previously to our removal from the metropolis.

I will not enter into a minute detail of the scene of this reading, though the recollection will never be effaced from my memory. Of the persons present who were destined to suffer capital punishment, eight were women. Four of them were taken from a single family, being a grandmother, a mother, and two daughters of the noble house of Alcala. They had all been beautiful of person, and of a graceful figure; the youngest of the daughters was in the nineteenth year of her age. Their crime, together with that of the majority of their fellow-sufferers, was obstinate and impenitent Lutheranism. The seats of the women were separated from the rest, and fronted with a close lattice. The men were twenty-two in number, and their appearance was truly impressive. Their persons were neglected, and their figures emaciated; their eyes were sunk and ghastly, and their complexions of a sallow and death-like white. Most of them were crippled by their long confinement and the severities they had endured, and were supported to their seats, upon an elevated scaffolding with benches raised one above another, by two apparators, one on each side of the condemned heretic. God of mercy and benevolence! is it possible that this scene should be regarded as thy triumph, and the execution destined to follow, as a sacrifice acceptable in thy sight? If these papers of mine are ever produced to light, may it not happen that they shall first be read by a distant posterity, who will refuse to believe that their fathers were ever mad enough to subject each other to so horrible a treatment, merely because they were unable to adopt each other's opinions? Oh, no! human affairs, like the waves of the ocean, are merely in a state of ebb and flow: "there is nothing new under the sun:" two centuries perhaps after Philip the Second shall be gathered to his ancestors he died in 159, men shall learn over again to persecute each other for conscience sake; other anabaptists or levellers shall furnish pretexts for new persecutions; other inquisitors shall arise in the most enlightened tracts of Europe; and professors from their chair, sheltering their intolerance under the great names of Aristotle and Cicero, shall instruct their scholars, that a heterodox doctrine is the worst of crimes, and that the philanthropy and purity of heart in which it is maintained, only render its defenders the more worthy to be extirpated.

What were the ideas and reflections of my fellows, seated on the benches above, below, and on either side of me, I am unable to affirm; my own could not fail to be pungent and distressing. I understood continually more and more of the mysterious and unuttered history, of the stranger who died in the summer-house of the lake of Constance: I found that I was only acting over again what he had experienced before me. His legacies had served to involve me in the bitterest and most unheard of miseries, but were wholly destitute of ability to rescue from the evils themselves created. Unbounded wealth I found to have no power to bribe the dastard slaves of religious bigotry; and the elixir of immortality, though it could cure disease, and put to flight the approaches of age, was impotent to repel the fervour of devouring flames. I might have been happy——I was happy when the stranger found me. I might have lived to a virtuous and venerable old age, and have died in the arms of my posterity. The stranger had given me wealth, and I was now poorer than the peasant who wanders amidst polar snows. The stranger had given me immortality, and in a few days I was to expire in excruciating tortures. He found me tranquil, contented, in the midst of simple, yet inestimable pleasures; he breathed into me the restless sentiment of ambition; and it was that sentiment which at length had placed me on high in the chapel of the prison of the Catholic Inquisition.

Our progress to Valladolid was slow and solemn, and occupied a space of no less than four days. On the evening of the fourth day we approached that city. The king and his court came out to meet us. He saluted the inquisitor general with all the demonstrations of the deepest submission and humility; and then, having yielded him the place of honour, turned round his horse, and accompanied us to Valladolid. The cavalcade that attended the king broke into two files, and received us in the midst of them. The whole city seemed to empty itself on this memorable occasion; and the multitudes that crowded along the road, and were scattered in the neighbouring fields, were innumerable. The day was now closed; and the procession went forward amidst the light of a thousand torches. We, the condemned of the inquisition, had been conducted from the metropolis upon tumbrils; but, as we arrived at the gates of Valladolid, we were commanded, for the greater humiliation, to alight and proceed on foot to the place of our confinement, as many as could not walk without assistance being supported by the attendants. We were neither chained nor bound; the practice of the inquisition being to deliver the condemned upon such occasions into the hands of two sureties each, who placed their charge in the middle between them; and men of the most respectable characters were accustomed from religious motives to sue for this melancholy office.

Dejected and despairing I entered the streets of the city, no object present to the eyes of my mind but that of my approaching execution. The crowd was vast; the confusion inexpressible. As we passed by the end of a narrow lane, the horse of one of the guards who rode exactly in a line with me, plunged and reared in a violent manner, and at length threw his rider upon the pavement. Others of the horse-guards attempted to catch the bridle of the enraged animal. They rushed against each other. Several of the crowd were thrown down, and trampled under the horses' feet. The shrieks of these, and the loud cries and exclamations of the bystanders, mingled in confused and discordant chorus. No sound, no object could be distinguished. From the excess of the tumult a sudden thought darted into my mind, where all, an instant before, had been relaxation and despair. Two or three of the horses pushed forward in a particular direction. A moment after they resiled with equal violence, and left a wide, but transitory gap. My project was no sooner conceived than executed. Weak as I had just now felt myself, a supernatural tide of strength seemed to come over me. I sprung away with all imaginable impetuosity, and rushed down the lane I have just mentioned. Every one amidst the confusion was attentive to his personal safety, and several minutes elapsed before I was missed.

CHAPTER XXXIII.

In the lane every thing was silent, and the darkness was extreme. Man, woman, and child were gone out to view the procession. For some time I could scarcely distinguish a single object; the doors and windows were all closed. I now chanced to come to an open door; within I saw no one but an old man, who was busy over some metallic work at a chafing-dish of fire. I had no room for choice; I expected every moment to hear the myrmidons of the inquisition at my heels. I rushed in; I impetuously closed the door, and bolted it; I then seized the old man by the collar of his shirt with a determined grasp, and swore vehemently that I would annihilate him that instant, if he did not consent to afford me assistance. Though for some time I had perhaps been feebler than he, the terror that now drove me on, rendered me comparatively a giant. He intreated me to permit him to breathe, and promised to do whatever I should desire. I looked round the apartment, and saw a rapier hanging against the wall, of which I instantly proceeded to make myself master. While I was doing this, my involuntary host, who was extremely terrified at my procedure, nimbly attempted to slip by me and rush into the street. With difficulty I caught hold of his arm, and, pulling him back, put the point of my rapier to his breast, solemnly assuring him that no consideration on earth should save him from my fury, if he attempted to escape a second time. He immediately dropped on his knees, and with the most piteous accents intreated me to spare his life. I told him that I was no robber, that I did not intend him the slightest harm, and that, if he would implicitly yield to my direction, he might assure himself he never should have reason to repent his compliance. By this declaration the terrors of the old man were somewhat appeased. I took the opportunity of this calm to go to the street door, which I instantly locked, and put the key in my bosom.

Nothing but the most fortunate concurrence of circumstances could have thus forwarded my escape. The rearing of the horse of the life-guardsman was purely accidental. The concourse and press of the crowd from all sides could alone have rendered this circumstance of any magnitude. The gap which was made by the pushing forwards and resiling of the horses continued barely long enough for me to spring through, and closed again in an instant. It is astonishing that the thought of escape should have thus suddenly darted into my mind, which, but a moment before, was in a state of dejection, equally incompatible with activity and with hope. That in the lane down which I rushed I should have met no human creature, and that the first open door I saw should lead to the residence of a decrepid old man, who appeared to be its single inhabitant, were occurrences equally extraordinary, yet seem to have been both indispensable to my safety.

One point more concurred with this fortunate train, and assisted to still the palpitations of my beating heart: I perceived, by certain indications in the countenance of my host, that he was by parentage a Jew. I presently concluded, that he was what in Spain they denominate a new christian; for that otherwise he would not have been allowed to reside at large in a Spanish city. But, upon that supposition, I did not believe that christianity was very deeply mingled up in him with the vital principle: the converts of the inquisition are not conspicuous for their sincerity. Now, then, for the first time I thought, in the course of twelve years, I had opportunity to communicate with a man, whose soul was not enslaved to the blood-thirsty superstition of this devoted country. All I had seen during the period of my confinement were hyenas, tigers, and crocodiles—they were not men.

I had no sooner soothed my host into a temper to listen to my story, than I told him with all imaginable frankness whence I came, and to what I had been destined. The mention of sorcery however, and preternatural practices, I suppressed; for I suspected that persons of all religions entertained an equal horror against these. I suffered him to imagine that the allegation against me had been the crime of heresy: all sects of the christian superstition might be supposed equally obnoxious or acceptable to a Jew. I emphatically appealed to the persecutions which had been so long directed against the religion of his ancestors, and observed how disgraceful it would be in him to assist the operation of a principle, the effects of which his fathers had so deeply deplored, and so perfectly abhorred. I assured him that I would bring him into no danger, and that all I asked was the protection of a few hours: I would leave him in the course of the following day, and he should hear of me no more. I reminded him, that the danger he had to fear was in betraying, not in protecting me. The inquisition looked upon every new christian with an eye of the severest jealousy; and the mere fact, if known, that I had taken refuge in his house, would infallibly subject him to the purgation of a temporary imprisonment in their dungeons. It would be in vain for him to affirm that he had no choice in what had occurred; he was without a witness to confirm his relation, and the assertions of a man born of Jewish parents never obtained credit in the court of the inquisition. I added, with solemn asseverations, that the moment I set foot beyond the territory of Spain, I would remit to him the sum of six hundred pistoles as an acknowledgment for his kindness.

During the whole of my discourse, I watched his countenance with the utmost minuteness. It gradually relaxed from the terror which had at first appeared in it, to expressions of compassion and complacence. I saw nothing that ought to alarm me. When it was his turn to speak, he earnestly assured me that he took a warm interest in my story, and would cheerfully perform every thing I required. He was happy that my favourable stars had led me to his habitation, and would rejoice, to the latest hour of his existence, if they rendered him instrumental in preserving the life of a human being from so deplorable a catastrophe. While I talked to him, I easily perceived that the arguments I used, which produced the most sensible effect upon his features, were those of the dangers arising to him from betraying me, and the reward of six hundred pistoles which I promised him in the event of my success. His motives however were blended together in his mind; and he had no sooner formed a determination, grounded perhaps upon the meanest considerations, than he became eloquent in a panegyric of his own benevolence, by which he was not, I believe, more anxious to impose upon me, than to put the change upon himself. I considered all that he said, his gestures, and the very tones of his voice, with eager anxiety; the terror of the inquisition penetrated to the marrow in my bones; and the fate awarded against me by that court became inexpressibly more horrible to my thoughts, now that I saw the probability of escaping it. Every thing that I observed in the Jew was apparently fair, plausible, and encouraging; but nothing had power to quell the agitations of my apprehensive soul.

We were still engaged in discussing the topics I have mentioned, when I was suddenly alarmed by the noise of some one stirring in the inner apartment. I had looked into this room, and had perceived nothing but the bed upon which the old man nightly reposed himself. I sprung up however at the sound, and, perceiving that the door had a bolt on the outside, I eagerly fastened it. I then turned to Mordecai, such previously to his conversion had been the name of my host: "Wretch," said I, "did not you assure me that there was no one but yourself in the house?" "Oh," cried Mordecai, "it is my child! it is my child! she went into the inner apartment, and has fallen asleep on the bed." "Beware!" I answered; "the slightest falsehood more shall instantly be expiated in your blood." "I call Abraham to witness," rejoined the once more terrified Jew, "it is my child! only my child!" "Tell me," cried I, with severity of accent, "how old is this child?" "Only five years," said Mordecai: "my dear Leah died when her babe was no more than a year old; and, though we had several children, this single one has survived her." "Speak to your child; let me hear her voice!" He spoke to her, and she answered, "Father, I want to come out." I was satisfied it was the voice of a little girl. I turned to the Jew: "Take care," said I, "how you deceive me now; is there no other person in that room?" He imprecated a curse on himself if there were: I opened the door with caution, and the little girl came forward. As soon as I saw her, I seized her with a rapid motion, and retired back to a chair. "Man," said I, "you have trifled with me too rashly; you have not considered what I am escaped from, and what I have to fear; from this moment this child shall be the pledge of my safety; I will not part with her an instant as long as I remain in your house; and with this rapier in my hand I will pierce her to the heart, the moment I am led to imagine that I am no longer in safety." The Jew trembled at my resolution; the emotions of a father worked in his features, and glistened in his eye. "At least let me kiss her!" said he. "Be it so!" replied I: "one embrace, and then, till the dawn of the coming day, she remains with me." I released my hold; the child rushed to her father, and he caught her in his arms. "My dear Leah," cried Mordecai, "now a sainted spirit in the bosom of our father Abraham! I call God to witness between us, that, if all my caution and vigilance can prevent it, not a hair of this child shall be injured! Stranger, you little know by how strong a motive you have now engaged me to your cause. We poor Jews, hunted on the face of the earth, the abhorrence and execration of mankind, have nothing but family affections to support us under our multiplied disgraces; and family affections are entwined with our existence, the fondest and best-loved part of ourselves. The God of Abraham bless you, my child! Now, sir, speak! what is it you require of me?"

I told the Jew that I must have a suit of clothes conformable to the appearance of a Spanish cavalier, and certain medical ingredients that I named to him, together with his chafing-dish of coals to prepare them; and, that done, I would then impose on him no further trouble. Having received his instructions, he immediately set out to procure what I demanded. He took with him the key of the house; and, as soon as he was gone, I retired with the child into the inner apartment, and fastened the door. At first I applied myself to tranquillise the child, who had been somewhat alarmed at what she had heard and seen: this was no very difficult task. She presently left me, to amuse herself with some playthings that lay scattered in a corner of the apartment. My heart was now comparatively at ease; I saw the powerful hold I had on the fidelity of the Jew, and firmly persuaded myself that I had no treachery to fear on his part. Thus circumstanced, the exertion and activity with which I had lately been imbued left me; and I insensibly sunk into a sort of slumber.

The night was now far advanced, and I was still reclined insensible upon Mordecai's bed, when suddenly a jargon of various sounds seemed from all sides to assail me. My mind was confused; I heard something, but seemed wholly unconscious what I was, and where. I wanted to escape from the disturbance; but it continued, and even increased. At length I was forced to command my attention; and the first thing I perceived was a beating at the door of the chamber. The little girl was come to the bedside, and endeavouring to shake me. "Sir, sir," she cried in an eager accent, "my father wants to come in, and I cannot slip the bolt of the door." By slow degrees I began to comprehend my situation, and to recollect what had happened immediately before. I felt greatly alarmed; I feared by the disturbance that Mordecai had not returned alone. I essayed to speak; my organs refused their office. I endeavoured to move; my limbs felt palsied, and absolutely lifeless. I experienced a sinking and sickness of heart that seemed to be the immediate precursor of death. By listening occasionally to the discourse which the father and the daughter began to hold with each other, I became satisfied that Mordecai was without a companion. I endeavoured to make the little girl understand that I was incapable of rising from the bed; and, having at length succeeded, she communicated the information to her father. With considerable trouble he loosened the door at its hinges, and entered the room. I found myself in the extremest degree feeble and languid; the Jew however assiduously administered to me of cordials he had in his possession, and by degrees I felt myself considerably restored.

Now, for the first time, I was at leisure to attend to the state of my strength and my health. My confinement in the inquisition, and the treatment I had experienced, had before rendered me feeble, and almost helpless; but these appeared to be circumstances scarcely worthy of attention, in the situation in which I was then placed. The impulse I felt, in the midst of the confusion in the grand street of Valladolid, produced in me an energy and power of exertion which nothing but the actual experience of the fact could have persuaded me was possible. This energy, once begun, appeared to have the faculty of prolonging itself; and I did not relapse into imbecility, till the occasion seemed to be exhausted which called for my exertion. I examined myself by a mirror with which Mordecai furnished me: I found my hair as white as snow, and my face ploughed with a thousand furrows. I was now fifty-four, an age which, with moderate exercise and a vigorous constitution, often appears like the prime of human existence; but whoever had looked upon me in my present condition, would not have hesitated to affirm that I had reached the eightieth year of my age. I examined with dispassionate remark the state of my intellect: I was persuaded that it had subsided into childishness. My mind had been as much cribbed and immured as my body. I was the mere shadow of a man, of no more power and worth than that which a magic lantern produces upon a wall. These are thy works, Superstition!—this the genuine and proper operation of what is called Christianity! Let the reader judge of what I had passed through and known within those cursed walls by the effects; I have already refused, I continue to refuse, to tell what I suffered, and how those effects were produced. Enough of compassion, enough of complaint: I will confine myself, as far as I am able, to simple history.

Being recovered, as far as the cordials and attention of Mordecai were capable of recovering me, I desired for the remainder of the night to be alone, except that I was still resolved to retain the little Jewess as the pledge of my safety. I was greatly obliged to my host for the punctuality he had already displayed: he had found considerable difficulty in procuring the articles of which I stood in need, owing partly to the lateness of the hour, and partly to the presence of the king, and the general hurry and confusion which had been produced by the solemn entry of the inquisition. His efforts too to recover me from the languor and lethargy into which I had sunk, had a character of generosity; and perhaps I ought now to have trusted him without a hostage. But my heart was too earnestly bent upon accomplishing its present object, to afford harbour to the punctilios of delicacy. The same earnestness caused me to insist upon Mordecai's repairing the injury which the hinges of the door had sustained; and I was careful to satisfy myself that every thing was restored to a state of perfect security.

I was now once again alone. The little girl, who had been unusually disturbed, and roused at an unseasonable hour, sunk into a profound sleep. I heard the noise which Mordecai made in undressing himself, and composing his limbs upon a mattrass, which he had dragged for the present occasion into the front room, and spread before the hearth. I soon found by the hardness of his breathing that he also was asleep. I unfolded the papers he had brought me; they consisted of various medical ingredients I had directed him to procure; there were also two or three vials, containing syrups and essences. I had near me a pair of scales with which to weigh my ingredients; a vessel of water; the chafing-dish of my host, in which the fire was nearly extinguished; and a small taper, with some charcoal to relight the fire, in case of necessity. While I was occupied in surveying these articles and arranging my materials, a sort of torpor came suddenly over me, so as to allow me no time for resistance. I sunk upon the bed. I remained thus for about half an hour, seemingly without the power of collecting my thoughts. At length I started, felt alarmed, and applied my utmost force of mind to rouse my exertions. While I drove, or attempted to drive, my animal spirits from limb to limb, and from part to part, as if to enquire into the general condition of my frame, I became convinced that I was dying. Let not the reader be surprised at this: twelve years' imprisonment, in a narrow and unwholesome cell, may well account for so sudden a catastrophe. Strange and paradoxical as it may seem, I believe it will be found in the experiment that the calm and security which succeed to great internal injuries are more dangerous than the pangs and hardships that went before. I was now thoroughly alarmed: I applied myself, with all vigilance and expedition to the compounding my materials. The fire was gone out; the taper was glimmering in the socket: to swallow the julep when I had prepared it, seemed to be the last effort of which my organs and muscles were capable. It was the elixir of immortality, exactly made up according to the prescription of the stranger.

Whether from the potency of the medicine, or the effect of imagination, I felt revived the moment I had swallowed it. I placed myself deliberately in Mordecai's bed, and drew over me the bed-clothes. I fell asleep almost instantly. I believe my first sleep was perfectly sound and insensible; but in no long time I was visited with the pleasantest dreams imaginable. Nothing was distinct; nothing was attended with the consciousness of my former identity; but every thing was gay, cheerful, invigorating, and delicious. I wandered amidst verdant lawns, and flower-enamelled gardens. I was saluted with the singing of a thousand birds, and the murmuring of a thousand fountains. Kids, fawns, and lambs frisked and gamboled before me. At a distance, through an opening in the trees, I discerned nymphs and their swains dancing a variety of antic measures. I advanced towards them; they approached towards me. Fifes, oboes, recorders, and instruments of a hundred names, commenced a cheerful and melodious concert. Myself and the dancers now were met; they placed me in the midst of them. They began a choral song; the motion of their limbs conformed to their numbers. I was the theme of the general chaunt; they ascribed to me the beauty of Apollo, the strength of Hercules, the invention of Mercury, and the youth of Bacchus.

My sleep was not long; in a few hours I awakened. With difficulty I recognised the objects about me, and recollected where I had been. It seemed to me that my heart had never beat so vigorously, nor my spirits flowed so gay. I was all elasticity and life; I could scarcely hold myself quiet; I felt impelled to bound and leap like a kid upon the mountains. I perceived that my little Jewess was still asleep; she had been unusually fatigued the night before. I know not whether Mordecai's hour of rising were come; if it were, he was careful not to disturb his guest. I put on the garments he had prepared; I gazed upon the mirror he had left in my apartment. I can recollect no sensation in the course of my life, so unexpected and surprising as what I felt at that moment. The evening before, I had seen my hair white, and my face ploughed with furrows; I looked fourscore. What I beheld now was totally different, yet altogether familiar; it was myself, myself as I had appeared on the day of my marriage with Marguerite de Damville; the eyes, the mouth, the hair, the complexion, every circumstance, point by point, the same. I leaped a gulf of thirty-two years. I waked from a dream, troublesome and distressful beyond all description; but it vanished, like the shades of night upon the burst of a glorious morning in July, and left not a trace behind. I knew not how to take away my eyes from the mirror before me.

I soon began to consider that, if it were astonishing to me that, through all the regions of my countenance, I could discover no trace of what I had been the night before, it would be still more astonishing to my host. This sort of sensation I had not the smallest ambition to produce: one of the advantages of the metamorphosis I had sustained, consisted in its tendency, in the eyes of all that saw me, to cut off every species of connection between my present and my former self. It fortunately happened that the room in which I slept, being constructed upon the model of many others in Spain, had a stair at the further end, with a trap-door in the ceiling, for the purpose of enabling the inhabitant to ascend on the roof in the cool of the day. The roofs were flat, and so constructed, that there was little difficulty in passing along them from house to house, from one end of the street to the other. I availed myself of the opportunity, and took leave of the residence of my land host in a way perfectly unceremonious, determined however speedily to transmit to him the reward I had promised. It may easily be believed that Mordecai was not less rejoiced at the absence of a guest whom the vigilance of the inquisition rendered an uncommonly dangerous one, than I was to quit his habitation. I closed the trap after me, and clambered from roof to roof to a considerable distance. At length I encountered the occasion of an open window, and fortunately descended, unseen by any human being, into the street. Having with difficulty succeeded, on this occasion of public solemnity, in engaging an apartment in one of the hotels of Valladolid, I sent into it, as soon as I was able, a chest, containing every necessary of apparel, and particularly a suit of clothes. I then changed my dress, and threw the clothes which Mordecai had provided into the chest I had purchased. As long as they continued safely locked up, and the key in my possession, no faculty possessed by any human creature could detect my identity, and expose me afresh to my former jailors. The only peril under which I had before laboured, was from Mordecai, who, if he had seen me in the garments he had procured, might have recognised them; and, though a peril from this source came barely within the limits of possibility, it was easily avoided, and I therefore chose to avoid it.

I passed the whole of this day in a species of enjoyment, which, as it has no parallel in the ordinary transactions of mankind, so are there no terms in the received languages of the world that are adequate to the description of it. It has often been a subject of melancholy and complaint among mortals, that, while the whole vegetable system contains in it a principle of perpetual renewal, man alone,—the ornament and lord of the universe, man,—knows no return to youth. When the sun declines in the west, the flowers droop, and fold up their frail and delicate leaves; but soon the eyelids of the morn are again opened, and again they rejoice in his invigorating beams. Upon the approach of winter, the beech, the ash, and the monarch-oak, scatter their withered foliage over the plains; but spring reappears, and nakedness is no longer their reproach, and they clothe themselves anew in their leafy honours. With what a melancholy sensation does the old man survey his decaying limbs! To me, he cries, there is no second morning, and no returning spring. My head, pressed down with years, shall never again erect itself in conscious manhood. These hoary locks shall no more be adorned with the auburn of glossy youth. My weather-beaten trunk shall at no time clothe itself with a smoother rind. A recruited marrow shall never fill these bones, nor a more vigorous sap circulate through my unstrung limbs. I recollect what I was in the prime of manhood, with vain regrets; the memory answers no other end than to torment and upbraid me.

The useless wish of the old man, the object of his hopeless sigh, was mine. Common and every-day blessings have little value in the eye of their possessor. The young man squanders the endowments of youth, and knows not to prize them. If the young man had once been old, if the old man could again be young, then, and then only, they would justly estimate their wealth. The springy limb, the bounding frame, the vigour that sets fatigue at defiance, and revels in pleasures unexhausted, would then by the near and conscious comparison, of feebleness and lassitude, the drooping limb, the aching head, and the frame decayed in all its senses, be well understood. Such was my situation. Yesterday I was fourscore; to-day I was twenty. Yesterday I was a prisoner, crippled in every articulation; to-day I was a citizen of the world, capable of all its delights. To-morrow I was destined to have been dragged to the stake with ignominy, and to suffer intolerable anguish amidst the shouts and huzzas of an unfeeling populace; to-morrow I was at liberty to employ as I pleased, to choose the theatre upon which it should be spent, and the gratifications that should be crowded into it. What was most material, my mind was grown young with my body. Weary of eternal struggle, I had lately resigned the contest, and sunk under the ill-fortune that relentlessly pursued me. Now I felt within me a superfluity of vigour; I panted for something to contend with, and something to conquer. My senses unfolded themselves to all the curiosity of remark; my thoughts seemed capable of industry unwearied, and investigation the most constant and invincible. Ambition revived in my bosom; I longed for new engagements and new relations; I desired to perform something, that I might myself regard with complacence, and that I might see the world start at and applaud.

I determined, for reasons that I shall presently have occasion to unfold, that my first visit should be to my daughters at my paternal estate of St. Leon. I proposed to spend two or three days in preparations for this journey. By mere accident, by a most censurable heedlessness, I became in some degree a spectator of the auto da fé in which I was destined to have been a victim. Unawares I had become entangled in the crowd, and could with difficulty escape, or even prevent my being carried nearer the centre of the scene. I saw the galleries and accommodations that had been erected for the spectators: I saw the windows and roofs of the houses crowded with beholders. The shrieks of the sufferers I could not hear; they were drowned in the infernal exultations of the multitude. But what was worst of all, I discerned some of the condemned, fixed as they were upon small boards, near the top of stakes about four yards high, and therefore greatly above the heads of the assembly, while the flames, abundantly fed with faggots and dry fuel, climbed aloft, and seemed eager to embrace their victims. As I have already said, there were thirty of these death-devoted frames; and, if my eye did not count them all, my fancy well supplied what sense was unable to discover. The impression I felt at that moment was horrible beyond all conception. I exerted my new-found strength, and pushed out of the press with irresistible vigour. If at that instant I could have felt exultation, even in the consciousness of my own safety, I should regard myself as the most execrable of monsters.

CHAPTER XXXIV.

The first employment in which I purposed to engage my new-found liberty and youth, was a visit to my daughters. I now carried a disguise perpetually about with me, that would render my journey incapable of proving injurious to them. My daughters were all that remained, if indeed they still remained, of my once idolised family. For twelve years I had continued totally ignorant of their fortune, and even of their existence. Part of the plan I had adopted for their advantage necessarily precluded me from all correspondence or communication with them or any one near them, that might satisfy and tranquillise the anxieties of a father. If it had been otherwise, deprived, as I had been, of the common benefits of light and air, and cast out from the society of mankind, I could have obtained no intelligence of their welfare. In visiting, I determined not to make myself known to them; yet, notwithstanding the greatness of this disadvantage, I felt that one of the most exquisite gratifications the earth could afford me was to behold my children. What a multitude of adventures and incidents might they not have encountered in the space of twelve years! Imagination and affection dwell impatiently on the interval; nor can any thing quiet the conjectures of him that loves, short of the most complete information. What a difference must twelve years have produced in the very persons and figures of creatures so young? With what mingled and exquisite emotions does the father contemplate his daughter, whom he left a child, grown up into a woman? He sees her with astonishment and rapture, displaying maturer beauties, discovering in her countenance new traces of knowledge and sentiment, and in her gesture and manners a character finished, matronly, and sedate. The very circumstance that I should visit them unknown, and converse intimately with them without being discovered, while it cut me off from many pure and ingenuous pleasures, added in some respects a new relish to the indulgence; for it gave it a character, singular, and perhaps unprecedented, in the history of mankind. I anticipated with eager transport the hour at which I should revisit the place of my birth, wander amidst the shades where my careless infancy had strayed, recognise objects made sacred to my heart by associations with my venerable mother and my adorable wife, now illumined with the presence of my children, and steal a joy, unsuspected and unknown, to which the very secrecy with which it was ravished would give a tenfold gust.

I embraced the nearest route, by Pampeluna and the Pyrenees, to the banks of the Garonne. One particular pleasure that I reaped during this tour, which the climate and scenery might alone have rendered delightful, consisted in the youthful sensation with which every thing I saw was enjoyed. Every one who can call to mind the amusements of his childhood will be conscious that during that period all his senses were in a tone adapted to convey the most exquisite gratification. This is not merely, as is vulgarly supposed, the result of the novelty and freshness with which at that time every thing strikes us. The extremities of the nerves are in a state of the most delicate susceptibility, upon which no touch, however slight and evanescent, is lost, and which makes us, upon every occasion favourable to enjoyment, gasp and tremble with the pleasure we imbibe. We feel it thrilling through every pulse, and communicating its tone to every part. Our attention is engrossed by a single object; or, if we are sensible to accompanying incidents, it spreads over them an animating sunshine, and totally varies their appearance and hue. Age, on the contrary, imperceptibly brings along with it callosity and sluggishness of sensation, our gratifications are coldly relished, and our desires feebly awakened. Such is the difference in our perception, of delicious fruits, of fragrant smells, of smooth and glossy surfaces, of the vividness of colour, and the heavenly sweetness of sound. If this be a just account, I leave the reader to imagine how I enjoyed my tour from Valladolid to the beautiful and romantic retirement of St. Leon.

There was however one sentiment with which I was at this time impressed, that I shall find it difficult to make the reader understand in the extent in which I felt it, and that formed a powerful drawback upon the pleasures I have just described. A short time ago I had been old; now I was young: I had quaffed of the elixir of immortality. The revolution this had produced in my sentiments was not less memorable than that which it had effected in my corporeal lineaments and my mental elasticity. It is so different a thing to conceive a proposition theoretically, and to experience it in practice! The case is parallel to that of the expectation which an ordinary Christian entertains of eternal bliss. It is an article in his creed; he repeats it every night when he lies down, and every morning when he rises. He would be both offended and surprised if you told him he was not persuaded of it; and yet how faint and indistinct a picture it produces in his intellectual retina! The affairs of the world strike him with all the force of vision; to them he cannot make himself a stranger and a pilgrim; he cannot transfer all his affections to the mere creature of his imagination, engendered in solitude, and nurtured by enthusiasm,—heaven. How different must have been the feelings of the celebrated apostle, who had been taken up into the third heaven, and had beheld the new Jerusalem with all its jaspers, its chrysolites, its emeralds, and its sapphires!

My situation was similar to this. I had long known, as far as reflection could assure me of it, that I possessed the elixir of immortality. But never till now had I felt the julep tingling in my veins, and known the effects of it in every joint and articulation of my frame. I before believed, I now felt, that I was immortal. The consequence of this intimate persuasion was not without its portion of melancholy. I still bore the figure and lineaments of a human creature; but I knew that I was not what I seemed. There was a greater distance between me and the best constructed and most consummate of the human species, than there is between him and an ant or a muskito, crushed by the first accidental tread, or consumed by the first spark wafted by the wind. I can no longer cheat my fancy; I know that I am alone. The creature does not exist with whom I have any common language, or any genuine sympathies. Society is a bitter and galling mockery to my heart; it only shows in more glaring colours my desolate condition. The nearer I attempt to draw any of the nominal ties of our nature, the more they start and shrink from my grasp. From this moment I could not shake off the terrible impression of my loneliness; no, not for an hour. Often does this impression induce me to regard my immortality with loathing indescribable; often do I wish to shelter myself from it in the sweet oblivion of the grave. From this hour I had no passions, no interests, no affections; my heart has never expanded with one natural emotion; I have never delivered myself up to the repose of one genuine amusement. If at any time I have had a glimpse of pleasure, it has irritated, only to deceive; it has increased the appetite, while it displayed in stronger colours my impotence to gratify it. What is worse, every added year has still subtracted something from the little poignancy and relish which the bowl of human life continued to retain. I have the power of assuming a youthful and glossy appearance whenever I think proper; but this is only a bitter mockery of the furrows ploughed in my heart. In so much of my adventures as remains for me to describe, I feel that I shall be obliged to employ the established terms of human description. I cannot interrupt the history of my sensations, by a recital of those pangs by which they have been every moment interrupted. The terms I must use may delude the reader into an imagination that I still participate of enjoyment and of hope. Be it so; they may cheat the reader; they cannot cheat myself!

Previously to my arrival in the vicinity of the Garonne, I equipped myself in the habit of an Armenian, and assumed the character of a merchant travelling from country to country for the sale of his commodities.

It was in the close of a wintry day in the bleak and cheerless month of December, that I first viewed from a distance the turrets of St. Leon. I procured myself accommodations for the night in the adjoining village. Being now, after so long an absence, within reach of the residence of these lovely treasures, I sought, without any direct consciousness of the sentiment, to delay our interview. When I entered the little auberge, sheltered under a small plantation of olives, I dreaded to hear the repetition of my family name. I longed most fervently to be informed of the welfare of my daughters, yet I could have died sooner than utter a single question on the subject. I found that that ardent love which had urged me with rapid steps from Valladolid to St. Leon, gradually, as the distance grew little, changed from an impetuous vehemence to hear of, and to see them, to fearful, awe-struck, motionless anxiety. Their light and airy figures, as I last saw them at Montauban in 1547, danced before the eyes of my imagination: what casualties, what calamities might not have overtaken them since! I was afraid almost to breathe, lest I should dissolve the unreal scene that played around me. How did I know that I did not indulge this cheerful imagination for the last time? Again and again in the course of the evening, I felt as if I could have wasted ages in this auberge and the neighbouring fields, still believing that my daughters inhabited yonder towers, still hovering round their fancied residence, but never daring to utter their name, lest it should be found the prelude to some fatal intelligence. How rich and refined a repast in some cases is uncertainty! It had the power to impart to these precious pledges a share of that immortality of which I was the destined monopolist.

Why had I not the courage never to overpass the limit at which I was now arrived, and, wherever I afterwards wandered on the various surface of the globe, still to be able to repeat to myself the complacent whisper, "I have visited my daughters in their separated abode, and my visit was productive of none but agreeable sensations?" My passions were too much afloat to suffer me really to rest in this patient, contemplative gratification. Before the morning's dawn, I walked forth, and turned my eyes towards the castle. I loitered from bank to bank, and from point to point. Daylight slowly broke in upon me, but all was silent and quiet in my paternal château. "The family is not yet stirring," said I to myself. I turned my steps to the spot where the ashes of my mother were mingled with their parent earth. The time that had intervened since her decease, the various fortunes and impressions I had experienced, had somewhat obliterated the vividness of her picture in my memory, and deadened the tremblingness of sensation with which I once thought of her. Yet enough was left, to make it an interesting moment to me, when I kneeled at her tomb. Why, oh why, as it had been with my great forefathers, was it not a moment of exultation to me, when I thus feelingly saluted the shade of a parent! He that exults in such an hour, must feel that he has illustrated his birth, and honoured his progenitors. I had done nothing of this: I was an exile on the face of the earth, had acquired no trophies, and accumulated no fame. I had none to honour, none even to know me; I had no family, I had no friend! These bitter recollections started up in array before me, and cut me to the heart. The spirit of my mother frowned upon her son; and I returned along the path by which I came, disgraced and disconsolate.

"I am now," said I, "in a fit temper to learn intelligence of my daughters: if they have been unhappy, to hear it will not make me more forlorn; if they have been fortunate, that knowledge, and that alone, may revive my courage." I hastened towards the avenue. I looked into the thickets and winding paths, as I passed. They communicated to me mingled pictures of my own boyish days, and of the amusements of the present inhabitants.

I told the nature of my pretended traffic to the servants of the house, and proposed an exhibition of my commodities; I was admitted, as I desired, to the apartment of their mistresses. I saw two young ladies, who appeared to be respectively about twenty-eight and twenty-four years of age, and whom without much difficulty I recognised for my daughters Louisa and Marguerite. Their situation and their ages identified them; and when afterwards I came to peruse their features attentively, I could easily discover traits of the amiable young woman and the playful child they had been when last we parted. I found them employed upon a piece of embroidery; a comely and respectable looking young woman, a servant, was sewing in another part of the room. Every thing about the ladies bespoke the ease of their circumstances, and the propriety of their sentiments. Both had on an elegant morning-habit; both had an air of sedateness and sobriety, that to my apprehension told that they had not lived unchastened by misfortune.

They each slightly looked up, as I was ushered into the apartment; they saluted me with a graceful and condescending bend of the head, such as we are accustomed to use to an inferior whom we are willing to put at his ease. What were my sensations, a father, disguised and unknown, in the presence of his children! I attempted to stand, as is usual for a tradesman, when he waits on his customers at their own house. I attempted to speak. My tongue refused its office; my legs tottered as if sustaining an unusual weight. Louisa observed me, and desired me to be seated. I had no power of choice; I accepted her civility. No sooner was I seated, than in spite of myself a flood of tears gushed from my eyes. She was astonished; she begged to know if I were indisposed; she requested me to make use of every assistance the house could afford. I now found my speech. I apologised for my behaviour; said I had felt suddenly ill, but that the tears I shed would prove the most effectual relief to me. My appearance, it may be proper to mention, was not that of a vulgar pedlar; it was tall, graceful, and ingenuous, with a certain air of refinement and politeness; my Armenian dress, though formed of uncostly materials, was such as to display my person to considerable advantage. Both the young ladies showed themselves interested in the symptoms of my distress. After a few minutes internal struggle, I rose, made an excuse for the abruptness of my departure, and requested permission to repeat my visit in the afternoon, when I should have something not unimportant to communicate to them.

I had seen two of my daughters; I had been satisfied that they still existed; I had witnessed their exterior health and beauty. As I withdrew, I laid my hand upon my heart, and congratulated myself: "Thus far," said I, "it is well!" I felt relieved from part of the weight that lay there. With my right hand I struck upon my forehead: "but, oh, where," cried I, "is my other daughter?" The thought came over me with the force of a demonstration: she is dead! A servant was attending me to the door; I requested to speak to the housekeeper; I was introduced to Mariana Chabot. She was struck with my appearance, as I believe my daughters had been, as if my features were those of some person with whom she was intimately acquainted. She would probably have mistaken me for my own son, but that I looked considerably too young. I intreated her to pardon my curiosity; but, I assured her, I had a particular reason to interest myself in the family of Monsieur St. Leon, and I therefore requested that she would have the goodness to inform me of their affairs, as far as she could with propriety communicate them to a person who was not so happy as to be in the catalogue of their acquaintance. I told her that I had just seen two of her ladies, but that I had understood there had been three, and I particularly desired some information as to the young lady who had not made her appearance in the parlour. My presentiment was true; the impression that smote me when I left the parlour, was her funeral knell; my beloved Julia was dead; she had been dead four years! If it had not been for the agitation of my mind when I visited the tomb of my venerable parent, I should have discovered her monument near that of her grandmother. That would have been too overwhelming a mode of learning the painful intelligence; I was glad at least to have escaped that!

In this and some subsequent conversations I held with this respectable matron, I learned a variety of particulars respecting my daughters. Madame Chabot expressed herself sorry that she had nothing pleasing to communicate. Her young ladies had been pursued by a train of misfortunes, though, heaven knew, they had merited every happiness. A few years after they had been settled at St. Leon, Julia had been addressed by a lover in every sense worthy of her. He was rich, noble, of a gallant spirit, of a cultivated understanding, and a truly kind and affectionate heart. Their attachment had been long and tried; habit and experience of each other's virtues had caused it to take a deep root. The father of the young man had destined him to marry the daughter of a duke and peer of the kingdom; but, finding his affections unalterably fixed, he had at length yielded, and sanctioned their mutual passion with his consent. Every thing was now prepared for the nuptials; a day was fixed, and the appointed time was fast approaching. Just at this juncture, the father changed his mind, and became more obstinate and inexorable than ever. A report had begun to be circulated that monsieur St. Leon, the father of the young ladies, was still alive. Madame Chabot expressed her fear that this report had originated in some indiscretion of Bernardin, who, however, had always proved himself a most zealous and faithful servant, and who had since paid the debt of nature. Be that as it might, the father of the lover of Julia was found no longer accessible to expostulation or entreaty. He was of an avaricious disposition, and he regarded the fortune of the young lady, which would otherwise have been considerable, as entirely alienated and annihilated by this flaw in the title. But what was more material, it by no means accorded with his ideas of nobility and honour, that the father-in-law of his only son should be a fugitive and a wanderer, with whose residence no one was acquainted, and of whom no one could tell whether he were living or dead. The manner in which the ladies had entered into the repossession of their paternal estate, when minutely investigated, was thought to have something in it of an ambiguous and unpleasant nature. It was well known that monsieur St. Leon had left the country in consequence of his having ruined himself by the vice of gaming. "Surely," said some, "it is a little mysterious, how his children came, after an interval of nine years, to be able to repurchase all he ever possessed." In short, the more the old vicomte was reasoned with, the more furious he grew. At length he made use of the power which the government of France vests in the father of a family, and shut up his son in one of the royal prisons. This was a fatal blow both to the chevalier and his mistress. Disappointed in the object of his warmest affections, maltreated and disgraced by the severity of a father, his health sensibly declined. Nothing however could shake the inflexibility of the vicomte; he would release his son upon no other terms than a renunciation of his love, terms which the sense of dignity and honour in the young gentleman, equally with his passion, forbade him to accept. To all representations of the necessity of granting liberty to his son, if he would not make himself answerable for his death, the vicomte sternly replied, "that he preferred his dying to the idea of his connecting himself with a family of dishonour." It was not till a few weeks before he expired, that the father had consented to his release from prison, and had removed him to one of his castles in a remote province. But the malady of the chevalier was found incurable; the vital principles of the system were fatally deranged. The lover died; and the consequences of this unhappy affair had put a premature close to the existence of the unfortunate Julia. Madame Chabot added that, the circumstance of this story having become a subject of public animadversion, it had had a most unfavourable effect on the prospects of the surviving sisters. They bore their situation with dignity; but they could not but feel the unhappy coincidence, which cut them off from the happiest condition of human life, an honourable and well assorted settlement in marriage.

While madame Chabot related to me the tragical history of Julia, I felt convulsed with passion, and more than once burst into an agony of tears. Fatal legacy! atrocious secrets of medicine and chemistry! every day opened to my astonished and terrified sight a wider prospect of their wasteful effects! A common degree of penetration might have shown me, that secrets of this character cut off their possessor from the dearest ties of human existence, and render him a solitary, cold, self-centered individual; his heart no longer able to pour itself into the bosom of a mistress or a friend; his bosom no longer qualified to receive upon equal terms the overflowing of a kindred heart. But no mere exercise of imagination, nothing short of the actual experience through which I had passed, could have adequately represented the mischiefs of a thousand various names, that issued from this Pandora's box, this extract of a universal panacea. I regarded myself as the murderer of these two lovers, than whom I concluded, from my personal observation of the one, and all that I heard of the other, two purer and more affectionate beings, more singularly qualified to form each other's happiness, had never existed. I felt as truly haunted with the ghosts of those I had murdered, as Nero or Caligula might have been; my wife, my son, my faithful negro; and now, in addition to these, the tender Julia and her unalterable admirer. I possessed the gift of immortal life; but I looked on myself as a monster that did not deserve to exist.

It is with difficulty that I shall be able to make the reader understand how much more severe the impression of this last catastrophe was made to me, by the place and time in which I received the intelligence. We are creatures of sensation: our worst calamities derive as much of their pungency from the accessories by which they are accompanied, as they do from their intrinsic evil. If I had heard this story at any other period, I am persuaded its effects would not have been half so painful. The idea of my daughters was faded in my sensorium, and whatever related to them, though really felt, and felt like a father, would have been felt with a less overpowering interest.

But now I had journeyed from Valladolid to the Garonne to behold them; I had surveyed the castle they inhabited; I had viewed the garden which they arranged with their hands; I had entered the parlour which they adorned with their presence. All this controlled the operation of absence and of distance; I felt at this moment as if I had been accustomed to see them every day, and to regard them as inseparable from my existence. I experienced, as it were, the united effect of familiarity and novelty; I felt the melancholy fate of Julia, with all the keenness of an inmate, and all the surprise of a long absent traveller. The very metamorphosis I had undergone gave new poignancy to my distress. Madame Chabot tortured me deliberately and at leisure, without the slightest consciousness of what she was doing; she believed she was pouring a tale of persons unknown into the ears of a native of the other hemisphere, at the moment that she was calling up in arms the strongest and most excruciating feelings of a father for his child. I on the other hand had the most violent struggle with myself, while I endeavoured to suppress the appearances of an emotion, which to the person who witnessed them must have been for ever unaccountable. As it was, and in spite of all my efforts, madame Chabot betrayed no little amazement at the agitation with which I listened to a story, in which, as she apprehended, I could have no personal interest.

What I heard from madame Chabot suggested to me a conduct, which I resolved to adopt under the present circumstances. In my next interview I told Louisa that I would now account to her for emotions which, at the time they occurred, must have appeared somewhat extraordinary. I owned that I had been acquainted with her father; I said that I had first met with him in a journey, in which I was then engaged through the province of Mesopotamia; that I had received from him, though a stranger, a singular obligation; that a sincere friendship between us had been the result of this event; that he died about two years since; that I had attended him in his last moments; that he had charged me with his dying recommendations and requests; and that my present journey into France had principally been instigated by a desire to visit his children. I then delivered into her hands various letters and papers, which I had counterfeited chiefly with the intention of supplying my daughters with legal evidence of the decease of their father.

Louisa listened to what I related with those marks of affection and sorrow, which are inseparable from the habits of a well constituted mind. The emotion she discovered led me farther than I first intended. I was urged by an irresistible impulse to practise, beyond what the occasion demanded, upon the feelings of her virtuous mind. I know not whether this is to be considered as a vain refinement and a criminal curiosity; but—I think—every generous spirit will excuse me, when it is recollected that this covert and imperfect proceeding was all that was left me to soothe the impatient cravings of a father's heart. From time to time I reminded her of particulars that it was scarcely possible any one but her father should know; I conjured up past scenes; I made all the revolutions of her youth pass successively in review before her; I touched all the pulses of her soul. Sometimes she was fixed in mute astonishment at the exactness of my information, and was ready to do me homage as some aerial genius, who condescended to clothe himself in this earthly figure; at other times astonishment was swallowed up in feeling, her soul dissolved in tenderness, and she appeared ready to faint into my arms. It is scarcely possible to depict the pleasurable sensations I drew from these intercourses; I know not whether they were entirely innocent; but this I know, that in me they produced a sentiment of innocence, and a sentiment of paradise. I felt sometimes as if I could have wasted ages in this sort of gratification.

As the executor of their father, my daughters received me with every mark of respect; but, after having already protracted my visit to them for the space of many days, I felt that I should be guilty of something alike hostile to their decorum and reputation, if I did not speedily bring it to a termination. I was a person unknown and almost without a name; nor could it be proper for a young woman to continue to receive the visits of a person of her own age and a different sex, upon the intimate and confidential footing upon which my visits were paid, except in the case of him whom she intends to make her husband. To considerations of this sort I was obliged to sacrifice the gratifications in which I had lately been indulging. My principal concern at St. Leon, from the time in which madame Chabot had communicated to me the real nature of my daughter's situation, was to remove those disadvantages in which my destiny and my errors had involved them: it would therefore have been the extreme of inconsistency in me, while I was healing one mischief, to prepare for them another. It is not indeed probable that I should long have been contented for myself with this anomalous and neutral situation, in which I more resembled a piece of furniture endowed with the faculty of noting the sensations of those around me, than the member of any human society. It was high time, as I thought, even in this point of view, that I should put an end to the inglorious scene, should appear in some real character, and engage in some real undertaking.

Influenced by these considerations, I now quitted the residence of my daughters. I had satisfied the longing curiosity of a father, had seen their situation, had witnessed their beauty, their accomplishments, and their virtues. If I had been afflicted at hearing of the premature fate of my eldest daughter, if I had been agonised by the reflection that I might justly regard myself as her murderer, who was so fitted to suffer this anguish as myself? The outcast of my species, what right had I to expect to be happy in my own person, or prosperous in any of my relations? The guilty cause of all this mischief, it was but suitable that it should be brought home to my own bosom, that it should tear and distract my own brain! Add to this, I was not without a hope that my journey would not be found useless to the survivors. By furnishing to them the proper documents to certify the death of their father, I flattered myself that I had cut them off more effectually than before from all connection with my unpropitious destiny, and had placed them nearly upon a footing with the other noble and unmarried heiresses of their native country. I have nothing further to relate in regard to these two amiable and excellent sisters. From the time that I quitted St. Leon upon this occasion, to the time in which I am now writing, the opportunity of making further enquiries respecting them has not occurred to me. If ever it does occur, I have only this one wish to entertain, which, if granted, will, I am sure, satisfy my fondest hopes,—May I find they have been as happy, as they so well deserve to be!

The parting between me and my daughters was not an unaffecting one. On my part, whose bosom was fraught with a thousand tender feelings, to which I could give no language, and of which those whom they principally concerned had not the slightest suspicion, it could not be unaffecting. Nor did Louisa and her younger sister look with an indifferent eye upon the bearer of the last sentiments of their father, the witness of his death, the executor of his will. There was something in the features of my countenance, a peculiar sort of conformation, a family resemblance to themselves, which it is probable they did not advert to, but which I am persuaded wrought within them to the full extent of the mysterious sympathies of our nature. I pretended to have been the familiar confident of their father; I told them of things at which they started and almost blushed to think that any one beyond the circuit of their dearest relations should have been privy. In the hour of our separation, they shed many tears, and embraced me with a warmth that might have well become sisters to a brother. Yet, shall I confess my weakness, a weakness in which I do not apprehend myself to be singular? It happens to few men to witness the manner in which the story of their own deaths is received. If it did, I believe we all of us have enough of vanity and personal feeling, however sincere a grief might show itself in the demeanour of survivors, to find it falling short of our appetites and demand. This I know, I was myself a party to this unreasonableness. My daughters received the intelligence of my death with a decorum and sensibility, which in the eyes of every impartial spectator would have reflected honour on their characters, a sensibility beyond what could have been imagined in daughters who now had not seen their father for twelve years. Yet it was an unpleasing reflection to me, thus to have occasion to gauge their love, and to say, This is the exact measure of their affection. I remained in this part of the world long enough to see my children consoled, and myself forgotten. Self-importance of man, upon how slight a basis do thy gigantic erections repose!

CHAPTER XXXV.

From St. Leon I proceeded to the kingdom of Hungary. To complete this journey I must pass through near twenty degrees of longitude. But that was a trivial consideration: what I most desired was to gain a new situation, and enter upon an untried scene. I had determined in my next experiment upon the endowments of the stranger, to make no half-formed efforts, and to suffer no mischiefs that drew their source from my own irresolution. I determined, as I have said, to forestall all opposition by my firmness, and to silence all objectors by the display of a more than princely magnificence. I thought it therefore eligible to remove to a scene, where no encounter with any one I had ever known might abash me, and no relation of any adventure I had ever met should follow me. The change of my figure, it is true, would render an encounter of this sort of little moment to my liberty or my reputation; but I was a new man, and I was desirous to engross and to feel the benefits that attend upon novelty.

There was another motive however secretly working at my heart, of a grander and more exalted cast, that made me prefer Hungary to all the countries of the earth. Hungary had been now, for upwards of a century, the great frontier of the Christian world,—the theatre upon which the followers of Mahomet contended against the followers of Jesus for destruction and for empire. My mind had from time to time brooded over this picture in the solitude and forlornness of my dungeon. I ruminated on all the calamities of Hungary, from the battle of Warna in 1444, to the battle of Mohacz in 1526; in both of which this generous nation had unsuccessfully achieved prodigies of valour, and, even by their defeats, had protracted the date of their own independence, and co-operated for the defence of the population and arts of Europe against a barbarous and blood-delighting foe. My thoughts dwelt with rapturous admiration upon the exploits of the heroic Huniades and his greater son. In the course of my many-coloured experience I had seen something of war, and was not totally unacquainted with its never-failing consequences. Meditating as I had done in the dungeons of the inquisition, if ever I recovered my personal liberty and my freedom of action, a journey into Hungary, my imagination had grown familiar with captured towns and smoking villages; with the gallant soldier stretched lifeless on the plain, and the defenceless mother and her offspring brutally insulted and massacred; with fields laid waste, and a people lifting up their hands for bread. Determined as I was to open at once all the stores of my wealth, I thought I could not find a nobler scene for its display. I resolved to pour the entire stream of my riches, like a mighty river, to fertilise these wasted plains, and revive their fainting inhabitants. Thus proceeding, should I not have a right to expect to find myself guarded by the faithful love of a people who would be indebted to my beneficence for every breath they drew? This was the proper scene in which for the possessor of the philosopher's stone to take up his abode. He who could feel his ambition satisfied in a more straitened field would, by so doing, prove himself unworthy of the mighty blessing.

Nothing occurred to me in my journey of importance enough to obtain a place in this history. When I arrived, I found the condition of the inhabitants even more wretched than the lawlessness of my imagination had represented it. In the battle of Mohacz the last of the line of their native sovereigns, together with the flower of his nobility, had fallen a victim to the merciless plague of war. What survived of eminent persons in the state assembled soon after in national diet, and elected, as they had been accustomed to do, one of the most illustrious among themselves to preside over the councils and to conduct the battles of their country. But the princes of the house of Austria, ever on the watch for the aggrandisement of their family, seized the opportunity of their disastrous situation to enslave the Hungarians to their sceptre. Charles the Fifth caused his brother Ferdinand, whose consort was only sister to the deceased monarch, to advance his claim to the vacant throne, and to enter the country with an imperial army. The native and elected sovereign found himself, in the weakened condition of his realm, unable to resist the Austrian arms, and was finally driven to the desperate expedient of calling in the Turk to his assistance. From this time, for now upwards of thirty years, the kingdom had been a prey to two foreign invaders, alternately taking and retaking her most considerable towns, and distributing with the strictest impartiality the miseries of war to her devoted inhabitants. Solyman the Magnificent, the present Ottoman emperor, in no long time threw off the mask; and, like his rival Ferdinand, professed to fight only for the enlargement of his own dominions; while the claims, the liberties, the constitution, and the prosperity of Hungary, were alike trodden under foot in the protracted and sanguinary struggle.

At the period at which I entered this unfortunate realm, the Turk was in possession of Buda, Gran, Temeswar, and many of the most considerable cities; and Ferdinand, who had now succeeded Charles in the imperial dignity, had been obliged to withdraw the seat of the national government from the first of these towns, the ancient metropolis, to the comparatively insignificant city of Presburg. The war between the two parties had more than once been interrupted; not indeed by the more stable accommodations of a treaty of peace, but by a truce variously concluded for the terms of six or of eight years. Short as was the period assigned to the suspension of arms, it was never suffered to reach its natural termination; but, after the interval of one or two summers, hostilities did not fail to break out again, with aggravated symptoms of resentment and animosity. The warfare that was now carried on had more in it of passion than vigour: it was of little moment to the interest of either of the princes under whose banners it was conducted; but it was not on that account the less, but rather the more, vexatious and distressing to the Hungarian people. It obeyed no rule; it operated in every direction; no place, no province, no town,—neither the church nor the palace, neither the cottage nor the castle,—could assure safety to those who sought its protection. A flying party, which was to-day in the west, would almost the next day make its appearance in the eastern extremity of the kingdom. Arts were neglected; civilisation was destroyed; the stern and haughty baron, free from restraint, would sally from his castle, sometimes in pursuit of plunder, sometimes of private resentment and revenge; the starving peasantry gladly enlisted in the band of a ferocious partisan for bread; the gangs of robbers, which the vigilant policy of better times had almost annihilated, rose again in importance, and swelled into regiments; and, while they assumed at pleasure the denomination of adherents to Ferdinand or to Solyman, perpetrated every species of excess with impunity. When a reflecting spectator surveys a country in a condition like this, he is tempted to wonder that the inhabitants still retain the courage to bestow on their fields any sort of cultivation, and that the licensed or the unlicensed robber still finds something over which to extend the fangs of his rapacity.

I had not long passed the gates of Vienna, before I began to observe the symptoms of that, which I had come from the Pyrenees and the Garonne to visit. The farther I advanced, the more melancholy was the scene I beheld. The country in some places entirely deserted; villages laid in ashes; cities reduced to the dimensions and insignificance of villages; fields fertilised or made rank with the manure of human blood; the roads broken up; the erections of human ingenuity almost obliterated; mills thrown down; rivers choked up and rendered stagnant; a few solitary plots of cultivation scattered amidst the mighty waste. The inhabitants I saw, appeared terrified, sickly, dejected, and despairing; there was scarcely one who earlier or later had not lost a father or a brother, whose wife had not been made the victim of brutal lust, or who had not seen his children butchered before his face. Persons of the more opulent classes could not travel the country in safety, without being armed and associated in companies and caravans. I was myself obliged to obtain the protection of parties of soldiers, who from time to time happened to be marching in the route I pursued. The savage neglect into which every thing was declining, produced in repeated instances a contagious air and pestilential diseases; while dearth and famine unrelentingly haunted the steps of those whom the sword and the pestilence had spared. Such is war: such are the evils nations willingly plunge into, or are compelled to endure, to pamper the senseless luxury or pride of a Ferdinand and a Solyman!

I proceeded, as I had originally determined to do, to Buda, the metropolis of the kingdom. It was in the hands of the Turk. It was of little importance to me whether the monarch of the soil were a Mahometan or a Christian; my mind was engrossed by considerations of a very different magnitude. I came to relieve and assist, to the utmost of my power, the inhabitants of the country in the extremity of their distress.

I had not proceeded thus far, without bestowing a certain strictness of reflection on the subject. I easily saw that, if I would confer a substantial benefit on this unfortunate nation, I had scarcely any other means for the purpose, than that of reviving among them a spirit of industry. I was aware that, in the strictness of the term, money was not wealth; that it could be neither eaten nor drunk; that it would not of itself either clothe the naked or shelter the houseless; and that it was unable, but by a circuitous operation, to increase the quantity of provisions or commodities that the country afforded. It was my business therefore not to proceed idly in the distribution of gold, but to meditate seriously my plan of operations.

I fixed myself in a spacious and beautiful mansion in the capital. This in the present distressed and depopulated condition of Hungary, it was not difficult to procure. The house I selected had for centuries been the principal residence of the illustrious family of Ragotski; but the present representative of that family, after having seen his sons, one after another, killed in the battles of his country, and his estates ruined by military depredation, had found himself compelled to fly in his old age, and had taken refuge with a distant branch of the same house in the great duchy of Lithuania. It was not necessary for me to proceed to any great extent in the first instance in the manufacture of my wealth; I had every facility for adding to my store from time to time as circumstances should demand.

I determined to open my operations with the article of building. There was sufficient need of it. One half of the houses, through most of the districts of Lower, or Western Hungary in particular, were ruined and untenantable. I did not begin with erecting palaces; I felt that the first claimants in the present emergency were the peasant and the cultivator. I was more desirous that the rustic than the prince should be well lodged and accommodated, provided with the means of rest after fatigue, and secured against the invasion of ungenial seasons.

My reasons for beginning with building were these:—It was my purpose to stimulate and revive the industry of the nation: I was desirous of doing this with the least practicable violence upon the inclinations and freedom of the inhabitants. Had I required of those to whom I addressed myself, that they should fertilise the earth, the seeds with which it should be impregnated might be wanting: I should have a nice balance to adjust between what was necessary for immediate subsistence, and what might be applied as the basis of future; a point better left to its spontaneous level: I might be impeded and controlled by a thousand circumstances and at every step. But the materials of building are to be found in every country; no seasons can impair, no malignity of man can annihilate them. Wherever there are quarries, there is stone; wherever there is clay, there are the means of manufacturing bricks. I was anxious to leave the rest of the great process of human accommodation to its course. While I employed labourers, and paid them their wages, there would be, in the mildest and most salutary mode, a continual influx of money into the market. The increase of the precious metals would give new alacrity to the operations of traffic; the buyers would come forward with double confidence; the venders would be eager to meet the activity and spirit of the demand. Ardour and hope would revisit the human mind; and the industry I created, and the accommodations of one kind at least to which I gave birth, would inoculate the other departments of the community with a similar industry. I came into Hungary in the spring of 1560; the season was favourable to seeding and cultivation; I seemed to enter on my undertaking with the happiest auspices.

Some time however must necessarily elapse between the period of impregnating the soil, and that of the future harvest. Though I laid it down therefore as a law to myself, to commit the least practicable violence upon the genuine action of human society in pursuit of the means of subsistence, I thought proper in a certain degree to engage in the importation of corn from Poland, Silesia, and other neighbouring countries. This seemed an eligible measure, if it were only that I might show others the way, and excite them by my example. I procured agents; I extended my concerns in various directions over the navigable rivers; I formed magazines. It would have been contrary to the genius of my undertaking, either to make a gratuitous distribution of what I purchased, or to sell it at such low prices as to drive other speculators, whose spirit of enterprise might happily co-operate with mine, out of the market. However indifferent I might feel to the receipt of pecuniary compensation, it was necessary that, in the concerns of barter and trade, I should assume the exterior of a merchant.

Nor did I wholly confine my exertions within the occupations of an architect and a corn-dealer. These, or rather the former of the two, I regarded as my true and genuine province; but I did not so far enslave myself to my own maxims, as to negative in all instances the direct demands of want. I was not anxious to convert a nation or an army of men into my personal adherents and retainers: I was rather desirous to avoid this as a dangerous source of obloquy. I did not therefore always decline, by pretended loans to assist other men to employ labourers as well as myself, to act upon their own designs, and prosecute their own fortune. The cries of the poor man, the widow, and the orphan, were sometimes too importunate, and too well justified by their unquestionable necessities, to allow me to withhold from them my alms. In a few instances I conveyed my supplies anonymously to persons, whose dignity of birth or whose proud independence would have been too grievously wounded if they had known their benefactor. I was cautious and apprehensive as to the direct dispensing of money, but not entirely bent against it; I regarded it as a precarious, but in some cases a necessary interference.

The impulse which, by these various measures, I was fortunate enough to generate, seemed to have the effect, so far at least as the sphere of my activity extended, to revive the almost expiring life of the country. Dejection and hopeless indolence, when I commenced my operations, were written in every face; the miserable inhabitants crawled along the roads or the street, their hands idly relaxed by their side, and their slow and painful steps scarcely supporting their lifeless trunk. When my plan became known, and I had already in a few instances reduced my maxims into practice, it was as if the mellow and spirit-stirring blast of a trumpet had wakened their sleeping souls. Their eyes lightened with intelligence; the tear of anguish was wiped from their faded cheeks; the smile of hope slowly expelled, and faintly succeeded to, the bitter expression of despair. Busy and active thoughts gave new motion to their limbs and quickness to their steps; the labourer was seen hastening from place to place; the sound of the hammer, the saw, and the various tools of the workman, was to be heard from every side.

The conduct I pursued necessarily fixed upon me a considerable portion of public attention. I was a foreigner, destitute of connections, and having no previous acquaintance with any individual in the country. I was in appearance a mere boy, a young man in all the flower and bloom of adolescence, and who must be supposed to have just entered into possession of his patrimony. These things tended to increase the public wonder, and to render the mystery of my proceedings more perplexing and obscure. In the age of genial warmth and melting softness, I did not appear accessible to those passions which haunt the days, and too often undermine the virtues, of youth. Youth is the season of benevolence; but benevolence is rarely, as seemed to be my case, the only fruit that youth is found to produce. There was a maturity and a justness of adaptation in my plans, not less foreign from what those who surrounded me would have expected me to display. The apparent disinterestedness and modesty of my proceedings were not lost upon the spectators. The consequence of all this was, that the sieur de Chatillon, such was the name I at this time assumed, was regarded as a phenomenon which could not be too much admired, or too loudly extolled. Wherever I appeared, the people followed me with their gratitude and blessings; ballads were written in my praise; the very children were taught with their infant tongues to lisp the virtues of the saviour of Hungary. My doors were besieged; my steps were watched; I could move no where without public observation. I was importuned with petitions without end; yet, if any petitioner showed himself presumptuous and intrusive, the whole multitude of bystanders was ready to repress his indiscretion, and teach him the respect that was due to their generous benefactor, who never refused any thing, but what it would be improper and injurious to grant.

Such was the treatment I experienced in Buda and the neighbouring districts. Whether I looked within or without, I was equally presented with incitements to self-approbation. I sent forth labour, accompanied with her best and loveliest companions, plenty and health, congratulation and contentment, to scatter blessings through the land. I felt that I was prompted to this conduct by none of the motives of vulgar ambition. I desired neither lordships nor estates, neither elevation of rank, nor extension of prerogative. Sufficient to myself, if I effected the happiness of the people, and they confessed me their benefactor, my every passion would then be gratified. The utmost boundary of my personal wishes proceeded no farther than this, that I might be honoured and loved. What I desired, I obtained; the youth I had procured to myself through the medium of the opus magnum, was like what we are told of the youth of Job:—"When I went out through the gate of the city, the young men saw me and hid themselves, and the aged arose and stood up; the nobles refrained from talking, and the princes laid their hands upon their mouths. When the ear heard me, then it blessed me; and when the eye saw me, it gave witness to my actions."

Here it may be thought I had ascended to that sphere which it was fit the possessor of the philosopher's stone should fill, and reaped the rewards to which a man thus endowed ought to be forward to entitle himself. Nor will I affirm that I was insensible to the gratifications of my present situation. Though I sought to escape from the applause that pursued me, yet there is something in the nature of the human mind, that makes it impossible for us to hear it without complacence. It was not however a boisterous and obtrusive acclamation that satisfied me. A certain inwrought modesty of nature made me listen to noisy commendations with a sentiment of shame. They seemed to be more than any thing I had done could deserve; or they seemed to be in a tone from which the delicacy of a virtuous mind shrinks back displeased. They were so obstreperous, as to take from me the power of hearing the sweeter verdict of my own conscience. No; it was the unbidden tear that glistened in the eye of my beneficiaries; the tongue that faltered beneath the essays of gratitude; the overwhelmed heart that had no power to express itself; the hand of the parent that was stretched out to his children, and dumbly said, These, these shall thank you!—it was these things, that I felt within as the balsam of my life, and the ambrosia of heaven.

CHAPTER XXXVI.

Yet, thus surrounded, and regaled with this animated praise, I was not content; I wanted a friend. I was alone amidst the innumerable multitudes of those I had blessed. I knew no cordiality; I could repose no confidence; I could find no equal. I was like a God, who dispenses his bounties profusely through twenty climates, but who at the same time sits, separate, elevated, and alone, in the highest heaven. The reader may, if he pleases, despise me for the confession; but I felt that I was not formed for the happiness of a God.

I was not however long sufficiently at leisure, thus to refine upon the deficiencies of my situation. I had engaged in a task of extreme delicacy, in which the smallest failure would draw along with it the most serious consequences. Mine was not an undertaking that had for its object, to supply those around me with luxuries, or to augment the stock of their cheerful relaxations and amusements; the very existence of my beneficiaries depended on its success. I had put myself in a considerable degree, with whatever diffidence and caution, in the room of the course of nature, and had taken the administration of the common benefits of human society into my hands. The populace are ever ready to construe this delegation in the strictest sense: unqualified to trace the wheels and combinations of the great machine, if prosperity is their lot, they willingly ascribe it to their protectors and governors; and if they are unfortunate, it is against them that the storm of their resentment is directed. The moment they are thus irritated, their impatience is too great to admit of correctives and remedies; in the fury of their disappointment, they disturb every thing, and render that irreparable and fatal, which was at first only doubtful and unpromising.

My proceedings, as I have already said, bore in the commencement the most benignant face, and seemed a revival of this despairing and unfortunate nation little less than miraculous. The regular labours in which the inhabitants became engaged, restored a healthful tone to their minds; the payments they duly received seemed to discharge them from all anxious solicitude; and, as by my own efforts and the enterprises of others, the market was supplied with provisions, they had no difficulty in exchanging these payments for the necessaries of life. The supply of the market at first was easy; the universal dejection that preceded, though it had not prevented all exertions for that purpose, had rendered those exertions too feeble for extensive success. The strenuous efforts that were now made were productive of a copious supply; but they rendered each importation more difficult than the importation before. The demand continued the same; the relief was every day more diminutive and precarious. The harvest was however advancing with the happiest auspices: and, though some time must yet be consumed in expectation, it was probable frugality and fortitude might enable the inhabitants to hold out till the season of plenty should arrive.

But fortitude is not the virtue of a populace. The higher had been their hopes, and the more unexpected their deliverance, with so much the more blank and melancholy a countenance they beheld this unexpected delay and retrogression. Not understanding the powers by which I acted, they blindly ascribed to me the faculty of doing whatever I pleased. As long as every thing went on prosperously, they were grateful; the moment a reverse occurred, they were inclined to murmur. They made no allowance for the limited capacities of a human creature: they imputed whatever was unpleasing to indifference or ill will. The price of commodities, after having for a while become moderate, now rapidly rose again: this was partly the consequence of the increased quantity of the precious metals, by means of which any assignable sum bore a less proportion to the provisions of the market than it had done before. Bread was at a very high price; and it occasionally happened to buyers who did not come early enough, that there was no bread to be purchased. The doors of the houses where it was sold, were besieged; the industrious poor appeared before them with the first faint dawn of the morning's light. Here they consumed hours of painful expectation, in grievous addition to the hours of their customary fatigue. The whole was a scene of anguish and calamity; the passions of those who composed it, mingled with the distress, and rendered it too heavy to be borne. Anticipating famine, they felt the mischiefs of it before it arrived. Never was the demand so urgent; it seemed as if the capacity of men's appetites was enlarged, and the cravings of hunger became more insatiable, in proportion to the smallness of the supply. To people thus circumstanced, it would have been vain to recommend frugality and moderation. They devoured the food with their eyes, while it was yet beyond the reach of their hands; and the lesson you read them, would have sounded in their ears as if you had bid them die to-day, to escape the danger of dying to-morrow.

The crowds which the necessity of purchasing bread brought together at certain hours, when assembled, naturally entered into the discussion of their present discontents. They were not satisfied with the discourse and jostling of the morning; the habits produced by these noisy assemblies had a secret charm with them, and drew them together at seasons of less urgent demand. They patroled the streets: they were loud in the expressions of their dissatisfaction. With the inconsequence incident to the lower orders of mankind, they threatened to destroy the mills, the markets, the places of sale, the means and materials by which their wants were to be supplied.

In the midst of these scenes of tumult and confusion, it is not to be imagined that I escaped uncensured. Far otherwise: in proportion to the gratitude and adoration with which they had lately regarded me, were their detestation and abhorrence now. My interference was spoken of with contempt and execration. For what purpose had I, a foreigner, come into their country, and intruded myself into their affairs? Why had I impiously taken them out of the hands of their heavenly Father, whose care was so constant, and whose relief so certain? It was on my part a despicable vanity and presumption, which the justice of Providence could not fail to avenge; and they must now suffer the punishment of my blasphemy. But they did not stop here. There was no horrible calumny which they did not invent, or give credit to, against me. They imputed to me the basest personal motives for what I had done. Under the hypocritical pretence, they cried, of being their benefactor and saviour, I was using them only for my private ends. I had become a purchaser and vender of corn, for the single purpose of increasing my fortune. The present scarcity, they were well assured, was artificial, and of my own contriving. I had magazines in different stations on the borders, which, when the price was risen to the standard of my avarice, and when half the people had fallen victims to my inhumanity, I purposed to dispose of to an immense profit.

Such were the aspersions to which my character became generally exposed. By the populace, who now experienced the unsatisfied cravings of hunger, and in whom my proceedings had excited hope, only to be followed by a more cruel disappointment, they were greedily credited. Many who knew their falsehood, were yet zealous to propagate them. Short as had been my residence in Hungary, I had made many enemies. It is to be feared that no man can be assiduous and indefatigable in the service of others, without incurring that consequence. I employed a great number of workmen; every one whom for whatever reason I refused to employ, every one who, being unqualified for the service I required, looked with an envious eye on the better fortune of his neighbour, was well disposed to be my enemy. Persons of no contemptible account in the community had been excited by expectations of profit to engage in the importation of corn: these persons viewed my efforts in the same department with a suspicious eye, and regarded a man who, however cautious in his proceedings, was not regulated by the same motive, as a most pernicious rival. My sudden elevation and importance in the country were viewed with not more astonishment than aversion by those whose importance I obscured. They could not hear with patience of an upstart, a boy, a stranger, one universally unknown, elbowing out the influence of all that was most illustrious and venerable in the community, and robbing them daily of their adherents and retainers. All these persons left no effort untried to defame my character.

The impulse once given, the turbulent disposition of the populace became every day more formidable. It is much easier to disseminate a temper of this sort than to quell it: my opulent foes might take alarm at its excesses, and desire to undo what they had done; but it was beyond their power. Every day I feared lest, from threats and invectives, the populace should proceed to violence: every night I thought I had reason to congratulate myself, that the day had passed without waste and spoil committed by them on the means of their subsistence, or was not marked with the destruction of their champion and benefactor. In some places a sort of petty sedition broke out among the labourers I employed: in the morning they refused to work: why should a man work, they muttered, when after all he may starve with the wages of his labour in his possession? At night they became impatient and furious, and demanded from my superintendents and storehouse-men the food, which in the morning they had refused to earn, and were therefore now unable to purchase. I had already had some experience in the nature of popular tumults; I had now no marchese Filosanto at hand to persuade me of their inefficacy; and, if I had, I should no longer have lent an ear to his serene and unsuspicious generosity. I felt the reality of the danger; I saw the storm as it blackened in my horizon, and was deeply convinced what it would be if it burst upon my head.

It may be imagined with what feelings I viewed my whole design on the point to be subverted, by the unruliness of those for whose benefit it had been planned. It is true I had now no darling relations to be involved in my fate, no incomparable wife, no daughters illustrious in innocence and beauty; yet my feelings were scarcely less pungent than they had been at the period of my catastrophe at Pisa. I had blamed myself in review, that, in my experiments at Constance, at Dresden, at Pisa, and at Madrid, I had not commenced upon a sufficiently ample scale, but had suffered myself to be frustrated by the ingloriousness of my precautions. That had not been my error in the present instance; yet my success now promised to be scarcely more flattering than upon former occasions. I had looked for happiness as the result of the benevolence and philanthropy I was exerting; I found only anxiety and a well grounded fear even for my personal safety. Let no man build on the expected gratitude of those he spends his strength to serve! Let him be beneficent if he will; but let him not depend for his happiness on the conviction of his rectitude and virtue that is to be impressed on the minds of others! There is a principle in the human breast, that easily induces them to regard every thing that can be done for them, as no more than their due, and speedily discharges them from the oppressive consciousness of obligation. There is a levity in the generality of men, that entails on them a continual oblivion of past benefits, and makes one recent disappointment of more importance in their eyes than an eternity of kindnesses and condescension. I shall have other instances of ingratitude to display in what yet remains to be related of my story.

My nights were restless; my thoughts were in arms. What was it that it became me to do in the present emergency? Sometimes, in the bitterness of my heart, hating myself, hating the endowments of the stranger, hating a race of beings who denied all credit to the most unheard-of exertions for their advantage, I determined to withdraw unobserved from my attendants and clients, and bid adieu to Hungary for ever. But whither was I to fly? What was I to do next? What experiment could I make of the purposes to which to apply the philosopher's stone, that I had not already made? These questions, to none of which I could give a satisfactory answer, checked the career of my passion, and gave pause to my thoughts.

Whatever I did, I was determined to do nothing rashly, nor to quit a great experiment without its having been fully tried. It was no light concern, no trivial child's-play, in which I had embarked. I had taken the welfare, perhaps the existence, of a great and heroic nation under my protection. In this glorious vocation it did not become me to be lightly discouraged. What if those I served and saved did not show themselves sufficiently sensible to the exertions I made for them? I ought to purify my bosom, on an occasion like this, from base and ignoble motives, and to deem myself sufficiently recompensed by my conscious virtue. What if the service in which I had engaged now appeared to be a service of hazard and peril? Is there any great undertaking that can be separated from this condition? If hastily, from cowardice, from pique, or from any other motive, I deserted the business on which I had entered, what was to become of my mistaken indeed, but in that case most unfortunate clients? The greater was the crisis to which they were exposed, the more were unremitted vigilance and uncommon powers necessary to guide them amidst its rocks and its quicksands. I saw thousands of men who for several weeks had fed, as it were, from the stores of my bounty. By a propensity inseparable from the human heart, I became attached to the work of my meditations, and the labour of my thoughts. All their fickleness, their injustice, even the atrocious calumnies they admitted and propagated against me, could not wean my attachment from beings, a great portion of whom, but for my interference, would, I believed, long ere this have expired of hunger.

In the peculiar and urgent circumstances in which I found myself, no expedient was so obvious as that of calling in the interference of the government under which I lived. It was necessary that the resources of national subsistence should be defended from the wanton spoil of those who, when they were annihilated, must inevitably perish. It was necessary that the benefactor of Hungary, who, I flattered myself, was still able to watch effectively for her advantage, should be protected from her misguided resentment. The alternative was singularly painful to my feelings. The pride with which my unparalleled endowments inspired me, was deeply wounded, when I was compelled to confess that I was not alone equal to the task I had undertaken, and that I must submit to call in a foreign auxiliary. I augured little favourable from the interference of government, which, if I implored, I could scarcely expect to guide, which was not likely to submit to my principle of rendering its interference the mildest and smallest that the nature of the case would admit; but, puffed up with presumption, and intoxicated with authority, would probably leave no concern of the public welfare uninvaded. Least of all, could I anticipate much of good from a Turkish government. But what could I do? I could discover no other expedient. Influenced by the views I have recited, I had hitherto kept myself as far from the observation of the political directors of the state as I could. But my cautiousness and reserve were now at an end. With my eyes open I exposed myself to all the evils that might attend on my proceeding.

I determined to apply to the bashaw of the province. Previously to my taking this step, I had the precaution to enquire his character. He was the genuine offspring of the Turkish system of government. His name was Muzaffer Bey. He was originally a Circassian slave; then a Janissary; and, rising by insensible gradation, had at length been appointed bashaw of Buda, which, as being the immediate frontier between Austria and the Porte, was at this time the most arduous situation in the gift of the sultan. He was esteemed a good soldier; he had been early distinguished by his dexterity in military exercises; he had since seen much service; and, in every situation in which he was placed, had earned commendation and honour. He was abstemious and hardy; for himself, he neither pampered his appetites nor shrunk from severity; and he had as little indulgence for those under his command as for his own person. Yet he was indebted for his present eminence more to the arts of the courtier, than to his merits in the field. His chief care had ever been to recommend himself to those above him, and to obtain the good will of his equals; for the opinion of his inferiors he gave himself little concern. With considerable ability, he laboured under no check from either principle or ingenuous pride; and therefore was extremely successful in his attacks on the inclination of those he sought. The habits of his mind had modified the lines of his countenance and the tones of his voice. Except to his dependants and the poor he almost always spoke with a smile upon his face, and his enunciation was silver-tongued, oily, copious, and insinuating. If he ever adopted a different manner, the variation was only in the means not the end; and, when he seemed to travel by an opposite road, the goal at which he aimed was the same. He never consulted any oracle but that of his apparent interest; if he had any insolence in his nature, he regarded his slaves and those under his military command as affording a sufficient sphere for its exercise; he had no affections to disturb him from his bent; he had no passions but the self-complacency of superior cunning, and the sordid love of pelf.

This account of the man with whom I had to deal was far from encouraging; but I had no alternative. I sent to signify my desire to confer with him; or, to speak more accurately, to ask, in the Eastern manner when it would be agreeable to him to receive a present of which I requested his acceptance. He appointed the morning of the following day. I prepared a gift, such as might tend to conciliate his favour, without marking in the donor the possession of immoderate wealth. It consisted of silks and muslins, with a small piece of plate of exquisite workmanship. My present was borne by two of my servants. We were ushered to the bashaw in his private apartment; there were two or three persons in attendance upon him. They examined my present together; and, without condescending to express much approbation, I could nevertheless discern that the bashaw was pleased with it. This ceremony concluded; Muzaffer ordered what I had brought to be taken into a different apartment; and, every other person withdrawing, we were left alone.

While the bashaw was examining my gift, I took the opportunity of considering his person. He appeared to be about sixty years of age; his complexion dark and muddy; his features coarse and distorted; his mustachoes remarkably large; his person, though bony and muscular, considerably below the middle size; and his figure ungainly and ungraceful. I felt surprised that such a man should ever have been an excellent soldier, or have risen from a low rank to one of the first situations of the empire. To look at him, he seemed better formed for the vice of a comedy, than the ruler of a nation. He raised his eyes towards me askance, as he sat leaning on his elbow, and said,

"You call yourself—?"

"The sieur de Chatillon."

"And your age—?"

"Is two and twenty."

"I am glad you are come to me. I intended to have sent for you, and you have saved me the trouble."

I made many apologies for my intrusion, but added that I had a petition to prefer, and I hoped he would favour me with a hearing.

"Not at all, not at all; do not call it an intrusion: it is necessary I should be acquainted with you." He proceeded:—

"You have undertaken to confer great benefits on the subjects of the grand signior, my master; to rescue them from famine. Young, rich, a stranger, unknown to my master, unknown to his subjects, I understand that you have spared no labour or expense to bring about their welfare. This is really a very extraordinary case; your merit is unprecedented; I do not feel myself competent to reward it."

I answered that I laid no claim to uncommon merit; that every temper had its particular gratifications; and that I found as real a luxury in the proceedings he had remarked, as other men did in the excesses of the table, or the promiscuous enjoyments of the harem.

"It is out of my power," continued he, "to remunerate you as you deserve; I must send you to Constantinople."

I perceived that this was the first essay of his artifice. I informed him which I have no doubt he knew well enough before, that I had no desire to go to Constantinople. I wished to remain where I was, and to finish what I had begun.

"What, you have not done then?" suddenly and with an abrupt voice exclaimed the bashaw. "By Mahomet, a man of a reasonable appetite in your place might be satisfied. Have not you filled the streets with riots, and the country with rebellion? Do not the populace assemble in crowds, insulting every one they meet, and talking of nothing but fire and devastation, the bowstring and the cimeter? Be so good, my dear sir; as to inform me what further you may have in view?"

"Reverend bashaw," cried I with submission, yet with firmness, "I have none of these things in view. But a moment ago you did justice to my intentions. They are those of beneficence, and beneficence only."

"I know nothing about that. I have nothing to do with honest men's blunders; I look to the effects they produce."

"These effects, most mighty sir, are temporary; they are the clouds that will often obscure for an instant the brightest sunshine. Condescend to lend me your generous assistance, and all will be well."

"Do not tell me of clouds and sunshine. This is, to my thinking, not an April shower, but an earthquake and a hurricane. If we are all to be swallowed up or whirled into the air, it is no consolation to me, that the day after we are gone, every thing shall be as fair and serene as paradise itself."

"Remember, sir, that when I came into Hungary, I found its inhabitants in the most desperate condition, miserable, wasted and starving. Have I not already suspended this evil for months?"

"Yes, I do remember. You are one of those busy-bodies, who never see an evil without imagining they are the persons to correct it, intruding into every thing, and subverting every thing. The superintendence of the public welfare is a mystery to which none are competent, but those whom Mahomet has raised to the situation of statesmen. Your interference is blasphemy against the spirit of our religion, and deserves to be encountered with the most exemplary punishment."

"Good God! then, is it in this country a crime to feed the hungry, to clothe the naked, and shelter the houseless?"

"Sieur de Chatillon," retorted the bashaw, "you appear to be unacquainted with the maxims of Turkish policy, the wisest and most beneficent in the world. If none of the disturbances had happened at which I have so much reason to be alarmed, still, in relieving the people in the manner you have done, you have incurred the guilt of high treason against the sultan. Know, sir, that, through the whole extent of his dominions, there is but one proprietor, and that is our illustrious monarch. You say, that you wish to be the benefactor of his subjects, and the judge of your own proceedings: such sentiments are direct rebellion against the glorious constitution of Ottoman. The sovereign of Constantinople will have no benefactor in the countries he presides over, but himself. Like the invisible ruler of the universe, he acts by second causes; he allows his ministers to be the instruments of his beneficence; but all must be ascribed to him, must flow from his will, and be placed under his control. You, who have formed a plan of public benefit without consulting him, and have presumed, like a luminary of the world, to move in an orbit of your own, have in strictness of construction forfeited your life to his justice; and I consult rather the clemency of his nature than the maxims of his policy, if I suffer you to go from this palace with your head upon your shoulders."

Without permitting myself to be too much moved by the imperious language addressed to me, I complained to the bashaw of the rigorous and arbitrary character of what he stated to be the maxims of the Turkish government. I solemnly protested that I had no private or personal object in view. The effect of my operations would be to give new strength and energy to his master's dominions. By diffusing happiness among his subjects, by reviving industry, and scattering plenty, prosperity, and ease, all disaffection would be rooted out; and the people, who are never minute in scanning the cause of their enjoyments, would bless the sceptre under which they were made to participate such manifold benefits. If the policy of the divan led them in any degree to interfere, they ought rather to crown my measures with their applause, than wantonly to throw obstacles in the way of what I purposed. I asked however no reward, I demanded no favour for myself; all I desired was that the sultan would assist me in securing to his people those benefits, the dissemination of which I had so auspiciously begun.

The bashaw, without taking any direct notice of this expostulation, answered, that I was not aware of the maxims of his government, to which, in consideration of my seeming generosity and rectitude, he was willing to give the mildest interpretation. "It is however," continued he, "to the last degree idle in you to imagine, that you can be permitted to go on unobserved, and that the sultan and his representatives are to take no account of your proceeding. The great instrument for ruling mankind is by their passions and their opinions. The man from whom they believe they have the most to fear and the most to hope, will always be their master. Whatever be your secret or your professed designs, you go on from day to day making yourself partisans, and enlisting the subjects of the sultan among your personal retainers. What security has he for your submission and loyalty? How shall he know that, when you have acquired the advantages of a powerful leader, you will not go over to the enemy, or, in the present distracted condition of the province, even have the audacity to set up for yourself? If therefore, by an unexampled clemency of construction, I decline to reduce you into the passive machine of my master's will, it is at least incumbent on me, that I should take account of your powers, and possess myself of the schedule of your property. By this means only can I watch your progress, and take care that you do not suddenly become too powerful for a subject. Are you prepared to satisfy me on this head?"

On this question I hesitated for a moment; I had not exactly anticipated the enquiry; at length I requested the delay of a few days, and then I promised that all his demands should be satisfied. The bashaw resumed:—

"Sieur de Chatillon, I remark your hesitation, and I draw from it no favourable augury. These indirect and involuntary indications are more worthy of my attention than all the studied and elaborate information you shall think proper to give me. Sir, you are a man of darkness, and every thing that relates to you is enveloped in mystery. You come hither with no apparent motive; you have no connections of blood in Hungary; you have no acquaintance with any eminent person of the Hungarian nation. I have had my spies on you, though I have not hitherto thought proper to summon you to my presence. You have purchased no property in the province; I cannot learn that you have any correspondences or resources from abroad. I have been at the pains to procure an account of your expenditure during the three months you have resided among us; much of that expenditure has been obscure, clandestine, and indirect; but I believe you will find my estimate, which you are at liberty to inspect and remark upon, tolerably correct. Your disbursements for three months, exceed the amount of two years' income of the richest subject that even the credulous monarchs of Christendom suffer within their dominions. What am I to think of this? How can I be sufficiently vigilant respecting a man, whose expenditure is immense, and whose wealth can neither be traced to its source, nor ascertained in its amount?"

I was not slow in conjecturing the result which the bashaw proposed to himself from our present conference. I was confirmed in my conjecture by the circumstance of his choosing that the discussion between us should be apart from all witnesses. He regarded me as a boy, and had therefore practised upon me all those arts which might most effectually excite in me fear and alarm. He found however that, under the external indications of youth and inexperience, I possessed the wariness that added years most powerfully inculcate, and the self-possession of a mind thoroughly awake to its situation and its resources. This must have been to the minister before whom I stood a memorable phenomenon. But curiosity is not a Turkish passion; and the single object of the bashaw in the present instance, was to make the mysteriousness of my circumstances a pretext for extorting money. I submitted with as little seeming reluctance as possible to the necessity of the case; I requested the good offices of Muzaffer to protect my benefactions; and begged permission to make him the compliment of a handsome sum of money, by way of convincing him that I was worthy of his friendship.

This business was easily adjusted between us. I found him perfectly skilled in the duties of a public office, and by no means under the dominion of visionary scruples. He told me he was now convinced that I was a well meaning man, and a good subject; he said, that nothing could tend more effectually to demonstrate my innocence, than my showing that I understood the duties and concerns of a minister of state; and that for his own part he was never so happy, as when he was thus able to reconcile his private interests with the good and faithful service of his master. There was nothing that demanded a more unremitted vigilance, or a more skilful management, than such a situation as his; and it would be most unreasonable, either in the sovereign that appointed him, or the subjects over whom he was placed, to expect him to be indifferent to the emoluments and perquisites of his function. He complimented me warmly upon the disinterestedness and liberality of my exertions. He thought himself particularly fortunate in having so public-spirited an individual within the circuit of his jurisdiction. In fine, he hoped he should be honoured with my personal acquaintance, and assured me that nothing could make him more happy than the frequent repetition of my visits.

We now perfectly understood one another; and it was apparent that I had to do with a man, who, for what he deemed an adequate consideration, would willingly lend me the authority and countenance of his office, and suffer me to guide him in any of the functions I might conceive necessary for the execution of my projects. Guards were agreed to be placed upon the magazines where corn was still contained, and from place to place on the banks of the rivers, where the depredations of a misguided populace were most to be apprehended. Finding the bashaw so perfectly willing to comply with my requisitions, I further obtained from him the direction of several squadrons of cavalry for the protection of the crops, which from the consequences of my interference now began on all sides to variegate the scene. This was a most important service. When the corn was first committed to the earth, it was out of the reach of military devastation. But, as time glided silently on, the case became materially altered; the enemy might from forecast desire to reap the harvest of what he had not sown, or from malice to destroy that without which the Turk would perhaps be unable to retain his newly acquired territory. This had in reality been the principal cause, before my arrival in Hungary, of the very general neglect into which agriculture had fallen. Muzaffer, than whom no person could now be more polite and condescending, allowed me to determine the number and nature of the troops I required; and added that, though he could not openly put them under my direction, the slightest intimation I might think proper to convey to him, should at any time decide their march, and regulate their quarters.

CHAPTER XXXVII.

In my conference with the bashaw I may seem to have secured more than one point of material importance; yet it was difficult for any man to be in a state less consolatory or more full of danger and menace, than I was at this moment. By my vigilance and the power which thus I had acquired, I prevented indeed the inhabitants from wantonly destroying the means of their own subsistence; but, the more I was their benefactor, the more I appeared to become odious to their thoughts. My negotiation with the bashaw, whatever other benefit might accrue from it, did not tend to increase the resources of the country; I was obliged to witness many scenes of wretchedness. He that would assist mankind in their adversity, must harden his heart to be the spectator of the distress that he can, and that he cannot, relieve. But whatever I beheld of this sort, the majority of the bystanders obstinately persisted to ascribe to my deliberate malignity. The military aid I found myself necessitated to introduce by no means tended to disarm the prejudices of my clients. In one or two instances, but no more, slight tumults arose, and a few of the rioters fell a prey to their own wickedness and folly. These misfortunes were cast as reproach upon me; and I was pursued with clamours and curses. I found it requisite to obtain a guard for my person. I was abhorred by those for whom all my vigilance was exerted, and insulted by the mouths that I supplied with the necessaries of existence.

Nor was this my only source of alarm and uneasiness in my present situation. I was by no means a dupe to the ostentatious civility of the bashaw. I perfectly understood his insinuation when he invited the frequent repetition of my visits. I knew that, however dearly I purchased his friendship and patronage, I should still have to purchase them again and again. His extortions upon me admitted of no limits, except from his own modesty, or the estimate he might form of my invisible resources. Bribery itself afforded me no complete security; and, now that I had become an object of curiosity and remark, he had sufficiently shown me I was at the mercy of his caprice, or that of his master, for my liberty, and even for my life.

Yet, could I have resolved to quit Hungary, and seek the protection of some more regular government, what benefit should I derive from a removal? Mystery was the great and unconquerable bane of my situation, and from the poisonous influence of mystery, the most regular system of government was not competent to protect me. It would be idle to imagine that, in any country on earth, a stranger would be permitted to launch into such expenses as those in which I was engaged, without becoming an object of suspicion, and being made liable to continual interruption in his measures. Yet, unless allowed to use the resources I possessed, of what advantage was it to be the depository of wealth without a bound? Was it to be wished for a man under my circumstances, to have a family, or to be without a family? When I had one, I found the legacy of the stranger robbing me of every comfort of that sort, with the most calamitous aggravations. When I was stripped of wife and children, though no man could prize those benefits more dearly than I prized them, I took to myself the consolation, that at least now I should risk no one's happiness but my own; and that, for a person exercising my endowments, it was perhaps requisite to be free from every shackle and incumbrance. I found however the topic from which I had consoled myself, in reality the source of a new misfortune. I had the wealth of a nobleman; but I was deprived of his adventitious attributes. I had no illustrious ancestry to boast; I had neither lineage nor parent; I had neither wife nor children, in whom mutually to reflect and see reflected the elevatedness and generosity of my station. I had not even the ordinary advantage, which is within the reach of almost every man, of connections and acquaintance, friends handed down to me as a branch of my patrimonial inheritance, friends whose value experience enabled me to ascertain, and friends with whom long habits of familiarity had given birth to reciprocal endearment. The bashaw had imputed to me the design of forming a party. Alas! these, which are the great materials for cementing party attachments, were totally denied me. I had no bonds of alliance but those which money afforded, the coarsest, the meanest, the least flattering, and the most brittle of those ligatures, that afford the semblance of uniting man with man.

CHAPTER XXXVIII.

Aware of the difficulties which unavoidably sprung out of the nature of my situation, I resolved immediately to endeavour to supply them to the best of my power. I conceived that there was no consideration so urgent upon me at the present moment, as that I should without loss of time create to myself connections that might balance and keep at bay the sallies of arbitrary rule, and that I should weave with my own hand the cords of friendship.

I had no sooner formed this project, than an individual suggested himself to my reflections, whom I judged to be, by a singular concurrence of circumstances, happily fitted to be the subject of my experiment, and admirably qualified to afford me protection in the most unfavourable events. The name of this man was Bethlem Gabor. He had been some time before brought to me by one of his friends, and he was a man whom for a thousand reasons it was impossible to see and converse with, without receiving the most indelible impression. He was the lineal representative of one of the most illustrious houses in Hungary. His vocation, like that of the majority of the Hungarian nobility, had been arms; but, in the midst of a fraternity all of whom were warlike, he stood conspicuous and alone. His courage, though cool and deliberate, almost mounted to a degree of desperate rashness; and the fertility of his invention, and the variety of his stratagems did not fall short of his courage. The celerity of his measures was equally distinguished; distance was no bar to him; and he had no sooner conceived a project, however arduous, than it was executed. He had formed under his own eye a band of men like himself, impetuous yet deliberate, swift in execution, silent in march, invincible to hardship, contemners of fatigue, of difficulties, of hunger, and of thirst. When introduced to me, he was upwards of fifty years of age. He was more than six feet in stature; and yet he was built as if it had been a colossus, destined to sustain the weight of the starry heavens. His voice was like thunder; and he never uttered a word, but it seemed to shake his manly chest. His head and chin were clothed with a thick and shaggy hair, in colour a dead black. He had suffered considerable mutilation in the services through which he had passed; of one of his hands three fingers were gone; the sight of his right eye was extinguished, and the cheek half shot away, while the same explosion had burned his complexion into a colour that was universally dun or black. His nose was scarred, and his lips were thick and large. Bethlem Gabor, though universally respected for the honour and magnanimity of a soldier, was not less remarkable for habits of reserve and taciturnity. But these habits misfortune had caused to become more deeply ingrafted in his nature. During one of his military excursions, a party of marauders had in his absence surprised his castle, burned it to the ground, and savagely murdered his wife and children, and every living creature within the walls. The same stroke that rendered him childless made him also a beggar. He had been regarded for his proceedings as an adherent to the Turkish standard, but he had always tenaciously maintained the most complete independence. The adversity that had now fallen upon him was too great. He would not become a pensioner of the sultan; despair had taken fast possession of his heart. He disbanded the body of men he had formed, and wandered a solitary outcast upon the face of his country. For some time he seemed to have a savage complacence in conceiving that the evil he had suffered was past all remedy, and in spurning at those palliations and disguises with which vulgar souls are accustomed to assuage their woe. Yet the energy of his nature would not suffer him to rest: he wandered an outcast; but every day engendered some new thought or passion: and it appeared probable that he would not yet quit the stage of existence till he had left behind him the remembrances of a terrible and desolating revenge.

It may seem strange that such a man as I have described should be the individual I selected out of the whole Hungarian nation to make my friend. It may seem that his qualities were better adapted to repel than attract. My choice would not appear strange, if the reader could have conversed with him, as I did. He was hideous to the sight; and he never addressed himself to speak, that I did not feel my very heart shudder within me. Seldom did he allow himself to open his thoughts; but, when he did, great God! what supernatural eloquence seemed to inspire and enshroud him! Not that upon such occasions he was copious and Ciceronian, but that every muscle and every limb seemed to live, and to quiver with the thoughts he expressed. The hearer could not refuse to venerate, as well as fear him. I never pitied him; Bethlem Gabor's was a soul that soared to a sightless distance above the sphere of pity; I can scarcely say I sympathised with him; but, when I listened to his complaints, rather let me say his invectives, I was astonished, overwhelmed, and motionless. The secret of the effects he thus produced, lay in his own way of feeling the incidents he described. Look at him, when he sat alone, wrapped in meditation, you would say, "That is a man of iron; though adversity pour her fiercest darts upon him, he is invulnerable; he is of too colossal a structure to be accessible to human feelings and human affections." Listen to his narrative, or rather to the bursts of passion, which with him supplied the place and performed the functions of narrative, you would soon confess your mistake. While he spoke, he ceased to be a man, and became something more amazing. When he alluded to what he had endured, you did not compassionate him, for you felt that he was a creature of another nature; but you confessed, that never man seemed to have suffered so much, or to savour with such bitterness the cup of woe. He did not love his wife or his children as any other man would do; he probably never dandled or fondled them; his love was speechless; and disdaining the common modes of exhibition, it might sometimes be mistaken for indifference. But it brooded over and clung round his heart; and, when it was disturbed, when the strong ties of domestic charity were by the merciless hand of war snapped asunder, you then saw its voluminous folds spread and convulsed before you, gigantic and immeasurable. He cursed their murderers; he cursed mankind; he rose up in fierce defiance of eternal providence; and your blood curdled within you as he spoke. Such was Bethlem Gabor: I could not help admiring him: his greatness excited my wonder and my reverence; and, while his manners awed and overwhelmed me, I felt an inexplicable attachment to his person still increasing in my bosom.

On his part, my kindness and partiality appeared scarcely less pleasing to Bethlem Gabor, than his character and discourse were fascinating to me. He had found himself without a confidant or a friend. His wife and his children in a certain degree understood him; and, though he had an atmosphere of repulsion beyond which no mortal ever penetrated, they came to the edge of that, and rested there; they trembled involuntarily at his aspect, but at the same time they adored and they loved him. The rest of the world viewed him from a more fearful distance; respected him, but dared not even in fancy be familiar with him. When therefore he lost his family, he lost his all. He roamed the earth in solitude, and all men made room for him as he passed. I was the first who, since the fatal event that had made him childless and a beggar, had courted his society, and invited his communications. I had dared to take the lion by the paw, and seat myself next him in his den. There was a similarity in our fortunes that secretly endeared him to me. We had each by the malice of a hostile destiny, though in a very different manner, been deprived of our families; we were each of us alone. Fated each to be hereafter for ever alone; we blended ourselves the one with the other as perfectly as we could. Often over our gloomy bowl we mingled groans, and sweetened our draught as we drank it with maledictions. In the school of Bethlem Gabor I became acquainted with the delights of melancholy——of a melancholy, not that contracted, but that swelled the soul—of a melancholy that looked down upon the world with indignation, and that relieved its secret load with curses and execrations. We frequently continued whole nights in the participation of these bitter joys; and were surprised, still at our serious board, by the light of the morrow's sun.

I have now, I believe, fully accounted for our intimacy, and displayed the ligatures that secretly bound us to each other. It is scarcely necessary to add, that my understanding confirmed what my heart impelled. Bethlem Gabor appeared to me the fittest man in the world upon whom to fix for my friend. We were qualified mutually to benefit each other. My kindness, my unremitted attentions, the earnestness with which I listened to and soothed his griefs, mitigated their agony. I proposed, when I could once more reconcile and incite him to activity, to repair his castle, and restore his fortune. On the other hand, he was, of all the persons I could have pitched upon, the ablest to protect me. By his birth he ranked among the first men of his country; by his ability, at least as a partisan soldier, a character at that time highly esteemed, he rose above them all.

For some time I regarded Bethlem Gabor as entirely my friend, and I consulted him in every thing, in which, compatibly with the legacy of the stranger of the summer-house, I could consult him. I told him of the suspicions of the bashaw, and the precariousness of my safety. I demanded his advice as to the best method of securing it. Ought I to regard it as a more effectual or as a cheaper expedient, to attempt to purchase the countenance of the sultan, instead of condescending to bribe his minister? Ought I to set up for myself, and by rendering myself the independent prince of one of the Hungarian provinces, defy the Turk, or at least endeavour to negotiate with him from a more respectable and commanding situation? I said more than enough under these heads, as it afterwards appeared, to awaken strange imaginations in a mind of so much penetration as that of Bethlem Gabor. In fine, I demanded of him whether, in case of any great and formidable danger falling on me, he would to the utmost of his power afford me protection? When the question was first started, he swore to me with his customary impressiveness and energy that he would.

While I was thus employed in consulting him, and opening to him as far as was practicable my prospects and fears, I did not less succeed in dissipating or suspending the despair of his melancholy. It was of benefit to him in this respect, that, by opening to him my affairs, I from time to time called off his attention from his personal misfortunes. I proposed to him the rebuilding his castle, and I at length obtained his permission to send off a corps of workmen for that purpose. Beside the castle in which his wife and children had been murdered, and which the marauders had nearly destroyed, he had one considerably stronger, though void of all recommendation from cheerfulness or beauty, in the more northerly part of the kingdom. This we visited together. I restored the condition of his fields; with considerable difficulty I replaced the cattle he had lost, by purchases in Poland; and I revived his dilapidated revenues. At first he felt an invincible repugnance to the receiving any advantage from the bounty of another; but by continual remonstrances I was able to persuade him, that he owed me nothing, and that what I did was no more than was required from me by a regard for my own safety.

If ever on the face of the earth there lived a misanthrope, Bethlem Gabor was the man. Never for a moment did he forget or forgive the sanguinary catastrophe of his family; and for his own misfortunes he seemed to have vowed vengeance against the whole human race. He almost hated the very face of man; and, when expressions of cheerfulness, peace, and contentment discovered themselves in his presence, I could see, by the hideous working of his features, that his spirit experienced intolerable agonies. To him such expressions were tones horribly discordant; all was uproar and havoc within his own bosom, and the gaiety of other men inspired him with sentiments of invincible antipathy. He never saw a festive board without an inclination to overturn it; or a father encircled with a smiling family, without feeling his soul thrill with suggestions of murder. Something, I know not what, withheld his hand: it might be some remaining atom of humanity: it might be—for his whole character was contemplative and close—it might be that he regarded that as a pitiful and impotent revenge, which should cause him the next hour to be locked up as a madman, or put to death as criminal. Horrible as was his personal aspect, and wild and savage as was his mind, yet, as I have already said, I felt myself attached to him. I knew that all the unsocial propensities that animated him, were the offspring of love, were the sentiments of a lioness bereaved of her young; and I found an undescribable and exhaustless pleasure in examining the sublime desolation of a mighty soul.

Bethlem Gabor had at first regarded me with some degree of partiality. Kindness in almost all cases begets kindness; he could not see how much I interested myself about and how much I courted him, without feeling for me a sentiment different from that he confessed for other men. I saw however after some time, with inexpressible grief, that his regard for me, instead of increasing, suffered perceptible diminution. Our propensities were opposed to each other. He rejoiced in disorder and desolation as in his congenial element; my present pursuit was the restoration of public order and prosperity. He repeatedly expostulated with me on this. I had sometimes in our conversations, in the bitterness of my recollections, exclaimed on myself as the most unfortunate and most persecuted of men, though without entering into an explanation of my sufferings. He reminded me of these exclamations. He reproached me as a contemptible and pusillanimous wretch, that I did not, like him, resolve amply and memorably to revenge my own sufferings upon my species at large. In his estimate, the poorest and most servile of all maxims was, that of the author of the christian religion, to repay injury with favour, and curses with benediction.

I perceived with grief that the kindness towards me that had been excited in Bethlem Gabor's mind, rather declined than augmented; but I was very far from being aware of the degree in which, as I afterwards found, this sentiment had relapsed into its opposite. It seems, I inflicted on him a daily torture by my daily efforts for the dissemination of happiness. Of these he had not been at first completely aware. His mind had been too much absorbed in its own feelings to attend very distinctly to any thing I did, unless it were done in his presence. But, in proportion as I soothed his sorrows, and made him my confidant, the film was removed; and all that he saw had the peculiar misfortune to excite at once his contempt and his rage. The finishing stroke that I gave to the animosity which, unknown to me, was now brooding and engendering in his breast, consisted in my bestowing an important benefit upon one, against whom he had entertained a long and eternal feud.

CHAPTER XXXIX.

While Bethlem Gabor became every day more confirmed in his antipathy against me, I reposed in him an unsuspecting confidence—a confidence more extensive than I had, since the singular and fatal acquisition I had made, reposed in any other man. Frequently for a considerable time together he resided under my roof; frequently we went forth together in those excursions which either my projects or his views rendered it necessary for us to make. In his character of a nobleman of great consideration in his native country, he was now rising like a phœnix from its ashes. His castles were repairing; his property was restored; the list of his retainers daily became more numerous; he revived and carefully recruited the martial band, which, in the first exacerbations of his despair, he had dismissed from his service. My purse and all that I had were his; he never made a demand upon me that I did not instantly supply; I reaped a particular pleasure from the largeness and frequency of his requisitions; there was nothing for which I was more anxious, than to bind him to me in indissoluble ties of gratitude and affection.

Little, alas! did I understand the compound of tenderness and ferocity, of decisiveness and inscrutability, with which I was now concerned. My friend, such I esteemed him, had been absent some time; I expected his return to my residence at Buda; and anxious to pay him every mark of attention and respect, I set out to meet him. It was scarcely safe, during the existing hostilities between the Austrians and the Turks, to travel any where without a guard; I had the precaution in the present instance to take with me an attendance of twenty men.

It was after having partaken of a slight and early dinner that I set out on my excursion. The season was remarkably fine, and the air genial and balsamic. I scarcely ever commenced any tour with more agreeable sensations. The harvest was already ripe; and, as I passed along, I saw reapers from time to time entering upon the first essay of their interesting occupation. I felt that I had at length surmounted one of those difficulties, with which I had been so strongly assailed, and to which I had refused to yield. If I were not free from apprehensions from the arbitrary nature of the government under which I lived, I believed however that I had nothing further to dread from the misconstruction and animosity of the nation I preserved. My anxiety as to whether I should be able to substantiate the benefit I had sought to confer, was at an end; and I had little doubt that, with the plenteous crops which were on the point of being gathered, my popularity would return, and the gratitude of my clients become more ardent than ever. It was a delicious enjoyment that I now experienced; the pleasures that the eye unavoidably takes in from the spectacle of a luxuriant autumn, became blended in my mind with the ideas of famine put to flight, my own rectitude vindicated, and the benevolent purposes realised, the prosecution of which had cost me so profound a heartache.

We at length passed the lines of the soldiers planted for the defence of the soil against the depredations of the enemy. I had calculated that I should meet my guest a few leagues from Buda; I was deceived in my estimate. The day however of his arrival was fixed; I could not be mistaken in his route; I resolved not to turn back without meeting him. The road I took led upon the borders of that part of Hungary which owned the Austrian yoke; the shades of night were fast gathering round us, and we heard at a distance the alarm-guns and the drums of the enemy. I was not however a novice in the appearances of a country, the seat of military excursions and war; and, if my mind were not wholly free from perturbation and uncertainty, I at least resolved not to be turned aside from my purpose. We travelled two hours longer; still no notice of the approach of Bethlem Gabor. At length a question was started whether we were still in the right road, and I thought it advisable to hold a sort of council of war to deliberate respecting our further proceedings. Having assembled my attendants for that purpose, I was now first struck with the apprehensions and timidity which they unanimously betrayed. They had been drawn out rather for show, and to keep accidental stragglers in awe, than with the expectation of actual service. I became sensible that nothing was to be hoped from their resistance in the event of an action; and the utmost I could aim at was in the mean time to hold them together by the sentiment of a common danger.

It was resolved to return; I began to be apprehensive that Bethlem Gabor had been prevented by some unexpected occurrence from observing his appointment. Scarcely had we faced about, before we heard a body of cavalry approaching us. I called to my party to halt. I soon discerned, from symptoms not difficult to be remarked by a careful observer, that the party at hand was composed of Austro-Hungarians. We had every thing to fear from them. I held myself bound under these circumstances first to make experiment of the fleetness of our horses. I however charged my people to keep together, and not to suffer the enemy, by means of our inadvertence and folly, to make an easy prize of us one after another. In a short time I found that our pursuers sensibly gained ground upon us. I was mounted upon an excellent beast, and could easily have rode away from my troop, while they would have been placed as a sort of intercepting object between me and the enemy. But I had too much of a military spirit not instantly to reject so inglorious an expedient. I called a second time to my attendants to halt. I judged that the party of our antagonists was less numerous than ours. I was convinced that our common safety depended upon our concerted resistance. Filled with the gallantry that my situation inspired, I did not perceive, till it was too late, that my present call to halt was attended to by few; even those few rather hung back, divided between apprehension and shame. I was the foremost, and, before I was aware, I found myself, through the means of the darkness, enveloped by the enemy. From my appearance they judged that I was the master, and the rest my attendants; they contented themselves therefore with the prize they had made, and did not give themselves the trouble to pursue the fugitives. They eagerly enquired of me who I was; and, comparing my answers with various circumstances which rumour had brought to their ear, they easily concluded that I was the rich stranger of Buda. The character they had heard of me did not produce in these freebooters any sentiments of forbearance, or demonstrations of respect; the only point about which persons of their habits were concerned, was how they should make the greatest advantage of what the fortune of war had thrown in their way.

While they were consulting, and various expedients were started by one and another for this purpose, a second alarm was given, and one of the party being despatched to reconnoitre, presently returned with intelligence, that the persons approaching were horsemen of the enemy, and that they amounted, as he guessed, to forty in number. Upon this information the party whose prisoner I was, agreed to return with all expedition by the way they had come, and commanded me upon pain of death to proceed in their company. This menace had not the effect to deprive me of courage or presence of mind; and I easily conceived that the readiest way to deliver myself from my embarrassment would be to join at the first opportunity the band of Turco-Hungarians, whose approach had occasioned our sudden retreat. The darkness of the night was favourable to my purpose; and, taking advantage of a sudden winding in the road, I slackened all at once the pace of my horse without being observed by my companions, who, as the enemy approached, had now their thoughts almost wholly intent upon the safety of their retreat. They passed me; and I no sooner perceived that to be the case, than, covered from their observation by the intervening inclosure, I turned my horse, and gradually, as my distance from my keepers increased, urged him to a fuller speed. It was not long before I came up with the band which had produced our alarm; and hailing them with the acclamation, "Long live the mighty sultan!" was without difficulty admitted into their troop. I instantly understood to my great joy that this was the party of Bethlem Gabor that I had come out to meet.

He received me with much cordiality, and seemed greatly rejoiced that fortune had made him the instrument of my rescue. He proposed however that, having met on the road, I should now, instead of proceeding to Buda, return with him to his northern castle, from which our distance was scarcely greater than from the metropolis. The proposal was such as I had not expected, nor could I well comprehend the purpose with which it was made. But the habitual demeanour of Bethlem Gabor neither accorded with his minutely assigning a reason for what he did, nor was calculated to encourage enquiry in another. I saw no material objection, and therefore felt little scruple in yielding to his desires. Our brief consultation on this point passed at some little distance from the rest of the troop.

When the morning broke, the first thing that excited my attention was the appearance of his followers. They were full forty in number, well mounted, of a large and athletic figure, with sun-burnt faces, immense whiskers and a ferocious countenance. I thought I had never seen so tremendous a band. To me they were every one of them strangers; of all the persons that surrounded me, the only one of whom I had the slightest knowledge was Bethlem Gabor himself. I know not why it was, but I no sooner beheld my situation than I was struck with alarm. I saw myself completely in the power of a man who three months before was ignorant even of my existence. I had not a single attendant of my own, not an individual with me over whom I had personal authority or command. I had no reason to distrust my host; towards me his demeanour had ever been frank, confidential, and manly; I had every imaginable claim upon his generosity and his gratitude. But our senses are often the masters of our mind, and reason vainly opposes itself to the liveliness of their impressions. Every time that I lifted my eyes, and saw myself hemmed in by these barbarians, my heart seemed involuntarily to fail me. Bethlem Gabor too appeared to neglect me; he had never shown himself so little obliging and attentive as at this moment; and, aided by the rest of the scene, I thought I had never beheld him so deformed or so tremendous. I was more than half inclined to wish myself again a prisoner with the Austrians.

When we arrived at the castle, we were all of us fatigued and hungry; we had roamed during the whole night. A repast was prepared; we sat down to partake of it. "Excuse me," said Bethlem Gabor, in a low voice as he passed me, "that I this night offer you the fare of a soldier; to-morrow you shall be accommodated in a different manner." The words were innocent; the proceeding natural; but there was a mysterious gloom, at least as I thought, in the tone in which he spoke, that electrified me. The hall in which we supped was spacious and lofty; the naked walls and rafters were imbrowned with age. Though it was daybreak as we entered, the windows were still darkened, and the apartment was illuminated only by the partial glare of lamps depending from the roof. As I sat at table with the troop of my host, I appeared to myself as if inclosed in a cavern of banditti. Though excellent partisans, skilful in execution, and perfect in their discipline, they were unpolished in their manners and brutal in their conversation. I had been inured from infancy to all the refinement that the age in which I lived had any where to boast; and, amidst the various evils I had suffered, that of being associated with the vulgar and the base had never presented itself. While they uttered, now a loathsome jest, and now a sanguinary ejaculation, I became ashamed of my species, and the pride of manhood perished within me. They however paid little attention either to my feelings or my person; and, accustomed as I had been, whether with friends or enemies, to be regarded as of some importance, I found myself unaccountably and suddenly dwindled into a cipher. I felt it like a release from the state of a galley-slave, when Bethlem Gabor proposed that we should break up our meeting and retire to rest.

CHAPTER XL.

A succession of gloomy thoughts revolved in my mind for some time after I was left to myself. I was however overcome with fatigue, and, after an interval of harassing meditations, insensibly fell asleep. I was awakened after some hours' repose, by the presence of Bethlem Gabor standing by the side of my couch. He invited me to rise, and, when I had attired myself, started the plan of our visiting together the various apartments of the castle, a small part of which only had been seen by me when I was last at this place. Among other things, he told me, there was a subterranean of most wonderful extent, interspersed with a variety of cells and lurking places, of which no man had to his knowledge ever ascertained the number.

The same dreary complexion of thought followed me to-day, which had been first produced in me upon my reception into the troop of Bethlem Gabor the preceding night. My sensations were of the most depressing and discomfiting nature; I felt as if I were the slave of some dark, mysterious tyrant, and dragged along supinely wherever he motioned me to go. I tasked myself seriously; I reasoned with myself. I felt that it was no idle and every-day part that I was called to sustain; and I resolved that I would not be ruined by my own inactivity and cowardice. Yet, when I examined the question dispassionately, I could not find that I had any occasion for courage, and I confessed that it was not less censurable, to discover a useless spirit of mistrust and defiance, than to desert one's preservation where resistance was demanded. What reason had I to suspect a man between whom and myself there had prevailed so much mutual confidence? None, none, I replied, but the causeless and superstitious misgivings of my own mind! Even if I had ground to distrust him, what remedy had I against his ill faith, placed as I was in the midst of his own domains, and surrounded by men devoted to his service? To discover apprehension under such circumstances, was to excite animosity.—These reasonings particularly occurred to my mind, as I stood waiting for the torch, which he had himself gone to procure that he might attend me to the subterranean caverns.—I had as yet seen no one, since we broke up from our nightly repast, but my host. "We will breakfast," said he, "when we return from viewing these curiosities."

We crept along a succession of dark and gloomy vaults, almost in silence. Bethlem Gabor, though he led me on, and discharged the office of a guide, seemed to have small inclination to assume that of an interpreter. This was sufficiently in unison with his ordinary character, to have little claim to excite surprise. Yet the reader will not on reflection greatly wonder that my present situation was far from agreeable. I was alone in passages which, to judge from any discoverable token, you would scarcely imagine had for ages been trod by a human creature. The voice was lost amidst the damps of these immense caverns; nor was it possible by any exertion to call the hand of man to your aid. My guide was an individual whom calamity had prompted to quarrel with the world; of strong feelings indeed, of capacious thought; but rugged, ferocious, brutal, and inaccessible to prayer. I had chosen him for my protector and ally; I had never intended to put myself in his power. There was a mystery in his carriage, a something not to be explained, a shell that no human forces could penetrate, that was mortal to confidence, and might quail the stoutest.

I thought there would be no end to our pilgrimage. At length we came to a strong door, cross-barred and secured with a frame of iron. Bethlem Gabor unlocked it. We had no sooner entered, that it impetuously closed behind us. "What is that?" said I, startled at the loudness of the report. "Come on," cried my host; "it is only the wind whistling through the caverns: the spring-bolt is shot, but I have the key in my hand!" At the opposite end of the apartment was another door with an ascent of five steps leading to it. Bethlem Gabor unlocked that also, and then faced about with the torch in his hand: I was close behind him. "Stay where you are!" said he with a furious accent, and thrust me violently from him. The violence was unexpected: I staggered from the top of the steps to the bottom. This door closed with as loud a report as the other; Bethlem Gabor disappeared; I was left in darkness.

For an instant I doubted whether the situation in which I thus found myself were the result of design or of accident. The shutting of the door might be ascribed to the latter: the action however, and the words of my host did not admit of that interpretation. I stood motionless, astonished, and almost incapable of reflection. What an incredible reverse was thus the creature of a moment! Yesterday I possessed unbounded treasures, and the hearts of the whole Turco-Hungarian nation. Yesterday, as I rode forth on this fatal excursion, I beheld the food of a mighty people, mature for consumption, the growth of my exertions; and it will not be thought surprising that my heart leaped within me at the sight. Who would not have envied the unparalleled eminence at which I had arrived? My triumphs were attended with no melancholy exceptions to damp their joy. They were the children of no intrigue; they were manly, frank, ingenuous, and honourable. My laurels were stained with no drop of blood, were tarnished with no tears of the widow and the orphan. How much more noble to rescue mankind from famine and death, than to violate the honest pride of their nature with the exhibition of victories and trophies!

Yet, truly considered, there was nothing abrupt in the reverse under which I was now suffering. The whole was a chain, every link of which was indissolubly connected from one end to the other. My attempt to rescue a people from the horrors of famine necessarily exposed me to unfavourable accidents and misconstruction. It inevitably led to my application to the government for its aid. It could not fail to excite the alarms and jealousies of government as to the tendency of my proceedings. By exhibiting me as the possessor of immense wealth, with very limited means for the protection of that wealth, it marked me a prey to a rapacious viceroy or his more despotic master. When I became sensible of the precarious situation in which I stood towards the powers of the state, could I have fallen upon a more natural expedient, than the endeavour to cover myself with the shield of friendship and gratitude in the person of one of its nobles? But this expedient would almost infallibly lead to the placing myself sooner or later in the power of the man whose friendship I sought. I had done so, and this was the termination of my views and my projects!

I now well understood the purpose of that inattention and neglect with which Bethlem Gabor had treated me the preceding evening, the uneasiness resulting from which I had blamed in myself at the time, as the dictate of weakness and unworthy suspicion. Yesterday I had been placed under the safeguard of a nation; every man in Buda and its environs was familiar with my person; every man would have been ready almost to sacrifice his life to procure my safety. Now I was far from the scene of my philanthropical exertions; no one in the troop of Bethlem Gabor knew who I was; he had appeared to treat me the preceding evening with indifference and contempt; if they saw me no more, no curiosity would by that circumstance be excited in their minds. My clients on the other hand in the vicinity of the metropolis, however great an interest they might take in my fortune, had no clue that could lead them to the knowledge of it. They must suppose me a prisoner with the Austrians, or that I had been killed, in resisting to become their prisoner. I was cut off from all assistance and discovery, and left as much in the power of my treacherous ally, as if I had been alone with him, oppressed with the utmost disparity of personal force, in the remotest island of the Pacific Ocean.

Such were the reflections that early suggested themselves to my mind in the solitude and darkness in which I was thus unexpectedly involved. Meanwhile one tedious hour succeeded to another, and I remained unintruded on and unnoticed. I could form no conjecture as to the object of Bethlem Gabor in the atrocious perfidy he had committed. Could he have any resentment against me, and did he meditate revenge? He had received from me nothing but benefits. Did he employ restraint on my person as the means of extortion? I could not conceive that he could have any clue leading him to the discovery of my grand secret; and, short of this, my bounties had been so exuberant, as, I imagined, left him nothing to wish. In this wilderness of conjecture I however fixed upon extortion as a motive less incredible than revenge. I impatiently waited, till the appearance of my tyrant should free me from some part of my present uncertainty.

He did not appear. In the mean time I was in a condition feeble and exhausted. The exercise of yesterday, the hourly-baffled expectation of meeting him whom I had called my friend, the alternation of being first taken prisoner and afterwards rescued, had extremely fatigued me. We had travelled during the whole night. Yet the unaccountable dejection of mind under which I laboured on our arrival at Bethlem Gabor's castle had prevented me from taking almost any share in the coarse repast that had then been set before us. The entrance of my host in the morning had rendered my slumbers short. As I followed him to my dungeon, unconscious whither I went, my limbs ached, and my heart ached still more. I was ill prepared for a fast of thirty-six hours which the brutality of my jailor inflicted upon me. After having long expected him in vain, I gave myself up to despair. What a termination of life for him who possessed the philosopher's stone!

I cannot do justice to the sensations that now took possession of my mind. It was not the deadly calm of despair, for I still expected every moment when Bethlem Gabor would appear. I believed than he would, and I believed that he would not, leave me to perish. I listened with eager attention to every sound, and my soul floated on the howling winds. In vain! nothing came of it; there was no alteration in the sound, or only those vicissitudes to which the howling of the wind is unavoidably subject. I then turned away in anguish; I cursed; I stamped with my feet; I smote my forehead with my closed hand; I tore my hair. Anon another sound arrested my attention; it was a different howling; it seemed to be like a human voice; my fancy created to me the tread of a human foot. I listened with more intentness of soul than ever. It was again in vain!

No, no; he will not come! he will never come. Why should I agitate myself to no purpose? Let me lie down and die!—I reasoned with myself. Why should I wish to live? I am nothing to any human being: I am alone in the boundless universe; I have no tie to existence. St. Leon has no wife; St. Leon has no child; he has neither connection nor friend in the world. Even in this wretched vision of the philosopher's stone, have I not tried it enough? have I any hopes from it? is it not time that I should throw away that and existence together?—My meditations were ineffectual. I suppose it is the case with all men thus violently thrust out of life in the full possession of their faculties—I know it was the case with me,—the more peremptory was my summoner, the more obstinately I clung to the worthless toy.

At length I laid myself down on the floor; and, if I occasionally listened, I no longer ran to the walls and the doors to catch the uncertain sounds. The gnawings I now felt within were intolerable. They were at one period so severe, that I can compare them to nothing, but the sensation of having swallowed a glowing ember. Afterwards, the weakness of nature would no longer feed this excruciating pain, and it subsided into a starting and convulsive throb; the pain was diversified with intervals of a death-like and insupportable sickness.—But, no; I will not attempt to describe the horrors of hunger sublimed by despair, where the torture of the mind gives new pungency and uproar to the corporeal anguish. The image, as it now presents itself to my recollection, is too dreadful.

At last I sunk into a state of insensibility; and the agony I had suffered seemed drawn to its final close. The busy turmoil, the feverish dream of human existence was at an end. I shut my eyes, and I believed I should open them no more.

CHAPTER XLI.

How long I endured this suspension of the vital faculties I cannot tell. The next impression on my sensorium, subsequent to those I have described, was a sort of external twitching and violence that seemed to persecute me. It was an importunity from which I felt desirous to escape; I longed to be undisturbed and at rest. The intruder on my quiet would not leave me; and I at length roused myself, as if to put away my cause of molestation. My thoughts were all confounded and obscure; I knew not where, I could scarcely be said to know who, I was. A little more effort brought with it a further capacity of perception; I saw before me, what was now the chief object of my mortal aversion, the figure of Bethlem Gabor. It was some time longer, before I became aware that he had been employed in taking up my apparently lifeless corpse, placing it on a stone-bench in the side of the cave, and chaining it to the wall. He observed the motions that indicated in me returning life: he remarked the stare of my glassy and rayless eyes; he now spoke with a stern and unpitying voice—"There is food; there is a light; eat!" Having thus said, he left me.

What a cruel and remorseless treatment! He cared not for my life; he disdained to make the slightest exertion to restore me; he left it to chance whether I should revive or perish. The figure of a dying man that I presented, did not make one fibre of his bosom bend or quiver.

I revived; I ate. By degrees I recovered from the deadly languor which had invaded my senses. In about twelve hours longer Bethlem Gabor returned with a new supply of sustenance. I was now strong enough to be able to converse with him. I heard the heavy sound of opening locks and removing bolts before he entered, and I summoned my faculties to expostulate with him.

"Why am I here? What is the meaning of the unworthy way in which you treat me?"

"It is,"—he regarded me with a truculent aspect, as if he would pierce through my heart,—"because I hate you!"

"You hate me? Good God! is it possible? What evil have I done to you? What good have I not done you? What supplies have I refused you? What occasions have I neglected of studying your advantage, your interest, and your honour? If thus your hatred is purchased, how shall that man demean himself who is to purchase your love?"

"Oh, think not my hatred idle or capricious! Heaven knows, I would have refrained from hating you if I had been able; I struggled against it with all the energies of my soul. But you have committed towards me the most mortal offences that man ever endured. There is an antipathy between your nature and mine, that all the menstruums in the world could never bring to coalesce."

"Eternal Providence! and what is the source of this antipathy?"

"And do you profess ignorance? Have you not gone on day after day with the full consciousness and will to torment me? Have I not warned you, and expostulated with you times without number?"

"Of what have you warned me?"

"I hate mankind. I was not born to hate them. I have no native obliquity of character. I have no diabolical maliciousness of constitution. But they have forced me to hate them, and the debt of abhorrence shall be amply paid.

"I loved as never mortal loved. No human heart was ever so devoted, and centred, and enveloped in the kindly affections of family and parentage as mine has been. Was not my wife, were not my children, murdered? When I came home to feast my eyes and tranquillise my soul with the sight of them, did I not find all waste and desolation? Did I not find their bodies naked, pale, disfigured with wounds, plunged in blood, and already putrid? This was the welcome I looked for! This was the object I so speeded to see! No, never was a moment like that! My whole nature was changed in an instant. My eyes were blasted and dried to horn. My blood froze in my well stored veins. I have no longer delight but in human misery.

"My revenge is not causeless; this was not the act of individuals. All men, in the place of these murderers, would have done as they did. They are in a league together. Human pity and forbearance never had a harbour but in my breast; and I have now abjured them. With something more of inwrought vigour and energy, I will become like to my brethren. All men are excited by the same motives, urged by the same temptations, influenced by the same inducements. Why should I attempt a futile distinction, when nature had made none? All men bear the same figure; I cannot view the human figure without a torture the most dreadful."

"I always knew," answered I, "your general hatred of mankind; but your manners and your behaviour persuaded me that you exempted me from the general censure."

"I wished to do so; you made the attempt impossible. You told me, that you had suffered the same misfortunes which I had; that you, by the injustice and persecutions of men, had also lost your wife and your children. I hailed you as a brother; in my heart I swore to you eternal friendship; I said, we will carry on this holy warfare together. We communicated to each other our mutual sorrows; with you, and you only, I found moments of consolation.

"Soon I discovered my mistake. Instead of, like me, seeking occasions of glorious mischief and vengeance, you took upon yourself to be the benefactor and parent of mankind. What vocation had you to the task? With the spirit of a slave who, the more he is beaten, becomes the more servile and submissive, you remunerated injuries with benefits. I found that there was not within you one atom of generous sentiment, one honest glow of fervent indignation. Chicken-hearted wretch! poor, soulless poltroon! to say the best of you, to your insensate heart it was the same whether you were treated with reverence or scorn. I saw you hunted, hooted at, and pursued by the people you fed; you held on your course, and fed them still. I was compelled to witness or to hear of your senseless liberalities every day I lived. Could I submit to this torment, and not endeavour to remove it? I hate the man in whom kindness produces no responsive affection, and injustice no swell, no glow of resentment. I hated you the more, because, having suffered what I had suffered, your feelings and conduct on the occasion have been the reverse of mine. Your character, I thank God! is of all beings the most opposite to that of Bethlem Gabor.

"At length you filled up the measure of the various thwartings with which you daily insulted me. There was one native of Hungary between whom and me there subsisted an open and eternal war. I relate in no human ear the cause of my animosity to that man. Suffice it, that it was deep, immeasurable, inexpiable. With a refinement of cruelty and insult difficult to conceive, you chose that man for one of the objects of your beneficence. Would I consent to see my name joined in pension list with my mortal enemy? The injury you inflicted on me would have been less if you had stabbed me to the heart. Less? That would have been a blessing. I impose on myself the task of living for my revenge: but never shall I deem that man my foe, who should rid me of all this tumult of passions, and this insupportable load of existence together.

"You have heard my motives. You may wonder at, you may censure them: but they are human. I have nothing further to say to you now: you have no need to recur to expostulation; expostulation never moved the heart of Bethlem Gabor. Hereafter you shall hear more!"

Thus speaking, he left me; and I must confess, with whatever disgrace to my sagacity, he opened upon me a new world. I conceived not, till now, the faintest suspicion of what had been labouring in his bosom. Amidst all my experience of the varieties of human character, this was a species that had never fallen under my observation before. What a painful and mortifying occurrence is it in human life, when we have lived with a man from day to day, when we have conversed with him familiarly, and seen him in all the changes of circumstance, and when we flatter ourselves we have penetrated all the recesses of his heart, suddenly to start upon something portentous that brooded there, of which to that moment we had not the lightest suspicion! I am not the only individual to whom this event has occurred.

In a subsequent visit of Bethlem Gabor to my cell (for he only attended me with provisions, he would intrust the secret of my confinement to no other mortal), I intreated him to inform me with what intention he retained me a prisoner, and to fix a price on my ransom. To this overture he appeared to yield some degree of attention. He made no explicit answer, but asked with an inquisitive and severe tone, in what manner I imagined I could procure money in my dungeon?

"Let us agree upon the terms, and set me at large. You have never found me deceitful, and you shall not find me deceitful now."

"Do not hope I will consent to that. I ask you again, in what manner do you imagine you can procure money in your dungeon?"

I reflected for a moment. Liberty is ineffably sweet; and whatever followed, upon the present overture, I was determined not to neglect the faintest prospect that led to a termination of my confinement.

"There is," answered I, "in my mansion at Buda, a chest which, if it can be brought to me hither, will enable me to supply your demands. I have the key in my custody, and no key but my own will unlock the treasure."

"Give me the key!" replied Bethlem Gabor.

"No," rejoined I, "it is in my custody; it is not upon my person: I have taken care of that. No human hand shall touch it but my own."

"And how can I cause this chest to be brought to you without risking a discovery of your situation, or that I had a concern in your disappearance?"

"Of that," said I, "judge for yourself. I have made a proposition to you, and I have done enough. I will have no share in the detail of its execution."

"Well," said Bethlem Gabor, after having ruminated a moment, "the chest you shall have; I undertake that. Describe it."

I described the chest, and its situation in my house, with a minuteness that made mistake impossible.

After a considerable time it was brought to me. It was too bulky and ponderous to be introduced into my cell by a single arm. But Bethlem Gabor, having first caused me unconsciously to swallow a powerful opiate, found no difficulty, either to conceal my person in the dark shadows of this ragged subterranean, or to cause some of his followers to place the chest within my reach, believing that they placed it in a vacant apartment. I awoke, and found it at hand. I was secure that the lock was such a one as could not be forced; but I examined the different surfaces, to see whether violence of any other sort had been exercised on it. There were marks of damage, but not sufficiently unequivocal to enable me to form a certain judgment on this point. The chest contained, not gold, but the implements for making and fashioning gold. Allowing for the distance from which it was brought, they appeared to be pretty exactly in the state in which I left them. I had never placed much confidence in this expedient for softening the heart of Bethlem Gabor; but I perceived that it would serve at worst to divert my thoughts, and, by exciting in me some share of expectation, might call off my attention from the miseries of my present condition. Embracing the occasions when I was most secure against the intrusion of my jailor, I provided myself with the sum that had been previously agreed on between us. My task being finished, I carefully displayed the produce of my labour, against the next time Bethlem Gabor should visit my cell. He viewed it with an air of sullen and gloomy triumph; he removed it from the cave which was my habitation, to an apartment of this subterraneous abode, little distant from my own. When he had concluded this employment, it seemed to be a just inference, that he was to give me my liberty. He did no such thing. Without uttering a word, he closed the door of my cavern, locked it, and departed.

When Bethlem Gabor next entered my cell, I reproached him with this, as with the breach of a solemn engagement. His first answer was an infernal laugh, expressive of derision, hard-heartedness, and contempt. By and by, however, he condescended to explain himself more fully.

"I made no engagement," cried he. "You talked of a ransom, and I suffered you to talk. I made you no answer; I gave you no encouragement. Boy, I deceived you not! No; though my heart pants for vengeance and for misery, I will never be guilty of treachery; I will break no engagements; I am a knight and a soldier. You have given me ten thousand ducats; what are ten thousand ducats to me? Do you think I am uninformed of your secret? I opened your chest; I found no gold; its contents were crucibles, minerals, chemical preparations, and the tools of an artist. You are possessed of the grand arcanum, the philosophers stone. If I had a doubt of it before, the transaction of yesterday converted conjecture into certainty. And did you suppose, idiot, driveller that you are, that I would take ten thousand ducats in commutation for wealth inexhaustible? No; you are my prisoner, and may choose, in this infallible dilemma, whether you will remain my slave, to supply me daily resources as I shall daily think proper to demand, or at once make over to me your whole mystery, and place me in this respect on a level with yourself."

It was now my part to be peremptory and firm.

"I refuse," said I, "every part of your dilemma, and all that you can propose to me. Do you talk of my remaining your slave, to supply you with daily resources? Do you imagine that, shut up in this dungeon, I will nevertheless labour for your gratification? Do you believe that that gift, which I received as the instrument of my own happiness and the benefit of mankind, shall be made the pledge of my perpetual imprisonment?

"With regard to imparting to you the secret you suppose me to possess, I answer without hesitation, that, dearly as I prize liberty, and numerous as are the motives you may think I have to prize it, I will not purchase my liberty at that rate. I would rather spend the days of eternity in this cavern, than comply with your proposal. The gift of the philosopher's stone, the moment a man possesses it, purifies his mind from sordid and ignoble inducements. The endowment which raises him so much above his species, makes him glory in his superiority, and cherish his innocence. He cannot, if he would, mingle in the low passions and pursuits of the generality of mankind. For myself, I value too much the verdict of my own heart, ever to allow myself to be influenced in the main concerns of my existence by menaces and compulsion. Beside, this gift I received for holy and beneficent purposes; to such it is consecrated; and if I ever impart it, I must select its depository with all the assiduity and penetration it is practicable for me to exert. You I will henceforth benefit no more. You hate me; my disapprobation of you is fixed and irrevocable. I weep to think how much I have been deceived in you; I weep to think how many high and heroic qualities in your breast are now converted into malignity and venom.—You the possessor of the philosopher's stone! You tell me, the sole pursuit of the rest of your life is revenge and human misery. What an image do you raise in my mind, if, with such dispositions, you possessed the means which the acquisition of riches inexhaustible would confer on you? And do you believe that any consideration on earth could induce me to realise such an image?"

"As you please," replied Bethlem Gabor indignantly. "I have nothing to propose to you. Think you that, either as my enemy or my slave, and I hold you for both, I would descend to negotiate with you? I simply told you your situation. Yours be the consequences of your wilfulness and folly!

"One mistake however that I see you make respecting my purposes, I will remove. You seem to suppose that, if you were to communicate to me your secret, I would then set you at liberty. No, by heavens! This cavern is your abode for ever. You shall never go forth from it alive; and, when you are dead, here your flesh shall moulder, and your skeleton shall rest, as long as the world remains. Look round your walls! Enter fully into possession of your final home! I know that to keep you here and alive my prisoner, I must in a certain sense imprison myself. But at that I do not murmur. I shall have the gratification of beholding my foe, and seeing him daily wither in disappointment. You wish to be a father to the human race; and I shall deem the scope of my misanthropy almost satisfied, while, in your restraint, I image myself as making the human race an orphan. Never shall Bethlem Gabor set at large a man of your unnatural and gall-less disposition, and your powers for the indulgence of that disposition.

"Sieur de Chatillon, I do not want your secret: it suffices that I know you possess it. Have I not yourself in my keeping? It will be more joy to me rudely to issue my commands, and to see you complying with them in spite of the most heartfelt reluctance, than to possess the richest gift on earth in the fullest independence. Think you Bethlem

Gabor incompetent to tame the tenant of this wretched cavern? Boy, you are my prisoner; you shall be my creature. I will humble you at my feet, and teach you to implore my bounty for the most miserable pittance. Look to it! You know your destiny! Do not provoke my fury, without a foresight of the consequences!"

I will enter into little further detail of this my wretched imprisonment in the wilds of Hungary. It was not destitute of its varieties; and I could, if I pleased, fill a volume with the artifices and the violence of my gloomy superintendent. I could fill volumes with the detail of the multiplied expedients, the furious menaces, the gigantic starts and rhapsodies of passion, by which he alternately urged me to compliance and concession. But I will not. I will bring to an end the history of Bethlem Gabor; and then, having detailed the surprising events that immediately followed it, will close the page of St. Leon's history for ever. I stood like a rock. Shut out from all other gratifications, I at least resolved to accumulate in my own person all the energies of resistance. If I were to unfold the story, I could command the reader's astonishment, his admiration; but the object of these papers is to record, not my merits, but my fate.

How different was my imprisonment in the cavern of the man-abhorring palatine, from that which I had experienced in the dungeons of the inquisition! There an inexorable apathy prevailed: my tyrants were indifferent whether I died or lived; filled with the sense of their religious elevation, they held on the even gravity of their course, and counted my groans and my tears neither for remorse nor pleasure. The variety I experienced in their dungeons was the growth of my own thoughts: from without I encountered no interruption; it was not to be ascribed to those who held me in durance, if my faculties were not lethargied into death. Bethlem Gabor possessed no share of their apathy; his malice was ever alive, his hatred ever ingenious and new in its devices. He had a purpose to answer,—to extort from me the supply of his necessities and projects. It was not so much perhaps that he stood in need of this, as that he placed a pride in it, and had fiercely resolved to show me that I was unreservedly his slave. His animosity against me was so fixed and insatiable, that nothing that was pain to me was indifferent to him. If at any time he saw me subsiding into insensibility, he failed not to exert himself to sting me into life again.

The consequence of this was somewhat different from what Bethlem Gabor expected. Desponding as I was, weary of life, and almost finally alienated from the all-coveted gift of the philosopher's stone, if he had left me to myself, I should very probably have sought in insensibility relief from the torment of my own thoughts. But he taught me a better lesson. Refusing me the indulgence of torpor, he obliged me to string myself to resistance. He gave me a passion; he gave me an object; he gave me comparative happiness. I was roused to opposition; I was resolved that, placed, as I seemed to be, at his mercy, I would yield him no atom of his desires. Thus employed, I found in my employment pride. Perpetual occasion presented itself for fortitude; and I gradually ascended to the sweets of consistency, perseverance, and self-gratulation. I had for years been inured to satisfy myself with a sparing stock of pleasures; and I was less at a loss to expand and ramify those which I now possessed, than almost any other man would have been in my situation. If my attendant train of sensations was scanty, Bethlem Gabor took care to afford them a perpetual supply of food and employment, and I was comparatively little exposed to the pain of vacuity. When he saw that I was inflexible, and that he could no longer gain from me the smallest compliance with his will, he raged against me with terrifying fury. Was it a crime in me, that this fury in my tyrant produced the operation of a sedative and a cordial? There was no malignity in the joy it gave me. I had much aversion for Bethlem Gabor, but no hatred. I took no pleasure in his agonies, because they were agonies. My sympathies towards him now, I confess, were small; but the joy I felt was because his fury told me, was the unwilling evidence of my own value. I left him to assail the mound I opposed to his desires as he pleased; it remained strong and unaffected as the sea-beaten promontory.—From the inefficacy of his efforts, I sometimes took occasion to remonstrate with my jailor, and demand the restoration of my liberty; but Bethlem Gabor was not a man whom arguments and expostulations like these could move. In spite of himself however I commanded his wonder, if not his esteem. He regarded the contrast as almost incredible, between the boy-aspect under which he saw me, and the inflexibility and resources of my time-instructed mind.

The contentment that I have here described in myself, was however a creature of the imagination, the forced progeny of uncommon effort. It was no natural state of the soul. My mind would sometimes wander beyond the limits of my cavern, and remember that there were other persons beside Bethlem Gabor and myself in the world. I recollected the situation in which I had left my great project for the reviviscence of Hungary, and rejoiced to remember that it was already in such forwardness, as, I hoped, no longer to stand in absolute need of my assistance. Yet what I had done was but a small portion, a dismembered branch, of what I had meditated to do, and what every person of a generous and enterprising mind, who had been in possession of the philosopher's stone, would have designed. Why was I thus stopped in the commencement of a career so auspiciously begun, and to which an ardent fancy, would prescribe no limits? Why was every power of the social constitution, every caprice of the multitude, every insidious project of the noble, thus instantly in arms against so liberal and grand an undertaking? Nor could I help repining at the perverseness of my fate, which had decreed that I should savour all the bitterness incidentally resulting from my plan, and not be permitted so much as to taste the applause and reward that ought to grow out of its completion. Thousands of men were at this instant indebted to my generosity and exertions for every blessing they enjoyed; and I was cast forth as the refuse of the earth, pining under the alternate succession of solitude, negligence, and malice, my very existence and the manner of it unknown, except to one individual, who had, from the strangest and most unexpected motives, sworn eternal hostility to me.

Bethlem Gabor had resolved that, so long as he lived, I should remain a prisoner: when he died, if he continued my only jailor, the single individual acquainted with the place of my confinement, the probable issue was that I should perish with hunger. Twelve years before, I should have contemplated this attitude and condition of existence with indescribable horror. But within that time I had been better taught. I had received an education, I thank them, in the dungeons of the Spanish inquisition; and, if that be properly considered, it will not be wondered at that I was superior to ordinary terrors. Early in my present situation the presentiment had suggested itself to me that, by some striking event, I should be rescued from my present confinement; and, improbable as the suggestion was, it made an indelible impression on my mind. I had originated in, or it had produced, a dream, the scenes of which had appeared particularly luminous and vivid. I imagined I saw a knight, cased complete in proof, enter my prison. A smile of angelic kindness beamed on his countenance. He embraced me with ardour; he made a sign to me to follow him. I felt that I had seen him somewhere, that he had been my intimate friend. Yet all the efforts I made in sleep, or afterwards when I was awake, were unavailing to remove the mystery that hung upon his features. I rose to obey him; the ground trembled under my feet like an earthquake. Presently, with the incoherency usually attendant on a dream, the figure changed to that of a female of unblemished grace and beauty; it unfolded a pair of radiant wings; we ascended together in the air; I looked down, and saw the castle of Bethlem Gabor a prey to devouring flames.—Here ended my dream. I soon felt that I could reason myself out of all confidence in the presages of this wild and incongruous vision. But I refused to do it; my consolations were not so plenteous in this frightful solitude as that I should willingly part with one so delicious. Reason, thus applied, I contemplated as an abhorred intruder. It was, for a long time, part of my occupation in every day to ruminate on this vision, not with the sternness of a syllogist, but with the colouring of a painter, and the rapture of a bard. From thus obstinately dwelling on it in the day, it happened that it became again and again and again my vision of the night. Slumbers like these were truly refreshing, and armed and nerved me for the contentions of my tyrant. Sacred and adorable power of fancy, that can thus purify and irradiate the damps of a dungeon, and extract from midnight glooms and impervious darkness perceptions more lovely and inspiriting than noontide splendour!

CHAPTER XLII.

I had now continued here for several months, and in all that time had received no external impressions but such as related to the cell I inhabited, and the misanthropical savage by whom it was visited. One evening that Bethlem Gabor entered my dungeon, I observed in him an air of unusual disturbance. Where apathy reigns, the intercourse between those over whom it presides will be marked with a death-like uniformity; but wherever the furious passions take their turn, they will occasionally subside into a semblance of familiarity and benevolence. There was something in the countenance of my tyrant that made me for a moment forget the complicated injuries I had received from him. "What is it that has disturbed you?" cried I. There was no answer. There was a knitting in his brow, and a contraction in his features, that showed me his silence was an effort. He departed however, and had already passed the threshold of my dungeon. The door was in his hand. He returned. "Chatillon," said he, "perhaps you will never see me more!"

"My castle is besieged. I have passed through dangers of a thousand names, and I ought not to be made serious by that which now assails me. But a gloomy presentiment hangs upon my mind. The busy phantom of life has lasted too long, and I am sick at heart. In the worst event I will not be made a prisoner; I will die fighting.

"I feel as if this were the last day of my existence; and, upon the brink of the grave, animosity and ferociousness die away in my soul. In this solemn moment, my original character returns here (striking his heart) to take possession of its native home; a character, stern and serious, if you will; but not sanguinary, not cruel, not treacherous or unjust. Between you and me there is a deadly antipathy; but you did not make yourself; you intended me friendship and advantage; the sufferings you have experienced from me in return have been sufficiently severe. If I die defending my walls, and you remain thus, you will perish with hunger. I had intended it should be so; but I am now willing to remit this part of your fate. I will enter into a compromise with you; I will trust to your fidelity, and your honour. I will take off your chains; I will bring you a timepiece and torches; I will leave with you the key of the spring lock of your cavern,—provided you will engage your word to me that you will not attempt to make use of your advantages till the expiration of twenty-four hours."

To these terms I assented without hesitation. The chains fell from my wrists and my ancles; I stood up once more unshackled, and in respect of my limbs a free man. When Bethlem Gabor was on the point to depart, my soul melted within me. I took hold of his hand; my fingers trembled; I grasped and pressed the fingers of my tyrant. I cannot describe what then passed in my bosom. No man can understand my sensations, who had not been in my situation, who had not passed through a treatment, arbitrary, ferocious, and inhuman, and had not then seen the being who had wounded him so unpardonably, suddenly changing his character, commiserating his fate, and rescuing him from destruction.

From this time I saw Bethlem Gabor no more; he died, as he had sworn to do, in the last dike of his fortress. His self-balanced and mighty soul could not submit to the condition of a prisoner; he was nothing, if he were not free as the air, and wild as the winds. I may be mistaken; but this appears to me to have been a great and admirable man. He had within him all the ingredients of sublimity; and surely the ingredients of sublimity are the materials of heroic virtue. I have much cause of complaint against him; he conceived towards me an animosity the most barbarous and unprovoked; but, in writing this narrative, I have placed my pride in controlling the suggestions of resentment, and I have endeavoured to do him justice.

I had engaged to wait twenty-four hours; I waited only six. I know not how the reader will decide upon the morality of my conduct; but I own I had not the force, I believe I may call it the insensibility, to remain in my dungeon any longer. There was no doubt that, if Bethlem Gabor returned a conqueror, the term of my imprisonment would be renewed, and all his former menaces continued in force. What should I deserve to have thought of me, if I could sit down idly, and tamely wait the return of my jailor? No! liberty is one of the rights that I put on when I put on the form of a man, and no event is of power to dissolve or abdicate that right. Of what validity was the promise that Bethlem Gabor extorted from me by compulsion, and as the condition of that which he had no title to withhold? What gratitude did I owe to this man, who treated me with every contumely, and shrunk from nothing but the thought of causing me to perish with hunger? Whatever became of my attempt to escape, I could at least in this vast subterranean hide myself from the face of him who had injured me. I had a provision of phosphorus in my chest; and could therefore extinguish my torch upon the slightest alarm, and relume it at pleasure. What was the value of life, situated as I was situated? It was better to perish in the attempt to escape, than linger on for ever in perpetual imprisonment. As a further resource I left a billet in my dungeon (for for this also I had implements) intreating Bethlem Gabor by every motive of compassion and humanity to provide for me the means of sustenance as usual. Having taken these precautions, I lighted a fresh torch; and, unlocking the door, and thrusting the key into my girdle, set out upon my expedition. Though Bethlem Gabor had stipulated for twenty-four hours, the siege might even now be over, and I trembled every instant lest my jailor should return.

I wandered for a considerable time among the alleys and windings of this immeasurable cavern. I had the precaution to mark the sides of the vault with characters and tokens as I passed, that, if necessary, I might be able to find the way back to my dungeon: this might prove an indispensable resource, to prevent me from perishing with hunger. Once or twice I changed my route, inferring from a comparison of circumstances, the best I could make, that I was not in the direction of the castle from which Bethlem Gabor had led me to my imprisonment. In all this wandering I had seen nothing, I had heard nothing, which could demonstrate to me that I was approaching the habitation of man. I had groped my way for near two hours, when on a sudden I heard a loud and tremendous shout that almost stunned me, and that from its uncommon shock could be at no great distance from the place where I stood. This was succeeded by a terrifying glare of light. I extinguished my torch, both that I might be better qualified to observe, and that I might be less in danger of discovery by any one who should approach me unawares. The shouts were several times repeated. The light I found to proceed from that end of the vault towards which I had been advancing, and, by the best conjectures I could form, I concluded the outlet into the castle to be at no great distance. I heard the crackling of the flames, and the fall of rafters and beams. Presently I discerned a volume of smoke approaching me, and found that, if I remained long in my present station, I should incur the risk of being suffocated. I formed my resolution. I concluded that Bethlem Gabor's castle was taken, and set on fire by the Austrians. I believed that my persecutor was already no more: to this faith I was undoubtedly prompted by the presentiment which he had communicated to me. I saw that it would be impossible for me to emerge into light, till the flames should abate. I once more therefore lighted my torch, and returned by the straightest road I could find to my dungeon. Arrived there, I proposed to pass the interval quietly, in the cavern where I had so long felt the weight of the Hungarian's chains. Suddenly however the suggestion occurred to me, may not my conjectures be false? may not Bethlem Gabor yet repel the enemy, and return to me from amidst the ruins of his falling castle? The thought was sickness and extinction to my heart. Hope! beautiful as are thy visions, in how much anguish and agony do they clothe the terrors of disappointment! Never had Bethlem Gabor been half so dreadful to me as now. I shrunk away; I took with me the fragments of provision that yet remained; I hid myself; I deemed no cell remote enough to conceal me from the inhuman persecution of my tyrant.

I continued in the subterranean all that day and all the succeeding night. Once in this period I attempted to reconnoitre the avenue of my escape, but I found the situation still so heated and suffocating that I did not venture to proceed. At length I came forth from this den of horrors, and again beheld the light of the sun. The path had already been sufficiently explored by me, and I no longer found any material obstacles. I now saw that my conjectures were true: the castle of my ferocious adversary was a pile of ruins. The walls indeed for the most part remained, but choked with fragments of the falling edifice, blackened with the flames, and penetrated in every direction by the light of day. With difficulty I climbed over the ruins, which opposed my egress from the subterranean, and rendered my passage to the outside of the castle an affair of peril and caution. Here the first object that struck me was some tents, probably of the soldiers who had been employed in this work of destruction. I was hailed by a sentinel, and I demanded that he would conduct me to his commander. He led me to the centre of the little encampment, and I stood in the presence of his chief. I lifted my eye to behold him, and was petrified with such astonishment as till that hour I had never felt. It was Charles, my son, my only son, the darling of his mother, the idol of my soul!

CHAPTER XLIII.

It may seem extraordinary that I should instantly have known him. He was sitting at a table, covered with papers, and with one or two aides-de-camp waiting to receive his orders. He was clothed in complete armour, and his casque was resting on the ground by his side. When I entered, his eye was fixed on a despatch that day received from the great palatine of Hungary; but, in little more than a minute, he raised his head, and his countenance was completely presented to my view. It was fifteen years since I had beheld it; he was then scarcely above half his present age, a mere stripling, in whom the first blush of manhood had awakened the sentiment of independence and an honour impatient of a shade; he was now a leader of warlike bands, his complexion olived over with service, and his eye rendered steady with observation and thought. But I knew him; I knew him in a moment. My soul, with the rapidity of lightning, told me who he was. Not all the arts in the world could have hid him from me; not all the tales that delusion ever framed could have baffled me; I could have challenged him against the earth!

I have already had occasion to explain the complexity of my feelings, when, after a long absence, I visited the heiresses of the house of St. Leon. The sweets of recognition, that transporting effervescence of the mind, where the heart bounds to meet a kindred heart, where emotions and tears mingle in speechless encounter, where all is gazing love and strict embrace,—these pleasures were denied me. I stood stiff and motionless in the presence of my child. My heart might burst; but it must not, and it could not communicate its feelings.

After an instant's pause of overwhelming sensation, I sunk back on myself, and considered my own figure. It happened that, exactly opposite to me, in the tent of my son, hung his armour, and over the rest his polished shield, in which I saw my own person clearly reflected. The youth of my figure indeed was still visible; but the hardships of my dungeon had imprinted themselves in glaring characters on my face. My beard was neglected, my hair was matted and shaggy, my complexion was of a strong and deadly yellow. My appearance to a considerable degree told my story without the need of words. Charles enquired of those who brought me, where they had found this wretched and unhappy figure; and was told that I had been seen a few minutes before coming out from the ruins of Bethlem Gabor's castle. He humanely and naturally concluded, that I was a victim on whom the tyrant had exercised his ferocity, and that I had been shut up in some dungeon of the fortress: it was impossible that any person above ground in the castle should have come out alive from the operation of the flames. He commanded that I should be led to a neighbouring tent and taken care of. After having been refreshed with food and rest, and attired with other apparel, he directed that I should be brought to him again, that he might hear my story.

Under these circumstances there was nothing for which I was more anxious, than that I might recruit myself, and shake off as quickly as possible the effects of my confinement. Cordials were brought me, and I tasted of them: I bathed in a neighbouring stream: one of my son's attendants removed my beard, and arranged my hair. I now desired to be left alone, that I might take some needful repose. I could not sleep; but I reclined my limbs upon a couch, and began to collect my thoughts.

I saw myself in one hour the sport of the most complete reverse of fortune that could happen to a mortal. I had been the prisoner of a cavern so wild and pathless, as almost to defy the utmost extent of human sagacity to explore its recesses. From this cavern, but for the sudden and extraordinary event which had just occurred, I could never have come forth alive. All sober calculation would have taught me to expect that I should have remained there, chained up like a savage tiger in his cage, as long as Bethlem Gabor existed; and that, when he died, I should perish, unheard, unknown; no creature that lived suspecting my situation, no lapse of ages ever bringing to light my dismal catastrophe. The remorse and relenting of Bethlem Gabor towards me seemed so little to accord with any thing that I had personally witnessed of his habits and his mind, that even now I feel myself totally unable to account for it. As it was however, I was once again free. From the state of an outlaw imprisoned for life, I suddenly saw myself at large, inspirited by the light of the sun, and refreshed by his genial rays, in the full possession of youth and all its faculties, enabled to return amidst my clients of Buda, or to seek some new adventure, in any corner of the earth to which my inclination led me. There is no man, however overwhelmed with calamities, however persecuted with endless disappointment, however disgusted with life and all its specious allurements, to whom so sudden and admirable a change would not convey some portion of elasticity and joy.

But there was one thought that entirely occupied me. I cannot describe how my soul yearned towards this my only son: the sentiment, even now as I write, is an oppression I am scarcely able to sustain. Willingly, most willingly, would I have traversed every region of the globe, if so I might have discovered his unknown retreat: and now suddenly, without the smallest effort on my part, he was placed before me. His last solemn parting, his abjuration of my society and intercourse for ever, rose to my memory, and gave a zest inexpressible to our present encounter. At the thought that my son was in the neighbouring tent, all earthly objects beside faded from my mind, and appeared uninteresting and contemptible. I instantly resolved to devote myself to his service, and to place all my enjoyment in the contemplation of his happiness, and the secret consciousness of promoting it. He had, if I may so express myself, in my own person forbidden me his presence: in my now altered figure I might disobey his injunction without fearing his rebuke. Let not the reader condemn me, that, endowed as I was with unlimited powers of action, I preferred a single individual, my own son, to all the world beside. Philanthropy is a godlike virtue, and can never be too loudly commended, or too ardently enjoined; but natural affection winds itself in so many folds about the heart, and is the parent of so complicated, so various and exquisite emotions, that he who should attempt to divest himself of it, will find that he is divesting himself of all that is most to be coveted in existence. It is not a selfish propensity; on the contrary, I will venture to affirm that the generosity it breathes is its greatest charm. Beside, in my case I considered my own existence as blasted; and I could therefore find nothing better than to forget myself in my son. I had made a sufficient experiment of the philosopher's stone, and all my experiments had miscarried. My latest trials in attempting to be the benefactor of nations and mankind, not only had been themselves abortive, but contained in them shrewd indications that no similar plan could ever succeed. I therefore discarded, for the present at least, all ambitious and comprehensive views, and believed that I ought to be well content, if I could prove the unknown benefactor of the son of Marguerite de Damville. I entered into a solemn engagement with myself that I would forget and trample upon every personal concern, and be the victim and the sacrifice, if need were, of the happiness of my child. Dismissing my project of becoming a factor for the Hungarian people, I determined to lay aside the name of Chatillon, and cut off every indication that might connect my present existence with that of the rich stranger of Buda. One of the advantages I possessed for that purpose was, that no creature in Hungary had the slightest suspicion that the sieur de Chatillon had ever been the prisoner of Bethlem Gabor.

Having thus arranged my thoughts, I now called for the garments that had been assigned me. They were supplied me from the stock of my son; and, when I had put them on, I overheard the attendants whispering to each other their astonishment, at the striking resemblance between their master and myself. When I came once more into the tent of their captain, and stood as in the former instance before his shield, I did not wonder at their remark. The coincidence of our features was so great, that, had we passed through a strange place in each other's company, I should infallibly have been regarded as his younger brother. Yet there was something of Marguerite in the countenance of Charles that I wanted. When I recovered, as in a short time afterwards I did, my vigour and health, I was more blooming than he; but there was something graceful, ingenuous and prepossessing in his aspect, which I could by no means boast in an equal degree, and which might have carried him unhurt and honoured through the world. We shall see some of the effects of this in what I shall presently have occasion to relate.

When my son required of me to declare who I was, I told him, as I had already determined to do, that I was a cadet of the house of Aubigny in France; that, after having passed through several other countries, I had come into Poland with the floating and half formed purpose of entering as a volunteer against the Turk; but that, before my plan was completely arranged, having been led, by my juvenile ardour in a hunting party, far within the frontier of Hungary, I had been so unfortunate as to become a prisoner to the troopers of Bethlem Gabor. I added that, when introduced to their chief, I had given him so much offence, by the firmness of my manner, and my refusing to comply with certain propositions he made me, that he had thrust me into a dungeon, from which, but for the gallant exertions of the present detachment, I should never have come out alive.

Charles heard my story with attention and interest. He called on me to resume my courage and my hopes, and to be confident that my sufferings were now at an end. He told me, that he was a Frenchman as well as myself, and like myself, had been a soldier of fortune. He felt, he said, a powerful sympathy in my tale; there was something in my countenance that irresistibly won his kindness; and, if I would put myself under his protection, he did not doubt to be the means of my future success. He spoke with great asperity of Bethlem Gabor, who, as an intrepid, indefatigable and sanguinary partisan, had been the author of greater mischiefs to the Christian cause, than any of the immediate servants of the sultan of Constantinople. He congratulated himself that the same action that had delivered the world from so murderous a renegado, had rendered him the preserver of a youth of so much enterprise and worth, as he doubted not I should prove. He said, there was but one other man in Hungary, who had been so effectual an enemy to the cause of truth and Christianity as Bethlem Gabor. The name of this man he understood was Chatillon, and he grieved to say that he bore the appellation of a Frenchman. To the eternal disgrace of the nation that gave him birth, he had joined the Turkish standard, and, by exertions difficult to be comprehended, had rescued the infidels from famine at a time when, but for his inauspicious interference, Buda, and perhaps every strong town in Hungary, were on the point of falling into the hands of the Christians. It was this same man who had revived the resources of Bethlem Gabor, after they had once before, by his own fortunate exertions, been routed out; and whom I might therefore in some sense consider as the author of my calamities, as well as the inveterate foe of Christendom. Such a wretch as this was scarcely entitled to the common benefit of the laws of war: and he would not answer for himself if Chatillon had fallen into his power, to what extremity his holy resentment against this degenerate fellow-countryman might have hurried him. Providence however had overtaken him in his impious career; and he had fallen obscurely, as he had lived basely, in a night skirmish with a party of marauders from the Austrian camp.—The reader may believe that I did not a little rejoice that, in announcing myself a few moments before, I had taken the name, not of Chatillon, but D'Aubigny. What I heard however occasioned in me a profound reflection on the capriciousness of honour and fame, and the strange contrarieties with which opposite prejudices cause the same action to be viewed. I could not repress the vehemence of my emotions, while I was thus calumniated and vilified for actions, which I had firmly believed no malice could misrepresent, and fondly supposed that all sects and ages, as far as their record extended, would agree to admire.

In another point of view, the invective which my son thus unconsciously poured in my ears, had the effect of making me regard with a more complacent satisfaction the plan I had formed of devoting myself to his service. Here I pursued no delusive meteor of fame; the very essence of my project lay in its obscurity. Kings and prelates, armies and churches, would no longer find an interest in disputing about my measures; I should indulge the secret promptings of my soul, undisturbed alike by the censure of the world, and its applause. It was thus that, under every change of fortune, I continued to soothe my soul with delusive dreams.

Meanwhile my project went on with the happiest auspices. The friendship between me and Charles continued hourly to increase. As a Frenchman, whom chance had introduced to his acquaintance in a distant country, it was natural that he should feel a strong bias of affection towards me. But that sort of fraternal resemblance which the most inattentive spectator remarked in us, operated forcibly to the increase of Charles's attachment. He would often, in the ingenuous opening of his soul towards me, call me his brother, and swear that I should for ever experience from him a brother's love. Charles had by this time completed the thirty-second year of his age; I was, in appearance, at least ten years younger than he. There is something in this degree of disparity, that greatly contributes to the cultivation of kindness, and is adapted to the engendering a thousand interesting sentiments. Frequently would he exclaim, "Our fortunes, my dear Henry," that was the name I assumed, "have been in a considerable degree similar: we were both of us early cast on the world; I indeed at the immature age of seventeen. I entered the world without an adviser or a friend; but my destiny was favourable, and I escaped its quicksands and its rocks. I have now by a concurrence of happy circumstances obtained a place among honourable men and soldiers, and for what is to come may reasonably regard myself with some degree of confidence. You are yet in one of the most dangerous periods of human life; your work is all to do; your battles are yet to fight. Suffer me, my dear friend, to represent your better genius, and act an elder brother's part. You shall find me no ignorant Mentor, and no ungentle one."

Nothing could be more gratifying to me than to see the shoots of affection thus springing up spontaneously in Charles's bosom. I willingly humoured the generous deception that he was putting on himself, and heard with transports inconceivable his assurances of kindness and protection. We rode, and we walked together; we were in a manner inseparable. When he went out to reconnoitre, I was his chosen companion; when he inspected the discipline and condition of his soldiers, he applied that opportunity to initiate me in the science of war; when he expected to encounter the enemy, he placed me immediately by his side.

Sometimes he would open his heart to me, and dwell with a melancholy delight upon his secret sorrows. "It is no wonder, my Henry," he would say, "that I feel this uncommon attachment to you. I am alone in the world. I have no father, no mother, and no brethren. I am an exile from my country, and cut off for ever from those of my own lineage and blood. It is with inexpressible delight that I thus cheat the malice of my fate, and hold you to my bosom as if you were indeed my brother. I would not part with the fiction for the mines of Peru; and I know not whether I do not cultivate it more assiduously, and regard it with a sentiment of more anxiety and zeal, because it is a fiction, than I should do if it were a reality. I had indeed," added Charles, "a mother!"—And, when he had started this theme, he would dwell for ever on her praises. I easily saw that never son loved a mother more cordially, than Charles loved the all-accomplished Marguerite. With what sentiments did I hear her eulogium? I could not join in her praises; I could not be supposed to know her. I stood there, as the statue of Prometheus might have done, if, after being informed with a living soul, the Gods had seen fit to chain its limbs in everlasting marble. The passion within me panted and laboured for a vent; but I was invincibly silent. With what sentiments did I hear her eulogium? Every word of it was a dagger to my heart; every word said, "And thou, villain, wert not thou her murderer?" more painfully, than the fiercest reproaches could have done.

When Charles had celebrated with an eloquence truly divine this incomparable mother, a sudden pang of memory would make him start into rage.——"And this mother I left! Of this mother I cannot tell whether she is alive or dead! What shall I say? the crime, or the not less fatal error of my father, separated me from this mother! I loved my father: I loved him because he was my father; I had great obligations to him; he once had virtues. But my mother,—if I could have found her in the wildest desert of Africa, and have known her virtues, a stranger to my blood, descended from the remotest tribe of the human race, I should have chosen her for my friend, my preceptress and my guide, beyond all that youth and beauty, with their most radiant charms, could tender to my acceptance!"

Thus unconsciously, yet ingeniously, did my dear son from time to time torture his father's heart. I could not even deliver him from the gloomy and wretched uncertainty, whether this mother were alive or dead. With one word I could have composed his soul into a sober grief; I could have said, Your adorable mother at length rests from her sorrows; she is no longer the victim of a misguided and a cruel father; you have no longer occasion to brood over that most disconsolate of reflections, "I know not what anguish may be at this moment suffered by her who is entitled to all my duty and all my affection." With one word I might have told this; and that word I dared not utter.

CHAPTER XLIV.

My son related to me his history, and made me the depository of his feelings and reflections. The name of St. Leon indeed never passed his lips; I felt that he had consigned that to inviolable oblivion. The appellation he bore in the army was the chevalier de Damville. Soon after he abandoned me at Dresden, he had entered as a volunteer in the imperial army. Charles the Fifth was at that time assembling forces to encounter the confederates of the league of Smalcalde. In this situation my son was eminently fortunate. He was distinguished for uncommon enterprise and courage in some of the first actions of the war, and early attracted the notice of Gian-Battista Castaldo, count of Piadena, who held an eminent command under the emperor. In this army my son was a party to the decisive battle of Muhlberg, in April, 1547. Four years afterwards, Castaldo was appointed commander in chief against the Turks in Hungary, and the French chevalier accompanied his patron to this new scene of military enterprise. Charles had felt dissatisfied with the grounds and motives of war between the Catholics and Protestants of Germany, men worshipping the same Saviour, and appealing to the same authorities, but many of them at least, from the most upright and ingenuous scruples, differing in their interpretation of those authorities. But, in their contentions between the crescent and the cross, he entered with unbounded enthusiasm into all the feelings that constitute a champion or a martyr. He conceived that whatever was dear to the human race in this world or the next hung on the issue; he regarded the grandeur of the cause as purifying his efforts and consecrating his name; and, when he lifted his sword in vindication of an expiring God, he felt himself steeled with more than mortal energy.

My son dwelt on the merits of his patron with a degree of veneration and love that knew no bounds. Castaldo was ranked by the consenting voice of mankind with the most accomplished generals of the age in which he lived. "I knew him," said Charles, "in his most private hours, and stood next to and observed him in the greatest and most critical occasions of his life. It was the least of his merits that he distinguished me, that he took me up friendless and an orphan, that under every circumstance he was more than a father to me; that he corrected my faults, that he guided me with his advice, that he instructed me with his wisdom, and supported me by his countenance. Castaldo was the most persevering and indefatigable of mankind; no difficulties could undermine his apparent serenity; no accumulation of dangers could appal or perplex him. Victory never robbed him of his caution; misfortune and defeat never destroyed the grandeur and elasticity of his soul. I firmly believe that no general had ever a more discouraging variety of counteractions to struggle with. The enemy was barbarous and sanguinary, yet firm and undismayed, in the full vigour of their political health, under the rule of the ablest of their sovereigns. The nobles of the country Castaldo had to defend had almost all of them been alienated, one after another, by the tricking and ill-judged politics of the house of Austria. The nation was ruined, houseless and starving. Many of the officers who served under my general were the basest of poltroons; but they were imposed upon him by his court; he was compelled to place them in important trusts; and, even when in the most dastardly way they betrayed those trusts, they were by some pitiful intrigue sheltered from his discipline and his justice. The forces of Castaldo were mutinous and ungovernable; and he was almost constantly denied the funds requisite for their pay.

"For two years the count of Piadena struggled with these complicated difficulties. When he had obtained a hard-earned advantage at one extremity of the kingdom, he found it rendered useless by some treachery or incapacity in the other extremity, which it was instantly necessary he should hasten to repair. He quelled four alarming mutinies by his firmness, his resources, and the prudent combination of his calmness and severity. In the midst of one of his most arduous situations he suddenly received intelligence that the states of Hungary, which were at that time assembled, were debating whether they should enter into a treaty with Solyman for the purpose of placing their country under the Turkish sceptre. He immediately flew to the place of council; the decision in favour of Solyman was drawn up and ready to be adopted; but Castaldo, by his presence, his authority, and his eloquence, recalled the states to their duty, and prevented them from eternally staining the Christian name. Surrounded with these difficulties, opposed to an enemy many times more numerous than the forces he could bring against them, and whose wants were all plentifully supplied, Castaldo by his single abilities kept the balance even, or rather caused it to incline in favour of the Christian scale. But what," added Charles, "avails the most consummate merit! How may the most incessant and undaunted exertions be shadowed by the veil of obscurity! The world judges by events; success is necessary to procure the palm of fame. After two years of such labours as I witnessed and glory to describe, a mutiny broke out among the mercenary troops, more formidable than any that preceded; it was no longer even in the abilities of Castaldo to quell. 'We honour and respect you,' said the mutineers, 'but we will no more serve without pay: we have been baffled two years; we will march to the gates of Vienna, and demand from Ferdinand, our sovereign, why we are thus denied the arrears that are due to us.' They chose leaders for this expedition among themselves. The great Castaldo, whose peculiar talent it is to accommodate himself to events, and never by any misfortune to be deprived of his invention and resources, saw what it was that became him. Having in vain tried every method for retaining his troops in Hungary, he offered himself to lead them to Vienna. Then was seen the true ascendancy of a noble mind. Goaded with want and distress, they had been deaf to the remonstrances of their general when he sought to direct them against the enemy. But, when they saw him submitting himself to their rage and impatience, and fearlessly intrusting his safety to those who had before refused even to listen to him, and who had reason to fear his retribution as their accuser and judge, they were awed and speechless. They almost repented of their frenzy, and were half determined to return to their duty. Their remorse indeed was imperfect and ineffectual; but Castaldo led this band of mutineers through the heart of the kingdom, with as many symptoms of regularity, modesty, and order, as if they had been the best paid, the promptest and most loyal army in the world."

My son spoke in terms of the warmest enthusiasm of the defence of Erlau, in the period of Castaldo's last and most arduous campaign against the Turks. In respect of fortifications the town was scarcely competent to resist the feeblest enemy; but its deficiency in this point was supplied by the constancy and valour of its garrison and inhabitants. The very women displayed an enterprise, that the more vigorous sex have seldom exhibited. In one instance, a heroine of this sort was seen fighting in the presence of her mother and her husband. Her husband fell dead by her side. "Let us, my daughter," said the mother, "remove the body, and devote the rest of our care to its honourable funeral."—"May God," returned the impassioned widow, "never suffer the earth to cover my husband's corse, till his death has been amply revenged; this is the hour of battle, not a time for funeral and for tears!" So speaking, and seizing the sword and shield of the breathless champion, she rushed upon the enemy; nor did she quit the breach till, by the slaughter of three Turks who were ascending the scaling ladders, she had appeased the fury in her breast, and the ghost of her departed husband. Then raising the corpse, and pressing it to her bosom, she drew it to the great church of the city, and paid to it the last honours with all possible magnificence. Many other examples of a heroism not inferior to this were displayed on the same occasion. "And shall I," added Charles, in a sally of glorious enthusiasm, "ever desert a cause which has been thus honoured? Shall I betray a soil which has been immortalised by such illustrious actions? Shall I join myself to the renegado Bethlem Gabor, and the execrable Chatillon? No: such virtue as I have described never could have been conceived, but in the bosom of truth! Great as is the pious devotion I feel for that God who died on the cross for the salvation of mankind, I own my weakness, if it be a weakness, his cause is scarcely less endeared to me by the sublime exertions of his heroic followers, than by his own adorable condescension and mercy.

"When the glorious Castaldo departed with his rebellious army for the metropolis of Germany, there was nothing I more earnestly desired than to accompany his march. For seven years he had conferred on me the benefits, and shown towards me the affection, of a father; and I could not think of being separated from him without the extremest anguish. Beside, I regarded it as little less than sacrilege, to quit his side at a time that he was exposed to the furious suggestions of a host of robbers and banditti. But he would not allow me to abandon my post. 'Some time,' said he, 'we must separate, and you must stand alone. I have been long enough your instructor; and, if my lessons or my example can produce improvement in you, they must have performed that office already.' He treated with disdain the thought of the danger to which he might be exposed, and his need of a faithful guard; a thought which he had detected in the midst of my anxieties, but which I had not the courage to mention. 'This,' said he, 'is your genuine sphere. You are a young man, burning with the zeal of truth and religion. You are inspired with the enthusiasm of a champion and a martyr. Heaven knows how willingly I would have spent my blood for the overthrow of Mahomet and his blasphemous impieties. To me this is not permitted; to you it is. I shall be engaged in the painful scenes of civil contention between Christian and Christian, misguided and inflamed by the human inventions of Luther and of Calvin. You have before you a clearer and a brighter field; and, I confidently persuade myself, you will be found worthy of your happier destiny.'—The count of Piadena bestowed me, so he was pleased to express himself, upon Nadasti, the great palatine of the realm, as the most precious pledge of his friendship that it was in his power to confer.

"Since the retreat of Castaldo, the Christian standard has obtained little more either of attention or aid from our lawful sovereign, now the possessor of the imperial throne. Ferdinand for a great part of this time has had his negotiators at Constantinople, whom the insulting Turk has condescended neither sincerely to treat with, nor to dismiss. The Christian army in Hungary has been left to its own resources; but zeal has supplied the place of magazines, and religious ardour has taught us to omit no occasion of annoying and distressing the enemy. The most considerable occurrence of this period, has been the siege of Ziget about four years ago. Solyman, taking advantage of certain factious broils among our hereditary nobility, appointed at that time one of his eunuchs bashaw of Buda; and, having placed a numerous army under his command, dismissed him from the foot of his throne with this arrogant injunction, not to enter the capital of his province, till he had first sent the keys of Ziget as an offering to his royal master. Horvati, the Christian governor of this fortification, is one of the most accomplished and the bravest of our native commanders; and, Nadasti having sent him a reinforcement the better to enable him to support the threatened siege, I was in the number of the soldiers appointed on this service. The trenches were opened early in June, and the siege continued for the space of seven weeks. The bashaw, though an eunuch, in person stunted, and of monstrous deformity, was distinguished for an uncommon degree of audacity and perseverance. Four times he filled the dikes of the fortification with wood and earth; and as often, by means of a furious sally of the besieged, the materials, which had thus with vast expense of industry and labour been accumulated, were set fire to and consumed. On the twelfth day of the siege he gained possession of the town, and drove us back into the citadel; but on the day following we recovered the ground we had lost, and from that time the town was his no more. The actions of these days were the severest of the whole siege; we fought the enemy street by street, and inch by inch; the great fountain in the market-place ran with blood; we ascended hills of the dead, which the infidels opposed as a barrier to our further progress; I seized two Turkish standards; and, though wounded, pursued the enemy through the eastern gate, and returned in triumph. Nadasti in the sixth week of the siege marched to our relief; but he was met and worsted by the bashaw, who returned victorious to the foot of the walls. During the whole of the siege mutual animosity was cherished by every species of contrivance, and the heads of the distinguished dead were exhibited on both sides as spectacles of abhorrence and terror. The inflamed passions of the combatants several times found a vent in listed duels: Horvati, the governor, killed in one of these encounters a gigantic Turk, who had sent a proud defiance to our host. I procured myself honour upon a similar occasion; and the scarf which I now wear, composed the turban of the infidel I slew. At length the disappointed bashaw was obliged to raise the siege; and he soon after died of grief and mortification in his palace at Buda. I confess I recollect the Christian exploits in the defence of Ziget, in which I also had a share, with rapture and delight; they will serve to awaken in me new animation, when hereafter the coldness of ordinary life might strike palsy to my soul. I shall never think I have lived in vain, after having contributed, in however humble a place, to arrest the career of insolence and impiety which, under the standard of the crescent, threatened to over-run the whole Christian world."

Such were the adventures and such the sentiments of the gallant chevalier de Damville. I had been a warrior in my youth, and the discourse he held was sufficiently congenial to my earliest propensities. I saw indeed that he had gained, in the zeal of a soldier of the cross, a source of martial heroism, to which my military history had been a stranger. But, though I could not entirely enter into this sentiment of his, and indeed regarded it as an infatuation and delusion, I did not the less admire the grandeur of soul with which this heroic fable inspired him. There was no present propensity in my heart that led me to delight in deeds of blood and war; I saw them in their genuine colours without varnish or disguise; I hated and loathed them from my very inmost soul; but, notwithstanding this, I was sensible to the lustre which military zeal cast round the character of my son. Nor is this incredible or absurd; the qualities of a generous and enterprising champion are truly admirable, though the direction they have received should be worthy of eternal regret.

Charles de Damville was my friend; and, when I say this, I cannot help stopping a moment for the indulgence of reflecting on the contrast between my present intercourse with my son, and my late connection with Bethlem Gabor. I had sought the friendship of the Hungarian partisan, partly because I wanted a protector and an ally, but partly also because in my soul I looked up to and admired the man. I called Bethlem Gabor my friend; I persuaded myself that I had cogent reasons for calling him so. But there was little sympathy between us; he was wrapped up in his own contemplations; he was withered by his own calamities; our souls scarcely touched in a single point. No, no; this is not friendship.

Friendship is a necessity of our nature, the stimulating and restless want of every susceptible heart. How wretched an imposture in this point of view does human life for the most part appear! With boyish eyes, full of sanguine spirits and hope, we look round us for a friend; we sink into the grave, broken down with years and infirmities, and still have not found the object of our search. We talk to one man, and he does not understand us; we address ourselves to another, and we find him the unreal similitude only of what we believed him to be. We ally ourselves to a man of intellect and of worth; upon further experience we cannot deny him either of these qualities; but the more we know each other, the less we find of resemblance; he is cold, where we are warm; he is harsh, where we are melted into the tenderest sympathy; what fills us with rapture, is regarded by him with indifference; we finish with a distant respect, where we looked for a commingling soul: this is not friendship. We know of other men, we have viewed their countenances, we have occasionally sat in their society: we believe it is impossible we should not find in them the object we sought. But disparity of situation and dissimilitude of connections prove as effectual a barrier to intimacy, as if we were inhabitants of different planets.

It is one of the most striking characteristics of the nature of man, that we are eternally apt to grow dead and insensible to the thing we have not. Half our faculties become palsied, before we are in the slightest degree aware that we are not what we were, and what we might be. There are philosophers who regard this as the peculiar privilege of man, a wise provision of Providence to render us contented and easy with our lot in existence. For my part, I do not envy, and I have never aspired to, the happiness of ignorance and stupidity. But, be it a blessing or a curse, the phenomenon is undoubted. Present me with some inestimable benefit, that my nature fitted me to enjoy, but that my fortune has long denied me to partake, and I instantly rise as from an oppressive lethargy. Before, it may be, I felt myself uneasy; but I knew of no remedy, I dreamed it was my nature, I did not put forth a finger for relief. But now, that I have drawn the unexpected prize, I grow astonished at my former blindness; I become suddenly sensible of my powers and my worth; the blood that slept in my heart, circulates, and distends every vein; I tread on air; I feel a calm, yet ravishing delight; I know what kind of an endowment life is, to a being in whom sentiment and affection are awakened to their genuine action.

This was the effect of the mutual attachment produced between me and Charles. I looked into him, and saw a man; I saw expansive powers of intellect and true sensibility of heart. To be esteemed and loved and protected by such a man; to have him to take one by the hand, to enquire into one's sorrows, to interest himself in one's anxieties, to exult in one's good fortune and one's joys; this and this only deserves the name of existence.

I had however a painful drawback upon my satisfaction. It was my fate since the visit of the stranger of the lake of Constance, to rejoice for moments and to lament for years. I could not at first ascend to that purity and eminence of friendship to forget myself; I could not but painfully feel the contrast between me and my son. How happy was Charles, how respectable, how self-approving, how cheerful of heart: I shall presently have occasion to speak of a still further addition to his happiness! I looked indeed young, fair, blooming, a stranger to care: but I had a secret worm gnawing at my vitals. This very deceitfulness of my countenance was a bitter aggravation to my remorse. I never saw my features reflected in the polished shield without feeling myself struck to the core. Charles had walked right onward in the paths of honour; he feared no detection; he had no secret consciousness that gave the lie to the voice of applause, partiality, and friendship. But I was all a lie; I was no youth; I was no man; I was no member of the great community of my species. The past and the future were equally a burthen to my thoughts. To the eye that saw me I was a youth flushed with hope, and panting for existence. In my soul I knew, and I only knew, that I was a worn out veteran, battered with the storms of life, having tried every thing and rejected every thing, and discarded for ever by hope and joy. When I walked forth leaning on the arm of him who delighted to call me his younger brother, this was the consciousness that hunted my steps and blasted me with its aspect whichever way we turned.

CHAPTER XLV.

Among the various confidences reposed in me by my son, one was his love. The object of his attachment was a young lady of quality, named Pandora, niece to Nadasti, great palatine of Hungary. In consequence of the earnest recommendation of Castaldo in 1553, Nadasti had taken my son under his particular protection, and Charles's principal home at the periods when the army was dispersed in winter-quarters was at the palatine's house in the city of Presburg. Here his manners had become more polished, and his taste more refined. Till then, bred in tents, and living amidst the clangour of arms, he had been a mere soldier, rough, generous, manly, and brave. But Nadasti was an elegant scholar, smitten with that ardent love of classical and ancient lore which has so eminently distinguished the sixteenth century. He assembled round him men of letters from various parts of Europe; and, under his auspices, the days of Matthias Corvinus, king of Hungary, seemed to be revived, whose love of literature was such, that he kept three hundred transcribers in his house, constantly employed in multiplying copies of the precious relics of Roman and Athenian learning. The consort of Nadasti was one of the most accomplished matrons of the age in which she lived, and her three daughters were patterns of every polite and amiable accomplishment. Such was the school into which the chevalier de Damville entered at the age of twenty-five, immediately after the retreat of Castaldo. This may seem an age somewhat late for new-modelling the character, but Charles had an enterprising and aspiring temper; and he soon became a distinguished ornament of courts and the society of ladies. Castaldo had taught him all he knew, the temper, the manners, and the science of a military chieftain: the palace of Nadasti finished and completed the education of my son.

Pandora was only fourteen years of age when Charles de Damville first became a sort of inmate of the house of her uncle. She at that time lived with her father; but he being afterwards killed in the battle which Nadasti fought for the relief of Ziget, Pandora occupied an apartment in the palatine palace. From the first hour he saw her, a mere child as it were, accompanied by her governess, Charles confessed to me that he had beheld her with eyes of distinction. He had said to himself, This little girl will hereafter be a jewel worthy of the crown of an emperor. He had found something inexpressibly attractive in the starry brightness of her complexion; her air he regarded as both lighter and more graceful than any thing he had ever before seen; and her speaking and humid eye seemed to him the very emblem of sensibility and sweetness. If, at the girlish and immature season of fourteen, he had ascribed to her all these perfections, it will easily be supposed that, as she increased in stature as the beauties of form unfolded themselves in her, and she advanced in sentiment and a lovely consciousness of her worth, the partiality of Charles became more deep and unalterable. But the orphan niece of Nadasti was altogether without a portion; and the great palatine would have seen with more complacency the chevalier de Damville addressing his pretensions to one of his daughters.

Charles confessed to me that the passion he nourished had been fruitful of pleasures and griefs, of hope and perplexity. It was now almost a year since Pandora and himself had confessed a mutual affection. The confession had not been the result of design on either side: both had wished to suppress it; Pandora from virgin dignity and reserve; and Charles, because he saw not how their affection could be crowned with success, and he dreaded, more than any misery to himself, to be the author of degradation and misery to her he loved. But what is ever uppermost in the heart will at some time or other betray itself. Their sympathetic and accordant feelings upon a point so deeply interesting to both, rendered them eagle-eyed to discern the smallest indications. They had had a thousand opportunities, and a thousand opportunities had been resisted. They became more than usually silent and reserved towards each other; they shunned to meet, and, when they met, avoided each other's eyes. One day a casual encounter in a solitary retreat, which each had sought principally with intention to escape the presence of the other, had taken them off their guard. They were mutually hesitating and perplexed; each discerned more unequivocal indications than had ever occurred before of the state of the other's sentiments; the entire accord snapped as it were at once the chains of reserve; and each, after a short interval of hesitation, spoke with an eloquence, hitherto untried, the language of love. The difference of years between them gave a zest to the communication. Pandora seemed to be throwing herself upon the protection of an elder brother, of a guardian, one in whose prudence she confided as the antidote of her inexperience; Charles felt his maturer years as imposing on him more severely that sacred integrity, the obligation of which, at least as society is at present constituted, seems in the majority of cases to grow out of the relative situation of the sexes, of the protectorship of the one, and the dependence of the other.

"And now," exclaimed Charles, "what am I to do? what am I to desire? It would be affectation in me to conceal from myself on an occasion like this, that the reputation I have acquired both in the arts of peace and war is such, as to have caused Nadasti to set his heart upon my becoming his son-in-law. The great palatine, though in many respects generous and liberal, has that inflexibleness of opinion, which is perhaps more apt to grow up in the hearts of scholars, than in other departments of society. He is grave and solemn; all his habits are of a majestic and lordly nature; and I have small reason to hope that I shall find him accessible to my representations. He is little subject to sallies of passion; his own propensities are wholly under the control of his judgment; and it is not likely that he will make allowance for the ardent affections of other minds. Pandora is entirely dependent on him; in any case the portion she would receive from him would be very inadequate to her worth; but, discarded and discountenanced by him who has the absolute rule of Christian Hungary, what can she expect? I am myself destitute of fortune; my provision as a soldier will be very inadequate to the wants of the first and softest of her sex. But even of that provision Nadasti will deprive me, if I marry in opposition to his pleasure. Shall I make Pandora the inhabitant of tents and encampments; shall I expose her to all the changes and hazards of a military life; shall I drag her as the attendant of a soldier of fortune through every climate of Europe? No, by heavens! I should regard myself as the most selfish and the basest of mankind, if I could deliberate on such a question. Never shall the charmer of my soul owe a single privation to her Charles. I love her with so pure and entire a passion, that I prefer her prosperity to every earthly good. Nor is it merely necessary to my attachment that she should live in plenty and ease; I require that my Pandora should be seen in her native lustre, that she should be surrounded with every appendage due to her merit, that she should command applause from the mercenary, and homage from the superficial. Her praise is the only music I enjoy. I could not bear to hear her name coupled with levity and scorn. I could not bear that, where she appeared, every eye should not be turned to her with reverence and honour. My passion, I confess it, is that of a disciple of liberal arts and a nobleman, not that of an Arcadian."

The period of the campaign now drew to an end, and Charles, having requested me to accompany him, set out for his usual winter retreat in the city of Presburg. I saw Pandora. Never in my life had I beheld any thing so sweetly simple. I had always been an admirer of the sex; but the perfections of Pandora were of a nature that I had not observed in any other woman. Her symmetry was so perfect, the pearly lustre of her skin so admirable, and her form and carriage so light and ethereal, that at first view it was difficult to persuade one's self that she was framed of the same gross materials as the rest of the species. She seemed not constructed to endure the shocks of the world, and the rude assaults of ill humour or neglect, of censure or adversity. Her voice was of the sweetest, the clearest and softest tone I ever heard. There was a peculiar naïveté in her accents, that riveted your soul in irresistible fetters. Her conversation, for in the sequel I enjoyed much of her conversation, had a very uncommon zest. She seemed to have no art, and what she uttered appeared as if wholly unchecked by consideration or reserve. You were persuaded that she always delivered without restraint the first thing that occurred to her mind; yet in what she said there was so much good sense, so much true feeling, and, as the occasion allowed, so much whim and imagination, that you could not discover how any of her words could be changed but for a worse. This circumstance strikingly contrasted with the childish simplicity, or rather the feminine softness and sylph-like delicacy, of her manner and her tone. The opposition of appearance between her and my son made a strong impression upon me. He was a perfect soldier, with an ample chest, broad shoulders, and a figure, though graceful and well proportioned, yet so strong, that it seemed framed to contend with and to conquer the wrestlers in the Grecian games. His complexion, shaded with luxuriant curls of manly hair, was itself made brown with the rigours of climate. Pandora was so heavenly fair, so sweetly delicate and slender, that you would have thought she would be withered and destroyed in his embrace, like the frailest ornament of the garden before the northern breeze. But courage to choose what is rugged and manlike is often characteristic of the softest of her sex.

I speedily contracted an intimate commerce with the beautiful Pandora. I was naturally desirous to be as consummate a judge as possible of those perfections, which I believed fated to determine the future happiness of my son. When sufficiently satisfied in that respect, I still continued the indulgence, and found a pure and exquisite pleasure in the daily contemplation of accomplishments that were to prove the materials of his gratification and delight, whose gratification I preferred to my own. I had a still further view in this commerce. I was anxious to be perfectly informed of the connections and family of Pandora, that upon them I might build a project I had deeply at heart, of bestowing on her, in the least questionable and exceptionable manner, a dowry, that should place her upon an equality with her cousins, the daughters of Nadasti, and deliver my son from all apprehension of the unpleasing consequences to result from the resentment of the great palatine. Nadasti was opulent, and the portions of his daughters very considerable; and, however inclined, I could not exceed this limit without risking the entire miscarriage of my project. Charles thought nothing too rich either in situation or income to do honour to the mistress of his soul; but, separately from this enthusiastic sentiment, both he and Pandora had too just a taste, not to prefer the simple majesty of ancient nobility, to the expensive ostentations of modern refinement.

Having digested my plan I was obliged to travel as far as Venice for the execution of it. The mother of Pandora had been a Venetian, and the uncle of her mother was one of the adventurers who had sailed with Pizarro for the conquest of Peru. He had died before the completion of that business, and had left behind him no relative so near to him in blood as the lovely Pandora. By a singular piece of good fortune, I encountered at Venice an individual who had sailed in the same ship with the young lady's uncle. The uncle having died prematurely, the share he might otherwise have obtained of the spoils of Peru was sunk in the shares of the rest, and nothing was allowed to remain that might have descended to his heirs. His friend and countryman I found, though once rich with the booty he made, had by a series of calamities, before he reached his native home, been reduced to a state of poverty. The vicissitudes he experienced, had produced in him the effect of a very uncommon eagerness for acquisition. This man I fixed on for my instrument; I opened to him my plan, and offered him a very ample gratification, provided he acted successfully the part I assigned him. In concert with each other we digested and forged the various documents that were best calculated to give credibility to the tale. Having completed our arrangement, I set out for Presburg without a moment's delay, and directed my Venetian not to follow till after a stipulated interval. He was not to enter into full possession of his reward till he had completed the task he had undertaken. It was fixed that no person in Hungary should be acquainted with my visit to Venice, but only be allowed to understand generally, that I had been engaged for a certain time in an excursion of amusement. So hard is the fate of the possessor of the philosopher's stone, and so limited his power, as to have rendered all these precautions on my part indispensably necessary. Had not the various circumstances concurred, the detail of which is here stated, the birth of Pandora's mother in a maritime state, the expedition of Pizarro to Peru, her uncle's engaging in this expedition and dying before it was completed, and my own casual rencounter with his compagnon du voyage, my project would too probably have been baffled. A direct gift of the fortune I designed would never have been admitted of; and, had not the coincidence been eminently favourable, even though I should have succeeded in misleading every other party, I could not hope to have eluded the perspicacity and jealous honour of my son.

When I returned to Presburg, I again renewed my intercourse with Pandora. The passion entertained by Damville for the beautiful orphan was a secret to every person at court; they had managed so discreetly as to have avoided every hint of suspicion; and, as it was universally known that the great palatine had an eye on this gallant soldier for one of his daughters, few persons entertained a doubt that my son would speedily declare his election among the co-heiresses of Nadasti. On the other hand, in the friendly intercourse between me and Pandora, neither she nor myself felt that there was any thing to conceal, and it was therefore a matter of complete notoriety. My blooming youth of appearance was remarked; by the majority of bystanders we were judged formed for each other; and, before I was aware, the beautiful Hungarian was awarded to me by the general voice as my destined bride. When however I became acquainted with the rumour, I was contented to smile at it; the consciousness in my own breast how far the public sagacity had wandered in its guess, gave to that guess, in my apprehension, a certain air of whimsical and amusing.

CHAPTER XLVI.

Such was the situation of the affair of Pandora, and I daily looked for the arrival of my Venetian confederate, when suddenly I remarked an alteration in the carriage of my beautiful ally. She had hitherto, on all occasions, sought my conversation; she now appeared sedulously to avoid me. Her manner had been characterised by the gaiety, the sprightliness and general good humour, incident to her age, and congenial to her disposition. She was now melancholy. Her melancholy assumed a tone correspondent to the habits of her mind, and was peculiar and individual. It had an ingenuous and defenceless air, inexpressibly calculated to excite interest. It seemed to ask, what have I done to deserve to be melancholy? You felt for her, as for a spotless lily depressed by the unpitying storm. You saw, that those enchanting features were never made for a face of sorrow, and that that bewitching voice ought never to have been modulated into an expression of heaviness.

I was in the highest degree anxious to learn the cause of this revolution, and was the farthest in the world from suspecting its real foundation. I pursued Pandora with so much importunity, and demanded an interview with such irresistible earnestness, that she at length consented to grant it. We met in a remote part of the garden. "Why, Henry," said she, "do you thus persecute me? You are my evil genius, the cause of the greatest calamity that could ever have overtaken me."

I started. "For heaven's sake, beautiful Pandora, what do you mean?"

"I love the chevalier de Damville. I have loved him long; he is dearer to me than life; and he has cast me off for ever!"

"And am I the cause?"

"Yes, you, and you alone. I had for some time observed a change in his behaviour, that he was uncommonly grave, serious, and reserved. I endeavoured to soothe him; I redoubled my blandishments in our next season of unreserved discourse; I tenderly enquired into the source of his grief.

"For a long time he resisted my importunity. At length, 'Faithless girl,' said he, 'have you the cruelty to ask the meaning of my depression? This is the extremity of insult. Is it not enough that I know your inconstancy? Is it not enough that I have found you, like the rest of your frivolous sex, the mere slave of your sense of sight, regardless of vows, regardless of an affection which despised all interests but that of tenderness and love, caught by the first appearance of something younger, softer, and more courtly, than I pretend or desire to be? Will nothing satisfy you but the confession of my unhappiness from my own mouth? Do you require expostulation, intreaty, and despair, from your discarded lover, to fill up the measure of your triumph?'

"For a long time I was totally at a loss to apprehend my dear chevalier's meaning.

"'No,' continued he, 'I am not jealous. There is no temper I hold in such sovereign contempt as jealousy. I am not of a disposition easily to conceive umbrage, or lightly to doubt the protestations of the woman I adore. I have been blind too long. But I see that you are eternally together. I see that you take advantage of the distance at which the despotic temper of Nadasti keeps us from each other, to give all your time to my favoured rival. You seem never to be happy out of his society. I was first led to throw off the dulness of my unsuspecting security, by the general voice of the public. The whole court gives you to each other. Not a creature it holds, but has discerned that passion, which you have the insolence to expect to conceal from me. Since I have been awakened from my security, I have seen it a thousand times. I have seen your eyes seek and encounter each other. I have seen them suddenly lighted up by your interchanging glances. I have seen the signs of your mutual intelligence. I have seen with what impatience, the moment you could escape from the crowded circle, you have joined each other, and retired together. Ungenerous Pandora!

"'But do not imagine I will enter the lists with the gaudy butterfly who has now attracted your favour. I have told you already that I am not formed for jealousy. I am not the sort of man you have supposed me to be. I have loved you much; I have loved you long. But I would tear out my heart from my manly breast, if I believed it yet retained an atom of passion for you. I know what it was I loved; I loved a character of frankness, of ingenuousness, of simplicity, which I fondly imagined was yours, but which I now find was the creature of my own fancy. The Pandora that stands before me; the child of art; the base wretch that could take advantage of my forbearance in regard to her uncle, which was adopted purely out of love to her; the unfeeling coquette that would wish to retain me in her chains when she had discarded me from her affections; this creature I never did love, and I never will. I know how deeply rooted the habit has been in my bosom of regarding you as the thing you are not; I know how bitter it is to a temper like mine to detect so unlooked-for a delusion; I know what it will cost me to cast you off for ever. But I never yet proposed to myself a conquest over my own weakness that I did not gain, nor will I now. If you were to discard this wretched D'Aubigny to-morrow, if you were convinced of and contrite for your error, I must ingenuously tell you, no time, no penitence could restore you to my admiration. I had set up an imaginary idol in my bosom; but you have convinced me of its brittleness, and dashed it to pieces.'

"I endeavoured," continued Pandora, "by every imaginable protestation to convince my late faithful lover of his mistake. But it was to no purpose; all I could say only tended to swell the tide of his fearful resentment."

"'Be silent,' cried he: 'add no further to the catalogue of your wanton and causeless delusions. Do not make me hate too much what I once so blindly and ardently adored. I feel that I have an enemy within me, that would fain co-operate with your deceptions and hypocrisy. I find that man, treacherous to himself, is formed by nature to be the fool of your artful sex. But I will subdue this propensity in me, though I die for it. I may be wretched; but I will not despise myself. Have I not seen your falsehood? Have not all my senses been witnesses of your guilt? The miracle is that I could have been duped so long. I have heard this stripling lover of yours inexhaustible in your praises, and dwelling upon them with an ardour that nothing but passion could have inspired. I have seen, as I have already told you, the intelligence of your eyes. I have seen those melting glances, I have heard those tender and familiar tones between you, that bespoke the most perfect confidence and the most entire mingling of heart. If I did not believe this, I should believe worse of you. I should think your heart not merely capricious, but an absolute prostitute; prepared to bestow upon hundreds those sweet, those nameless tendernesses of accent and countenance, which I fondly imagined were reserved for me alone. I should regard you as the worst and most pernicious acquisition that could fall to the lot of a man. 'Go, Pandora,' added he: 'my heart is chaste; my soul is firm. I can no longer be deceived by you; I will not dispute your charms with the idle boy you have now thought proper to favour.' And, saying thus, he burst from me in an agony of impatience.

"Alas!" continued the sweet and ingenuous Pandora, "my dear Henry, what shall I do? How shall I remove the unreasonable imaginations of this noble mind? Bear me witness, Heaven! nothing could be more innocent than the correspondence I allowed myself to hold with you. My adorable Charles was continually calling you brother; I scarcely ever heard him speak of you by any other appellation. I regarded Charles as my husband; I already viewed you in anticipation as the brother of my lord. Excluded as I was from frequent conversation with him whom I most loved, I endeavoured to supply the deficiency by an unreserved communication with you. The extreme resemblance of your persons increased my gratification. You were his picture, his speaking image. While I looked at you, I said, 'Such once was my Charles, before he was the great man, the gallant soldier, the accomplished cavalier, the adored object, that now engrosses my affections.' Beside, I knew that Charles loved you as much as he did any man on earth, and that knowledge made you dear to me. You were constantly eager to dwell upon and describe his excellences; could I fail to be pleased with your conversation? I own that the pleasure I took in it was unbounded, and the emotions it awakened in my affectionate heart delicious. But all this, candidly explained, was only an additional proof of the tenderness and constancy of my earliest attachment.

"And now, ever since the fatal day in which this conversation passed with my Charles, he is absent from court, and I know not whither he is gone. He has disdained to seek any further explanation, nor do I know how to appeal to his calmer feelings and more deliberate mind. One thing however I had determined on, and that was, Henry, strictly to avoid your society.

"I trust, wherever my Charles is, he will hear of this. I owe this expiation to his agonised feelings, and to the appearances that in some degree justify his misconstruction. I will wait patiently, till the simplicity and singleness of my conduct have cleared my faith. If I should otherwise have found pleasure and relief in your society, I will make a merit with myself of sacrificing this to the apprehensive delicacy of my Charles's mind. In this single instance your importunity has prevailed with me to dispense with my rule: you were not to blame, and I thought upon more mature reflection that I owed you an explanation. But henceforth, if you have any kindness for me, or value for him who has acted and felt towards you like a brother, I must entreat you to co-operate with me in this, and that, whether in public or private, we may bestow no notice on each other, and avoid all opportunities of communication. To persuade you to this, was indeed a principal inducement with me so far to deviate from the rule I had laid down to myself, as to admit this conversation."

I was extremely affected with the unhappiness of Pandora. I exerted myself to console her. I promised that nothing on my part should be wanting to remove every shadow of doubt that hung upon her fidelity, and I exhorted her to believe that every thing would infallibly terminate in the way most honourable and gratifying to herself. Pandora listened to me, and dried her tears. The conversation was interesting and soothing to us both; we regarded it as the last unreserved and sympathetic communication we should ever have with each other; it insensibly grew longer and longer, and we knew not how to put an end to it. We were still in this state of irresolution when, looking up, I perceived Charles de Damville approaching from the further end of the walk that led to the alcove.

I would have withdrawn. I was anxious to remove the unjust suspicion that hung upon his mind; but the instant that presented to him so strong an apparent confirmation of them, the instant that by so doing must have worked up his soul into tumult, did not appear a favourable one for explanation. To withdraw was impossible. Pandora had discerned her lover at the same moment with myself. She was seized with a faintness. She would have sunk to the ground; but I caught her in my arms. I rested with one knee on the earth; her head was reclined on my bosom. Charles approached with a quicker pace.

"Rise," said he. "This is beyond my hopes. I left Presburg with the purpose of not revisiting it for years; but, as I proceeded further and further from a place which had lately been the centre of my affections, I began to doubt whether I had not acted with precipitation, and to believe that there was yet some uncertainty hanging on my fate. The seemingly earnest protestations of this delusive syren rung in my ears; mechanically, without any formed resolution, I changed my course, and returned on my steps. My doubts are now at an end. I find you taking instant advantage of my absence to throw yourselves into each other's arms. The feelings I so lately uttered in your presence, Pandora, would have kept you apart, if my feelings had been in the least sacred in your eyes, if all my surmises had not been too true."—He took by the hand the weeping Pandora, and led her to the seat which a little before she had quitted.

"Why all this artifice? Why all this deceit? It is said that we are not masters of our own hearts, and that no human passion is formed to endure for ever. Influenced by these maxims, I could have pardoned your inconstancy, too fair, too fickle Pandora! but why strain every nerve, to make me believe you still retained a passion you had discarded, to subject me to the lingering torture of deceit, instead of communicating to me a truth, agonising indeed to human frailty, but calculated to inspire fortitude and decision? This I cannot excuse: this racks me with the bitterest of disappointments, disappointment in the virtues I had ascribed to you; and convinces me, that you are neither worthy of me, nor worthy of happiness.

"And you too, D'Aubigny, you have acted a part in this unworthy plot, I rescued you from prison, from a dungeon from which, a few hours before, you had no hope of coming forth alive. I took you under my protection, when you had no friend; I placed you next myself; I conceived for you the affection of a brother; I loved you, next in degree to the mistress of my soul. In return for all that I have done, and all that I felt for you, you have with insidious heart and every base disguise, seduced from me the woman of my choice. Why not frankly and ingenuously have demanded her at my hands? The heart is free; your reciprocal passion, though I might have regretted it, I should have been unable to blame; it is the cloak that you have drawn over it, that proves the baseness of its origin. Do you think I had not the courage cheerfully and without a murmur to resign to you this illustrious fair one? I feel that I was worthy to be openly treated. Had I seen in you a mutual and ingenuous passion, I would not have been the bar to its just consummation. I would not have sought the person of a woman, whose heart, in spite perhaps of her better resolutions, was given to another. I should loathe myself for ever, were I capable of such a part. It was the sympathetic sentiment towards me, beating in accord to the sentiment of my own bosom, that I once saw in Pandora, and not either her peerless beauties, or the excellences I imputed to her mind, that formed the master-charm which fascinated my soul. I feel that I had the force, in the negation of my own happiness, to have drawn comfort and compensation from the happiness of two creatures I so dearly loved, as D'Aubigny and Pandora.

"But this alleviation in the midst of what you have condemned me to suffer, you have ungenerously denied me."——

I sought to interrupt my son. I could no longer bear to see him involved in so painful an error, and not exert every nerve to rescue him from it. But his passions were wrought higher than mine: he would not suffer me to speak.

"Be silent, D'Aubigny! I cannot brook to be interrupted now. My heart is full; and I must have leave to utter the sentiments that agitate and distend it."

He advanced towards Pandora. He took hold of her hand.

"Rise, madam. I shall not long trouble you with the boisterous impetuousness of my passions. Do not resist me now!"

She rose, and followed him; her face still covered with her handkerchief, and drowned in tears. He led her to the front of the alcove: he motioned me to approach; with his other hand he took hold of mine. He seemed to lift Pandora's hand to his lips, as if to kiss it; with a sudden start he put it down again; he held it below the level of his breast.

During this scene, Pandora and myself were speechless. Most women, in the situation of Pandora, would, I suppose, have spoken, and have been eager to vindicate themselves from so groundless an imputation. But what she did was peculiar to the delicacy and defencelessness of her personal character. She was overwhelmed, and incapable of effort. For my own part, my feelings were uncommonly complicated. My apparent situation was a plain one, the situation of a youth mistaken by his friend for the seducer of the mistress of that friend; and had my feelings been merely relative to this situation, I could undoubtedly have spoken without embarrassment. But with this were involved the sentiments originating in my secret character, the sentiments of a man anxious to benefit, and who had devoted himself to the interests of another; of a father tremblingly alive to the happiness of his son, and eager to dive into his soul, that he might the more sensibly admire his virtues, and with a more enlightened skill secure his fortune. I was silent: Charles de Damville proceeded:—

"Thus," said he, "I join your hands; thus I withdraw all my claims upon Pandora; thus I remove every impediment to your wishes. This, Pandora,—this, D'Aubigny, I was capable of, if you had treated me honourably, and avowed an honest passion. You do not know Charles de Damville. You have treated me, as none but the most groveling soul could deserve to be treated. Had you been ingenuous, I should have a consolation in what I am doing, that now I cannot have. I can no longer persuade myself that I am joining two worthy hearts to each other. I can no longer relieve the bitterness of my own disappointment, by the image of your future felicity. May I be mistaken! May you be truly happy in each other! You cannot be happy beyond the wishes formed in your favour, by him who will remember, to the latest hour of his existence, how much his heart was devoted to you both."

Saying this, he burst away from us abruptly, and disappeared. At first, as I listened to the heroic language of my son, I asked myself whether it were the expression of a warm heart or a cold one. It costs nothing to a cold heart to ape the language of heroism, and to pretend to make the greatest sacrifices, when its constitution has rendered all effort unnecessary to the feat. But I looked in the face of Charles, and forgot my doubts. His voice he had indeed wound up to the tone of his speech; it was a little tremulous, but in the main firm, serious, deliberate, and elevated. But his countenance was the picture of distress. There sat enthroned, defying all banishment and disguise, the anguish of his soul. His eye was haggard; his complexion was colourless and wan. He had been absent several days from Presburg; his appearance told me that he could scarcely either have eaten or slept during the period of his absence. He might talk of the generosity with which he could resign Pandora; I read in his face what that resignation had cost, and would go on to cost him. Ingenuous, noble-hearted Charles! I doubted whether, but for a reverse of the events he apprehended, he would be able to survive it.

He had no sooner left us, than I applied myself to comfort Pandora. I swore to her that, in spite of every temporary cloud, I would yet witness the union of her and her adored chevalier. I assured her that I would not rest, till I had forced Damville to hear me, and compelled him to credit the sincerity of my tale.

How many things were there, that, in the scene which had just passed, I might have urged in answer to Damville, but respecting which my situation imposed upon me the most rigorous silence! I might have said, "You call yourself my protector, my benefactor, my patron; the real relation between us is the reverse of the picture you have drawn. I want not your protection; I am qualified, if I please, to be a patron to all the world. I am meditating the most generous things in your behalf: this perfidious friend, as you deem him, has devoted all his thoughts, and postponed all his gratifications, that he might prove himself substantially and in the most important particulars your friend."

More than this I might have said. I might have said, "I am your father. I have no inclinations, no passions contravening your gratification. I love you with more than a father's love; I transfer to you all the affection I entertained for your peerless, murdered mother! All my study is your happiness. You are to me the whole world, and more than the whole world. Extensive and singular as are my prerogatives, I fold them up; I forget them all; and think of you alone."

I cannot give a stronger proof than is contained in what I have here stated, of the misery of my condition. I was cheated, as I have once before remarked, with the form of a man, but had nothing of the substance. I was endowed with the faculty of speech, but was cut off from its proper and genuine use. I was utterly alone in the world, separated by an insurmountable barrier from every being of my species. No man could understand me; no man could sympathise with me; no man could form the remotest guess at what was passing in my breast. I had the use of words; I could address my fellow-beings; I could enter into dialogue with them. I could discourse of every indifferent thing that the universe contained; I could talk of every thing but my own feelings. This, and not the dungeon of Bethlem Gabor, is the true solitude. Let no man, after me, pant for the acquisition of the philosopher's stone!

Charles de Damville had again left Presburg, the very instant he quitted the alcove. When I inquired for him in the palace, I received this afflicting intelligence. I did not hesitate a moment in resolving that I would pursue his steps. It was of the utmost consequence that I should overtake him; all that was most interesting to me hung upon our interview. The preparations however of my journey, though followed with ardour, inevitably reduced me to the being some hours in the rear of my son. I was continually in his track, but could not come up with him: to judge from events, you would have supposed that he had as strong a motive to fly, as I had to pursue. He led me along the course of the Danube, to the source of that far-famed and munificent river.

I reached the passage of the Rhine, and was on the point of crossing into Alsace. But here I lost all notice of Charles; no enquiry I could make was effectual to procure me the slightest intelligence. He had not crossed the river; he had proceeded neither to the right nor the left along its banks. I was disappointed, mortified, and distressed. What was I to do next? Could I return to Pandora? What tale must I relate to this adorable creature, whom I had urged to depend upon my exertions? Could I leave her however to the anguish and uncertainty that must follow upon her hearing no more either from her lover or myself?

I think I never felt more truly depressed than in this conjuncture. Most amply, most critically did the curse of the opus magnum attend upon my projects, and render all my exertions abortive. It was the same, whether my plans were formed upon a larger or a smaller scale. When I endeavoured to live in total obscurity in Madrid, when I undertook to be the steward and the father of the people of Hungary, and now that, with a chastised ambition I sought, what is permitted to all other human creatures, to provide for the honourable settlement of my only son, still, still my evil genius pursued me, and blasted every concern in which I presumed to interfere. I had intruded between two faithful lovers: unfortunate they had been indeed, and considerable obstacles were interposed to their felicity; but obstacles are commonly found to yield to firmness and constancy; and, without my fatal interference, Charles and Pandora would one day have been happy. If by adverse fates they had hitherto been kept asunder, still they understood each other, and rejoiced in their mutual confidence and attachment. This, the consolation of all their sorrows and disappointments, it was mine to have destroyed. The globe, for aught I knew, would speedily be interposed between them, and here I stood in the middle point, like one of those invincible repulsive powers hid in the storehouse of nature, forbidding to them all future retrogression to each other.

CHAPTER XLVII.

The picture which my distracted fancy thus set before the eye of my mind, was not altogether verified in the event. After a thousand fruitless inquiries and perquisitions, I found, to my utter astonishment, that Charles, arresting his career at the town of Fribourg, had returned upon his steps, and sought a second time the metropolis of Austrian Hungary. This was of the class of those events which we sometimes meet with in the world, that baffle all calculation, and strike us like magic, or like madness, in their authors.

I had nothing to do, as I conceived, on this occasion, but to follow the example of my son, and like him to resume the route of Presburg. I yet hoped to witness, if not to co-operate in, the reconciliation of Charles and Pandora. My spirits in this respect were revived, and my prospects made brighter, by the thoughts that these virtuous and meritorious lovers were at last likely to be once again inclosed within the cincture of the same city. Add to which, my Venetian confederate had not yet made his appearance at Presburg; and not only was I under engagements to give him the meeting there, but it was also clear that his errand could not be brought to its proper close without my assistance.

I once more entered the city to which Pandora owed her birth. Charles de Damville had preceded my arrival several days. I should without delay have repaired to his apartments, but that I found at my own lodgings a letter from Benedetto Cabriera of Venice, informing me that he was now in Presburg, and to avoid all cause for suspicion, had taken up his residence in a remote quarter of the town. From the enquiries I made, I became satisfied that my son had in some degree resumed his usual occupations, and that there was no appearance of his again immediately quitting the metropolis. I therefore felt my transaction with Cabriera more urgent than an immediate conference with Charles. Though I had sought that conference with earnest expedition, yet I dreaded it. It might require the maturest consideration and the nicest management, to render it effectual for the purposes I sought. I found from certain intelligence that Damville and Pandora had yet had no explanation with each other. I therefore regarded my exertions for that purpose as a final effort; and I was willing that every thing should be in train, and the portion of Pandora fully adjusted, before I entered upon that interesting scene. With Cabriera I had little difficulty. The documents and evidences of his tale we had concerted at Venice; and I presently found that he told his story so plausibly, and supported it so consistently, that it was admitted by every one without the smallest suspicion.

No sooner had Cabriera opened his business to the parties to whom the cognisance of it most properly belonged, than I once more presented myself to the beautiful and engaging niece of Nadasti. The instant I entered her apartment, I was shocked with the extreme change of her personal appearance. All the airiness, alertness and vivacity, that had once so exquisitely adorned her, were gone. The roses in her cheek were faded, and had given place to a delicate, but sickly paleness. Her arms, though always what is called white, had before been round, and had been distinguished by the purest hue of health. They were now emaciated, skinny, and colourless. Her eyes were hollow, and her eyelids inflamed with weeping. All these changes had taken place in about five weeks that had elapsed since I saw her last. I was so struck with the sight, that I involuntarily started, and could scarcely command myself enough to refrain from tears. It was plain that she carried an arrow in her bosom, which one hand only in the universe could extract with safety. As I approached, she raised her lovely head that had been depressed with grief, and lifted her white arms with an expression of despair.

"Come nearer, my sweet Henry," said she, "I rejoice to see you; though you have proved my worst enemy, the destroyer of my peace. But your intentions, my kind boy, my brother, for such I will still call you, have always been good and innocent. But, ah, Henry, you have deluded me; you urged me to banish despair; and every day I see more reason to despair."

I asked if she had not seen the chevalier since his return to Presburg.

"It were better for me," replied Pandora, "if I had not seen him. What has really happened, is worse than if I had been denied to see him. I have met him every day in the apartments of my aunt. To an indifferent eye it would have appeared as if he neither sought nor avoided me. He carries himself towards me with a cold and constrained civility. But he neither demands an interview, nor allows me the opportunity to utter a word to him in private. Oh, D'Aubigny, I see too well that I have lost him for ever. When he fled my presence, when he resolved to seek some distant region, cruel as that conduct was, it convinced me that I was of some importance to him. But now he passes by me in stern neglect; he has utterly driven me from his heart. Indeed, my brother, this last blow is too much; I feel that I shall never recover it."

"And does the chevalier," cried I, "appear at his ease? Does he exhibit the wonted symptoms of his health and triumphant spirit?"

"Away; too pleasing deluder!" replied Pandora. "Cheat me not with false hopes! flatter me not with unreal expectations! Damville does not appear to be well or happy. But you have deceived me too much; the disappointments that you prepared for me are too excruciating. I feel now at no time so high a degree of gloomy satisfaction and composure, as when I press despair firmly to my breast.

"But you, Henry," continued she, "are probably uninformed of my last and severest misfortune. I had a great uncle in the list of the adventurers that achieved the conquest of Peru; he has died, and unexpectedly bequeathed me a fortune, that sets the portionless Pandora upon a level with the wealthy heiresses of the great palatine himself. For a long time want of fortune was the only obstacle that stood between me and all my hopes of happiness. Now that poverty is no longer an evil to me, and wealth no longer desirable, I have obtained this unwelcome acquisition. You can have no conception how painful a sensation is produced by this mockery, the gift of ample possessions to the votary of despair."

I endeavoured somewhat to encourage Pandora; but she obstinately rejected my soothings. I was the less importunate on this subject, as, since the return of my son, I persisted to persuade myself that I should soon have something more substantial to offer her on his part, than mere guesses and conjectures. The day after this conversation, I boldly sought the presence of the chevalier. Till then, I had, since our return to Presburg, avoided to meet him. I now resolved to force from him a hearing; to assure him, with the most solemn asseverations, of my own innocence, and the constancy of his mistress; to represent to him in how eminent a degree the newly acquired estate of Pandora was calculated to facilitate their mutual wishes; and finally, to offer him any pledge he should desire of the sincerity of my declarations, even to the banishing myself from the presence and intercourse of him and the lovely Pandora for ever.

When I saw my son, his appearance and air advanced a forcible claim on my compassion. I will not now describe them. Suffice it, that they completely proved, how true was the sympathy, even to the minutest particulars, between him and his mistress. The difference was only in kind, and not in degree: hers a defenceless, a delicate and truly feminine grief; while his, amidst all its aggravations, had something in it of the champion and the hero. When he felt most severely, he seemed to disdain himself for what he felt; and, though his struggles were excruciating, he resolutely smoothed his manly front, and the loftiness of his spirit produced on his cheek a generous and a settled blush.

I have just said that I had resolved to force from him a hearing. I was mistaken in my calculations on this point. Dejected as his habits had lately been, he no sooner saw me, than he advanced towards me with a fierce and imperative demeanour, that absolutely startled me.

"How is it, man!" cried he, "that you are at this hour out of custody?"

"Custody!" interdicted and astonished, repeated I.

"Yes, custody! If such a wretch as thou art, be permitted to go at large, what human institution, what human possessions, shall ever be secure?"

"Good God," said I, "what am I to understand by your present rage? I know that you have considered me as your personal enemy and the underminer of your happiness. But, when first you accused me of this crime, you treated me in a manner less violent and disdainful than that which you now employ."

"I brook not to explain. Read that letter. I received it at Fribourg. That letter brought me back from the confines of France to the spot where now we meet."

I took up the letter. Its contents were nearly as follow:—

LETTER.

"My dear Friend,—You will permit me to call you so, since to me, and me only, you have recently thought proper to confide your projects, and your unfortunate passion for the charming Pandora. What you related to me on the subject convinced me how much she was unworthy of your love, and how basely she has conducted herself towards you. Yet you will yourself feel some compassion for her, when you learn who it is upon whom she has bestowed this unmerited preference. Know then that this wretched D'Aubigny is no other than the notorious Chatillon, the infamous impostor, who, by his machinations about a year ago preserved the Turkish provinces of Hungary from being conquered by the christian arms. The man is moreover a magician, the pretended or real possessor of the philosopher's stone. He is therefore doubly worthy of death, first as a traitor, the abettor and comforter of the common enemy of the christian faith, and, secondly, as a dealer in the black art, and a man notoriously sold and delivered over to the devil.

"I have received this information from the most unquestionable authority. A soldier in my old corps, who has lately escaped from a Turkish prison, no sooner saw him than he identified his person. I happened to be near the fellow at the moment, when, by an unexpected exclamation, he betrayed his discovery. It immediately struck me that the circumstance might be of importance to your interests; and, therefore, taking the soldier aside, I charged him not to mention to any one what he had observed. To render his secrecy the more secure, I have since removed him to a garrison at some distance from Presburg; and I have myself mentioned the circumstance to no living creature, that I might first receive your instructions on the subject, and act in all respects concerning it as you shall judge proper. The blackness of the character of the man sets all exaggeration at defiance. This very individual, whom you liberated from the bowels of the earth, who by the most treacherous arts won your confidence, and upon whom you lavishly heaped every imaginable distinction, was all the while conscious to himself, that he was the character that of all that live you hated most; in one word, the renegado Chatillon. He acted consistently with his preceding conduct and his recent disingenuousness, when he seduced from you the affections of the woman of your choice.

"I am concerned to add, that, on the very day that I made this discovery, this Chatillon D'Aubigny disappeared from Presburg, nor can I by any effort learn whither he is gone. It is impossible he should have been informed by any human means of the detection that had happened. But indeed it is vain to attempt to form any reasonable conjecture, respecting a character so mysterious and inexplicable.

"Your devoted friend,

"Andrew, count of Bathori."

"Well, sir," seeing I had finished the perusal, "and what have you now to allege? When I saw you simply as the favoured lover of Pandora, however treacherous and dishonourable I might deem your conduct towards me, I quitted the field. I did not trust myself to be a judge in my own cause. I did not confide in my estimate of your unworthiness, when I was myself wholly concerned. I had some time before received an invitation from the duke d'Aumale, who was collecting a number of generous and high-spirited nobles to accompany Mary queen of Scots to the barbarous fields of her native realm. I at first declined, I now accepted, the invitation; I set out for Paris to join him. I found that letter waiting my arrival at Fribourg, and I returned. Deeply as Pandora has sunk in my esteem, I determined I would never allow her to be thrown away upon the infamous Chatillon.

"You haunt my steps. I heard of you again and again on my route as I returned from Fribourg. I arrive at Presburg, and presently after you again make your appearance. What further villanies have you to act? What new treacheries have you devised against me? This morning I consented to the representations of count Bathori, and agreed that you should be delivered up to justice. Why then are you not in custody?

"When I consider the mystery and inscrutableness of your character, I am lost in conjecture. You are said to be a magician, a dealer in the unhallowed secrets of alchymy and the elixir vitæ. In cases like this, all the ordinary rules of human sagacity and prudence are superseded, the wisest man is a fool, and the noblest spirit feels the very ground he stood on struck from under his feet. How can I know that the seduction of Pandora's affections is not owing to magical incantations, who in that case is rather an object for compassion than for censure? How can I tell that the fraternal resemblance borne by your features to my own, and the sudden and ardent partiality that rose in my breast when first I saw you, have not been produced by the most detested arts? Magic dissolves the whole principle and arrangement of human action, subverts all generous enthusiasm and dignity, and renders life itself loathsome and intolerable.

"This is to me the most painful of all subjects. I had a father whom I affectionately loved: he became the dupe of these infernal secrets. I had a mother, the paragon of the creation: that father murdered her. All the anguish I ever felt, has derived its source from alchymy and magic. While the infamous Chatillon thus stands before me, I feel all the long-forgotten wounds of my heart new opened, and the blood bursting afresh from every vein. I have rested, and been at peace; and now the red and venomed plague, that tarnished the years of my opening youth, returns to blast me. Begone, infamous, thrice-damned villain! and let me never see thee more!

"Wretch that you are!" continued Charles; for he saw me motioning to withdraw,—I felt that all further expostulation and discussion on my part was useless,—"wretch that you are! what is it that you are about to do? Think no to escape my vengeance! In the midst of all the tumultuous passions you waken in my breast, I still feel in myself the soldier and the man of honour. I am not a thief-taker or a bailiff. You are within my power, and that is your present protection. I will not now deliver you up to the justice of the state, but will hurl against you my personal defiance. I am willing to meet you man to man: I thirst to encounter you as my worst and most mortal foe, who has perpetrated against me the basest injuries, and excited in my bosom the most hateful sensations. Though you were fenced with all the legions of hell, I fear you not; and seeing that, after all that is past, you have once again intruded into my presence, I here bind myself by all that is sacred to pursue you to the death."

What could I answer to such an attack? I saw at once that the case, as to all future harmony between me and my son was desperate and irremediable. What hope could I entertain further? What had hitherto been the result of our ill-fated intercourse? Every offence and prejudice that can gall the human mind had been brought forward in it in turn. I had wounded Damville in the most sensible point of private life, and had blasted his hopes there where he stored them all. I had offended his most rooted political prepossessions, by aiding the Turk, and feeding a nation that perished with hunger. I was an equivocal character, assuming different names, and wandering over the world with different pretences. Last of all, I had revived in his mind the images of his father and his mother,—all that had once been most dear, and now was most painful, to his recollection; and had tortured his fancy with nameless horrors. These sentiments could never be removed. All the explanations in the world could never reconcile me to his mind; and I felt that I had that within, which, in what was to come, as it had in what was past, must for ever annihilate all confidence between us. At once therefore I accepted his challenge, arranged with him the terms of a hostile encounter on the following morning, and immediately after bid adieu to Presburg, and to the sight of every soul contained within its walls, for ever.

This is, I powerfully feel, the last adventure that I shall ever have the courage to commit to writing. A few minutes more, and I will lay down my pen, and resolve in the most solemn and sacred manner never to compose another line. Indeed, all other adventures must necessarily be frigid and uninteresting, compared with that which I have now described. Great God, what a fate was mine! Anxious as I had been to prove myself in the most momentous respects the benefactor of my son, dismissing all other thoughts and cares from my mind, journeying with this sole object in view, from Presburg to Venice, and from Venice to Presburg, from Hungary to the banks of the Rhine, and from the banks of the Rhine back again to Hungary,—the whole scene was now terminated by a declaration on his part, that nothing could appease the animosity he cherished against me, short of rioting in the blood of his father's heart. I was reduced to the necessity either of lifting my sword against my son, of running myself upon the point of his weapon, or of forfeiting the engagement between us, and suffering him to brand me as a coward in the face of Christendom. I mention not this, because the variety of objects of choice produced in me the slightest hesitation. Weary as I was of life, I could cheerfully have consented to die, but not to stain the sword of Charles de Damville with my vital blood. I prevented him from being the assassin of his father's life; I could not prevent him from being the assassin of his father's character. He was assiduous and indefatigable in spreading against me the blackest invectives, which he regarded as the most unerring truths. All Hungary has resounded for thirty years with the atrocities of the sieur de Chatillon; what is here recorded contains the whole and unvarnished truth on the subject. This narrative however shall never see the light, till the melancholy hour when Charles de Damville shall be no more.

Yet in the midst of the anguish, the disappointment of every cherished hope, which rends my soul, I have one consolation, and that an invaluable one, in the virtues, the glory, and the happiness of my son. I said I would forget every gratification and sentiment of my own in him; I am now more than ever instigated to do so. When I quitted Presburg, I left Cabriera behind me in that city, and I took care to obtain a parting interview with him. He afterwards gave me the meeting, as we then concerted, at Trieste in the duchy of Carniola. It happened, as I had flattered myself the event would prove, that, the visible source of umbrage being removed, Charles and Pandora in no long time came to a mutual understanding, and were finally made happy in each other. I had been the fortunate means of supplying to this excellent and incomparable creature the only defect under which she laboured, a want of fortune; her uncle, having no longer a pretence to oppose their mutual passion, united their hands; and, at the time of which I am speaking, they were regarded as the most graceful and accomplished couple in the whole Hungarian dominions. The chevalier de Damville is considered in that country as the great bulwark of the Christian frontier, and the most generous and illustrious pupil in the school of the Bayards and the Scanderbegs. Cabriera, worn out with years and fatigues, but still grasping and avaricious to his latest hour, expired in my arms in the city of Trieste; and by his death yielded me this contentment, that henceforth the only obvious means for detecting my beneficent fraud in securing the dower of Pandora was for ever removed.

That the reader may enter the more fully into my sentiment of congratulation upon the happiness of my son, and rise from the perusal of my narrative with a more soothing and pleasurable sensation, I will here shortly recapitulate the good qualities that had been unfolded in this truly extraordinary young man from his earliest infancy. He was a child, only nine years of age, at the period of the truly affecting and exemplary behaviour the reader may remember him to have displayed, while I was at Paris squandering the property of my family at the gaming-table. In the alienation of mind produced in me by that dreadful catastrophe, he was my constant attendant, my careful nurse, and my affectionate friend. When, twelve months after, we were driven by our calamities out of Switzerland, and I lay extended to all human appearance on the bed of death, Charles was the comforter of his mother, the friend of his sisters, and even, young as he was, contributed to the maintenance of my starving family by the labour of his infant hands. At Dresden, as yet no more than seventeen years of age, he was assailed by one of the severest trials with which the mind of man can in any case be beset. But he hesitated not a moment. Obliged to choose between poverty and innocence, with the sacrifice of all his habitudes, and the loss of every friend, on the one side, and wealth, new to his enjoyment, with ignominy or an equivocal character, on the other, his determination was instant and unalterable. Cast, at so immature an age, alone and portionless, upon the world, he almost immediately, by his gallantry, his winning qualities, and his virtues, gained to himself a friend in one of the greatest captains of the age. Unaided by the brilliancy of family or fortune, he acquired the character of the bravest soldier in Hungary, where all were brave. This last trial, to which I had been the undesigning means of subjecting him, was none of the least arduous. Love often entails imbecility on the noblest of mankind: but Charles surmounted the most perilous attacks of this all-conquering passion. When he thought Pandora unworthy, he tore himself from her, and would not admit a struggle. When he believed she loved another, he disdained to claim a heart that seemed alienated from him, and himself joined the hands of his mistress and his rival. He might have died; he could not disgrace himself. I was the hero's father!—but no! I am not blinded by paternal partiality;—but no! he was indeed what I thought him, as near the climax of dignity and virtue as the frailty of our nature will admit. His virtue was at length crowned with the most enviable reward the earth has to boast,—the faithful attachment of a noble-minded and accomplished woman. I am happy to close my eventful and somewhat melancholy story with so pleasing a termination. Whatever may have been the result of my personal experience of human life, I can never recollect the fate of Charles and Pandora without confessing with exultation, that this busy and anxious world of ours yet contains something in its stores that is worth living for.

THE END.

FOOTNOTES

To this story, in the book from which I have quoted it, is subjoined the following reference:—"Mémoires Historiques, 1687, tom. i. p. 365." Being desirous of giving my extract from the oldest authority, I caused the British Museum, and the libraries of Oxford and Cambridge, to be searched for this publication, but in vain. The story and the reference are, not improbably, both of them the fictions of the English writer.

Johnson's Occasional Prologue on Garrick's assuming the management of Drury-lane Theatre.

Charles V.

Henry VIII.

Antonio de Leyva.

The constable of Bourbon.

Mistresses of Francis I.

The battle of Cerisolles.

This incident is told, nearly in the words of St. Leon, by Thuanus, Historiæ Sui Temporis, lib. 2. cap. 14.

CPSIA information can be obtained
at www.ICGtesting.com
Printed in the USA
LVHW080030290721
694010LV00026B/702